NEW WORLD
TRIBE

FACES OF SACRIFICE

NEW WORLD
TRIBE

FACES OF SACRIFICE

Doc McKay, Jr.

LOCEM Books, Sandy Springs, Georgia

For Betty

A beast does not know that he is a beast, and the nearer a man gets to being a beast, the less he knows it.

— George MacDonald

We should not ask, "What is wrong with the world?" for that diagnosis has already been given. Rather, we should ask, "What has happened to the salt and light?"

— John R. W. Stott

…can these bones live?

— God, to the Hebrew Prophet Ezekiel

Chapter 1

Atl was fifteen when the Aztec priests came to drown his little sister, Yellow Orchid. She had given him marigolds for taking time to play. They wilted in his hands as he stood through the night, watching them get her ready.

Finally, *Tonatiah* began his rising in the East. His bright fingers steamed through the trees and across the water. The priests got into the canoes. They tied rocks around Yellow Orchid's waist and made her stand in the lake. She had to stretch her neck to keep her mouth in the air. Atl felt as if it were his own toes sinking in the loose bottom mud. Her ears were under, where the lake would have shut out all but the dense echoes of her people standing on the swamp-shore. Her soft black hair spread in the water and the flowers their mother had woven into it loosened and left.

One priest spoke loudly and the sides of the mountains threw back his words: she would fly with the gods. He pushed her face under. When he let her up, she gasped and wailed. He said that *Tlaloc* would add her tears to his great jar on the cloud mountain and pour them out for the plantings. Life for rain, rain for life. He pushed again and let her up again. He said that it was an honor for her and her people.

The fourth taking of tears stopped her wailing. The priest's fingers threw shadow-bands across his face as he opened both hands to Tonatiah's rising. A lone quetzal cried out above him. The flowers floated freely on the smoothing surface. Atl's mother wept without sound, and his own teeth clinched so hard he feared they would break.

Chapter 2

The old school bus Smith had chartered from Tegucigalpa's public transit system broke down for the third time in the middle of the old mountain road. The driver hopped out into the dust again, pulled one of his big rusty cans of water and a towel from the side compartment, and opened the hood.

The team stood under shady trees, all but DeSparr, who sat at a window inside, seething as usual, coal-black beard glistening with sweat.

"Come on out," said Rachel. "You'll be cooler."

He didn't look at her, but said, sharply, "Save your charity act for the natives." His jaw tightened. "Maybe they'll believe it."

"Maybe," said Howard, "they'll answer like humans." He meant it more to get at DeSparr than to side with Rachel.

Rachel seemed surprised, but not irked. She pulled her hair off her neck and said to DeSparr, "It's true. You'll be cooler." Then she lowered her face and said softly to Howard, "Every human is a human."

Howard said, "What d'you care about the jerk?"

Her smile had a comical crinkle on one side. "Who's the jerk?"

All he could think to say was, "Not me," and turned away. It already bugged him how she said things and did things she must have thought would make him a better person. He was fine like he was.

He watched the driver unscrew the radiator cap and use the towel to slap at it and wave the steam away, then helped him lift the can and pour the water.

Everyone got back into the bus as it once again cranked up noisily and lurched into action, leaning on the switchbacks, shaking and rattling violently when climbing. The driver rarely spoke. He calmly avoided the steep drop-offs while staring coolly ahead through plastic beads and crucifixes and mini-statues of saints swinging from the visors. He and the two porters, a translator, a cook, and thirteen team members, down from fourteen since Miss Margaret was dismissed, bounced and rocked with the supplies and equipment. Most avoided the hard metal seats by standing in the aisle, knees bent.

Team leader Smith, the oldest and tallest of them all, stood with his bald head lowered, ready with an announcement. His calm, shy ways were probably meant to play down his high position in his church. Most of the team were connected with one church or another. Howard had joined his parents' church when he was twelve, pretending to mean it so he could get a sip of grape juice when it passed along the pew.

"Folks?" said Smith. "Just a reminder…" He fiddled with his straw hat in his hands. "If we find this tribe, our mission is only to observe and take notes. No disturbing them or their ways. I'm sure we will all honor that." He looked at Haughton-Alsef and Pryce who planned to do a TV documentary. "And take pictures too, of course."

"Got it, old boy," said Haughton-Alsef. "Trust is all-important."

Howard made his way forward, where his old friend from Tech stood holding his bulging belly. "L.P., you don't look so good."

L.P. tried to grin. "Dynamite enchiladas."

Howard shook his head. "Just don't detonate in the bus." He sighed. "You've been binging since we were roomies."

"You should try it. You need a little meat on you."

"Keep it up and you'll get Montezuma's revenge and wish you were back in Atlanta selling computers and raking in all that dough."

"And you all would have to press on without me." L.P. obviously meant that facetiously. He added nothing to the mission and neither did Howard. They came along for the adventure.

"Press on." Howard lowered his voice. "I just hope one of these characters knows what we're doing." He looked around. "Strange mix."

"Smith and Haughton-Alsef wanted it that way," said L.P. "It's the only reason we get to go. They probably had to do a lot of scraping to find clueless volunteers like us. At least they made sure we had prep sessions. I don't know where they found Blake, for a survival expert."

"One survival expert," said Howard. "One."

L.P. shrugged happily and grinned. "We're idiots for doing this."

"Look, *you* talked *me* into it. It better be good."

"Aw, you know it will. Hey, I saw you and Rachel."

"What?" Howard shrugged. "No way. Nothing there."

"There's worse women."

Howard frowned. "She won't take you like you are. She tried to get Zoe not to sleep in a tent with Blake like they're planning, even though they've been living together in Atlanta for a year."

"Yeah, I heard. She probably doesn't want Zoe to get hurt. Or maybe she wants Blake for herself. He's the perfect guy for a woman. Almost never talks."

"I think it was more of a moral thing," said Howard. "Me, I like my freedom."

"Shh," said L.P. "Here she comes."

Howard got his paperback on Aztecs out of his pocket.

Rachel said, "I miss Miss Margaret. She knows jungles."

Howard shrugged. "Yeah." He had not agreed with the team's decision to dismiss Miss Margaret back in Tegucigalpa, especially doing it when she was off with Rachel touring Copán, but there were strong team feelings and it was an awkward subject.

"She left her mission in the Amazon jungles to join us," said Rachel. "Then got fired."

"Not fired. Dismissed with gratitude, or something like that."

She studied him. "I don't think you care."

"About Miss Margaret?" He shrugged. "She's tough enough."

Rachel sighed and glanced out a window. "Look at that!"

An old Indian with flowing white hair on an ancient motorcycle was trying to pass on the down-hill side.

"Driver!" said Rachel, hurrying forward, pointing at the biker.

The driver glanced in his side mirror, but never slowed or pulled over. Finally, at a wide place in the road, the biker pulled directly in front of the bus. Then the driver hit the brakes and gas often, tapping the horn when he got too close, but never cussing or speaking at all.

L.P. suddenly groaned, slid a hand down his brown beard, and plopped on a seat. Something crunched. He got up. Blake's three GPS receivers lay there smashed.

"Now you've done it," said Howard.

Zoe heard and looked. "Blake! Your satellite thingies!"

Blake made his way to the seat, absorbing the bumps with athletic agility, dogged with consternation over well-laid plans having once again gone awry through no fault of his own. He reached down and picked up one receiver at a time. Each was bent and cracked, green chips hanging loose. He stared out the window, distantly, then at L.P.

4

"Look," said L.P., still holding his stomach. He held a hand out toward the receivers as if it had been their fault. "The one in the middle busted the other two and the other two busted it." Finally he said, sheepishly, "In other words, if you didn't plan everything so perfect, if you'd only brought one, it woulda survived my fat fanny." He grinned, opened the window, stuck his head out, and vomited.

"Oh, gross!" said Zoe, and turned away.

L.P. sighed happily.

Blake sighed unhappily. "At least we still have a compass."

Zoe announced, "Blake can do like… dead reckoning. He did it on a sailboat with me." She suddenly snickered and grinned at Blake.

***

The bus rumbled and rattled through clouds of dust and sun-sparkled insects and finally plunged into El Pueblo Último, where they planned to put into the river. A rambling general store-stable-saloon-service station stood across a wide dirt street from a row of make-shift houses. Each metal roof had at least one brooding vulture. Several big loose-legged dogs walked the street, sniffing the dust.

"Folks?" said Smith, "Mr. Sands of California, who financed our expedition, sends his best wishes. As you know, we only have rumors of a tribe. We hope to find them." He smiled. "But if not, I think there's still much we can learn, and the experience should be memorable."

After the team unloaded the bus, Smith's assistant, whose name was Tiffany but who insisted she be called by the "Native American-friendly, peace-awareness" name Dove-Ti, woke up Beg. He was curled up on two seats. Howard thought it was like her, just out of seminary, to bring along a vagrant as a way of feeding him and demonstrating "the equality of all people." She didn't like the nickname L.P. gave him, but it was meant good-naturedly, and Beg took to it, so it caught on.

Beg stepped out of the bus and grinned toothlessly to any villagers he saw. He sat knobby-kneed on a doorstep next to a middle-aged woman nursing a baby. "Got bum elbow. Hurt. Need *pulque*."

Mid-afternoon the driver cranked up the bus and began rocking back up the dirt road, motor screaming. When the dust had drifted away, birds, insects, and animals, near and far, cawed, chirped, and howled.

The river was about the width of a subdivision street back home, and deep. Four sixteen-foot wooden rowboats had been delivered.

5

Three were already sinking from slow leaks. Several team members bailed them out, and Blake found a way to plug them. Then came the rain, heavy.

They all ran into the general store-stable-saloon-service station, and most bought what Blake recommended, two sets each of loose white cotton shirts and pants like those worn by the local Paya farmers.

The Indian that had passed them on the motorcycle stood behind the goods table stroking his long white hair and taking money. "You should not go into that woods," he said to Rachel.

She glanced at Smith. He said, "We are well-equipped." He looked at Blake. "Blake here, an experienced survival expert and trip planner, led our preparatory sessions. He has seen to the setting up of an emergency helicopter near the river." He eyed each person. "And I'm sure we've all taken our safety rules to heart. We depend on each other."

The women found a back room and changed to their new white outfits, all but Dove-Ti, who came out in her wide flowered shorts and loosely tied gray top, and Mrs. Crauder, who was quite proud of the moose-decorated sweat clothes she had bought in Atlanta when she and her just-retired husband signed up for the expedition.

Howard bought a sealable plastic bag for his book and a used, American-made, red-handled pocket knife.

After the men had changed, Smith lowered his head, partly from shyness and partly to let the rainwater drain from his straw hat. "I believe we have some loading to do."

"Lead on, great chief," said Mr. Crauder, voice like a truck-horn.

All but DeSparr and Beg helped carry the supplies to the boats. Most put away their umbrellas and got soaked.

"Get used to it," said Blake, as he and Howard and L.P. tied tarps over the newly packed supplies.

DeSparr sat straight up on a middle seat, his bone-white face shining from his soaked black business suit, black T-shirt, black hair and beard, staring up through the trees as a prisoner might through a high, barred opening.

And in the four clunky wooden boats, the thirteen on the team plus a translator, a cook, and two guide-porters, none of whom had ever been farther than that last village, pushed off into the Honduran mountains and woods and rivers and rain.

As they rounded a bend, Blake was the first to spot the shiny red and white stand-by helicopter. It made a strange sight parked in a jungle clearing. The pilot had a well-equipped one-man camp, and was laid back under a hanging tarp in his bright yellow jump-suit, listening to recorded music. A gas-powered generator chugged away. Several on the team waved, and he nodded and shouted, "¡Hola y adios, mis amigos!"

Then for two and a half days, DeSparr stared up into the trees, Beg stared down at his new team-issued boots, and the others hung over the gunwales staring at the woods expecting and seeing and gasping at monkeys and birds and big snakes and once, they thought, a jaguar. After three rough portages, lots of rapids demanding heavy pushing with big sticks, the overturning of two boats quickly righted with amazingly little lost, a night in tents on a flat, grassy knoll next to the river, and another in a hasty camp at a spooky spot surrounded by high rock cliffs and huge old trees, the seemingly unending rain ended, and the boats floated easily through the remnant mist until they rounded a sweeping bend and a wide, curving silt bar, ahead of which was a muffled but increasingly loud roar.

"Rapids!" shouted Blake quickly. "Get over!"

Pryce quit putting make-up on Haughton-Alsef in the lead boat and, with great effort, all the rowers got all four boats to the silt bar just in time. Everybody got their feet in the water and on the ground quickly and stood shaking off the sudden fright.

Blake tied all the boats to one of the huge trees lining the river.

L.P. named the silt bar "The Beach."

"'The precipice' is more like it," said Mrs. Crauder, boldly exploring the shore and peering over the edge. "I wish you would look."

Howard and others joined her. The river crashed forward and downward over rocky ledges, pushed from behind by its own relentless force, swallowed far below by its own thick mist.

"Are we where we're supposed to be?" said Smith to Blake.

Blake hesitated and Haughton-Alsef answered. "Rumors of the tribe have their general area about three days from that last town. Roughly here."

"Mr. Architect?" said Smith to Howard. "Tent sites? Should we sit down and discuss our options?"

Howard pointed at the flattest part of the silty rise, quickly, to avoid one of Smith's long meetings. "The stakes'll go in easy. Not many options here, anyway."

Smith took his hat off and studied it. "Your decision."

They unloaded ten two-man tents. Howard directed the

mounding of the silt and the trenching around each site. DeSparr insisted on sleeping alone. All agreed to let Smith, as team leader, and Beg, made somehow special by Dove-Ti's attention to him, have tents to themselves. They worked three hours into the night. Insects swarmed the lanterns. They set up a large tent for the supplies, the radio and its generator, the huge bag of plastic toys and trinkets they had brought to attract the rumored tribe, and DeSparr's boxes of medicines and medical equipment. They left the food in the boats, in locked metal boxes.

When they snuffed the lanterns and crawled in for the night, the rain came again.

"Perfect timing," said L.P. as he and Howard tried to sleep.

***

The rain lasted all night, and for five more days.

On the second day, at various times, most people got soaked and gritty repairing tents and tarps and trails, cutting bushes, digging a latrine, bailing boats, double-bagging garbage. They made none of the planned searches for the tribe. Blake crawled into the radio tent several times a day to talk to the stand-by helicopter pilot and to hear news of the outside world. He kept up with the tracking of a hurricane travelling slowly westward in the Caribbean, foretelling unusually heavy rainfall. He scouted several times and was able to sketch maps.

On the third day, Crauder looked over the maps. "This hen scratching any good? Does it tell us where we are?"

"Sun-less, star-less, GPS-less guesses." Blake glanced at L.P.

"What can I say?" said L.P., sheepishly patting his big butt.

Maria the Cook and the Crauders set up the stoves under a huge, sagging tarp which poured heavily off one side, but their meals were served hot — temperature and pepper.

Smith insisted, in his apologetic way, that no one leave the area or separate in any way, so not to get lost, and to avoid unknown dangers that could "render one a burden to the rest of the team." He held two long meetings under the tarp every day, whether they were needed or not, opening each with, "Let's decide the purpose of our meeting."

At each meeting, DeSparr stood in the rain next to a rotten stump, within hearing distance.

Everybody got grittier and smellier. Late in the afternoon of the fourth day, the women talked among themselves, then announced that

8

cleanliness was more important than life itself, and that they would risk snakes and other "jungle dangers" to go to the side stream and bathe.

Howard crawled into his rain-darkened tent, lit the lantern, and began reading his book.

L.P. crawled in. "Reading about Aztecs again?"

"Yep."

"Cool! Human sacrifices. Do you think they still happen?"

"You worried?"

"No They wouldn't want our little snow-white bodies."

"Little?"

"Hey, that's all muscle."

"What I've read," said Howard. "It's been five hundred years."

"But they did do it back when. Right?"

"Ripped hearts out for their gods. Drowned little kids to make it rain. Less mouths to feed. Get rid of political enemies."

"Sick."

"All legal," said Howard. "Everybody did it."

"Everybody did it, so it was okay?"

"I didn't say that. 'Sick' just doesn't seem like the right word."

"Well, anyway, five days of rain, they won't need to sacrifice anybody for a while."

Suddenly a chorus of screaming came from the pool area.

"The women," mumbled Howard. He and L.P. crawled out and ran through the camp.

Blake joined them, then Crauder. More screams.

They found the women crouched to their necks in the black water, apparently unharmed. Mrs. Crauder was still screaming.

"Dang, Pat!" said her husband. "What happened?"

Rachel pointed into the woods. "They were here."

"Little men!" screamed Mrs. Crauder. "Little naked men!"

"They had loinie-thingies," said Zoe. "I was like, hu-u-uh?"

"They took our boots and our pile of clothes," said Mrs. Crauder. "They robbed us!"

"Then they just, like… left," said Zoe.

"I coulda told ya," said Crauder. "How many?"

"Four or five," said Rachel. She looked at Howard. "Could you bring our spares?"

Howard and L.P. went back to the tents, gathered each woman's second set of clothes, took them back and faced away from the pool.

9

Blake and Crauder posted themselves on opposite sides, watching the woods. Finally Mrs. Crauder called out that they were ready, and they all walked into camp. There were only four spare boots, which were over-sized. Rachel and Maria the cook did without.

"You can have mine," said Howard to the two.

Maria the cook didn't understand, didn't speak English. Rachel said, "I could put both feet in one and she could put hers in the other, but we don't want to have to hop around everywhere."

Howard frowned. His feet were not that big. Let somebody cool like L.P. do the ribbing, not somebody set on knocking him.

"Just kidding," she said with the crinkled smile. "But no thanks."

***

Smith called a special meeting that night under the tarp, lit by lanterns. DeSparr sat apart again, where he had made a bench of hefty sticks carefully set across the rotten stump and a large rock.

"They were short," said Rachel. "Pot bellies. And they had spots painted all over their bodies."

"Jaguar spots," said Crauder's truck-horn. "I coulda told ya."

"The Jaguar-people," said L.P. "That's what we call 'em. The Jaguar-people."

"They just grabbed stuff," said Zoe. "And we were standing there in the like... open, bathing. They didn't even look at us."

Howard tried, but couldn't get a believable mental picture of Rachel and Zoe standing and bathing.

Crauder said to Rachel, "You shoulda let Maria the translator go barefoot. She's hired."

"You should see her feet," said Rachel. "Tender. She's a college girl. Lives in Tegucigalpa. Zoe and Maria and I will swap shoes around. Whoever needs to do some walking, you know."

The team decided to post night watches. Smith asked Blake to set up a safety perimeter. When Blake finished, he and Pryce kept the watch through the night.

***

The next morning, the fifth straight day of heavy rain, everybody woke to loud, desperate screeching. Howard and L.P. crawled out just in

10

time to see DeSparr throw both hands up and fall over backwards onto the supply tent, causing several of its stick-pegs to pop out of the rain-softened silt. He and the tent collapsed into a deflated heap.

"You been shot?" shouted Crauder loudly but facetiously.

"They're gone!" cried DeSparr. "All the antibiotics! Gone!"

Crauder pulled back the flaps. "The boxes! We've been robbed!"

They looked at Smith. He thought, and said, "We've got to sit down and talk about this."

Everyone gathered under the tarp except DeSparr, who stood oddly in the rain at his stump-bench, and Blake and Pryce, around whom the thieves had somehow sneaked. Those two stood in the rain watching the woods, just close enough to hear Smith, who sat rotating his straw hat in his hands.

Finally Smith said, "Why would they do this?".

"What I don't get," said L.P., "is what the Jaguar-people want with antibiotics. They don't even know what they are."

"They'll probably plant 'em to see what comes up," said Crauder. "Or bow down to them."

"They *would* have a strange religion," said Mrs. Crauder.

"Ah, but our Christian religion would seem strange to them," said Haughton-Alsef.

She frowned. "I can't think of anything strange about ours."

"Certainly whatever we do," said Dove-Ti, smiling soothingly, "I'm sure we will remember that all religions are valid."

"Once again," said DeSparr, loudly and sarcastically, "believers affirm the obsolescence of belief. This consortium of detached observers, so eager to find a tribe of wise old poverty-stricken sages, primitive and powerless, pristine and 'authentic' by virtue of their very remoteness…" each consonant punched the air, "…this team, so eager to proclaim noble savages exemplary models of the latest religious, environmental, and social theories, contrives to return triumphant with selected discoveries, or — should I say? — to add pages to résumés. Why don't you take back a sample or two of live Indians for observation at the universities, just as the old conquistadors did?"

Everyone stared at him dumbfounded.

"God!" said Pryce. "That would be strictly against the rules."

Mrs. Crauder widened her eyes and batted her lids at DeSparr. "You sound as if you wish you hadn't come." She smoothed her sweat pants and gave them a final pat.

DeSparr glared fixedly away, the skull-like face flushed as if lit by some flaming inner pressure. He turned and walked into the woods.

Blake left his post and followed, not too close.

Smith seemed annoyed, but said, "I believe we have some issues to discuss."

Haughton-Alsef puffed pleasantly on his empty pipe. "Our hope of returning to our own familiar portion of the globe with a richer understanding of the whole, should still be within reach."

"Oh," said Mrs. Crauder admiringly, "thank you for that."

Haughton-Alsef walked to DeSparr's stump-bench. He found a small rock, dropped it on the bench, and jumped back. The sticks suddenly turned black with ants swarming from the stump.

L.P. grinned at Howard.

"What?" said Howard.

L.P. just grinned.

After some minutes, the ants crawled back into the stump. Haughton-Alsef grinned and went back to the meeting-on-hold.

Smith was unusually irritated. "I hope Blake has Dr. DeSparr in his sights."

"I'm sure we all will in time, old boy," said Haughton-Alsef.

L.P. snickered.

Smith went over the importance of minding the safety perimeter. "...not only for the sake of individuals, but the entire team."

DeSparr showed again at the edge of the camp. Then Blake showed, not close, and walked casually to the meeting. DeSparr walked to his stick-bench, sat on it, laid one hand on his crossed knees, and the other on top of the first. Nothing happened. No ants. Nothing.

L.P. grinned too eagerly, too obviously, out of the corners of his eyes. DeSparr glared at him just as he winked at Howard, who turned away quickly, but then it was Howard DeSparr glared at.

Smith went on. "We have come to observe, not interfere."

Haughton-Alsef winked at several people and stepped once again, in the rain, to a spot behind DeSparr. He spoke to him casually, was ignored, and picked up a short, heavy stick. He leaned against a tree, studied the stick, turned it, then held it well above the bench.

Howard could clear himself by warning DeSparr. He opened his mouth, but too late. Haughton-Alsef dropped the stick, pretending to grope for it.

The black swarm came with fiery speed, over the bench and over the raincoat and into it and into the shirt and pants. DeSparr let out a squawk. He jumped and danced like a badly strung puppet. He feverishly brushed the clothes. The raincoat flew off. The shirttails flew out.

Crauder laughed before he could stop himself. L.P. snickered.

"Oh!" said Mrs. Crauder, and she and Rachel jumped to help.

"Get away!" said DeSparr, wildly brushing at the two and the ants. He ran, jerking and twisting, behind a big tree. The pants came flying out, then the shirt, among slapping sounds, squawks, and now and then a bare elbow or hairy knee.

Several people muffled laughs. Rachel crawled into DeSparr's tent and came out with a clean shirt and pair of pants. She handed them to Howard. "Give them to him."

"I didn't do this," said Howard, "I…" No use; she had seen L.P. wink. He walked to the tree and reached the shirt and pants around. "Doctor DeSparr? Take these." He held them in the steady rain for what seemed like minutes. Doing this only further connected him with the prank. When they were snatched from his hand, he stepped back.

Rachel stared at him, arms folded.

DeSparr finally appeared, newly clothed, everyone watching, and walked straight to his tent. He dipped once or twice, the result of one last ant or two, then with the maximum dignity achievable in squatting and crawling in the heavy rain, disappeared inside.

Zoe snickered, covering her mouth. Dove-Ti held back a grin, eyeing Haughton-Alsef as she might a cute, mischievous boy. Haughton-Alsef and L.P. looked at each other and laughed. Crauder hee-hawed. Raul and Pedro and the Marias seemed a little fearful of the future.

Rachel did not laugh. She stood at DeSparr's tent. "Dr. DeSparr. Are you all right?"

"Find another object for your sentimentality," said DeSparr.

"Oh," said Mrs. Crauder, worried. "Oh."

Rachel turned to Howard. "Won't you tell him you're sorry?"

"Rachel, I didn't do it." Why was he defending himself against what he was innocent of? "And he doesn't want to hear it."

"Dr. Haughton-Alsef?" she said. "L.P.? Tell him."

"Oh, now, my dear miss school teacher," said Haughton-Alsef. "Loosen up. Boys will be boys. A little fun never hurt anyone."

She said the obvious. "It wasn't fun for him." She picked up the thrown-down shirt and pants. Even in the rain Howard could tell her face was red.

Chapter 3

Atl and Deer of Stone had the say of Deer of Stone's father One-Cip', and dove most of the night, quietly, so not to let the Aztecs know. When they found Yellow Orchid they dragged her to shore. Mud was in her hair. Atl washed it and smoothed it back. They knelt and lowered her into the grave. Atl smelled the fresh-cut earth and felt the coolness. He would be strong. He raised her head gently. Her round face was cold and gray in the moonlight. He laid the wilted marigolds in her hair, then placed the little death-arc himself. It was only wood, since she was so young, but Balanced Turtle had carved it to fit, and it curved gently from one shoulder across the top of her head to the other. He choked and a sob came. He turned to one side, but he knew the others saw.

***

The next year was the year the Aztecs called One-Reed. Each day Atl was able to think less about the rigors and fears and humiliations of his youth training time in their gleaming city in the High Valley, the lip-ringed, face-scarred boys always ready for a fight, the priests with their blood-soaked hands to match their flowing cochineal-red robes, and the captured warriors thrown down the high steps of the temples, their hearts having been torn from their chests while they still lived.

Each day he was able to think more about the people of his village. Each morning when he left his mute mother for the *chinampa*, he saw in her eyes how she cared for him even more in the year since Yellow Orchid was taken for Tlaloc. Each day as he and Deer of Stone dug and hoed they learned from One-Cip' how to praise the plants. Sometimes Deer of Stone's sister Dahlia, who had as many years as Atl, would bring tortillas and cook fish, and each time Atl noticed changes in her talk and her look and her way of moving.

In the cool of a morning, One-Cip' called from the bank of the swamp. "We will travel to Cempoala." He had almost fifty years, his body was long and saggy, his legs thin and short, but he was strong, and he knew the trails, the peoples, and the tongues.

Atl parted the *maize* stalks at the edge of the chinampa. "Today?" The sound in his voice gave away his fear.

"The endless water," said One-Cip. "Crowds and plazas. The chief of the Totonacs lives there. He is three times larger than a man."

Atl was curious, but those things were not enough to ease his fear of any city in the Aztec Empire. Of course, he had to obey One-Cip. "Who else will go?"

"Deer of Stone and Dahlia." One-Cip' was the father of those two and would keep them all safe, Atl thought.

Atl picked up his hoe and waded back to the village to get the say of his mother. She was already weaving, her loom strapped to her waist and hooked to the post in front of their hut. Her face glowed as Tonatiah's fingers sliced the mist between the trees. Atl touched her arm, smooth and plump. He kissed her cheek and smelled the flowers in the wooden spools in her earlobes and watched the tiny metal beads in them flash. He stood back. Her eyes were brown like earth and clear like water. Though the gods had struck her mute before he could remember, he knew the meaning of each move, and now her smile told him that she was proud of him, that she would think of him until he came back, and that he must take good care and do as One-Cip' said.

He left her and ran through the village. It had seemed smaller since he came back from the High Valley. But fear or no fear, his people would be proud of him for going off again to a great city. He ran past the huts and maize-bins of Balanced Turtle, the artist, and of steady old A Fox is Mad, who smacked his chicle, and of Two-Rabbit and Marigold and their daughters Thoughtful Rose, who was thirteen and could scare you or make you happy with just her poems, and Pink, who was younger and spoiled.

He touched his cousin acorn-tree which his mother told him had reached out of the ground on the day he was born and which, when he was six, he had named "Tree of Us." A silly name, he thought now, but Tree of Us was sturdy, and taller than the huts, and made Atl feel tall and strong.

Maybe in Cempoala he would practice *Nahuatl* again, for it was the second tongue in towns from the endless water, which he had never seen, to far beyond the High Valley, which he hoped never to see again. He was glad One-Cip' had taught him and Deer of Stone and Dahlia the rhythms and smooth vowels and sharp clicks of that tongue, even though it brought memories of chilling Aztec glory, of the shining white temples on islands in the lake, of jaguars and eagles seeing out from stone, of proud *Tlaxcalans* taken up the towers for their hearts.

One-Cip' had told Atl and Deer of Stone to forget the bad and learn from the good. He had helped them get the say of the elders to build up their small chinampa-island in the swamp like the big ones they had been made to work in the High Valley.

The four of them sat next to a tree and backed up to their basket-packs filled with bright cloth Atl's mother had woven, and gourds and red and yellow peppers. They looped the tump-lines across their foreheads. They would bring back beans and grains of maize blessed by a priest, and good copper hoe blades.

They leaned forward under their loads and followed the stream, crossing twisted roots and wide rocks dotted with blue, pink, and yellow flowers. Now and then Tonatiah warmed them through the tree-tops.

Even with basket-packs bouncing, Atl chased Dahlia. Not as he had before. No longer would he pull her long black hair as in their childhood. Her ways were new. She would frown, then laugh, then run away and glance back at him. They both glanced often at her father One-Cip', who was strict about the boy-girl rules.

"Look," said Dahlia.

Ahead of them rose a thin column of blue smoke.

One-Cip' said, "Circle off the trail with me and be very quiet."

They climbed, crouching, to a rise where they could look down and see a group of men speaking Nahuatl and waving large feather-fans.

One-Cip' led the three on, and Deer of Stone began to strut. "They are fools," he said.

"They are not fools," said One-Cip'. "I do not think the sacrifices honorable. And I think that your life can be planned. But the Aztecs are not fools. These we passed are tribute-takers from the High Valley. They hold sway everywhere they go in the empire. And they can take whom they like for the sacrifices."

"Will we be in danger?" whispered Atl.

One-Cip' only said, "In Cempoala, do not draw attention."

16

When Tonatiah rested beneath the earth, and *Tezcatlipoca* smoked the sky, Atl and Deer of Stone and Dahlia and One-Cip' hung their basket-packs on the stubby arms of old pines, and bathed in a pool beside a small waterfall. Dahlia turned away, behind a large rock. When they finished bathing they built a fire and stretched out and listened to the voices of the forest.

Dahlia said, "Remember when the farmers from Coatepec came with gifts, and then told us how badly they needed water from us?"

Deer of Stone laughed. "Yes. They used their word for 'water.'"

"Which is '*atl*,'" said Dahlia, "in their Nahuatl. And Atl's mother hid him in the woods until they were gone." Dahlia looked at Atl. "How did you get a name like that?"

Atl shrugged.

One-Cip' said, "He was born on an unlucky day." He looked at Atl. "Your father did not want you named for that day, so he asked a priest what to do. The priest said, 'You could call him Atl, for the waters that rose and flooded that day.' And that became your name."

It was the first time Atl knew he was born on an unlucky day.

A cough-roar came from far away. One-Cip' said softly, "Jaguar, my uncle. You jump for the jugular. Your teeth are long and your spots are lovely."

They waited, and after as long as it would take a large animal to eat a small one they heard the cough again, but farther away. One-Cip' was the last to lie down, after rubbing his knees for a long time.

***

Tomorrow came. After the four ate dried maize, they took a steep rocky downhill path beside the stream. Dahlia stepped so lightly it seemed she only touched the ground because it was expected. Atl did not know how to talk to her now that she looked more like a mother than a girl. But he said, "How did your father lose his eye? If you don't mind telling."

"I don't mind," she said. "He told me that when he was a boy, he broke off a tree limb without praising it, and the sharp end sprang and gouged out his eye. It surprised everyone because, you know, One-

Cipactli is one of the lucky days."

"Yes."

"He doesn't like to talk about it, but once he told me that after that happened, he no longer trusted in his birth-day luck. He said that one day his brother told big lies, and a priest was fetched from Coatepec to cut a gap as wide as two teeth from his lower lip."

"The lifetime mark of a liar."

"Yes. And when Father saw that, he set himself a path of honesty. After some time he gained the ear of the elders. People began to trust him, even far away. That's how he earned profits and almost proved he had the luck back. But my mother, who he says was as pretty as an orchid, died giving birth to me."

"I know," was all Atl could think to say.

"Your mother," said Dahlia, "even though she cannot talk, is like my own now, the way she looks after Deer of Stone and me."

"And your father has taught me a lot of things. It's like…"

"Yes," said Dahlia, and they both laughed. "I love the cloth your mother weaves. Everyone likes the way she puts her bright colors together across the bands."

Atl said, "You know she uses the cotton your father brings each year from the Land of the Turkey and Deer."

Dahlia nodded. "Father says that Maya and Huaxtecs come from there to Cempoala, where we are going." Her eyes widened. "And there are trading booths as far as you can see."

He said, "Stone towers higher than trees."

They walked with smiles. The trail joined a wider one paved with stones. It led down to a wide flat swamp which vanished ahead of them into a gray-blue mist. One-Cip' made them drink as much water as they could stand, "…while it is still good."

Atl was the first to see the tops of the white temples of Cempoala rising above the mist in the trees. The air was hot and heavy now, and smelled like fish. White birds circled and cried out. The marshes spread into endless waters.

One-Cip' stood at a booth of roasting cacao beans. "Here!" The three grinned. Dahlia clasped her hands in front of her.

The girl in the booth said as she stirred a cacao froth, "Vanilla or Honey?"

One-Cip' looked at Dahlia.

Dahlia said, "What do you like?"

18

One-Cip' said, "Vanilla."

Then Dahlia and Atl and Deer of Stone all said, "Vanilla."

One-Cip' said to the girl, "Honey," and they all laughed, even the girl. They watched her pour the honey into the froth and One-Cip' paid her with more cacao beans — twice as many as she had put into their bowl. The girl checked them to make sure they had not been gutted and filled with dirt, then served the bowl.

"It has a cool, happy taste," said Dahlia.

They all nodded.

One-Cip' glanced, then stared, at the endless waters. "That's new." Wooden towers rose, swaying slowly, bristling with poles.

"The waters speak," said Dahlia, "and don't speak, and speak again." She stared at the avenue and began to say, "Look!" over and over, and louder each time.

Atl saw a tall man with pink skin standing at a jewelry stall. Dahlia giggled.

"What?" said Atl.

"Your mouth is hanging open!"

"His hair is as red as a marigold."

Then they saw other men in costumes like clowns. They saw brown hair and straw-colored and black. The skin of two men was almost black, not from burned scorpion-powder like the priests'.

Two little girls and a boy ran in the avenue picking up rose petals. There were thousands.

Dahlia tugged at One-Cip's arm and pointed across the plaza. More strangers stood with Totonacs on a platform.

"There is the chief of the Totonacs," said One-Cip'.

Atl's eyes widened. The chief was three times larger than most men, as One-Cip' had said, but in width, not height. His loincloth had disappeared in his hanging fat. The strangers called him '*Gordo*.'

Atl heard people talking, saying the strangers were warriors who controlled and rode beasts that were like huge stags, that they carried fire-breathing weapons that killed from farther than arrows could shoot.

One-Cip' said, "We will go to the next town."

Quiahuiztlan was smaller. Several strangers sat with Totonac leaders on a low stone platform near market stalls. The stranger in the middle had pink skin, and hair on his chin and lips. He was badly dressed for the wet heat in a stiff animal skin that had been blackened and decorated with swirling scratches. He seemed to be a leader, except

19

he wore no feathers. Some called him *el Capitán*, some Señor Cortés.

A tall, slender woman stood with them, talking as they talked. She was called Doña Marina. She would point to a man and he would talk, then she would talk and point to another and he would talk.

"She speaks the Yucatec form of Maya," said One-Cip'. Atl did not understand Maya, but he knew the Totonac and most of the Nahuatl. He guessed the other tongue was that of the strangers. The Totonacs called the strangers "Sant-yagos." Señor Cortés listened but said little. Finally they stopped talking and stood and stretched.

Dahlia pointed at Doña Marina's robe. "Atl's mother wove like that."

"Yes," said One-Cip'. "I traded her patterns in the Land of the Turkey and Deer."

Dahlia stepped toward Doña Marina. "I like your robe."

One-Cip' stopped her. "Don't draw attention."

A tall, friendly-looking Sant-yago said to Dahlia, in simple Nahuatl, "She does not know your tongue. But I will tell her."

One-Cip' said to Dahlia, "We do not know that man."

"But he speaks Nahuatl," said Dahlia. "And Maya."

"Always ask me first."

"Yes. I am sorry."

The man spoke to Doña Marina, who spoke to Cortés, who smiled at Dahlia.

Suddenly one Totonac stared down the avenue behind Atl.

Atl turned and the fear came again as he saw the Aztec tribute-takers One-Cip' had made them avoid earlier on the trail. Their faces were like stone carvings: sloping foreheads, hair pasted with dried blood and glistening oil, smelling of flowers and of death. Dahlia almost spoke, but One-Cip' stopped her with a firm hand on her shoulder.

One of the Aztecs looked directly at her, with sharp eyes. He spoke to a Totonac leader, who looked around at her, then smiled.

One-Cip' said, "Let's go. Leave this town now."

But one of the Totonacs, whose upper lip stuck out like a fish's mouth, signaled them to stop. He leaned close to Dahlia, staring. Atl felt a chill under his sweat. One-Cip' put his arm around Dahlia's shoulder. He reached his other hand around his back and pulled a small cloth bag from his tote-sack. Then he moved Dahlia behind him.

Young warriors showed in the avenue. They looked like those in the High Valley, with lip-rings and knife-scars on their faces.

Fish-mouth said to One-Cip', "They must have the girl."

One-Cip' held out the bag. His good eye glared. "All this gold instead." Atl didn't know that anyone in his village had gold.

The tall, friendly Sant-yago stepped close, to see into the bag. One Aztec sang out melodiously, "The gold and the girl!"

One-Cip' stiffened, but Fish Mouth took the gold from him. The tall Sant-yago studied the bag, then quietly left.

The young Totonac warriors closed in.

One-Cip' turned quickly to pick up Dahlia, but more lip-ringed warriors showed behind him.

The Aztec threw his head back and sang, "She is ours!"

Fish Mouth bowed and directed the warriors to Dahlia.

One-Cip' shouted, "The maize priests!"

The Totonac warriors stopped again. The Aztecs frowned.

"What?" said Atl, confused.

Atl could hear the translators explaining to Cortés. "*Centoetl* is the maize-god. His priests are pure and wise, respected everywhere. They only speak when asked. They eat no meat and spend their time painting stories of the years. When they are called for a hearing, it must be carried out. There is no higher court."

The Totonac leader sent for the priests of Centoetl. After a long time, two old men walked slowly to the center of the avenue. Their faces looked out from the disjointed mouths of fox-heads.

Atl wiped the sweat on his face. "Will they help?" he whispered.

One-Cip' said, "Not even the maize priests will defy the Aztecs. And they will consider, as they decide, that I am disloyal for not giving up Dahlia happily. But a hearing could buy us time."

"Time to do what?

One-Cip' looked around. "I do not know."

The priests of Centoetl made One-Cip' and the Totonac leader come to them. They asked and listened for a long time, then waved them away. One-Cip' came back and stood beside Dahlia. She seemed too scared to move. Even Deer of Stone could not hide his fear.

One priest spoke. His first sounds were weak and strained. He cleared his throat. "It is not good to Centoetl that innocent ones be killed. Thus life must be protected."

Atl took a deep breath and looked at One-Cip'.

One-Cip' whispered, "That was for the priest's face in front of the people."

"But," said the priest, "to protect life is a puzzle. One who is chosen for sacrifice, then freed, may be the worse for the wrath of unsatisfied gods. And everyone, having less maize, would take their sufferings out on the young one. For her to live would be harmful to her." He made a solemn face. "Centoetl is merciful and just. Thus the girl will be protected from harm by being sacrificed."

Atl almost cried out, "Two-talk!" but One-Cip' held him.

***

Cortés stood. He and other Sant-yagos stepped down to the plaza. His legs were oddly bowed. He spoke to the Town Chief. One of the Sant-yagos marked a hard tablet with a black stick. The translators' eyes widened as they passed the message from language to language, leaving out the Nahuatl. Atl heard it in Totonac. "Send a message to Gordo that the Totonacs are holding the Aztecs for their crimes. We will back you."

The Town Chief's mouth dropped. He looked around at the Sant-yagos in their silly costumes. Then he turned to a messenger and gave him a part of his bracelet and leaned close to him and whispered, hitting his fists together, then sent him running toward Cempoala. All the town watched the road and waited in silence. The Aztecs stood apart, smelling roses, sighing loudly, ignoring the Sant-yagos.

Soon the runner returned, shouting. He handed the chief a small dried skin with pictures. The chief calmed him, read the pictures, then gave an order to the warriors and they seized the Aztecs. The Sant-yagos watched, ready. The warriors shouted and danced around the captive Aztecs, who glared viciously at the Town Chief.

One-Cip' said, "I believe you are saved, Dahlia."

"But what does Cortés care about Dahlia?" said Atl.

"He cares nothing for her," said One-Cip'. "He has a plan. I do not know it. I have never seen this kind of defiance in the empire."

More Totonacs arrived from Cempoala, cheering and pushing at the Aztecs. Finally the Town Chief held his hands out and there was quiet and all eyes were on him and he said, "Do not gloat. These are only five. And this will not be taken lightly in the High Valley."

"We won!" shouted a warrior. "We have them!"

"Sacrifice!" shouted another.

"No!" said the Town Chief, then looked at Cortés, who nodded.

The Town Chief announced, "We shall keep these men the night, then take them to the Chief in Cempoala."

The warriors cheered again and tied up the captives.

"We will go," said One-Cip'. They hurried toward Cempoala, through the crowds coming from there.

"Where will you go?" said the tall, friendly Sant-yago, appearing suddenly beside them. "Are you from a nearby village?"

Dahlia pointed westward, but One-Cip' quickly pushed her hand down. He said to the man, "We will walk without you."

The man squinted where Dahlia had pointed, then bowed and left them.

"Do not forget," said One-Cip'. "These are strangers."

"Will they harm us?" said Atl.

"The leader Cortés looks silly but he has the lust for power. He must know of the Aztecs' gold. You saw how his mouth gained him the Totonacs for allies. When the Aztecs hear, the Totonacs will need him and his army. No turning back."

They passed two Sant-yagos talking seriously on a temple step. One was in the strange Sant-yago costume, the other in course brown cloth from his shoulders to the ground, drawn at the waist with a rope. His smooth hair was black, tied behind his head.

Chapter 4

Howard woke to an unusual quiet: no rain. It was the sixth day at the camp. A few knuckle-sized drops from the trees still knocked down on the canvas. The rapids were louder. He pulled a window-flap. In the misty shadows of the undergrowth, he saw an odd, curved silhouette.

Then he thought the ground shook.

He tapped L.P.'s shoulder. "Did you feel that?"

L.P. grunted and rolled over.

"L.P.," said Howard.

L.P. sat up. "Hey, did I tell you Maria the translator told Maria the cook she'd opt to help me instead of her? That is, if they'll let her?"

"No."

"When we loaded the boats she bumped me three times."

"She bumped you?"

"Yep. How do you figure that?"

"She's as clumsy as you."

"I'm serious. What'd she mean by it?"

"L.P., how old are you?"

"Thirty. You know that."

"And you can't read a woman?"

"Can you?"

Howard opened the tent flap again. "I'm only twenty-nine." The curved silhouette moved. He glimpsed a low, dim reflection, like an eye. Then all of it swelled and flowed. Too big for an ocelot. The canvas between it and him was nothing, but the expected fear didn't come. The eye was appealing, as if all it wanted was company. "Jaguar," he said.

"No way," said L.P.

Then the whole form moved away, and a throaty, coughing

sound came from farther out.

Howard said, "Evil."

"Huh?"

"The Aztecs ripping hearts out. Drowning kids. Not sick. Evil."

Thunder rumbled from the west. The ground shook again. They crawled out of the tent. Crauder stood at the river. DeSparr communed with trees at the edge of the camp.

"Maybe we should move the tents to higher ground." Howard pointed to a silt rise farther back. "Up there. It shouldn't take a day."

"I've got some ideas how we can do it," said L.P.

"Well, two days, then."

Before they finished stretching, Howard flattened two mosquitoes on his sleeve.

"Get 'em?"

"Yep. Enjoyed it. I figure they're exempt from the team oath."

"Team oath?"

"You know. No matter what the risk, we won't harm any 'natives or wildlife species.'"

Through a break in the trees where some of the fog had cleared, they saw broad new columns of rain slogging down the mountains.

L.P. sighed. "Your Aztecs must be drowning a lot of kids."

***

A new hissing wind shook the limbs and leaves all around. A big cold raindrop soaked into Howard's cotton shirt at the shoulder.

Suddenly Crauder wheeled and pointed up the river. Howard looked. A crooked wave, about a foot high, rolled out of the fog.

"Get out!" shouted Crauder. "Up the dune!"

Howard should have known. A little kid should have known. The hurricane passing in the Caribbean, the days and days of heavy rain. Too late to move the tents. He stuck his head in his tent and grabbed his book in its plastic bag.

The wave crested the bank and swept through the tents. Frustrated, complaining people crawled out.

Suddenly laughing roared from the edge of the camp. DeSparr, head back, mouth wide, jaw throbbing.

Another wave quickly followed, higher than the first. Crauder waded toward the supply tent. "Hey, people! This is no drill! Get out!"

"Oh!" shouted Dove-Ti from higher ground. "The boats!"

Howard looked. The big wooden rowboats, with the food and supplies, had broken loose and were rocking down the river, clunking against each other. He ran for them, but could only watch them crash and break up over the rapids and drop out of sight in the rain and mist.

Dove-Ti and Rachel and Mrs. Crauder awkwardly pulled the big bag of plastic trinkets out of the supply tent.

Howard handed Rachel his book in its bag. "Hold this for me?"

She seemed surprised, but took it and ran with the others for the dune. She looked back and shouted, "Doctor DeSparr! High ground!"

DeSparr's head barely moved, like a cat setting its ears. Then he laughed again, and as if the laughing had started it, the trees roared above them, and the rain came again, crashing through a million leaves.

"Go for the dune!" said Howard to Smith, who stood slumped.

Then Smith's jaw dropped when Crauder came out of the supply tent with a shiny pistol, dripping water. "Jud! What…?"

"C'mon," said Crauder, and ran for the dune, where most of the team stood now, feet apart, gray in the rain, forearms above their faces, watching.

DeSparr began a march, slogging not toward the dune, but the river, the long black raincoat flying cape-like in the wind, head back, skull-white face up, mouth red and toothy in the thick black beard, arms out as if he himself had invoked the stinging spray and rising water.

Another huge wave knocked DeSparr down and tumbled Howard and Smith and Blake and L.P. and the whole supply tent to the ground. They helplessly watched the tent, the radio, the generator, and the rest of the supplies tumble into the river and over the falls.

DeSparr somehow regained his footing and stepped, incredibly, into deeper water, the raincoat ballooning on trapped air.

Blake and L.P. ran to join the others, shouting "C'mon!"

Howard glimpsed Rachel on the dune, foot forward, calling out, arms stretched, his book swinging from one hand in its plastic bag. A painful thought came to him, that she, of all of them, would act.

DeSparr's mouth drew back and the eyes widened and reddened and darted left and right with the explosive spray and flying debris.

"Reverend Smith!" Howard pointed at DeSparr. Maybe Smith would offer a religious excuse to leave him. Then it occurred to Howard for the first time, that most of the team, including himself, didn't care if DeSparr, cynical and sarcastic, died, and the thought shocked him more than the sight of a grinning red-eyed man strutting into a rising flood.

Smith said, thinly, "This is a risk! Complex, not simple!"

"Please! Boil it down!" Howard wasn't going to risk anything.

"Well," Smith swayed side to side, "what's right for you?"

"To get out now!" Howard glanced at the dune. Rachel was not there, probably on her way to help him or DeSparr, dodging debris. All he could do was turn from the unsure Smith and slosh into the flood before she could get there. His boots sank in the silt. Even with the prodding from that distorted image of Rachel, each step he took needed a new excuse for the risk. He didn't care about DeSparr the man, no. Step. But DeSparr the doctor... The team needed its only doctor. Step. And a death would add confusion and there had been enough delay with all the rain. Step. But, really, he just didn't want the arrogant brain to get away before he could, someday, somehow, see it humbled.

DeSparr's whole body was so splashed and mud-sodden in the spreading raincoat that it was hard to tell where it stopped and the river started. The team's washtub came rocking and DeSparr grabbed it, then grabbed a ruined floating box of soap and a broken flashlight and threw them into the tub. He reached for a long stick, and stepped to higher bottom, where the flood was only to the knees, and somehow the whole body crawled into the tub, where there was just enough room for hips and legs folded over the useless supplies.

The water rose again. "Doctor DeSparr!"

DeSparr pushed with the stick. The tub slid jerkily into deeper water. Downstream, great shaking trees parted and fell, ripped from the earth in minutes by that which had nourished them for decades. A spiked jumble of twisted branches pricked Howard's arm as it passed.

"DeSparr!"

The doctor threw away the stick, the one means of navigating, and reached and grabbed instead the spiked branches and hugged them, laughing derisively, or in horror.

"DeSparr! Get out!" Maybe Howard could drag the tub to shore. But it spun faster toward the rapids. He couldn't move his legs against the relentless flow. And he couldn't let Rachel get there first.

DeSparr's resonant stage-voice shouted, in the spinning around, to its audience of wind and spray and dim remaining trees, laughing once more as if suddenly aware of one final irony, loud enough, even, for Howard to hear, "You can take it with...!" But a jerk of the tub stopped the voice, straightened the neck, raised the tendons, and the tub and the man and the non-grin rocked at the edge of the falls, tilted, and fell out of sight.

Another wave took Howard's footing.

***

Under, it was quieter, only a low metallic rumble. The mud-gritty flow twisted and bumped Howard against debris and stung his nose. His lungs sucked at his insides for what his insides could not provide. He flailed his elbows to protect against hard things, prickly things. He had a childish urge to apologize to the river for having built the camp too close to it, for having disturbed its smooth silt bar. But such an urge only called attention to the lack of any hearing or seeing or caring on the part of that river, which now held his future, his life. He shut his mouth to hold in what air was left and rolled himself into a tight ball.

He thought: there is no one else in this unthinking world where I'm spending my last minutes. Except there is DeSparr, whom I hate.

And he wanted to see and know that his enemy, who could hear and feel and think, was there, and wanted his enemy to know that he was there, hearing, feeling, thinking.

Then the river seemed no more to fall, but to churn and to hit him with tree-limbs and gravel, and to scrape him against boulders.

Then it threw him up and he saw DeSparr's wet-bearded head, close, bobbing, the mouth drawn back, red flesh pumping air, eyes wide and vacant, arms not swimming, but, incredibly, still hugging desperately the wad of spiked branches. Howard turned away and threw his arms wildly in all directions, to find something stable, but his left arm somehow locked with DeSparr's arm, and he couldn't free it. He paddled desperately with his right arm, and was finally able to grab a big passing limb-trunk, and it twisted violently and slid him, still locked with DeSparr, up to a flat spot on a large rock and to air.

Howard slipped several times but got to a place where he could sit. His arms and legs worked. He couldn't avoid making his own strange raspy noises, rocking with each breath, having a relentless need for air. There was blood on him but not from his mouth or nose. He propped DeSparr up. The doctor sat slumped, spitting, coughing, hugging the wad of spiked branches as if it were all that mattered.

Above them the flood soared loudly over the huge gash it had cut in the earth like an excavation for a highway. It splashed into the sky, falling over the acres of tree-denuded land, throwing trunks and limbs around, making new muddy streams in the still-heavy rain.

When Howard got his breath he said, "Dr. DeSparr!"

DeSparr coughed helplessly, like a child crying.

Howard leaned close. "Dr. DeSparr! Are you in there?"

DeSparr suddenly flailed an arm as if trying to swim in the rain, wincing and panting.

"What were you doing back there?"

DeSparr stopped. His eyes went red and blank.

The flood still rose. "We've got to get to higher ground."

DeSparr turned suddenly. "Why?"

"Drowning's bad for you." Howard enjoyed the sarcasm.

"Merge or drown!" said DeSparr, glaring at the muddy torrent. "None of this merged with me. Or drowned me. It only left me."

"Shut up."

DeSparr froze. He squeezed the branches as if they were his last hope. Blood dripped from them. He glared down at his slumped body. His throat made a sudden catching sound. "Leave me here."

Howard had not meant to save him. It had bothered him that Rachel may have meant to save him. "Get up!" he said, rising. He grabbed DeSparr from behind, avoiding the sharp, clutched branches. "Come on!" He lifted the crumpled body. He shoved it upward and the two of them began walking, stumbling, grabbing at trees and vines for support, knees wobbling. Water squished in Howard's boots. When they got high enough he let DeSparr go and sat down, gasping.

***

DeSparr had a whole forest in which to strut importantly away, to find his special place and sit and commune with his tree-gods, to show, after being saved from his own freaky self, the absurdity of his arrogance. But he sat beside Howard, gasping, wincing, bloody black clothes soaked and shining, head hanging.

Had Howard not been so beaten and lost, he would have left him and searched for the others. Were the others even alive? Now he felt more acutely the burning and aching. "Put the branches down," he said. "They're cutting you."

DeSparr hugged them tighter, rocking. "My mother." He swatted the air, angrily, as if it were blocking his voice from some vague audience. "She left me with people."

"Oh, great," said Howard, dropping his head between his knees.

"Weeks," said DeSparr to all the forest. "Months. I never knew how long it would be." He dug his fingers into the wet matting of leaves and brown beetles and came up with a handful of wet, black dirt. He smeared it on his face, where it streaked in the rain.

"Stop." Howard looked away disgusted.

"She and my father had agreed to have me aborted. How do I know? My 'dear' aunt yelled at my mother about it when I was seven. Abortion failed. I had to ask my second grade teacher what an abortion was. I'm sure everybody thinks it should have succeeded."

"Naw, naw." It always annoyed Howard for a man to fish for sympathy. But he was curious. "Your father agreed?"

"My father was a dope-head."

That shocked Howard. Not the fact, but the telling of it.

"Picture-taker." DeSparr rubbed the mud around his nose and eyes and beard. "Called himself 'Dead-eye.' And that's what I called him. Couldn't last two weeks on a job before he sold his camera for dope." He dug up another fistful of dirt. "I was nine when I first heard it. 'Dead-eye the dope-head.'" He hit at the air with the fistful of dirt. "The sneer-look." He started each sentence with a cough-cry. "'Where's your ma?' they would say. Then the sneers."

"Deal with it," said Howard, pushing aside a new, curious fear.

DeSparr raised his head defiantly. "I learned to sneer back. I had it on the sneerers. I thought, you see. Do you understand what it is to truly think? I discovered truths. Any marriage was simply prostitution, the family a burdensome result. And greed and power and social status? These were no different, no better, than my father's addiction. Of course! Even caffeine is addictive. Yes. All of it. The middle class, the hypocrisy of religion. Superstitions. Who didn't deserve a sneer? But," he said, "the consummate revelation came when I saw that their sneers, and the limited brains that produced them, were made up of nothing more than flesh. Flesh, don't you see? Flesh is matter. Fish. Ferns. Moss is matter. And guess what? Matter doesn't matter. This was gratification, not the fact, or even the fact that I knew it, but the fact that I knew it and they didn't."

As he talked, his look of terror grew wilder and he began to glare beyond and behind Howard, causing Howard to actually look behind himself to make sure some monstrous horror wasn't rising there.

30

"But," said DeSparr again with a serious frown, "the true dilemma of the matter was that since no one was more than matter, no one would matter, would they?" Then his eyes narrowed and he mumbled, "Not even I…" He paused, seeming to search for words. "It was ultimate equality in all its horror." He shut his mouth, as if afraid now of the plainness of his words and of the implications were they right, and as terrified by a new frankness from within himself as he had been at ease with whatever seeming demons had for all those years camped welcome there.

"So," he said, shaking off his fright, "could it be, that since I knew that we were all whats, not whos, and they didn't know it, and since I chose to think about it, and they didn't, that I was in fact a higher form of matter? I had found the thought-steps, the glorious steps, like those of the old Aztec temples, and stepped far above." He calmed for a moment. "The river could have drowned me. It wouldn't have mattered. Or it could have by some ultra-scientific twist of universal law merged me and my natural insight fully with itself and the trees. It does – did – seem possible." He waved an arm. "Talk about an oceanic experience."

He looked directly at Howard and sputtered, hands groping nervously as if it were his first and last chance to say his piece. "I would have become the first pan-personality. But you had to bull your way into that unfolding matrix."

Then suddenly he held out a hand toward the muddy, broken edge of land still being cut back by the raging flood. "Now bird-droppings full of seeds must rebuild this devastation. And reason, full of carefully selected facts, must rebuild for me, piece by piece, my precious proof that no one, no what, can ever be a who." He trailed off again and rocked back and forth, hugging the branches and wincing.

Then he frowned as if in pain. "Dead-eye flat on the kitchen floor with roaches and dope. Through med school I borrowed money and pictured him. Every completed course was a punch in his dead-eye face." He shook, then seemed to sink within himself. "People came to me," he said, beginning to use his stage voice again. "'Save me!' they cried. And they were only fleshy matter. But I was the matter that knew. And knowing raised me to the… gave me the…" His voice went to a scratchy whisper at the end of his breath, "gave me the privilege…" Then strangely he spoke two words with the ghostly hollow trick of sucking air. "To choose." He looked at Howard. "Can you imagine?"

It gave Howard chills. This was the team doctor, on whom alone

31

the team must depend for life-saving treatment.

DeSparr nodded seriously as if reading Howard's mind. "Horrible, isn't it?" He shuddered. "That river... It rejected me. But I concede that it had every right." He coughed despairingly.

The doctor, thought Howard, has taken personhood from humans and granted it to a river.

"Look," said Howard, without conviction, "We'll be okay."

"And all this," said DeSparr, "has me utterly..." he tightened his dirt-blackened fists in front of his face as if squeezing the words out of the air, "utterly..." he hugged the wad of branches, wincing and hitting them with his elbows, "utterly..." he shivered violently and his voice dove to a long rumbling air-sucking growl, "...alone."

Howard thought, but didn't want, to put his hand on DeSparr's shoulder, to say things he didn't know how to say, that he cared, or that he would be a friend, and oddly at that moment he almost saw in the tormented soul a kind of warmth. "So you did well in med school?"

"Immaterial," said the doctor, shutting him up again. It was as if Howard's speaking, rather than comforting DeSparr, had shaken him back into arrogance. In his tone and his eyes Howard could almost have believed there were demons returning, after running from DeSparr's momentary forthrightness, after leaving him to drown, seeing now that his life force was still intact and vulnerable, like meat for piranhas, unguarded by anything they might fear.

"You're bleeding," said Howard.

"Blood," said the mouth. "Dirt... Fire... Water... Air."

"Some of the others may be hurt. They'll need your help."

"I earned my skills. I say how they are to be distributed."

"You're a pro. You signed on. You have a responsibility."

The doctor's face rose and turned away, disgusted.

And that increased Howard's hollow fear should anyone become desperate for medical help. He leaned over his knees, careful not to press or stretch any sore places. He would rest ten minutes, then look for the others. The expedition would be over soon. He was ready for the helicopter and a normal doctor.

**

Two hours later the rain stopped. The team stood or sat or lay on higher ground, close but not touching, silent so not to be branded

32

upon any choice of words as crazy, Crauder and Rachel and Blake and L.P. having searched and found Howard and DeSparr, Crauder having jerked the spiked branches out of DeSparr's chest and arms, exposing deep cuts, Rachel having ripped off one of her own soaked but clean cotton sleeves for a tourniquet, Howard and others having carried the wilted doctor up the mountain as Rachel limped along wrapping the bloodiest gashes with her torn-off shirt tail.

Now DeSparr lay on the ground, and Rachel and Zoe cleaned and wrapped his wounds.

"Good thing Zoe's a trained nurse," said Rachel.

"Let him heal himself," said Howard. "The idiot."

"Everybody's health matters," said Rachel.

DeSparr raised up and cried, angrily, "Just name one thing, you who search the jungle for meaning, one thing anywhere in this mad universe, that does, in fact, matter!"

"Beer," said L.P., merrily. No one laughed.

"Cost," said Rachel softly and hesitantly, mystifying Howard and mysteriously ending that line of thought.

Finally L.P. pointed at the flood. "Unbelievable."

The tops of the few remaining trees swayed wildly above the crashing waves. The wide water movement made Howard uneasy, as if it were he and the team and the land careening in the opposite direction.

He said to L.P., "Do we know anything about the camp?"

"Formatted," said L.P.

"Everything?"

"All we've got's what we carried to the dune."

"Radio?"

"Couldn't find it. Or the generator or the compass or the medicine or the food except three cans of creamed corn Maria the cook saved along with her wooden spoons. Mrs. Crauder saved that bag of plastic toys for the tribe. What was all that with DeSparr?"

"Long story," said Howard. He glanced back at Rachel. "Why's she limping?"

"Rachel? She twisted her ankle."

Rachel looked up from tending DeSparr. "Not bad." She shook her head and made her crinkled, embarrassed grin, as if not sure how it could have happened.

Howard could still picture her stepping out from the dune, arms raised, calling. He couldn't resist saying, "You shouldn't take chances."

"Well, look at you," she said, and he should have known she would out-scold him.

Mrs. Crauder groaned and leaned on a tree with both hands.

Zoe said, "She sat on one of Maria the cook's wooden spoons. Poor thing broke it and cut her, like... self."

"Ouch. So you've got three patients."

"Had to treat her over there behind that big log. It's just very tender. Good thing Rachel's here, with her playground experience."

"All this takes the cake," said Rachel, "for playground accidents."

The bandages Rachel had torn off her shirt for DeSparr were soaked red. Zoe stood up and tore off the bottom of her shirt. Her midriff was smooth and tan. Howard and L.P. watched, then looked at each other, then did the same with their own, longer shirttails.

"This'll make it easier for the mosquitoes," said L.P.

Others tore their shirts and made a fair-sized pile of gritty rags. Rachel handed Howard his book. "You haven't forgotten this?"

"Oh," he said. It was still dry in its plastic bag. "Thanks."

She picked up the rags and took them to a small stream nearby. She piled them on a rock and went to her knees, favoring the ankle. She soaked a long rag in the stream, and scrubbed hard. She had no soap. She glanced at Howard, but he decided not to go and help her.

"'Bout the only thing worse than an unpredictable screw-up," said Crauder, staring at Howard who sited the tents on the silt, "is a predictable one."

"I must have missed when you predicted it," said Howard.

"Okay." Smith raised both hands. "Okay. Blake? What's saved?"

"Nothing," said Blake. "No tents, no compass."

"No hammocks," said Zoe. "No supplies. Not even the radio. We can't even like... make contact!"

"God! No cameras, either!" said Pryce.

"The wine!" said Beg. "Anybody know about the wine?"

"How'd you know we had wine?" said Smith.

Beg grinned, then frowned.

"I saw a wooden box floating away," said Zoe. "Was that it?"

"It was for a celebration when we're done," said Smith.

Birds and monkeys chirped and howled through the roaring of the flood. Rachel scrubbed away. There was still a sense of the presence of little men in the woods.

"Folks," said Smith, "don't forget the helicopter. The pilot will bring in a rescue team when he doesn't hear from us by contact time."

"But, like..." said Zoe, "when's contact time?"

"Day after tomorrow," said Smith. "We can sit down and talk about our options."

"But... how will they know where we are kind of thing?"

"The pilot should have a pretty good idea. He's in the 'copter back there – you remember. He'll pass any information to Tegucigalpa. He can give a pretty good idea of our location. You all know that if there's one thing we planned carefully," he glanced at Blake, "it was our safety. And even if the searchers don't hear anything from the pilot for ten days, they go to that town — what is it, Blake? — with the airstrip?"

"Las..."

"Las Derivas," said Zoe. "I know about that, but..."

"They wait for us there," said Smith. "We paid for that."

"Yes, but how far is it?" said Zoe. "Which way? Blake?"

Blake looked at the thick clouds. "Still can't tell."

Suddenly Dove-Ti's face went blank. She pointed at the flood.

Everyone looked. Upstream, stuck and almost hidden among the splintered trees, was the red and white helicopter, twisted and rocking in the heavy waves.

Blake started walking toward it. Others joined him silently. They reached a point where they each saw him at the same time, the pilot, hanging limp in the rain over a bent rotor blade. They stared, horrified.

"No way to get to him," said Blake.

"Oh!" said Zoe. "What does that mean? Nobody will know. Right? Nobody will come after us. They'll be going like... 'Where are they?' Oh, the poor guy! He was... I mean, I never really talked to him or anything, but... Wasn't he local? Oh... He may have had a fam..."

A loud crack came from downstream, a tree breaking up and rolling over in the flood, and a series of echoes, and a sudden crying out of scattering birds.

Chapter 5

Tomás Santillana knelt at the base of Cempoala's tallest pyramid. He shouted, "Padre Díaz! Get help! This man is trapped!" He caressed the arm of the unconscious man. "He is a Totonac priest!"

Soldiers formed noisy ranks in the grand avenue.

Díaz blinked nervously. "They won't listen. The men saw Cortés hang those who listened to me before."

"They know it was he, not you, who had all our ships burned. And he will not hang a priest."

"But he will hang the men," said Díaz. "We are all trapped." He pointed at the broken stone jaguars and birds and snakes lying around. "I am sorry this poor man chose to jump under that rock, but…"

"He tried to save it when Cortés had it thrown down. It is an icon of his people! A carved jaguar head. Look at it!"

"I know, Tomás. It is exquisite. Truly, I…"

"Fernando!" shouted Tomás to his old friend nearby. "Get some men to help!"

Díaz used the hobbling arrival of the officer Fernando Sera as an opportunity to excuse himself. Fernando took off his iron helmet and tucked it under his arm. He found four men and ordered them to push the jaguar head away. But as if it had been a signal, the Totonac priest let out a long hollow sigh and did not breathe again. Tomás felt the man's wrist. No pulse. A rush of memories came from twenty years before: the limp wrist of Rosa, her half-naked body lying in the stream near the tavern. He laid his fingers on the eyelids and pulled them down.

Fernando dismissed the men. He was as short at thirty-four as he had been at fourteen, back in Spain, when he and Tomás were students at the university in Salamanca. But his officer's uniform shone, and he still had the feisty look, oddly emphasized by his hobbling limp.

Tomás stood, tall and skinny next to Fernando. "Thank you anyway." His foot and knee caught in the long brown robe. He had never gotten used to it.

A grinning crossbowman strutted past. "To serve God!" He gave Fernando a jovial salute, "and get rich!"

Tomás winced. "Sounds like the names Cortés gives to towns." He tried to smirk. "'Rich Town of the True Cross?' Really."

"Point of law," said Fernando. "Set up a town. Give it a noble name. Have the royal ear."

"But Governor Velasquez commissioned him, from Cuba."

"Would you rather report to a governor or a king?"

"I am not sure I understand."

"Actually, Padre Díaz told me... Will you swear to secrecy?"

"Fernando. You are my old friend."

"I will tell you that Velasquez rescinded his orders to Cortés."

"Rescinded...?"

"After he heard that Cortés hand-picked the best conquistadores in the Islands."

"But — does that mean we are illegal?"

"Not technically. And believe me, Cortés knows the law. He heard about the rescindment from his informants and was able to sail before he got the actual note."

"I wondered why we left in such a hurry."

"Then founding and naming that little town up the coast gave him the right to report directly to His Majesty Carlos, even over the head of Velasquez."

"Odd mix of words. 'Rich Town of the True Cross.'"

Fernando pointed at the broken idols lying about where Cortés had ordered them thrown. "I think he proved his religious sincerity."

"No doubt the idols bothered him," said Tomás.

Fernando turned away slowly and raised his head. Sunlight flashed from the helmet under his elbow. He rested his other hand in the small of his back. "Did the idols not bother you?"

"They were only symbols."

"But pagan, Tomás. And you a *padre* — or something."

"Not ordained. Remember? No official capacity."

Fernando softened and grinned. His pocked cheeks pushed up against his rectangular eyes. "Holding out hope for a lady?"

Tomás winced again. He knew his ears stuck out. Again a

thought of Rosa came. It had been twenty years.

Fernando laughed and straightened. "No one should get hurt, if that is worrying you."

Tomás, then Fernando, looked down at the dead Totonac Priest. Tomás said, "Unless, of course, they resist."

"Tomás." Fernando cleared his throat. "True, Cortés was angry. But he knows what he is doing. When we threw down the idols, these blackened priests did not like it. This one was brave, I will give him that. But most of them did not get violent with us."

"Because you held them! You had to remove '*Gordo*' bodily!"

Fernando chuckled. "It took four of us to lift him."

"Even if we did not use violence, what right..."

"Listen, Tomás. Cortés is a genius. Those Aztec tribute-takers he ordered the Totonacas to capture? He let two of them go that night. You can bet they went straight to the High Valley, as he knew they would, to that emperor Motecu... Motecuhzoma. The Aztecas must be mad as hell. Defiance from the provinces. Now the whole Totonac nation, for their own protection, have no choice but to side with us."

"Side with us," said Tomás.

"Yes. It is brilliant."

"For what purpose?"

"You know the purpose," said Fernando, crisply. "To conquer for Christ."

"And what will Christ think," said Tomás, "of the harm we do?"

Fernando stiffened. "No resisting, no harming."

"And if they do resist?"

"Then it would be their own fault."

"Oh, Fernando. Even if we 'conquer' without harming anyone, what then? Make them say they believe? What if they do not? Do we kill them? Enslave them? What if they say it but do not mean it? That is not faith. We will subvert our mission."

"What is our mission?" said Fernando. "These people sacrifice humans, eat human flesh. You should be more angry with this paganism, more zealous for reform than any of us."

"Anger and zeal never reform!" said Tomás, angrily and zealously.

Fernando did not laugh. "Then what does?"

"Love."

"Love!"

"Yes. Listen to them, take time with them, know them."

Fernando rested his hand on the hilt of his sword. "Are cannibals who sacrifice humans so lovable to you?"

"You know that Christ's is a different love. He loves the unlovely."

"Actually," Fernando smiled, "some of these little ladies are not at all unlovely."

"And Christ's is a giving kind of love, Fernando. You know it. Not a taking kind."

"I will try to remember your admonition, Tomás."

"Christ's admonition," said Tomás, "not mine."

"Anyway, Tomás, do not forget: we are sanctioned by the king."

"My king is Jesus." It was a decision Tomás had finally made in Hispaniola. "These people have not harmed or threatened us."

"Tomás," said Fernando, firmly. "Díaz survived the hanging of the rebels only because he is ordained."

"I know. And I am not. And I know that you are my friend, Fernando."

"Of course, but you had better watch who may overhear you."

"I will be careful."

Fernando grabbed Tomás' shoulders. "Tomás." He searched for words. "I do care what you think." He let go, studied his friend, then stepped down, controlling his limp, into the line of troops.

Tomás called to him, "By the way, do you remember Mendez?"

Fernando stopped. "Ramiro Mendez. Yes. I have heard bits and pieces since the university. In trouble with creditors and constables and irate husbands." He frowned. "Why?"

"I saw him yesterday. Here in Cempoala. I am sure of it."

"Is he a soldier?" said Fernando. "He is not one of mine."

"I did not talk to him but he was carrying a helmet and sword."

"As if we do not have enough problems."

"People do change," said Tomás. "You know the little scar on the lip of Cortés?"

"Yes."

"He got it falling over a garden wall, running from a husband."

"I have heard several versions of that story."

"Anyone can change."

Fernando grinned. "Let us hope Mendez directs his malice to the enemy."

"The 'enemy,'" said Tomás, but Fernando was busy inspecting.

Salty gusts from the sea swirled clouds of dust around the temples and to the mountains. Gulls cried out. Sunlight flashed from the edges of swords, officers shouted, dogs barked, iron clattered. Pairs of soldiers made mock combat. Some coughed and held their stomachs.

The capitáns began calling for order. The clanging and talking stopped. Red-haired Pedro de Alvarado stood on a low temple platform and shouted instructions about overnight equipment. He closed with a rousing call to arms for King and Christ.

Tomás had often imagined, when he was at the university, back in Spain, what it must have been like at the capitulation of Granada, to see the mounting of the royal banners of Castille and Aragon billowing finally above the towers of the Alhambra. He remembered the talk of rich lands across the sea, the thrill of conquest.

Those things did not thrill him now. Thoughts of the university often went back twenty years, painfully, to his first year there, and the summer night in the tavern outside Salamanca, the night of Rosa.

***

He was fifteen. Crickets and frogs chirped and croaked along the Rio Tormes.

He and Fernando sat straight up on the crude wooden bench, nervous and uncomfortable in the brown lantern-light. Mendez, between them, leaned back against the rough, plastered wall. They watched two women dance to the syncopated strums and thumps of the musician on his vihuela de mano.

Girls never noticed Tomás. His chin was small, his nose, neck, and feet long and skinny. His mother had referred several times to his "piercing eyes of a child."

Mendez had bought a full wineskin and now he raised it and ran a finger around its middle and proclaimed, "The earth is round and full." He seemed to know everything. He looked at the two from the corner of his eye and smiled knowingly and winsomely. "Freedom!"

Tomás hoped the professors would not find out he was there, but mixing with Mendez could help him with his studies. The upper-classman was gifted with words, more from intelligent ease, it was said, than serious study. He was the best grammar and Latin student. He had impressed everyone with lengthy and accurate translations from Caesar

40

and the Vulgate, seeming obsessed with words and meanings and translations from the Greek and Hebrew. He entertained the younger students, mocking the professors subtly enough for safety and obviously enough for snickering. But they were fickle about their heroes, and it was obvious he was becoming increasingly bored with his studies.

Suddenly a girl appeared at the door, panting, a farm girl, in a long brown skirt and a course white blouse lapped and tucked into her waistband. She was awkward and girlish in spite of her mature figure. She glanced urgently at Tomás. "My mother! She fell and..."

Mendez jumped up, winked at the other two, and turned to the girl. He was tall, and had a twinkle in his deep-set eyes. He placed one foot in front of the other and bowed slightly. "I will help you, my lady."

Tomás laughed. To call a farm girl a lady! They did not know her. She did not know them. They would act out the chivalric images in their own way, with a farm girl as an audience — no, the boys would be their own audience, she a prop. Laughter eased his conscience. "And I!" he blurted, repeating Mendez' hilarious offer, "I will help you, my lady." He did not mean to snort. He looked at Mendez for approval, but Mendez only leered at the girl.

She turned quickly to Tomás. "I am Rosa. Come and help." She hurried outside.

Mendez followed. "We will help our fair maiden in distress."

The boys glanced at each other, grinned, burst into exaggerated dancing motions, and trailed out onto the moonlit road.

Fernando put his thumbs at his ears and wiggled his fingers. "Are you a Christian girl?"

Tomás roared with too-loud laughter. They had just had lessons about the inquisition. "I am the inquisitor-general!" he shouted, and his voice cracked. "I am Tomás!"

"Tomás de Torquemada!" said Fernando. Even Mendez laughed at that one.

Rosa walked fast, breathing hard. "My mother is in much pain."

"Oh," said Mendez, "she will need cloth for bandages!" He pulled the front of her blouse.

"Stop!" she shouted, and walked faster.

Mendez suddenly grabbed her blouse from behind and pulled. She stumbled backwards, then turned and swung at him. He laughed. His long arm kept her away but still held the blouse. Then, in the swinging and turning, and Mendez' adroit pulling, the blouse slid down her arms and off. Fernando frowned. Tomás looked away quickly.

"Leave me alone!" She turned and folded her arms and shouted, "Give it to me!" She began to cry. "My mother made it."

Tomás felt bad for her, but when Mendez pursed his lips and held the blouse up and said, "Her mother made it," his expression could have been mock sympathy for its loss or disdain for its quality, and Tomás thought it was the funniest acting he had ever seen.

Then, with calm authority, Fernando said, "Give it to her."

Mendez ignored him and held the blouse high. "Reach!"

"Give it to her!" Fernando shouted.

Suddenly, Mendez threw the blouse down, spun, and grabbed Fernando's neck with both hands. "You've destroyed the moment!" He forced him backwards to the dark edge of the river bank and pushed him down it. "You're no man!" He turned and chased Rosa. Tomás left Fernando and ran after the dazzling Mendez.

Mendez caught Rosa and held her.

"Leave me alone!" She cried, keeping her balance. She pointed at a tiny flicker on a rise a half mile down the road, above the trees. She glanced again at Tomás. "That is my house!"

Mendez pushed her to the stream bank.

Tomás studied the faint light. Her mother's unseen presence reached through the trees with the mist. She would have cared for Rosa as Rosa cared for her, as Tomás cared for his mother who cared for him. He was suddenly, surprisingly embarrassed for Rosa trying to hide her bare chest. He ran and stood beside her.

Mendez shouted, "Push her!"

Her eyes were fearful and distant now. The lowest class against university students. Tomás cried, "Her mother needs help!"

"You are no man!" Mendez shoved Tomás aside and grabbed Rosa again and pushed her down the bank as he had Fernando. She disappeared between two great oak trees. Tomás heard a loud thump and a small splash, then only the gurgling of the stream.

Fernando arrived, hobbling, holding a knee. "What happened?"

Tomás could just make out Rosa's limp body, face under the water. He and Fernando jumped down to the rock and pulled her out.

Tomás felt her wrist. No pulse. Her arms and torso were strangely blue-white. His own blood rushed in his ears, louder than the stream splashed. He looked away and stood to block Mendez' view.

Mendez said, "Nothing happened. We have been in the tavern."

"She is dead!" Tomás shouted.

"Shut up!"

"Her mother is hurt!" Tomás pointed to the flickering light down the road.

Fernando studied Rosa once more, then turned and hobbled back toward the tavern.

Tomás had never seen a dead human. She had been warm, alert, responsible. Her voice and her movements had been new to him.

"Fernando did it!" said Mendez. "Pushed her down the bank. Just playing around, you know? Did not mean to hurt her. She was drunk. Typical peasant. Hit her head on the rock. We can head him off!" He ran back toward the tavern.

Tomás hardly heard him. The thought of going to the mother of the dead Rosa was unbearable. But he turned and stomped jerkily along the road toward the house, wiping his eyes. He felt six years old with a too-big body. He could frighten the mother, coming out of the dark. He frightened himself. The road rose narrowly but gently in front of him and he saw the house on a steep hillside across a ravine. He knew the kind of house: crude and uncomfortable.

He heard a groaning, then barely saw, in the bottom of the ravine, a woman partly covered by a blanket. High on the opposite side was the dimming, flickering light. She was unattended the longer because he and the boys ignored the pleas of her daughter now dead.

He slid down to her. She grimaced and seemed to hold herself in place by effort, as if the earth provided no support.

"I cannot get up. I am hurt. Help me to the house."

"Where does it hurt?"

"My back. And my hip, there. My daughter is gone for help."

His throat caught, but he said, "You had better not move." He gathered leaves and straw and stuffed them under her.

"You are from the university?"

So it was obvious. Tomás said, "Do you have other children?"

"Only Rosa."

He could not tell her what happened. "I will go for help."

"Are you a Christian?" she said, seriously. It was the very question, not from a catechism or an inquisition, but with which he and the others had tormented her daughter now dead.

What answer? He was not a Moor or a Jew. But that was not her question. He could tell that hers was about his heart.

43

"I am baptized," he said, lamely. "Are you comfortable?"

"Pray for me." It was simple. All she wanted was, if he was a Christian, prayer. But a prayer ignoring the murder would be fake. God would be sadly and gravely aware of the omission. And if he mentioned it, Rosa's mother would hear.

He put a knee on the ground and a hand on her shoulder. "*Ave...*"

"No. Use words I know."

He felt Rosa's murder in the smell of creek water on his clothes, in the smell of his sweat. He felt it in the withholding of the news from the one who most should know it. He felt it in the now-disgusting image of the face of Mendez, and in the throbbing of his own heart.

"Praise God," he said, translating from the Latin. "Christ is King of kings." For the first time he was struck by the meaning of those last words, which he had said aloud: Christ was higher than their majesties Isabella and Ferdinand. It calmed him. An opening seemed to occur in the universe, even a sense of personal contact with its creator. "Help this woman be well. I have done things, eh... things not like you want. All power is yours. In the name of Jesus." That was the way they usually ended prayer at the university. "Amen."

It was stupid and choppy, but at least he admitted to God that he had displeased him without revealing the act to the mother.

"Thank you," she said and closed her eyes. "Can you stay until my daughter is back?"

With that, she unknowingly destroyed his new calm. He could leave. He had not told her his name. He would never see her again. He stood. She was uncomfortable but, unlike him, peaceful. That was probably because she thought her daughter would come. She did seem strong. She could probably handle things without his help.

He looked down the road, then back at her. Then back down the road.

***

"Very weak pulse," said the voice of Fernando. Tomás woke slowly. Fernando was kneeling, feeling the mother's wrist. Very weak."

Tomás sat up. "She... does not know... about Rosa."

"Rosa is alive. The musician and I went back to her. Her pulse returned. Here she is. Mendez has disappeared."

44

Tomás looked up at the musician, who stood there with his arm around Rosa, who leaned on his side, pale and tired, but breathing. Tomás wept. It was as if her recovery had been his own.

***

The burial service was simple and quiet but for the steady, vertical rain and the priest's gentle voice. It was in a grassy clearing below the turret-buttressed dome of the cathedral, not far from the old Roman bridge across the Rio Tormes.

There were seven people. Rosa stared at the clear rainwater running through the grass as the priest recited Latin prayers lamenting the too-early death. She wouldn't have known their meaning, but Tomás did. He was the enemy who had helped make them necessary.

Had she changed? Had she learned, in that one desperate night, of the carelessness, not heroic, not boyishly cute, but callous and horrible, in the human spirit? Had she learned it from Tomás and his friends? Students from the greatest university in Europe? Their credentials had given them a moral and intellectual upper hand, which led to moral and intellectual freedom, which led to moral and intellectual license and corruption.

He had faced the professors and the priests. Confessing to them had been difficult. Fernando wanted no part of it, had told him he was crazy. 'The girl' would not tell, he had said. And even if she did, the professors would not believe her over their own students. But Tomás could not sit in the lectures and pretend innocence. The dishonesty would rob his work of its meaning, as if he were busy about nothing.

Tomás was allowed to interrupt the forty days of prayers and community service prescribed by Padre Ruiz so he could attend the burial service. He could have given money instead. His family could have afforded it and the priest urged it. But he wanted to carry out the acts themselves.

When the service was over, he forced himself to approach Rosa. She was staring at the freshly broken earth as an aunt shielded her from the rain with a crude umbrella. He was conscious of his skinny neck and nose, and his big feet. Hair and water ran down his face.

"I'm sorry," he blurted.

Her round eyes didn't blink. "Thank you for helping Mamá."

"It was nothing," he said, wondering if anything was anything.

She said, "You had better get some shelter."

***

Tomás was shaken from these memories by the final calls of the officers from Cempoala's main temple platform and from far down the lines of conquistadores. Soldiers straightened. Hundreds of pikes and halberds jabbed the yellow sky. Winds whipped in from the sea. Men ran from behind a wall with long poles wrapped in colored cloth. Cheers rose from each unit as its pennant was unfurled.

In a line, along one side, came the capitáns: Pedro de Alvarado, Juan de Escalante, Cristobal de Olid, coughing, Juan Velasquez de Leon, Alonso de Avila, and Hernán Cortés, red-eyed with fever but unyielded. A tall Mayan woman walked beside Cortés and stopped with him each time he talked to a soldier. Finally, Rico, the most spirited of the horses, was brought to him in the lead position.

Tomás stepped down from the platform and joined padres Bartolomé de Olmedo and Juan Díaz as their non-ordained assistant. They all joined the 508 swordsmen, 32 crossbowmen, 15 cavalrymen, 14 cannoneers, 13 *harquebusiers*, 95 disgruntled sailors, and 2,000 Totonac warriors and porters.

Rico pranced nervously. Cortés bent forward in a spell of coughing. A soldier waited for him to mount, then handed him the banner, the one he had designed in Cuba, with its gold cross centered in white and blue flames. When he raised it, the wind caught it and spread its long power-and-religion motto echoing the Reconquest of Spain: "Comrades, Let us Follow the Cross, and With True Faith in this Symbol, Conquer." His eyes, like Rico's, shone wildly. He sat up straight, patted Rico's neck, and faced the westward trail to the mountains. A gull cried out. Waves rolled along the shore. Pennants fluttered. He drew his sword and pointed. Iron and leather rumbled. He cried out, his voice robbed of its usual force by the gusting wind, "You have heard of the High Valley of Mexico!" The men shouted. He and Rico turned halfway around and his voice gained strength and echoed from the steps of the temples. "The City of the Aztecas!"

46

Chapter 6

"The water's still rising," said Howard. "And we can't get to the chopper or the pilot."

"Higher ground," said Blake, "while there's still light."

Zoe looked up from tending DeSparr and called to Rachel who was still scrubbing cloths at the stream. "We're moving out!"

"Okay." Rachel gathered her work, teetered on the ankle, and looked back at the helicopter. "You hate to just leave him there."

"True," said DeSparr, limp and groggy. "We're short of food."

"Oh! Ugh!" said Zoe.

"You know what I meant," said Rachel.

Howard and Smith and L.P. picked up DeSparr, and Blake led them all up the mountainside through thick undergrowth. Howard's joints and bruises hurt, but all his limbs worked.

Crauder nudged Beg forward from time to time, whether he needed it or not. "We got jobs here," he said. "Get one."

They climbed out of the mangled gorge onto a roughly level clearing between the trunks of two huge fallen trees with black, broken limbs raised into the mist like groping hands.

"Camp Two-Log," said L.P.

The rain quit and a heavier fog started moving in.

"I love a fire," said Mrs. Crauder as they got settled.

"Dang, Pat!" said her husband. "There ain't a dry piece in a day's hike."

Blake walked toward the woods.

"Blake!" said Zoe. "Where are you going?"

Howard caught up.

Rachel set her scrubbed rags on one of the big logs. "Howard!"

Blake found a big hollow tree, crawled inside, and came out with an armload of dark, wavy strips of dry wood. Howard crawled in and broke off another armload.

When they were back, Blake stacked the smallest strips across each other. "No matches."

"Got this though," said Crauder, and he produced a cigarette lighter and a two-inch flame.

"You got any more of those?" said Blake.

"Just the one. Made it through the flood in my pocket."

"Hold on to it." Blake stacked the bigger strips on the smaller. They began to hiss and pop. Everyone stood closer as the night settled in. A warm smell of steam rose off wet clothes.

Zoe pulled DeSparr's bandages tight and warned him against moving. "You're going to need, like… stitches," she said. "You'll have to do it yourself." She turned to the team. "And, you know? We'll need to like… boil water."

"In what?" said Mrs. Crauder. "Our pans got lost."

Rachel pointed at the three cans of creamed corn Maria the cook had saved. "We could eat some corn, then use the can to boil water." She smoothed DeSparr's hair back and wiped away blood.

Howard opened a can with his pocket knife and set it on the fire.

After the corn had cooked, they each held the hot can in one of Rachel's washed cloths and, using one of the spoons Maria the cook saved, had about two slowly savored swallows of corn. Howard hated having to stop. When the can was empty, he washed and filled it in the little stream. He set it back on the fire and waited for bubbles.

Smith took his glasses off and looked at Blake and Crauder and officially cleared his throat. "Blake? Jud? We need to talk about our options." The three of them huddled to one side.

L.P. said to Rachel, "How's your ankle?"

"Sore. It'll be okay."

Howard said, "How's the doctor?"

"He's trying." The crinkled smile showed again. "Very trying."

Howard smiled. "Crazy as a bat."

"I don't know," she said, "He thinks he's… well, low."

"If you ask me, he thinks he's better'n the rest of us."

"I think that's just his way of proving he's not low."

"When we got out of the flood he smeared dirt on his face."

"I'm not surprised."

"And he said he feels all alone."

"Yes." She nodded. "Yes."

Dove-Ti spoke to the group in her calm, soothing way. "I've been thinking. Uhm... We should develop a dialogue with the forest people. We could agree to, uhm, let them keep some of the blister-packs, substitute some little rocks for the pills so they would still have something to rattle."

"That'll work!" shouted DeSparr, rising on his elbow. "They'll be so relieved that a pack of flooded-out idiots, pledged not to hurt a flea, will 'let' them and their ruthless warriors keep what they already have, that they'll be just gushingly happy to swap out the pills."

"There's no reason." said Dove-Ti, "to assume them to be uhm, 'ruthless warriors.'"

"Right, so just go pick up the antibiotics for us, would you?"

"Okay," said Smith as he and Blake and Jud finished their meeting. "Okay." He cleared his throat. "Now. What have we still got? Dr. Haughton-Alsef has his pipe."

"We're saved!" said DeSparr.

"And we still have our wristwatches."

"And silly me," said DeSparr, "afraid we'd miss a train!"

"They'll help in navigation," said Blake, "once we have sunlight."

Howard took off his busted watch. "Mine's no good."

"Wait," said Mrs. Crauder. "We can add it to the gift-bag."

Howard held up his pocket knife. "I still have this."

Mrs. Crauder pointed at Dove-Ti and squinted wonderingly at the folded black cloth she still held tightly under her arm. "And what would that be?" she said.

"Oh," said Dove-Ti. "It's uhm... my preaching frock. It's..."

"Glory!" said DeSparr. "They'll give us the antibiotics for a sermon!"

Smith held up a hand. "We need positive solutions."

Zoe pointed at his hand. "What's that like... book?"

Smith looked. "Oh, that." He turned the book up. It was soggy and coming apart. "That's my 'Robert's Rules of Order.'"

"Didn't you bring two books?"

"Well, the flood, you know. I needed a hand to break a fall."

"And the other one a Bible!" said DeSparr. "Mr. High Church Official!"

"He had to make a choice," said Crauder. "Let it be."

Dove-Ti said to Crauder, soothingly, "I saw what you sneaked

49

into your shirt. Uhm…"

"Good thing, too," he said. "That pistol'll be our power."

Smith said, quickly, "What else?"

"I've got these," said L.P., pulling three crumpled team photographs out of a plastic sandwich bag and holding them up.

"The ones we took at the airport," said Mrs. Crauder.

"Laminate them to our gravestones," said DeSparr.

Rachel said to DeSparr, "Are the bandages holding?"

DeSparr glared at her, troubled, it seemed, not over his bandages or physical pain or health, but over some private dilemma.

The little orange-yellow flame popped and slapped at the night air and waved enlarged shadows of heads and shoulders across the trees and fog. A distant crunching noise came from the flood, then a series of cracks and groans, another tree down, another wave of bird calls.

***

Smith said, "Blake and Jud and I have discerned that, besides these few things, nothing was saved. No food or medical supplies or equipment. No tents. No radio. No spare clothes. Not one hammock."

"What would we do," said DeSparr, "without our committee?"

"It's scary," said Zoe. "I'm like… what will we eat? Do we each have our same jobs kind of thing? Will we still try to make contact with those… people? Am I making sense? Do we keep our old agreements? No harm to any species? We're going to need food like… really bad. Do we just act the same as if we still had food and lived in nice little tents? Do we still search for these people and try to like… collect information? I mean, they are so creepy. And another question: should we get out of here now, before we like… starve? Do we even know how to get out? Do you see what I'm saying? This was supposed to be about information and contact, not just trying to survive."

"Survive?" said Mrs. Crauder. "Are we expected to do that too?"

Dove-Ti forced another smile. "We must never forget our vow not to harm any species or alter any cultural system. Everyone has a right to her own kind of happiness."

"You would have us die," said Crauder, "just so it can be said that this poor old jungle, which is making a pretty good mess of itself without our help, was never touched by human hands?"

Haughton-Alsef finally spoke. "What will history say if …"

"History!" said Crauder. "History's dang well proven it'll say what it dang well wants to say, no matter what you or I or anybody else does." He looked at Dove-Ti. "I say our pledge not to harm species never included game. These guides can fish, and probably hunt. Even we could learn. One thing a jungle has is plenty of food."

Dove-Ti, suddenly thoughtful, stomach growling, changed the subject. "Can't our guides hack a path for us through the jungle?"

"With what?" said Crauder.

She thought and said, "Howard, don't you have a pocket knife?" Crauder almost gagged laughing.

Haughton-Alsef said, "It seems to me especially important that we make pro-active but peaceful efforts at approaching the tribe. It's conceivable they could help us find our way out."

"Could it be," said DeSparr, leering at Haughton-Alsef, "that the loss of the cameras has cooled your quest?"

"God!" said Pryce, "Of course! The cameras were key. Without them what's the point of finding the tribe? Why did we bring me, and my skills to compose scenes? Or apply make-up for god's sake?"

"Nothing to do with it," said Haughton-Alsef, smiling pleasantly. "Of course I miss the cameras. But my concerns are as stated. Most importantly, we must establish trust with the people of this land, the Jaguar-people, if you will."

"I just had a nice thought," said Dove-Ti. "If we stay, that fire could uhm, attract the Forest People to us. And they must know we have nothing for them to steal anymore. They would have a heart. Help us. They know the forest, which we don't. Uhm…"

"Hospitality," said Haughton-Alsef, pleasantly and naturally, "is not untypical among primitive cultures."

"Not our savage little friends," said Crauder. "They've already shown us their kind of hospitality. They steal."

"I hardly think," said Haughton-Alsef, "that we can rightly call ourselves rational observers of a people while at the same time demonizing them, and calling them 'savages' simply because they express a different concept of sharing than some of us."

"Yeah," said Crauder. "A different concept: 'What's yours is ours.'"

Smith took off his straw hat and lowered his head slowly and rubbed the bald top of it. "I believe we can hash this out better after a good night's sleep."

Blake and Zoe curled up first, snuggling on the ground close to the fire, then the Crauders next to them, then all but DeSparr, who stood apart, and the watch, made up of L.P., Raul, Smith, and Pryce.

***

Howard woke to the forlorn, human-like wailing of the mountain roosters. He got up slowly, flinching from his bruises and scrapes and aching at the joints from sleeping on the ground. He rubbed his stubby whiskers. Smith stood with others around the ashes in the fire pit, groggy, squinting. The mist was warm and still.

Suddenly Raul showed, running up from the river. "He is gone!"

Smith scratched his head and put the hat on. "What? Who?"

"The pilot!"

"Oh!" Zoe pointed suddenly across the flood. "Look!"

Howard looked just in time to see a flash of dark green cloth move and vanish in the trees and undergrowth. Then another.

"Oh!" said Zoe. "They're carrying something! They're like... running in the... There they are!" She pointed again.

"They?" said Blake. "Who?"

"People in like... dark green," she said. She ran to one side and stopped. "They're carrying something, like, up on their shoulders."

"Dark green?" said Blake. "Soldiers?"

"Shoulders. No camo." She moved around, stretching her neck. "Loose cotton, like the farmers, you know? But not white. Green."

"Zoe?" said Smith. "Could they have been carrying a person?"

"Yes! On their shoulders! In yellow! That's so it! The pilot!"

"God!" said Pryce, glaring at Haughton-Alsef. "They're taking people now! I did not come here for this! This is the worst planned expedition I've ever been on, and okay, maybe it's the first one, but for your information I've seen movies."

"The Jaguar-guys'll steal anything they find," said Crauder.

"It wasn't them," said Zoe. She looked around. "We've got a new tribe, people. Just think about it. The ones who took our boots, the Jaguar-people? They just wore little loinie-thingies. These had clothes."

"Maybe the Jaggies wear clothes sometimes," said L.P.

Zoe sighed. "You men are so... If you go like... blue one day, you might go pink another, but I mean, if you go around like... naked, why would you all of a sudden go like... baggy dark green? Can you get

52

that? They are so not the Jaguar-people."

"Then they're the 'Shirts,'" said L.P. "The Greenshirts."

"But like…" said Zoe. "What do they want with a dead body?"

"God!" said Pryce. "That's it! They're cannibals! O god! I don't believe this! Cannibals! No one said! And my cameras are gone!"

"Cannibals don't wear clothing," said Mrs. Crauder. "I've seen movies too."

Zoe's face dropped to her hands. "What will they do with him?"

"The pilot?" said Crauder. "They'll eat 'im."

"Jud!" said Mrs. Crauder.

"And soon, too," said Crauder. "He'll spoil in a couple of days."

"Don't!" said Zoe, uncovering her face. "Just… Give the pilot a little dignity. If you died and somebody said you were like… buried, or… or cremated… Okay. But eaten?"

DeSparr said, "The fact is: we're all meat."

"Oh! Gross!" cried Zoe suddenly, shrinking from DeSparr.

"And we'll soon find ourselves hungry."

"Stop!" She swiped the air in front of her face. "Gross!"

"The jungle is different," said DeSparr. "When you get really hungry, you won't worry about the difference between a rabbit and a dead or hopelessly dying human."

"Don't even joke," said Rachel.

DeSparr was not joking. But Rachel's admonition shut the jaw.

Mrs. Crauder smoothed her sweatpants innocently. "What are we talking about?"

"Dang, Pat!" said her husband. "If something happened to one of us."

"No need for alarm," said Haughton-Alsef. "In any case, I think we all agree that an intelligent, scientific approach will best inform us."

"No decision about human life," said Rachel, face as red as DeSparr's. "Informed or not."

"I'm confused," said Mrs. Crauder. "New ideas are always better than old ideas. But this one doesn't seem better."

"Ah," said Haughton-Alsef. "It's better because we've moved forward. We have choices. It's the Twenty-first Century."

"The 'century' doesn't matter," said Rachel.

L.P. said, "Just don't anybody get sick or hurt."

"Please," said Zoe, "I think all of us have bunches of questions. Like, do we still try to get info on the tribe? Do we still give them those little plastic toys, after they robbed us? Am I making sense? And who are these new people in dark green? I mean, one tribe was enough, wasn't it? I'm like... hu-u-uh? What do we do about them? Do we give them gifts? Oh, my god, it's scary! It's like... majorly crucial that we work all this out! But can we bathe first? Does that make sense? I'm filthy."

"Then let's do what we need to do," said Smith. "We'll meet here in an hour.

***

At the meeting, Smith said, "Any thoughts about our options?"

"I don't want to go back to Atlanta," said Crauder, "saying all we did was get a pilot killed and lose everything we brought including our own puny butts."

"I think it will be wise," said Haughton-Alsef, "after carefully considering our security, the loss of all our supplies, and the potential abuse of this marvelous environment, to meet with our forest friends very near their home turf, and spend just enough time to offer gifts and convince them we only want directions out. Nothing more."

"This team is pathetic!" said DeSparr, propped on his elbows.

"So what would you suggest?" said Crauder. "That we all jump in the river?"

DeSparr reddened and his eyes narrowed and turned away.

"Okay," said Crauder, "let's make it easy for people to find us."

"Maybe somebody'll see that helicopter," said Zoe. "We heard an airplane the other day. Then they'll send somebody."

"Did you see the airplane?" said Blake.

"No. Too many trees and clouds."

"Same reason they can't see us."

"But," said Zoe, "couldn't we make a lot of smoke?"

"Same color as the clouds."

"If anybody sees smoke," said Crauder, "it'll be those cannibals."

"Nothing," said Dove-Ti, "has indicated the forest people are uhm, cannibals."

Smith's eyes were sadder than ever. "A vote. We can vote."

"Convenient for you," blurted DeSparr, "Voting gets you out of deciding and relieves you of responsibility for the outcome and..."

"You?" said Crauder to DeSparr. "After setting us back trying to drown yourself? We could have had the generator and radioed for help!"

"Right!" said DeSparr. "Blame it all on me, you who decide things with a gun!"

"That gun'll save your reprobate rump! And one thing that ain't gonna stop here is respect for our leader."

"'Leader!'" said DeSparr. "You mean the one who never takes a stand, who never takes sides, who offends no one, so that he rises to the top like thin air?"

Smith winced. "Thin air…" He cleared his throat and looked into his hat in his hands. Everyone watched. Finally he looked up. The tired, sad look began to leave him. "We have chores," he said. "We'll need volunteers. And I'll need to appoint and delegate."

Crauder sat back, grinning. "Here we go."

"Blake?" said Smith. "We need a new safety perimeter with watch points."

Blake got up and began pacing off distances.

Smith asked Mrs. Crauder to keep the water boiling. He asked her husband to search down river with Raul and Pedro for lost supplies. He asked Rachel and Zoe and Maria the cook to set up a laundry at the stream, Howard and L.P. to clear a path to it, then build some sort of shelter, Beg to keep the area swept and policed, and Haughton-Alsef, with Dove-Ti and Pryce, to dig a latrine downstream. "Stay within the safety perimeter, of course."

"But," said Haughton-Alsef. "We don't have a shovel, old boy."

"I think a good sturdy stick will do."

"Can't Raul and Pedro…"

"They'll help Jud look for lost supplies. Then they'll fish."

"Fish?" said Crauder. "Can there be any live fish left?"

Smith vaguely gritted his teeth. "I don't know." He looked around. "Everyone stay within the new safety perimeter. We've got two tribes out there now."

Rachel pointed at the heap of ashes. "We need some rocks or something around this." She glanced at Smith who nodded. It only took a few minutes, but several people gathered, sensing for the first time that they were laying claim to the new place.

***

L.P. said, as he and Howard cleared a trail to the stream, "Who are those Greenshirts? Why'd they take the pilot? And him dead? You think they wanta shrink his head? Eat him? Sacrifice him?"

"All I know is those dark green flashes we saw in the woods."

"You're reading about them in that book."

"They can't be the same after five hundred years."

They finished the trail and returned to the clearing. Howard pointed at two trees about twelve feet apart with major forks eight or ten feet above the ground. "We can rest roof beams in those crotches."

They managed to rest one end in one tree's fork, the other on the ground, then found another limb-beam and leaned it in the other tree's fork. They found plenty of dead limbs low on pine trees. It often took the weight of the two of them to break one off.

They found two fairly straight limbs with forks at their ends and stood them as posts about twelve feet from the two trees and rested the free ends of the beams on them, at a slope. They angle-braced them to the ground. They used small vines, though they were stiff and full of knotty joints, to tie everything. Across the two beams they laid and tied smaller limbs for purlins.

Rachel came. "Can I help? The laundry's all done."

"Well," said Howard. "We need sticks for side walls."

She shot up a tree like a monkey.

"Stiff sticks," said L.P. "But dead, so you can…"

She was already raining sticks down. "Like these?" She climbed several other trees and dropped more, faster than they could use them.

Howard got over his trained obsession with plumb and level, or trendy skewed angles, and actually saw a kind of beauty in the crooked beams and warped roof, as they echoed the lines of the rocks and woods and mountains.

He spotted a big curved piece of bark that had fallen off a tree nearby. "Terra-cotta."

They stripped more bark and took long pieces back to the clearing. Howard was able to cut and lay four shingles on the roof, half of them cupped upward and the other half downward, overlapping. He used short, stubby twigs for nails, drilling with his knife. He found a stick with a big hard knot on one end that made a sorry hammer.

Then Pedro and Raul and Crauder showed. Raul carried a wooden box. Pedro's cardboard one was soaked and falling apart. Out of it Crauder pulled a yellow candle. "We found this in the river."

"What is it?" said Pryce.

"Our supply of one gross of yellow eight-inch candles." He

grinned. "Got some matches, too." He pulled out a plastic bag with a couple of dozen little match-books.

Raul slowly tilted and drained the tightly bound wooden box. "What's that?" said L.P.

Beg grinned, eyes wide in happy anticipation.

"Twenty-four bottles of Australian shiraz," said Smith.

"Hee-hee," said Beg.

"For when we complete our mission," said Smith.

Blake walked out of the woods. "Whatcha got?" said L.P.

"Tannic bark. For soap."

Smith said, "Let's meet in an hour, when it's dark."

***

After the short twilight, they gathered around the fire.

"Well," said Smith when they had each reported on the progress of their work, "a productive day. Dove-Ti? Who's on watch tonight?"

"Uhm, Blake, Pedro, Pryce and uhm, Maria the translator."

"Let's don't talk," said Zoe, brightening, "so we can all like... sleep. Do you see what I'm saying? I don't mean we shouldn't talk about the problems and all, in the, you know, day-time — they're important — and actually, don't get me wrong, any kind of talking is nice, it's... you know, social, and helps us get things out in the open kind of thing, and I'm not like... being critical of anybody in particular, or actually of anybody at all, for that matter, naturally — it's just that talking could like... keep us awake, and we're going to need to get our sleep, those of us who want to, I mean — it's anybody's choice, of course, nobody has to..."

"Okay," said L.P. "Good idea."

Chapter 7

Tlaloc was busy on his mountain, throwing water from his jars, cooling the land, rattling the roof. The steady noise made all the world seem far away. The fire in the middle of the elders hut lit their faces and threw their shadows onto the walls behind them. Atl watched the dry smoke rise to the roof and weave through the undersides of the palm branches and drive away insects.

Everyone listened to One-Cip'. He told of the trip to Cempoala and the seizing of Dahlia. "I offered all I had," he said, "and they took it and still demanded her."

It hurt Atl to remember the loss of the gold, but he was proud to be allowed in the meeting, with Deer of Stone, as a witness. He looked around. The stubborn pride showed in Deer of Stone's jaw. Two-Rabbit was serious and attentive. Balanced Turtle's eyes were wide. A Fox is Mad chewed and smacked his chicle and spit out into the rain.

"We know little of the Sant-yagos," said One-Cip'. "They are few, but they carry deadly weapons and gather allies and itch for war with the Aztecs. The Aztecs call this year One Reed. They have always said that in this year all things will be new and in question."

Atl had finished all but a corner of the roof of his secret hut. He could work on that after the meeting since the rain relieved him from his gardening duties in the chinampa, and he did not mind getting wet.

Thoughtful Rose's skinny figure appeared in the door, silhouetted against the gray rain, holding a reed mat over her head. Atl wished it were Dahlia seeing him with the elders!

She said to Two-Rabbit, "Father, may I see Atl's mother?"

Two-Rabbit motioned her in. She set the mat at the door and tiptoed in and snuggled close to him and looked around with wide eyes.

The fire made cracking sounds.

Two-Rabbit said, as if orating, "Thoughtful Rose has eleven years. She will make a fine woman." He smiled at her. "She is a little head-strong sometimes."

She grinned.

Atl frowned. She had no right to grin at the stern faces.

Two-Rabbit whispered something in her ear.

She cleared her throat. "Will anyone be sad?" The men listened. "Will anyone lose heart?" Her voice was soft and her eyes thoughtful. "Can a man be sad with flowers for his wife? Can a woman be sad with meat she has prepared? Happy is the girl with the loom and the boy with the fishing net. Will anyone be sad?"

All the elders nodded and approved. It annoyed Atl that her poetry alone had affected their mood. But he was moved himself.

Two-Rabbit said, "When did you start asking my say to visit Atl's mother?"

She shrugged and grinned and shrank into his arm.

"Do you want attention? Now run fast, and do not get wet."

She got up. Atl was still annoyed but saw his chance to go work on his secret hut. "I will go to my mother, too," he said, and got up.

They ran holding the mat over their heads.

His mother was inside, grinding maize for tortillas. Her lack of speech did not hide her joy to see them.

Thoughtful Rose said, "May I work my loom?" Atl's mother nodded toward the corner post where the small bundles of sticks and colored strings hung. Thoughtful Rose swung hers out from the wall and unfolded it and slipped into the waist-strap.

Atl said, "I am going to the woods." His mother approved. She trusted him not to get into trouble, and he would always return such trust. He had not told her or anyone about the hut, but she would be proud when it was finished.

Atl stepped back out into the rain and down from the village to the stream-bank. The stream was in a hurry. He ran splashing. He liked making things. He had piles of carved animals and whistles and tools. He had made a *coa* with a flared end instead of pointed, to move more dirt. Deer of Stone and others had laughed. One-Cip' said that if he kept trying his ideas, some day one would be useful. That did not make Atl feel better. It was true the shape looked funny for a farmer to hold. But Atl used it anyway, even though the flared end made it harder to push into the ground.

When he rounded a bend and saw his hut he stopped suddenly.
The unfinished corner of the roof had been covered with large leaves.
He took slow quiet steps to the opening. When he looked inside he
made out, seated low on the dirt in a dark corner, the form of a girl, her
hair bunched at each ear.

"Dahlia!" he said. His secret was out. "This is not your hut!"

She sat motionless, arms around her knees, eyes up.

He stood in the rain to respect the boy-girl rules.

She was not frightened. She cocked her head and said gently,
"Shouldn't you get out of the rain?"

"I can't!" he said. "There's a girl in my hut!"

"I'll go outside," she said.

"Go outside? Why are you in my hut?" Rain streamed his hair.
"*Your* hut?"

Of course, she didn't know it was his. Now she knew every
secret. His anger left. How silly, she must think, to build a hut so far
from the village beside a stream where the ground is rough, where there
was no room for children to play or to set up a corn-bin or a sweat-
house or a loom. He had not thought of children until seeing her there.

"Dahlia, can you keep a secret?" He stepped inside, but did not
sit down. "I am building this."

Her eyes widened and seemed to receive more than he was
saying. She had swung on vines and argued and laughed with him and
Deer of Stone. Never had she listened like this.

"And my coa works fine," he said, proudly stretching the truth.

She smiled and did not fidget as he did.

Finally she said, of One-Cip', "I admire my father."

"So do I," he said, amazed that she shared such a feeling. "I
don't think he agrees with the sacrifices."

"Do you?" she said.

He took a deep breath. It was as if he must decide the rest of his
life. "Not all of it."

She did not blink. "Your mother is the sweetest woman in the
village," she said. "I wish she could talk. But she talks with her eyes."

Never had her words affected him so. "Yes."

"Have you ever hoped she and father would get married?"

Until today, he would have walked away from such silly talk. "I
have thought of that."

She said, "Her ear-spools? He brought them from the Land of

the Turkey and Deer."

He was surprised. "With the tiny beads? I didn't know…"

She looked out into the rain. "Do you not think Deer of Stone should grow up?"

He would not speak against her brother. "He is a good hunter."

"He is too proud. He will not talk to me about his hatred of the Aztecs."

"He loves the ways of our village."

"I like A Fox is Mad," she said. "I wish he would talk more. And not smack his chicle in public. But he is kind. Do you think so?"

"Yes."

"And I like Two-Rabbit, and Thoughtful Rose. Pink is spoiled, though. Do you think Marigold really went to the wood witch and asked her to bring harm on…?"

"I've heard that story," he said. "But how can anyone know?"

"My mother got sick and died when I was born, and at that time Marigold had no children."

"But that does not mean she was jealous."

"We have something alike," she said. "I have no mother. And you have no father." She said it in a way that made all the world seem balanced. Her round eyes made him feel odd inside. The noise from the rain was steady.

Finally he said, as gently as he could, "How is it you are here?"

She said, "I…" and paused.

He said, "Was it you that patched my roof?"

"Yes." Her eyes widened. "Is it alright?"

"Yes," he said. He knew it would not last. "Why are you here?"

She hesitated. "I know something you do not know."

He never liked challenges from her, but today he had to know. "What?"

"There is a jaguar around the bend of the stream," she said.

"There is not."

"She is big. I have come several times this year."

"How 'big'?"

"As big as this hut."

"No. Where?"

She rose and stood next to him and he stood straighter. He remembered when she had stood silently with him after his sister Yellow Orchid was drowned, and her arm had touched his arm, and her round

61

eyes had looked only at him. Now she pointed out and said, "There."

"I do not see her."

"Just below that tree."

He could smell the tiny flowers in her hair. He squinted into the rain. She leaned closer. "Coming out of the ground beside the stream."

Then he was surprised because he saw that he had been looking at the huge face all along, its ancient features worn and stained, thinking it was no more than the rock it had been carved from. "I see her." She was gray, with traces of color, snarling and showing her teeth. Her eyes seemed pained and old. There was a huge acorn tree on her, and its roots ran down the sides of her face like strands of hair.

Dahlia said, "I come here and then I have good luck." She turned and looked at Atl and as she did her hair brushed his face and he blinked and smiled and felt more odd inside. He looked at her and their faces almost touched and he could not think of anything to say. Neither of them spoke or blinked. The noise of the rain grew louder.

Then she grinned and bumped her nose against his and ran out into the rain and the rushing stream. He chased her and caught her and pulled her under, and she splashed him and he splashed her and they played and laughed in front of the old cracked face of the jaguar.

Chapter 8

Howard woke first when the mountain roosters began their forlorn wailing. He slept, then woke again when clouds drifted through the camp. A cool dew had formed on his skin and clothes. He was sore again from lying on the ground. His mouth was sour and gummy.

He woke L.P. and they sleepily joined Smith and the others from the night-watch, slapping mosquitoes. Blake had two cans of drinking water going at the fire.

"Chopper's still there," said L.P.

"Blake," said Smith, staring at the receding flood, "would there be a working radio in that... apparatus?"

Blake studied the downward terrain. "I'll check."

Smith glanced sheepishly at people rising and joining them. "No breakfast. Might as well get to work. Let's meet here about mid-day."

The chores began. By mid-day Howard and L.P. had almost shingled the lower half of the roof, and Rachel had woven an entire wall.

Blake climbed back up over the ledge, all muddy. "Chopper radio's busted."

Maria the cook marched out of the woods with a mango in each hand. She cut them with Howard's knife, wiping it on her white skirt. She spread a small cloth and laid the slices out.

"*Gracias*," said Mrs. Crauder. She asked Maria the translator, "Can she get more?"

"They are not so much in this woods."

Smith called his meeting. He said, "Raul and Pedro told me they hope to fish when the flood settles."

"I think," said Dove-Ti, "that this is a good time to talk about the gifts we brought. Perhaps the Jaguar People will be moved to return the favor in some way."

63

"Right," said Crauder. "They'll be so glad to have those plastic cowboys and Indians they'll probably kiss us on the mouth."

"Oh, but I agree with Dove-Ti," said Haughton-Alsef, pleasantly. "We must draw them out if we are to observe them."

"Look, folks," said Crauder, "we're dealing with a bunch of thieves. And their delicate little bunch of hallowed tribal elders or whatever they have to run their so-called culture doesn't care who steals what. And if they did, they'd throw all their grubby little rip-off artists in jail, or whatever they've got to lock 'em up in."

"Ah," said Haughton-Alsef. "It's well known that order and discipline among non-westernized Native American peoples are maintained with vastly different means than those illustrated by the heartless pits of incarceration we have imposed upon our own communities. One outstanding example is their system of exile. Non-violent, effective, liberating. No one is hurt. The community is restored to peace. The exiled offender has every freedom to live as best he determines for himself."

"Every freedom," said Crauder, "except to come back to his own family and friends."

"Returning is not allowed," said Haughton-Alsef. "His breaking of the social order is regarded as his choice to live elsewhere."

"That 'liberating' system didn't stop 'em from stealing our stuff."

"They would have a different concept of sharing than we, and it would be based on equality of reciprocation. We mustn't violate that concept. Rather, we must establish and maintain trust at all costs. To do otherwise would be obscene and unconscionable."

"Label it what you want," said Crauder. "They're thieves."

"Anyway," said Smith, holding his hands up, "the question is before us: do we still want to set out the gifts to attract and observe the tribe, after everything that has happened?"

Zoe paced back and forth in untied boots, "Blake has an idea."

Blake straightened. "Three parts. One: divide up. Two: set out gifts. Three: talk."

"Stake-out squads," said Zoe. "A few of us go out and set gifts in a good place and like… watch for signs of the tribe."

"And where does this 'stake-out squad' search?" said Crauder

"Not too far," said Blake. "It should be…"

"We'll go in a like… different direction each day," said Zoe, swinging her hair and taking a big breath. "And after each search we can talk about what we saw and make sure we all have it the same way in our heads. Right, Blake? Sort of word of mouth kind of thing? Careful memorization, like ancient people did. Checking each other's account each day. That way we can remember it all. And then later when we're like… in civilization, we can write it all down."

"You can be back by mid-afternoon," said Crauder.

Howard and L.P. and Rachel and Zoe and Blake volunteered.

"And Maria the translator," said Dove-Ti, "a local Honduran."

Maria looked a little scared but smiled and agreed with a nod.

"Beg!" said Crauder. "Your boots are small. Give'em to Rachel."

Beg handed his boots to Rachel. "A man could use a nip."

"Nope," said Crauder. "You could use a job."

The stake-out squad grabbed the bag of cheap gifts.

Zoe said, "Shouldn't we like… divide into pairs kind of thing?"

"I'm with L.P.," said Maria. L.P. blushed.

"I'm with Blake," said Zoe.

Rachel smiled at Howard and he finally exhaled and nodded.

***

They hiked on root-broken, rocky ground in the downstream direction and found a cleared, flat space away from the river.

Zoe grinned happily and glanced back toward the camp. "We've got ourselves a collection, haven't we? I mean like… I could see Pryce suddenly popping out of nowhere and jumping through here pointing his cameras at everything. That is, if he still like… had any cameras. And then his boss, I mean our, like… celebrity? Now he's pretty cool. Can you believe we have that man on our team? Has anybody ever actually seen him on TV? I think I did a couple of years ago."

Blake seemed annoyed. "Haughton-Alsef? Cool?"

"Well, cool in a like… older man sort of way. You know?"

"Uncool talker."

"Well, let him talk," said Zoe. "He's so… what? I mean, he's done all these like… documentaries. He knows the world. Can't you picture him, all nestled in front of a big like… stone fireplace, pipe in his hand, old book in his lap, shaggy dog at his feet?" She looked at Rachel. "Can't you picture it, Rachel?" Rachel smiled. Zoe pushed Blake playfully on the shoulder and leaned back and grinned at him.

Then Rachel made her funny, bewildered grin at Howard.

L.P. said, "Your 'cool older man' likes young Miss Dove-Ti. I've seen 'em go off in the woods more than once."

"Really?" Zoe flashed a happy, surprised smile.

Blake frowned. "Dove-Ti's an ordained minister."

"Makes it like... interesting," said Zoe, "huh? She dresses pretty bold for a preacher. Remember when we were in that little like... shop in Tegucigalpa? How she went for those local designs? Bright colors?"

"Tourist designs," said L.P. "The locals weren't wearing 'em."

"I'll bet some do. And you don't really have many tourists in Tegucigalpa, now do you? Anyway, when we were in that shop with Dove-Ti, remember? It was raining outside? A bus pulled up and who should get out but Miss Margaret? She was in her like... 'raincoat.'" Zoe giggled, then said, "And oh, Rachel, I know you like her and all, but, really, that black plastic raincoat, the kind you use once and then throw away? It was all crinkled up around her knees, sticking out. And she came in the shop and said, 'I thought you folks would be here,' like she thought we were silly for looking around in a nice shop like that."

"She liked the shop," said Rachel. "She was just glad to find us."

"I think she was always 'finding' us." Zoe rolled her eyes. "I mean there are times when you'd just like to dress up and do something fun like that and not..." she giggled good-naturedly, "...not have a disposable black raincoat sticking out everywhere, you know? I don't mean anything toward her, bless her heart, but I was pretty relieved when she didn't like... try to convert all the customers."

"She likes people," said Rachel.

"Well, anyway, to top it off, was it just me, or were any of you embarrassed when she picked out that black hat thing at the door?"

Rachel giggled. "She's so tiny and that sombrero brim hung out past her shoulders."

"It was the cheapest thing in the shop." Zoe was energized.

"And she offered the clerk half," said L.P. Everyone laughed.

"And," said Zoe, "Dr. Haughton-Alsef told her it would like... get all out of shape in the rain, and I knew it would, too, and I told her, and she said that was okay, it would still keep the rain off. And sure enough, when we went around that day, us with our umbrellas and her with her huge... thing, it did get all out of shape, and..." Zoe bobbed her head up and down, giggling, "...yes, it did keep the rain off!"

More laughter.

"And You know?" said Zoe. "That kind of thing didn't help her when it was time for us to like… decide about her."

"Do you really think that affected the decision?" said Rachel.

"Oh, no," said Zoe. "No. It just didn't help, is all I'm saying. I wish you and she had been there. I'm sure Copán was great. I would have gone myself, but I heard there was less shopping there. I know you liked her. We all did. She was… what? Cute."

"Yes," said Rachel. "And resourceful. My children liked her."

"That's right." said L.P. "You're a school teacher."

"Second grade. Miss Margaret brought meal worms for us."

"Wha-at?" said Zoe, laughing wide-eyed.

"It was one of our science projects. You know: metamorphosis."

"For like… second-graders?"

"Believe it or not," said Rachel, "they got it. The worms go through this process. They shed their outsides and turn into little bugs."

"That's smart," said Zoe, happily, "I'd rather be a bug than a worm!" The laughing was like a release of tension.

"Actually," said Rachel, "they don't really have a choice."

"Predestination in bug-world," said L.P.

"More like predetermination," said Blake, seriously.

Zoe looked at him blankly. "Oh, Blake. Entirely too many syllables." More laughter.

"What do you feed 'em?" said L.P. "Meal?"

Rachel grinned shyly at Howard. Her thin hands moved gently as she talked, the pale skin riding smoothly across the vessels and bones.

"Oh, dry cereal. A slice of apple. A wedge of…"

"A slice of apple?" said Zoe. "Hey, those little wormy-guys are almost human!" She was energized. "My god!" she said, "one of them might even evolve another step and become a Dr. DeSparr!"

All but Rachel, even Blake, laughed.

"Do you remember," said Zoe, "how he didn't like… say anything at that first prep session when it was his turn to introduce himself? Just stared at the ceiling? I said to myself, 'that man's going to be a like… case!' I knew!"

Rachel said, "He doesn't think much of himself."

"No?" said Zoe, brightly. "Mr. Ego sure fools me! The man brings it on himself. He's like… inconsiderate."

"That," said Blake, counting on his fingers, "is five syllables."

She looked at him, then burst into laughter again, and they all did. "But, oh god…" She covered her mouth. "When he walked into that river…" She rolled her eyes. "I was like…" she threw her hands out and relaxed her jaw, "…Huh-u-uh?"

"Just don't get sick or hurt," said L.P. "He's our only doctor."

Blake said, "We'd better get to our jobs."

"Let's split up," said Rachel. She and Howard hiked to the river, picked a spot where they could scan the woods for Jaguar-people, and set out their gifts. Below them, the muddy water beat against rocks and tossed up clouds of mist. He noticed a pink burn-mark on her wrist.

She held it up. "Want to know about this?"

He got his pocket knife and cut a dead stick, about the size of a pencil, dark like walnut and hollow, off one of the little trees. "If you want to tell." He squatted, elbows on his knees, and whittled.

She sat on a rock and picked up one of his shavings and turned it over in her hands. "I expect there are reasons why things happen. I was ten. Mamma had been up all night and day with my little brother. He had a fever. She was worn out. When I got home from school, Daddy was still at work. I tried to cook stew. I know it was my hand that moved, but it seemed like the pot. I heard this sizzling sound. Then I felt it and got into a state, screaming and yelling. Mamma looked awful, but she calmed me and got me and Brother in the car."

Howard cut short lengths and rounded them against a flat rock.

"The doctor scared me at first, but he stopped the hurting. When Daddy got home he was all over us, hugging and carrying on. The next day he bought me a bracelet, and Mamma a really nice necklace. Mamma hugged him. I stood with my big fat bandaged hand watching them. She treasured that necklace. What are you making?"

"What?" he said. "Oh. Beads." He tapped the knife in one of the holes. "If I had string…"

She looked around, then pulled several threads off the bottom of her shirt where it had already been torn for bandages for DeSparr. She twisted them together. "Last year," she said, "after Mamma died, I found a note saying she wanted me to have that necklace." She turned the bottom of her shirt farther up, showing him a small plastic bag safety-pinned to the inside. In it was a folded paper. "That's the note."

"Where's the necklace?"

"I'm afraid I lost it."

"Well," he said, "I'm sorry."

She smiled. "I'd rather have the note."

She handed him the string and he ran it through each bead.

"What was your dad like?" said Howard.

"Sweet. Tough. Quiet. Didn't make much. That's one reason Mamma held that necklace dear. He fell last year, soon after she died. Hip. Hardly talks now. He's staying with Brother while I'm gone."

"You take care of your dad?"

She nodded.

"The bracelet your dad gave you — did you lose it too?"

She combined her crinkled smile with a pout. "I'm afraid I did."

He folded his knife and put it and the beads in his pocket. She said, "Where'd you grow up?"

"Me? Hashart. It's part of Atlanta now, on the south side."

"I know of it. Are your parents still alive?"

"Yep. Mom does free-lance artwork. Great cook, too. Dad still runs his print shop."

"Does she do art work for him?"

"Nah. She's picky. Not much work at all. But good stuff."

"What does he print?"

"Anything that comes in. Well, no sleaze. He rents half of the old train station. Tracks are gone. He gets less business every year, but he doesn't need it. Invested well in the Nineties, when he had the Hashart Weekly and all the ads he could handle." Howard chuckled. "Dad only uses the old presses. Writes paper receipts. Just can't stop."

"What'd you do, growing up there? Besides school?"

"Sports. Sneaking into abandoned houses. Summer after sixth grade? I got my first job. On a panel truck. One of Dad's suppliers needed a helper. I ran boxes in. Hated it. The guy cussed the customers behind their backs. 'No s.o.b. tells me what to do. He'll find out who he's messing with.' I got up my twelve-year-old nerve and quit. When Dad found out, he made me go back and stick it out 'til the end of the summer. He said, 'That's what you said you'd do. So do it.'"

Rachel cocked her head. "You probably learned a few things."

"Some new cuss words and not to make commitments."

"Really? You committed to this trip."

"Yeah, L.P. talked me into it. Maybe, at twenty-nine, I thought I could give it a try. It had its appeal. The tribe. The unknown. Things were slow at the office, too."

"Why L.P.? Hasn't he done well selling computers?"

"Said he just wanted to do something 'pure analog.'"

The water roared below them. Birds called far away.

"I've wondered," she said, "how different these tribe people are. What would we be like if we had the same history and setting and all? Oh, I don't even know what they're like yet. I'm not making sense."

"Yes you are." Howard looked up. "Not much daylight left."

"Nope," said Rachel. "I wonder what the others may have seen."

They gathered the gifts and found the other 'stake-outers'. Nothing. Halfway back to camp, they all met Crauder sitting on a rock.

Rachel said, "Have you been sitting here ever since we left?"

"Aw, naw, naw. I knew you'd be okay."

At camp, they found Beg staggering drunk, singing about lost love, softly and badly. Smith was trying to cajole him.

L.P. and Crauder and Howard finally got him to sit down. He kept singing. Rachel took off her boots and put them on his feet.

"How'd he get into the wine?" said Crauder.

"It was my decision," said Dove-Ti. "Without being critical of any traditional attitudes some of us may hold, we, with our awareness of the value of cultural diversity and the need for tolerance, must avoid the unconscionable act of denying Odel his right to at least a moderate expression of his own lifestyle."

"Lifestyle?" said Crauder. "The man's a snot-nosed sot."

"I admonished him to drink responsibly," said Dove-Ti.

"Odel's past," said Haughton-Alsef, "is no basis for denying him choices that are as real a part of his lifestyle as, say, our obsession with this tribe is of ours. How would you like being denied our mission?"

"Get it right, man. This is butt-bustin' bad for him!"

"Have you noticed? He's happy. He was quite miserable before."

"And he'll be miserable after," said Crauder. He stood over Beg. "Is this you? A dipso? Get a job." Beg was already snoring.

Everybody crowded awkwardly into the hut and lay close.

L.P. whispered, "Howard? I got to, you know, talk to Maria."

"Oh, yeah?" whispered Howard. "You like her?"

"Hey, look at her."

"Yeah, yeah."

"How'd you and Rachel get along? But, oh, I forgot. You don't like her."

"Look, L.P., forget it." Howard shouldn't have talked about personal things with Rachel. She could bring them up to him later. He would be more careful.

Chapter 9

Atl breathed with the rhythm of his feet. Tonatiah's light would soon fall on the hunting mountain, and he would make his kill, and at the end of the day Dahlia would see him with it.

He heard Deer of Stone catch up in the dark, heard his whisper-laugh like leaves passing his ears. "Baby-face."

It was Atl's first mountain hunt, but he ran fast, and lifted his knees high not to trip, and touched his feet down softly to the rocks and the flat spaces between roots. All the men had spread, silent and quick. They had spoken to the animals and trees. The rainy time of One Reed had begun but tonight Tlaloc held back his jars of rain on his mountain. Atl's mother and the village and Dahlia were far behind.

True, Atl was the only baby-face, and the elders had named Deer of Stone, who had sixteen years, to be his teacher for the hunt, but when it was over, he would carry a cousin rabbit or fox on his shoulder and its blood would be smeared across his eyes by One-Cip' himself and after that, in every hunt, he would run with men's paint.

He heard One-Cip's grunt, far to his right, and turned to follow. His inside eye saw the other hunters running as he did, bows or spears in their hands, empty cotton sacks over their shoulders. Now and then a squirrel or a fox scurried. He made up shapes like Dahlia in the dark, as if she stood beside a tree or sat on a rock.

He searched the night with his ears and nose and knew where to turn, where to touch his feet down as the earth passed under him. He leaped like a deer, rock to rock, across a stream where the sky spread wide and black and the air hung cool. The moon's sister watched him from the water, breaking up and coming together.

His inside eye saw his mother's round, bright face among the flowers and squash and maize, her soft body bending, her strong arms

71

digging, lifting. Tomorrow would come and he would bring his kill to her. He was a man and would know what to do if his mother and his people were to call on him.

Finally Tezcatlipoca's smoke left the dew and the early air and Tonatiah climbed once more into the sky, and shone from behind Atl, and gave him the view of the hunting mountain. Atl knew its pointed shape, for One-Cip' had described it.

Other hunters ran from the woods. A wide stream was fast and noisy, and the few rocks for crossing were wet and slimy. Deer of Stone ordered Atl to follow him but Atl acted as if he did not hear and chose a different way on smaller rocks. He moved faster, to cross first, but failed to test each step. A rock turned and he fell. He held his bow up but lost his arrows, and when he had climbed out he could only find seven. His breechcloth was soaked. The early air was cold. He walked fast behind the others, studying the ground, head forward as if nothing had happened. He shouted, "Hurry up!" even though they were ahead of him. His voice cracked and Deer of Stone laughed.

Then One-Cip' stopped and waved his arm and looked left and right. He pointed at the base of the mountain and shouted, "Now!"

The hunters spread and found their places. Others from other villages showed and stood in the long curving line which vanished around each side of the mountain. Finally everyone was quiet. There was only the crackling of torches, bright even in Tonatiah's early light.

***

The drummer, on his knees, stared up the slope, leaned over the hollow log, and struck it. Other drummers struck their logs. The sounds were deep and loud. All the hunters began screeching harshly. They cried and whistled and cackled as the drums grew louder and faster.

Skinny rabbits appeared. Atl could almost taste the warm meat under the fur. One escaped between hunters. Others ran up the slope.

"My Uncle! Come near!" cried the hunters to the animals, offering respect in exchange for life. The drums and screams grew louder. A fox ran from behind a rock, and up. Antlers appeared for an instant. Atl made sounds, small and child-like at first. He was glad the others could not hear for all the noise. But trying made him bold. When he felt the mood he cackled like One-Cip', loudly, over and over, twining rhythmically and musically with the others.

The ring of hunters swayed side to side. "I am needy and poor," they cried to the animals. "Only you can help."

They took their first upward steps. Deer of Stone did not have to order Atl but he did. Drums pounded, voices screamed. There were more rabbits and foxes and even little wild dogs. Arms waved, torches flared. "My uncle! Come near! I must see you!"

"Mixcoatl!" cried some to an Aztec god. "Guide our spears!"

A fox jumped at another's neck with bared teeth, then ran away. The other lay bleeding. Animals had never behaved this way. Deer of Stone stepped close to the trembling fox which could lash out in her terror. "Go around!" shouted Atl, but Deer of Stone would not admit that Atl knew the animals. "She will bite!" A loud rush of air left her mouth. The boys jumped. She was dead. Atl's warnings had not been needed. Deer of Stone threw the dead fox into his sack and laughed again.

The other side of the circle of hunters closed smaller and tighter as they neared the top of the mountain. They shouted, "Forgive my intrusion! My cousin! Your beauty is not matched!" Animals cried, barked, ran up trees, into holes, out again, chased suddenly, leaped straight up as if to escape into the sky. "You are swift like the wind."

When Tonatiah gained his highest point the shouting and the drums stopped. The men stood shoulder to shoulder. The animals scampered and jumped. The men raised their spears and bows.

A fox ahead of Atl jumped at him, side to side, forward and back. Atl slowly drew an arrow over his shoulder and aimed and let it go. It missed, but hit a squirrel. The fox kept jumping. Atl drew and aimed again twice more and hit nothing. He picked up a small rock and angrily threw it at the fox and by chance hit it on the nose. It stopped jumping and crouched, and Atl let go another arrow and hit the heart. A hunter from another village proudly helped him put it in his sack. Atl felt sure of his skill. The hunter asked Atl to throw a rock at a rabbit he was trying to shoot. Atl hit it square in the head, and it fell dead, but the hunter still claimed it as his own.

The slaughter lasted until Tonatiah was near his dropping, and the hunters who had gathered their kills heaved their sacks and baskets onto their shoulders.

"He was almost killed by a pig," said Deer of Stone as they passed a bleeding man on their way down the mountain.

"Or it may have been a peccary," said Atl.

"Pig," said Deer of Stone. "There were no herds of peccary."

"How do you know?"

"I know. Also, Two hunters were killed today. One by an arrow shot too high across the circle. Do not forget that."

"I do not shoot high," said Atl.

"A jaguar killed the other hunter. It ran out of the brush."

"He should have let a jaguar pass through."

"He probably didn't speak to her kindly," said Deer of Stone. "They surprise you. Or maybe he tried to spear her. Her skin would have brought him a life of wealth."

"The life he lost," said Atl. Then he opened his sack. "I have — what do I have? — a rabbit, a fox, three squirrels, and a very big turtle. And I got all my arrows back! Look!"

"Not the three you lost in the stream." Deer of Stone chuckled.

"What did you get?" said Atl.

Deer of Stone shifted his sack on his shoulder. "Enough."

"How many?" said Atl.

"I helped others," said Deer of Stone.

"And so did I!" said Atl.

The hunters were tired but they walked fast. Three carried deer across their shoulders. Someday, Atl thought, he would be one of those.

By dark they would see the big fire and run shouting into the village. The women would smile and laugh. Atl's mother would hug him in front of the others as if he were a child and embarrass him. But One-Cip' would split open the fox Atl killed and draw its blood down across Atl's eyes in front of everybody. Next time it should be a deer, and he would wear the mark of a deer on every hunt.

The hunters walked faster, toward home. They would circle the fire and laugh and throw the animals up hot yellow in the black night. Dahlia would look up at Atl, and firelight and shadows would flash her face. Later she would listen to him tell of each part of the hunt.

Then he would go to his mother's hut and lie down and think of the day and the night and wonder what new questions the year One Reed would bring. He would close his eyes and see trees and streams and mountains. He would see antlers and fur and fire and raw meat. For these good things Yellow Orchid had been sacrificed. And for these good things his father, whom he could not remember, had been sacrificed.

And lying there, he would think of the look of Dahlia's round eyes, and of the future, and feel warm. And finally Ixtilton of children's sleep would rest on his shoulder.

The coming back was the best part of going.

***

As the hunters neared the village the air was still. The leaves did not wave at Atl and the trees and vines were sad. Atl tried to imagine the smell of flowers in his mother's ear-spool, but a strange odor in the air, like bad cooking, prevented it. Ahead was the last curve before the village. The hunters rounded it and stopped suddenly. Atl felt a great fear, a sickening chill. The trees above the village stood in silence, black and bare of leaves. The birds had left.

One-Cip' walked faster, then Atl and the others did the same. When they reached the high part of the path, Atl thought they had come to the wrong village. Most of the huts were burned black. There were no voices. Smoke drifted up. Then Atl made out his and his mother's hut, half of it fallen and black. He twisted his shoulders and dropped his sack. He ran forward, but was blinded by a flood of tears, and fell. When Deer of Stone passed him he got up. One-Cip' walked fast, stamping clumsily, eyes fixed on the ashes, frowning.

The bodies were black and the stench seemed a bad dream. In the houses still standing, dead bodies lay huddled, some tied with charred vines, and blood lay soaked in the mats and the dirt, as it had under the animals Atl had killed just that day. It was hard to tell who each of the burned bodies was. The women. The old men. The children.

One-Cip' called out. Atl and the others called out. No answers.

Embers glowed in the maize-bins. Tree of Us lay broken and black. The cloth Atl's mother wove still hung outside their hut, robbed of its bright colors by soot. The charred sticks of the loom Thoughtful Rose had kept for practice lay on the ground.

Atl was afraid to look, but One-Cip' held his shoulder and they looked inside and saw the misshapen plumpness of the charred body. An unburned part of his mother's cotton robe was stuck to it. It could not have been her. It could not have happened. She could not have had to endure it, and he not with her. It was a trick. One-Cip' had taken a wrong turn and they had come to a magic village like their own but not their own. Animals had been dressed up like his people.

Finally Atl's wailing came, loud. He felt the agony she must have

75

felt. *"Mother!"*

Some of the hunters ran into the forest, shouting angrily as if the killers were still nearby. One-Cip' said nothing for there was nothing to say. Others standing before the burned huts and charred bodies began crying out. Never had men cried. Two-House ran to the edge of the clearing and stabbed himself to death with his hunting knife in sight of all. "No!" shouted Atl, but glimpsed the look on Two-House's face and wondered what reason there was now to live. Then another horror came to his mind, and he shrieked in One-Cip's face, "Dahlia!"

One-Cip' pointed at his own hut, only partly burned. "She is not there."

"But where is she?" shouted Atl.

"Deer of Stone and others are looking for her," said One-Cip', pointing at the forest. "And for Thoughtful Rose and Pink. And the two babies and Shy Petals who was ready to have her baby."

Atl started to run and search, but One-Cip' held his shoulder. They stood like that for a long time, Atl crying out loudly.

Finally One-Cip' said, "We must bury your mother."

Atl could not stop crying. He searched the ground for answers, then the sky. When One-Cip' took his hand off his shoulder and called for coas to dig with, Atl felt something hanging over him that he had never known, a thing not like his village or his mother, an angry living swarm, drawing from him. He was sure it was not real but it was as if it were real.

The men who did not go off to search for survivors helped to bury the bodies. Balanced Turtle carved death-arcs in the plain shape. There were too many to take time for decoration. Once he stopped his carving and looked out across the wasted village. "The stream is dirty." Grime and ashes stuck to the banks and the chinampas. "I loved our clear stream," he said.

Nothing would ever be the same. Tonatiah would not even be able to push the darkness back and make a new day. Not even One-Cip' could know what would happen.

"The Aztecs," whispered someone.

"No," said One-Cip'. "The Aztecs burn only their own dead, and with order and beauty. What kind of people would burn the living?"

When it was time to put the dirt back into the hole, Atl made himself look at his mother's charred head and the death-arc. It was everything that death was, but he had cried all he could.

Tonatiah crawled behind the mountains. Tezcatlipoca smoked the sky. The blackened flowers in the chinampa slept. The air slept.

Atl and the others worked through the night. Over and over Atl had to push from his mind the home-thoughts he had had coming back from the hunt, of his mother's hugs which he wanted even though they embarrassed him, of the meat cooking, of the dark fire-lit eyes of Dahlia looking up at him as he danced with his kill.

Finally Tonatiah's fingers steamed through the trees, through a misting rain. No embers glowed. Balanced Turtle shaped the last death-arc and all the dead were buried, but the smell of burned flesh still hung in the air. The animals and birds did not return. The elders had met but the gods had given no signs. Many hunters had left in despair.

Atl could not stop thinking how his mother must have seen the horror as it came to her. He felt as if he were becoming nothing inside his chest. The angry swarm came to him again, and grew. It had many faces, like Aztec gods, proud and ugly, long-toothed, changing, leaving him, coming to him, robbing him of himself, judging as if they had known he had not been there when his mute mother needed him.

With his mother would go the village ways. Her eyes were soft and moist and clear, giving back the image of himself and his people, even shaping them. Now they were under the dirt. Still he did not cry.

Deer of Stone and other hunters returned from searching. They had found none of the missing. Husbands and brothers and fathers set out for longer searches. Deer of Stone walked to the edge of the village and shouted new words into the forest. "We will do this to you!"

Those still present looked to One-Cip'. He said, "We must go."

There were he and Atl and Deer of Stone and old A Fox is Mad and Balanced Turtle and Two-Rabbit whose Marigold was buried that morning, whose daughters Thoughtful Rose and Pink were missing, whose thinking seemed to have left him.

"Go where?" said Atl.

"Just go," said One-Cip'.

Atl stood in the rain at his mother's grave. "I will catch up."

*∗∗

The ashes smelled of death. The scorched trees around him seemed never to have been the trees of his village.

There was nothing from all his life in the village or in the High

Valley that could have made him ready for this. Nothing from his mother or from One-Cip'. Nothing from the old men or the gods, or from friends or travels, or from seeing or feeling.

And nothing could remove his heart-pain. He was helpless before the hanging, leering faces.

Then he thought that there would be nothing to lose in defying them. He would hold hatred for them. But as his hatred grew, they grew horns, and bigger claws, and courser hair, and more faces came out of trees and rocks and sky, glaring and throwing the hatred back at him.

Who killed his people? Who burned his village? The Aztecs could have done it to punish them for not showing joy over the sacrifices. But One-Cip' was right about their order and beauty. And if it had been them, they would have said so to all the world, to make the village an example. There were stories of bandits in the old time before the Aztecs came. But no bandits since. It could have been the Sant-yagos, but no corn or cloth had been taken.

There was nothing Atl could do. But if he and the others could know who the killers were, they would know whom to hate. It might take years but they could be secret as the killers had been, and track them down every one and return the pain and torture and death that they had brought to those he loved. The killers would wish they had never killed. He knew that it would not change the fact that his mother had suffered, but nothing would, and at least it would start to put his life back in balance. Hurt for hurt, life for life. The bold thought was the first small easing of the pain-fear. Even the glaring swarm of god-faces drew back and hid their eyes behind the claws of their prickly arms. But, oddly, they smiled at the same time.

To set his mind to this new way, he stood for the whole day without moving, though it seemed he should die for all the loss of himself. He thought of all the people he had known, all the work in the chinampa, all his inventions, all he had learned from his time in the High Valley. The night was the worst and longest he had ever known. The wet black ash-covered ground seemed in the dark a great gaping hole to the middle of the earth.

He had new thoughts, ways to solve problems, ways that do not cry, ways that look straight ahead and not to one side or the other.

He had much to learn. But he must find the killers. He must be certain of who they were before acting. They would look like the swarm of faces, long-toothed, horned, proud and ugly. By that they could be found. He felt a new peace, knowing now what his life would be.

He ran as he had never run and caught the others in less than a day. He talked to Deer of Stone, who also wanted to get back at the killers, and they agreed to work together patiently.

***

Ramiro Mendez thought: can my mother see from heaven? Can she have me punished from there? He knew she was in heaven because she had been close enough to the priests to get them to come and whip him when he would lie or steal or torment the landlord's little girl. Sometimes they would let him think they did not know. Then they would come. They were quite severe. She was close enough to one of them that he would meditate with her privately in her bedroom. She was certainly in heaven, for if she had done any wrong, the priests had always talked God into forgiving her. It had shown how frighteningly close to them she was, for some people had to give them gold for that.

He pointed Dog is Old to the edge of the waterfall, under the large pine branch. The old Indian was so stupid and worthless he had been thrown out of his own village.

Mendez' mother could not know what it meant to find a village of only women and children, how easy it would have been to relieve them of their gold, if only they had had any. Did she see how he and his little band responded to their devil-eyes and relieved them of their famous "radiant health?"

He should have predicted the irony. His other helpers had deserted the army and had now deserted him. One had even rolled on the ground in the pathetic torment of the repenting Christian. How ready was the thief for righteousness when there was no gold. Only Dog is Old and three other native helpers were left now, waiting to be paid.

The first "paid" helper's shoulder still showed in the pool far below. Mendez quickly pointed Dog is Old away from it, to the pine branch where he had tied the five small bags of dirt, which he told the helpers was gold. He had challenged them to come for their pay one at a time to prove they would not gang up on him. He was amazed at their gullibility. He was amazed at his own abilities with words and languages, even in this savage land.

Surely there was a wall around heaven and she could not see. If she had found priests there and told them to tell God, God would have sent the punishment by now. But then they could be waiting for the time of most effect, just when he thought he was free.

What parts of his years of misery had she sent as punishment? Had she seen him with Capitán Narvaez eight years before when they 'pacified' Camagüey? Was it too fine a point for her, or for Friar Las Casas who had tried to stop the frenzy, to see that they had only killed those Indians in whom they saw the devil? There had been no gold there either. And only gold would buy freedom to live as he pleased, just as only gold would stop God's wrath.

When Dog is Old stretched upward to untie the bag, Mendez quickly took off his own shirt. He must not delay. Surely his mother could not see. The man was a fool. Mendez grabbed him from behind and heard his own voice cry out, then the man's, as he pushed the knife through the thick old muscles and twisted it deep between the ribs.

The waterfall was loud. The work was ugly. It would gain him freedom from the fawning fool, but from nothing else. With gold he could have escaped to the coast, and back to Spain. Now he must come up with an excuse for his absence before returning to the army.

He hugged powerfully and worked the knife until the life was gone. Then he pushed the limp body out and let it drop. One of its feet did not clear the edge and slid back and almost tripped him. Did his mother get God to do that? No. God would not have failed.

He took one more bag from the branch and dropped it over the edge. Then he washed his chest of the blood. He put his unstained shirt back on for the second time and made sure the body floated away in the blood-reddened water. He "paid" one more of the remaining helpers, but the others disappeared before he came back for them.

Chapter 10

Howard woke, groaned, stretched, and got up. The sky had cleared. Maria the cook had graciously foraged in the woods and brought back papayas and cut them up. The team gathered.

Smith asked Dove-Ti to divide up the day's out-search teams.

She said, "Uhm... Blake may be able to get some bearings with this clear sky. And uhm, L.P. and Maria the translator? Can you go again? And Dr. Smith and myself. And Dr. DeSparr and Howard."

It hadn't occurred to Howard that he would be paired with DeSparr. And he couldn't think of a credible excuse to get out of it.

Dove-Ti handed out colorful squares of cloth from the bag of gifts. "These may attract them. Hang them out. And remember, keep silent. Don't frighten them away."

The six set out in a soft breeze. At the split-up point, L.P. and Maria the translator angled away from the river, Smith and Dove-Ti stayed, and DeSparr insisted that he and Howard follow a sizable stream fully back into the old woods.

As they walked, Howard tried to think of a way to ease the tension about the ant-prank. Rachel had wanted him to understand DeSparr's need for respect. But what Howard felt was hate, not the kind that intends physical harm, though down deep he had a vague urge to punch the jutting jaw. He wouldn't. The strange brain would regard it as a prize, a symbol of Howard's intellectual inferiority.

And Howard could strike at nothing DeSparr loved for he loved nothing. It was ironic. His people-are-only-objects theory must have been frustrating, since people had to be more than objects in order to know that they were only objects. DeSparr needed people if only to prove to them that he didn't.

The two came to an open area. The stream was wide there, and calm, four or five feet deep. Trees towered around it.

Howard took off his boots and socks and waded to the middle, where a big limb stood, its base jammed between rocks. The water was cool and clear. The surface sparkled. His feet underneath were distorted by refraction and looked like some grayish gel among the pebbles. He hung four cloth squares on the limb. They stood out against the gray-green woods like brightly colored flags at an international exhibition. He shook his feet off on the bank and put the socks and boots back on.

He joined DeSparr behind a big rock. He didn't move. To drive off mosquitoes, he only flicked his muscle, like an animal. The team had newly agreed not to talk once settled at the stake-outs, but it was odd that two people crouched together in a strange land would not.

The tops of the trees swayed one at a time in the light breeze as if passing a whispered message among themselves.

The brush behind them creaked. Howard turned only his head, then squawked. DeSparr turned detachedly, then sucked air, loudly. Three little men with spears and painted faces stood ten feet away.

Bracelets, necklaces, and tattoos decorated their red-gold skin. Their hair was straight and shiny and black, hanging to the ears, cut in a line all around. Their faces were focused but otherwise hard to read. They wore only loin cloths except for a young important-looking one who wore unlaced boots. Two more showed, then more, and more.

The little men squatted and swayed left and right, silently, not in unison, leaning forward, necks stretched, eyes large and round, mouths relaxed, spears held out from their sides. A few shook their shoulders to make their jewelry jingle. Several held their hands above their heads, clawing the air like children trying to look fierce. The near-silence and the near-comical exaggeration intensified the sense of danger. Adults who would behave that way might do anything. Several of them glanced at each other often as if for reassurance. They made no sound until one took a deep breath and barked. Then all of them started barking.

Howard stood slowly. He felt light-headed as the blood rushed to his legs. The men backed up one or two steps, still swaying and barking. Thin white lines splayed from their mouths like cat whiskers, and tiny dark shadow-lines under them made a three-dimensional look. Several flanks were painted orange, with black spots.

Finally the one in boots came forward shouting importantly, waving his arms, jerking his head. He leaned backward and forward as he shouted. He often raised a foot and stomped. He barked and one of his comrades handed him a spear. He shoved its point at Howard, not enough to make contact. Howard jumped, feeling his stomach muscles tighten. The man poked at DeSparr in the same way. Howard couldn't tell if he was serious or just trying to scare them and make his comrades laugh, which they did.

DeSparr's face was tense, slightly raised. How would the little men react to arrogance? Would they even recognize it as such?

The man stepped aside when an older man came forward barking. His voice was nasal and harsh. He was about five feet tall. Over his shoulder was the furry skin of a large jaguar. He barked up at Howard and DeSparr with unabashed authority and disgust. He wore Rachel's original pair of boots, unlaced.

Howard couldn't read his eyes. They were like hard black stones in narrow openings of folded, leathery skin. His jowls hung largely but there was not much chin. His belly was big and round and hung low, pulling thinly stretched skin. His legs were skinny and knobby and short, knees bent, feet apart. He stepped busily in place as he barked. He wore animal-tooth anklets, bracelets, necklaces, and earrings. His thick, black hair failed to diminish his ancient appearance. Several times he stopped barking and stared at the woods or the stream and scratched the inside of his thigh.

He must have finally realized that Howard and DeSparr didn't understand him. He clamped his mouth shut. He kept glancing at the woods behind him. No one spoke. It was awkward, but Howard dared not speak or move.

∗∗∗

A commotion in the woods ended the silence. Four more little men tumbled out of the undergrowth trying to carry a squirming animal which looked like a small pig. It was dark gray and muscular and had a huge fierce head and mouth with big sharp teeth. It squealed horribly. Avoiding the teeth seemed to be the main problem in carrying it. The old man watched, slouched, as if the sight were nothing unusual. The others leaned on their spears and laughed and aped the squealing. Once, the thing almost got away and two men fell to the ground but one kept his grip and the other three managed to pick it up again.

When the four finally reached the old man, struggling with the animal, he barked at them and they carried it to the stream, dancing for balance. They held it out over the water and it wiggled and squealed. The old man barked again and they ceremoniously plunged the animal into the water and all but one fell in with it, scrambling to hold it under while keeping their own heads up. There was a lot of splashing. The others, except for the old man, laughed loudly.

The animal managed to surface several times, just long enough to get a breath and let out a harsh, resonant squeal. But as comical as the men appeared, the struggle finally ended and they prevailed. They heaved the drowned thing up and dragged it to the bank.

The old man pulled the jaguar skin off his shoulder and looked around at the other Jaguar-men, taunting them while still frowning authoritatively. They chuckled. He chose one of them who had an unusually healthy set of large teeth. He handed him the skin and the others whooped and grinned and cheered him on as he threw the skin over his back, and dropped to his hands and knees. He made child-like growls and prowled around the dead beast, jumping falsely now and then to make the crowd yelp and laugh. Finally he leaped onto the pig and burrowed his face into its hairy neck. He gnawed and pulled. He jumped up and strutted around the clearing, a clump of skin and course hair in his teeth, blood dripping from his lips.

The four who had drowned the thing picked it up and laid it on the ground between the old man and Howard and DeSparr. A pool of blood spread in the dirt under its neck. The old man pointed at it and then at the two and then back at it, and barked again. He paused often, as if for answers. The only interpretation Howard could make was that he and DeSparr were next. The teeth of the little men looked jagged and rough. He ran his right hand up his left arm, gripping, and was sure that, skinny as he was, a man could have several meals on that arm alone.

His first reaction to the thought was to distract himself as if it were only academic. He said to DeSparr, "Ever…" He had to clear his throat, and was surprised how shaky his voice was. "Ever thought about… drowning?" There was no response. If the arrogant figure would squirm, Howard in his fearful state would forgive everything. Then he wondered what there was to forgive. Neither the arrogance nor the contempt had deprived him of any measurable thing.

The young man in boots stared, then pointed, at Howard, hand hanging lazily from wrist, finger up. His mouth laughed, but not his eyes, which darted strangely. His laugh was high-pitched and nasal.

He and the old man began talking dramatically to each other, the

84

old man motioning angrily. Both of them pointed now at the dead beast, now at Howard and DeSparr.

Howard remembered the oath not to harm anyone. It seemed crazy to think that he, or he and DeSparr, could have overpowered fifteen or twenty armed Jaguar-men and done them harm.

He had heard of people facing death and the thoughts that come. He didn't have dramatic visions of his life before his eyes. In fact he had a natural resistance to the idea that his own death could actually happen. Not where his mom and dad wouldn't know, where the team wouldn't, or his truest friend L.P., or Rachel.

Surely, he thought, something innate in his body or soul, or some ordering system of the universe, would protect him as it had for twenty-nine years, him who had family and friends, who had a license to practice architecture in Georgia and Ohio, who hadn't figured out what the important questions of life were, let alone the answers.

Had anything in his life earned him protection from a painful death? How would his life be assessed? Who would assess it? Would there even be an assessment? What difference would it make what he had done or not done? What if DeSparr were right? Nothing mattered?

But, no more time to think. Several of the men approached DeSparr, rocking their heads side to side, barking and motioning for him to follow them to the stream.

"No," said the mouth, and a finger rose quickly, as if to say, "just a minute." Then the finger inclined smoothly toward Howard. "Him," said the mouth, and Howard couldn't believe the blatancy, even from DeSparr. Of course the little men couldn't understand the words, but the finger and both hands sweeping several times in Howard's direction made the meaning obvious.

Howard's hatred for the man must have always been obvious. That was probably why DeSparr so easily blamed him for the ant trick. And DeSparr must have been humiliated by Howard's thwarting the brazen suicide attempt in the flood. But worst of all, Howard thought, DeSparr would never forgive him for hearing the confessions afterward.

DeSparr actually smiled at the Jaguar-men, a sort of international greeting smile, disgustingly out of character. Still, he pointed at Howard.

They came for Howard, smiling as DeSparr had. It was that easy. DeSparr's hate, now intending real harm, gave Howard the right, he thought, to act on his own hate. "That one!" he shouted, pointing at the smug DeSparr. "Yes, you, DeSparr." He made broad, crazy motions with his hands. If the universe wouldn't provide justice, he would. DeSparr would not get away with sacrificing Howard, his history, his future, his beating heart, to save his arrogant self.

Then DeSparr's uncharacteristic international grin spread benignly to Howard. "Don't excite them," whispered the doctor. "They want to kill us."

Before Howard could reply, the men motioned for them and led them both to the stream. Howard was as afraid as he was angry. Should he pray? They made a circle around the two. Pray to what? DeSparr's gracious smiling enraged him. Was there a god of haters?

The old man walked to them and turned and pointed at the ground in front of them, still barking. Four men brought the dead pig, bent down gently, placed it there carefully, as in a ceremony, then stood and backed away. The old man pointed at it and barked at the two again. He was either angry or threatening, or emphatically and seriously instructing. He stopped now and then, as if for a response.

Then he motioned to Howard, indicating he should turn and face the water. Four little men approached.

Why do condemned men go obediently to the death chamber? Why not run? What was the difference in how you died? If you ran, you at least had a chance, however small. And what could be worse than drowning? DeSparr's earlier admonition not to excite them gave Howard an idea. He remembered a shriek he had developed in high school, a kind of laughing shriek, like a witch. It was very loud and resonant. He did it one Halloween in front of the principal's house, with laughing friends, riding by at midnight, naively thinking the principal would be mystified.

There was little chance it would help, but it was better than nothing. He got up the nerve, out of desperation, and jumped, throwing his arms out and up, and the shriek came, successfully loud, more resonant than ever. All but the old man crouched, suddenly, spears forward. Encouraged by their inaction, he did it again, over and over, and they were gone, into the woods. He kept it up, unable to absorb the fact that all the bare little back sides disappeared so quickly and quietly, and hadn't cracked a stick or rustled a leaf. The old man didn't vanish, but stood defiant, Socrates on the battlefield, sobered by the flight of his comrades. Then he turned and waddled slowly away, and even the sagging rump had dignity. Howard and DeSparr stood alone over the drowned animal.

DeSparr avoided Howard's eyes, as if importantly occupied.
"'Him?'" said Howard, glaring, aping the blatant betrayal.
DeSparr ignored the incomplete sentence.

Howard said, "You pointed them to me."

DeSparr turned farther away and clasped his hands behind his back. He looked at the sky. "If you observe the earth from space, you will see water and... let's call it a great fungus."

"You said..." Howard inhaled deeply and shouted, 'Hi-i-im!'" He sounded ridiculous.

"To see things in perspective, picture the scattering solar systems, the galaxies. Is there an origin? A source of priorities? If there is, we can call it 'dead' center."

Howard was livid. "You pointed..."

"Did you know," said DeSparr, "that millions of living things die on this planet every day? It's covered with fungi. One dies. A million die. Living planet? Just as easily a dying one."

"You didn't want your own living self to die!"

"Even fungi have built-in auto-survival mechanisms."

Howard was surprised that DeSparr had listened. And it bugged him, but also calmed him, that the brain couldn't come up with good or relevant answers. And something else bugged him: the memory of the look on the faces of the little men, a particular aspect of it, a surprise, a disappointed or disillusioned surprise, as of well-intentioned people being spit upon, and Howard began to think that he had misinterpreted, in his over-frightened state, their meaning, misjudged their intentions. He began to think that the dead pig lying before them wrapped in the dignity of ceremony, its body a sacrifice, washed in the river, fresh in its unmarred plumpness, hadn't been a threat at all, but a gift.

"The pig could have been a gift," he said, with awed shock.

After a pause to think, DeSparr said, "Finally you see it."

DeSparr had warned of the men's intention to kill. He had pointed them to Howard. He was lying. And that was, like the international greeting smile, startlingly out of character. And not just the lie, but, by lying, the acknowledgement of the lingering wrongness, the guilt, without which there would have been no need for the lie. Was DeSparr one of those who would lie even when he knew you knew he was lying as long as there was no way to prove it?

DeSparr went on. "It was in payment for the boots."

Now Howard began to doubt the gift theory. Even if the Jaguar-men did want to pay for the boots, they would have paid whom they owed, the team in their camp, not two stragglers in the woods. And they had not behaved at all like people offering gifts or trade goods. They had shown hostility. The old man barked with disgust and contempt. The young one poked at Howard with a spear. They even took Howard and DeSparr down to the same pool in which they had drowned the pig. No, the pig was not a gift, or a payment.

He was still certain that lying was rare for the doctor. But if people were whats and not whos, then even though honesty had its practical value, dishonesty could be guiltlessly used as needed. So there was no future in arguing. He said, "We'd better get out of here. They may come back. And we can use this thing." He picked up the animal's front legs. Its hair was course. It was heavier than he expected. He had to lay the wet back of its huge head, as warm and almost as scary in death as in life, on his thigh. Its mouth gaped, sharp teeth bared.

DeSparr hesitated, then grabbed and lifted the splayed hind legs.

As they walked, Howard heard something big move in the undergrowth to one side, then minutes later a distant, throaty coughing.

***

When they had joined the other stake-outers and returned to camp, the questions came faster than they could answer them.

"That," said DeSparr, as if to a large audience, "is a peccary."

Maria the cook, Raul, and Pedro hung the peccary from a limb by its hind legs. Blood poured from the neck-wound. They boiled water in a can, poured it steaming on a small area of skin, and scraped hair off using Howard's pocket knife. By twilight, the whole peccary glowed pink-white.

Howard and L.P. gathered rocks, enlarged the fireplace, and made a rotisserie of heavy forked branches. The peccary was too thick to cook whole, but they got enough of the outside of it done and they all began pulling off slivers. Everybody exclaimed how good it was.

"I have something to say," said Smith, on one knee. He took off his straw hat and fiddled with it. "This is most important." He leaned forward, earnest and deliberate. "After what Doctor DeSparr and Howard have experienced, we must solemnly maintain our vow to keep to the safety perimeter Blake has marked out for us. It is absolutely inviolate. We agreed to it. Even within it, no one goes away from the camp alone, not even two or three. Only groups of five or more."

"If anybody violates it," said Crauder, "it's their own hide."

"Actually," said Smith. "It's not just their own hide. Don't forget: if something happens to one, it's a major burden for all. Problems arise. Search parties must be formed. Time is lost. An injured person must be attended to, his or her part of the work made up for. The ability of all of us to travel, even to survive, will be compromised. To violate the perimeter is not just mischievous, but dangerous to us all." He put his hat on. "I say this because we need to make a search, not too far, in case any lost supplies are still left. Raul, the river's down. Can you take four or five people? Stay close and safe?"

"*Si*," said Raul.

Rachel borrowed Mrs. Crauder's boots, and she and Howard followed. At the riverbank, she took a boot off. "These are too big."

Howard handed her a piece of white cloth from his pocket. "Thanks." She stuffed it in the boot. "Look. Shh."

Across the river, on a low branch, lay a jaguar. It saw them, got up awkwardly, and jumped to the ground painfully. It lifted its head slowly and uttered a long, broken groan, as a deposed but still defiant emperor might. Its mouth never quite shut as the groan died. The lowered head and ears twisted as if listening for a reply. Its eyes squeezed shut, then opened. It turned and walked away along the bank, head dipping and twisting each time its weight shifted to its bad front leg. It disappeared in the undergrowth. A strong image stayed with Howard. The living with the limping. The living alone with the limping.

***

"We didn't find any supplies," said Howard to Smith as they gathered again around the fire. "Saw a big cat."

"The sons and daughters of *el tigre* stay in the low country," said Raul. "But the old one comes to these mountains. He is still quick."

"Mercy!" said Mrs. Crauder.

"He was a lord of the woods. Now he is tired. Now he walks about and seeks the weak, lone thing which does not suspect. The animal or the fish or the bird. He can change all things for the prey in the moment. You cannot know the way how he will do it."

"Jaguars do avoid humans," said Blake.

"Maybe," said Raul. "But they say that the old one has no more the paradise, and when his hunger is great, he will jump the man."

"Mercy," said Mrs. Crauder again.

When Rachel finished her sliver of meat, she took the boots off and began scraping mud off with a little rock. She tucked the white cloth Howard had given her into the laces of one of them, then carried them and set them behind one of the big logs. "Mrs. Crauder?" she said, "The boots are here if you need them." She came and sat with Howard and clasped her hands at her bare ankles and rested her chin on her knees.

Howard said, "Hiding them from the Jaguar-guys?"

She nodded. "I'm afraid I made a bad scratch with that rock."

"To go with all our other scratches," said Howard.

A stick hissed and oozed bubbles. The yellow-gray smoke billowed and disappeared into the black sky. In the fire's pulsing, the people around it livened and dimmed, and the tree-trunks around the clearing seemed oddly to advance and retreat.

"Look at us," said Rachel. "We're lost." The fire made, through her torn cotton shirt, a golden glow that crept softly, with her breathing, up and down the curve of her neck and under her chin.

Howard nodded. "Got any ideas?"

"Pray."

He took that to mean she had no ideas.

She said, "How about you?"

He shook his head. "At least we have food for a couple of days."

"I like peccary," she said.

***

Something new showed between the tree-trunks, vague bulbous shapes, brownish-red, glowing and pulsing, forming, with the trunks, a kind of egg-and-dart necklace around the clearing. The shapes were long bellies, swaying slowly in the shadows. Howard felt a chill, and whispered to Rachel, "Don't panic, but look." She saw and didn't panic. He whispered the same to L.P. and the three told the others, quietly.

Before Raul saw them, he stood and threw new kindling on the fire, which made it pop and crack and flare up quickly and show off the meat on the spit. The bellies showed clearly now: the Jaguar-people, and lots of them. At the brighter firelight some stepped behind others.

Their red-gold skin seemed translucent. They stood with feet apart, faces and eyes glowing behind streaks of paint, long bony fingers

90

gripping and regripping tall spears and bows.

Finally one spoke, Shorty, the young one that had been so animated with DeSparr and Howard at the drowning of the peccary. "Sho-lo-peet!" Others in the circle laughed nervously, making fun, or trying to. They must have known about the flooding of the camp.

Shorty wore the army boots and the other pair was on the old man, who stood in them as before, pot-bellied and stony-faced.

"Yao-yees-cay," said Shorty grinning facetiously over his shoulder. The others pointed at the team and laughed like conquerors sharing a defeated-enemy joke. They stepped forward. Around some of their necks hung red plastic cowboys on strings.

Smith rose slowly, staring directly at Shorty. Shorty raised his bow and arrow and repeatedly and dramatically poked the air, directly at Smith, probably because he was the tallest.

Haughton-Alsef ducked behind Pryce, then Pryce ducked behind him, then they both ducked behind Mrs. Crauder. That frightened her, and all three lined up behind her husband.

Crauder patted his pants pocket. "Don't forget what I've got."

The old man spoke to Shorty in a severe, nasal voice. Shorty lowered the bow. The old man stared at Smith, then lazily raised an arm and pointed along the team's feet and barked.

A dozen Jaguar-men came forward, staring at the team's boots.

"I coulda told ya!" said Crauder. He struggled to pull the pistol out of his pocket. "Get out of here!" He swung his arm to wave them away. He finally got the pistol and pointed it at them. They grinned and kept coming. He shoved it forward and said, "Go!" He was shaking.

"Jud!" said Mrs. Crauder.

"Put that away!" said Smith.

"I'll shoot!" said Crauder.

The Jaguar-men seemed to enjoy his antics.

"I'll shoot!" Crauder held the pistol with both hands, shaking, pointing it directly at the tallest Jaguar-man. The man reached and took it as if accepting an important gift. Crauder slumped. The man smiled, turned it over in his hands, and held it up. The others stared blankly.

Then the old man took it, turned it over, scraped the ground with it, and grunted. He motioned and the Jaguar-men began picking and pulling at the team's clothes and the men's beards. They grinned and nodded as they stole. Howard slid his boot-laces out of their eyelets and put them in his pants pocket next to his knife. They could be useful later. But by the time the men got to him they were taking not only boots but socks and pants and shirts and watches. They didn't take eyeglasses or hats or Haughton-Alsef's pipe.

When they were through, they backed off and stood again in a circle around the team, holding their wadded loot under their arms. The old man stared at Smith, seemed to chew on something, and poked lazily at the peccary with his spear.

Howard rubbed his toes in the cool dirt. The team had little more than underwear left. The Americans' skin, next to the red-gold of the Jaguar-men, was a discordant blue-white. Crauder, hairy as a coconut, snorted and muttered. Zoe's skimpy pink underwear barely interrupted the sweeping curves of her unblemished tan. Haughton-Alsef's thin arms held tightly his pack of notes folded over a pencil. Mrs. Crauder was pouty, pink, and pudgy. Dove-Ti was white as curdled milk in her red satin panties. She and Maria the cook had no bras. Rachel's smooth, sleek skin was almost as white as her plain underwear.

Smith took off his hat. "The Lord's my shepherd."

Howard was surprised he would quote scripture in his drawers. "…Yea, though I walk through death's dark vale…"

Rachel joined Smith quoting. "…For thou art with me…"

"Thou!" said Haughton-Alsef, nervously. "Where is that kindly old icon who only wants everyone to support the building program?"

"Any 'thou' around here," said L.P., "is a practical joker."

"Maybe he's getting back at us for something," said Howard.

"Or he wants our attention," said Rachel.

The old man barked orders and a dozen of the Jaguar-men gathered the loot, including the pistol and the steaming, half-cooked peccary, which they held by the hooves, gingerly swapping hands, and ran into the woods. The others stood staring at the team.

Finally Smith raised his arms, his straw hat in one hand, and said, "We have come in peace. Zoe? Can you figure this language at all?"

"What I've heard," she said, "makes me think of Nahuatl."

Haughton-Alsef said, "Nahuatl is Mexican. Ancient Aztec."

"I know," she said, but that's what it sounds like. And there are still a million speakers today." She tried hand motions. The old man showed no interest for a while, then spoke, stony-faced.

Zoe's mouth dropped.

"What did he say?" said Smith.

"I don't know, but it's definitely close to Nahuatl. With time…"

DeSparr said, "Look at their necks. Some of the necklace-strings have empty blister packs. They've eaten the antibiotics."

"Or planted them," said Crauder.

Just then there was a sudden commotion in the woods. Six Jaguar-men reappeared, carrying the limp body of a boy by wrists and ankles, the way others had carried the peccary. He looked about twelve or thirteen, in a typical loincloth. Howard felt a tired, sick shock.

The old man directed the men as they laid the boy, unconscious but breathing, in front of Smith. Then he signaled the woods and two more Jaguar-men showed, carrying something small in their upturned palms as in a ceremony, a kind of knife. For a knife it was large and wide. It was roughly chipped out of what looked like stone or bone. On one side of it were somehow fastened a row of rootless human teeth and a round, black stone set in a larger round white stone, like an eye, all of it making the profile of a strangely warped, frighteningly wanton face. The old man took the knife, squatted, and held it over the boy's heart.

Howard said, "No," as if the word were known in all languages.

Rachel cut the air horizontally with her hand.

Crauder said, loudly, "No!"

"We are the alien," said Haughton-Alsef. "The fly in the ointment. We have no right to interfere with their customs and ceremonies. We are only to observe."

"We agreed," said Dove-Ti. "No changing them. No harm."

"That's right," said Rachel, indicating the boy. "No 'harm.'"

"It's they that meant to, uhm… hurt him," said Dove-Ti. "Their act, not ours. If we stop it, then it's we harming their culture."

"The world's full of problems," said Haughton-Alsef. "This boy's a drop in the ocean."

Rachel knelt and brushed the boy's hair. "He's in front of us."

The old man laid the backs of his hands on the boy's chest and slid them out from under the knife. It lay at a skewed angle across the sternum. He aligned it with the boy's length, pointing at his heart. He stood up and barked and looked around at Smith and the team and waved his arms as if to drive off some obnoxious odor. Then he and all the Jaguar-men disappeared into the woods quickly and quietly.

The firelight glinted from the jagged edge of the knife rocking with the boy's unconscious breaths. Its edges were stained with what looked like old, black, partially rubbed-out blood.

Crauder was the first to speak. "You know what that sorry

knife's for, don't you? They mean 'im to be our next meal."

"Jud!" said his wife.

"The ritual sacrifice of humans," said Haughton-Alsef, "is a part of many long-established cultures. Traditional. Ceremonial. Strict. It doesn't mean they're violent. But it may mean we have been presented with an opportunity." He sucked loudly on his empty pipe. "As I've said before, there is practiced among aboriginal societies, quite religiously, what is known as reciprocation. Absolutely crucial that they balance debt, whether it's incurred deliberately or accidentally. We have chosen to enter their world-space. They have made it clear, with the knife — which, by the way, is not 'sorry,' but an exquisite work of art — that the boy will provide us with a healthy repast."

"Stop!" said Zoe. "Don't joke! I'll like… starve first."

"Could some," said Mrs. Crauder, "be suggesting that we…"

Dove-Ti held her hand over her mouth and stared at the boy. He was out cold.

Rachel knelt and brushed his hair. She picked up the knife and boldly walked past Haughton-Alsef and laid it on one of the big logs. "Oh!" She glanced behind the log. "Mrs. Crauder's boots are still here! Where I left them. And here's Beg!"

Howard was exhausted, as it seemed everyone was, in spite of, or maybe because of, the arguing. But he got up and looked. Beg was asleep behind the log, still in his clothes and boots.

"So all is not lost," said Smith. "Let's get a night's sleep."

"With that boy lying there like that?" said Mrs. Crauder.

"We need watches for the night, for him, and for the perimeter." He and Dove-Ti appointed them. Some curled up at the embers, some in the hut. Few slept. The boy slept.

Chapter 11

Tomás Santillana sat on the west slope of a scrubby hill under the bare twisted limbs of a short thick oak. On the other side soldiers and horses and Totonac warriors and porters all settled in, exhausted by the first mountain crossings.

Before him were brown plains splotched with black lava flows and crawling cloud shadows. It reminded him vaguely of Extremadura, in Spain, west of Salamanca. He wondered if it gave Cortés thoughts of Medellín, his home. Beyond the plains, beyond the distant snowy peaks, in a high valley, it was said, lay Tenochtitlán, the City of the Aztecas.

In his lap lay Padre Olmedo's Latin Bible. He paused to admire the carvings on its thick wooden covers, then opened it.

"Tomás!" shouted Fernando, limping boldly up the hill. He stopped and took in the view. "Nice place to loaf!"

"Oh? And you've found a break, somehow, in your busy day."

"I'm on watch. And I can do that from here." He sat down, armor clattering. "Thanks for breaking up the fight yesterday."

Tomás shrugged. "Alonso and Gonzo. What a pair. Close friends, always fighting."

"I saw you talking to them afterwards. Was it about their faith?"

"To no avail, I'm afraid."

Fernando laughed, then pointed at the Bible. "Olmedo's Vulgate. Why such heavy reading?"

Tomás flipped pages. "Long story. You probably remember the girl in Salamanca. Rosa. After her mother's funeral, after my penance was done, I left the university. You saw me off."

"I remember. You seemed aimless. Did you settle anywhere?"

"Amsterdam. I loaded ships for three years. The beer was good. I wrote my family. I thought about Rosa. I met Joost de Shoonhoven, a wool weaver and a teacher with the Brethren of the Common Life. Fernando, have you heard of the priest Desiderious Erasmus?"

"I think so."

"Joost gave me a little book by him. I only skimmed it. Finally I went back to Spain. Home. Do you remember the priest who assigned my penance? Padre Ruiz?"

"I never understood why you chose him for confession."

"It was a mistake. He used my mention of Rosa as an excuse to meet her. Then he tried to make her his mistress. Gifts. An apartment. She did not answer my letters. I was disappointed. Then mad. I went back, to Salamanca, to Padre Ruiz, and fired questions. I mentioned his vows, the church, the penance he had assigned me. I asked him what his penance would be for having a mistress. He told me to be careful what I said about him. I let him know I had had enough of religion and stormed out and mouthed about it all around town. I also bolstered my spirits with spirits. Within a week I was in prison."

"You?"

Tomás closed the Bible and laid it on the grass. "For drunkenness at first. Then I had visitors. Do you remember, at the university, how vague and distant the word 'heresy' seemed?"

"Tomás!"

"They showed me a list of things they found in my room. They had marked pages in the little book by Erasmus, like where it said a personal faith in Jesus is more important than the church. After they framed a case, they took me to an inquisitor. He decided that 'a learned and faithful man' would 'help me search my conscience.'"

"The rack or the water?"

"Both. They took me somewhere underground. It was so dark I could not see the roof among all the beams and cross-braces. Did you know that, held on your back with an iron trap between your teeth and water poured in, you cannot help but swallow?"

Fernando frowned. "I saw a public *auto de fe*. They burned the face of a *converso*. He had to breathe the flames right into his nose and throat. Did they plan an auto de fe for you?"

"Me? Eventually, but no fire. They made me watch several, and that did have an effect. I asked what they wanted, what words. They started reading through the Gospel of Matthew. I could not listen well, but I heard where Jesus said to several corrupt religious leaders, '…some of my followers you will chase from town to town: some you will kill;

96

others you will flog; upon you will be all the righteous blood…' I asked them which of us were the floggers and which the killers."

"They liked that."

"They gave me extra water for that. Eventually one of the 'learned and faithful men' said to me, 'Your name is Tomás.' He turned to the Gospel of John and read where the doubter whose name was the same as mine saw the nail scars in Jesus's wrists and cried, 'My Lord and my God!' and Jesus said, 'Blessed are they who have not even seen, yet believe.' Fernando, I thought it was Jesus speaking to me. I asked for forgiveness, I…"

"Forgiveness?" said Fernando. "What for? The drunkenness?"

"You would be surprised."

"How convenient! Live it up, then get forgiveness. Full license!"

"No! Fernando! That forgiveness — Jesus earned it by his own suffering. When you see it, you want to please him. It is not just the rules. It is his company. And out of that, the good company of people. When you get down to it, that's what we are made for."

Fernando smiled. "Well, anyway, they did not kill you."

"No. I started shouting over and over, 'My Lord and my God.' I did it for days. I think they got tired of it. One of them got me to write it down and sign it. He showed it to the others. They called it a confession, but not of heresy. They confiscated my property and scheduled me for the next auto de fe but only flogged me and let me go."

"I would have thought all that would turn you against religion."

"It did. But not against Jesus."

"Wait. No. Please do not try to explain."

"I am not sure I can."

"So this is why you like to read Olmedo's Bible."

"Yes."

"And you have since been the faithful believer I now know?"

"No. I left the prison with much zeal and little direction. I heard how lawyers were needed in Hispaniola. Traders, landowners, slavers, capitáns, all needed contracts drawn up. I sailed there and did quite well. Remember Iago? At the university? How loudly he argued against slavery, praised Her Majesty's ruling against it? The horrors he named?"

"Which he had never seen."

"He is in Hispaniola now. A wealthy *encomendero*. I am afraid he used my help in finding loopholes in the law. He is cruel, Fernando, cruel to his Indian workers. He breaks up families. It was when I heard him tell them, half-heartedly, as he was required under the laws of *encomienda*, about the love of Christ, that I finally saw the irony, the hypocrisy, and the extent of my own complicity."

"Everyone knows:" said Fernando, "slavery is against the law."

"But the natives are naive, and we are far from home."

Fernando pointed across the valley. Several Indians sat on a ridge at a fallen tree. "They are lucky they are not slaves of the Aztecas!"

"The Aztecas are slavers. We are slavers and hypocrites."

"I have not finished," said Fernando.

"Sorry."

"And human sacrifices, Tomás, human sacrifices."

"I know, I know."

"Their leaders, their priests, eat human flesh. Can you change that without force?"

"I hope so."

Fernando took a deep breath. "Will you tone me down, as Olmedo does Cortés?"

"I agree with Padre Olmedo. Why destroy idols? Why replace them with images of the Virgin? Symbols obscure substance. Jesus said it is the heart that matters. And that cannot be forced. And, I might add, Cortés listens to Olmedo. Sometimes."

"I listen to you," said Fernando. "You were always a rock. But for me, quitting this expedition would mean resigning my commission. And that would mean no future and no chance at the gold."

"How do you know? God may want you rich."

"I am afraid it is I that wants me rich."

"Fernando," said Tomás, "You are my most honest friend."

Officers shouted commands. Fernando picked up his helmet and began limping down the hill. His sword and stiff leg swung awkwardly but confidently. He turned once to Tomás, almost lost his balance, then smiled and saluted.

***

"It has been twelve days," said Atl. "We have found nothing." He was tired and sore. He had not slept well. "I do not like this place. It is cold and there is nothing to eat."

They stood on a ridge next to a fallen tree. Below them lay bare, twisted valleys and brown plains scattered with black rocks. Beyond them, Atl could see Popocatepetl and its hanging gray smoke. His skin stung remembering the snow and ice in the cold windy pass between it and Ixtaccihuatl. Far away now, both mountains were almost as blue as the sky.

"Rain seldom comes here," said One-Cip'.

To the south, Atl could see the white top of Orizaba. The first time he saw it was when his mother showed him from the high land near their village. He blocked the memories of her and of Dahlia. He tried to replace them with plans for the killers when he would find them.

Two-Rabbit and Atl huddled in torn cotton quilting they had found in a deserted Sant-yago camp. Deer of Stone refused to wear anything that smelled of the Sant-yagos. A Fox is Mad picked at bushes for berries.

Balanced Turtle spoke with hope. "When we have found the women, then we must find a clear stream, where we can settle."

Deer of Stone said, "We will kill the killers first. Look." On a hill across the valley, under a bare acorn tree, sat two Sant-yagos, one in a brown robe, one in the leather costume. A cloud of dust rose from the far side, iron clattered, and out of that dust came Sant-yagos and Totonacs carrying long spears and all sorts of strange objects. "Even if the Sant-yagos are not the killers, they might know who is."

One-Cip' said, "A Huaxtec told me they give food to porters and guides."

"Can we ask them what they know?" said Atl. "If they did it, we will see it in their eyes."

"If they did it, they will do it to us," said Deer of Stone.

One-Cip' nodded to the west. "They go to the High Valley. But first, they must pass through the land of the Tlaxcalans."

"Will the Tlaxcalans war with them?"

"I do not know. I believe their final goal is the Empire."

"They will never defeat the Aztecs," said Deer of Stone.

"Cortés succeeds well with just his mouth," said One-Cip'.

A Fox is Mad turned and sat under a tree. "I am getting a nap."

"We will all need rest," said One-Cip'.

Atl lay down and closed his eyes, but when the others slept, he crept away. He ran along the side of the ridge, behind the trees, toward the sounds of the Sant-yagos. If Dahlia were there, she would see his speed and stealth. It was not easy to put thoughts of her out of his mind.

He found a row of large rocks and scrub bushes and tried to

watch, torn between his curiosity and his relentless need for sleep.

***

The vest was colored black and carved with fine swirls. It looked thick and tough and able to slow or stop an arrow. The orange hair of the rider swept in waves from under the iron hat, bouncing with the steps of the huge beast, which snorted and sweated and swung its head side to side. Dust rose from the feet of fourteen other beasts and from the feet of the thousands of men stretched out as far as Atl could see. Totonac scouts walked far ahead.

When the army had moved close to Atl's people he ran and woke them. "Look!"

They all watched from behind the rocks. Atl was proud he had seen them first. He wished he could share in their boldness.

One-Cip' composed himself. "Look for our women."

Two-Rabbit said, sadly, "What if they are not there?"

"Then maybe the Sant-yagos will help us find them."

The soldiers seemed grim, even sickly. The Totonac porters seemed tired. Cortés himself rode high on his snorting beast. Beside him walked the interpreter woman from the Land of the Turkey and Deer.

Atl saw the iron logs that were said to kill from a distance. Groups of men pulled them and they glided over rocks and through wash holes on pairs of walking circles made of wood. Others pulled loaded wooden boxes on larger walking circles. It was like toys he had seen at trading booths in Cempoala. Before his eyes, they carried loads!

One box on circles rolled up a rock and turned over and spilled its load of bundles into the mud of an arroyo. Atl was shocked at the loss. But oddly, the soldiers laughed as they waited. Some sat down. Atl felt hate and fear and envy. If these were not the killers, and if he were bold enough to go to them, he would wish to be like them.

He saw none of the missing women or girls.

"Our women are gone," said A Fox is Mad. "Our way of life."

For a long time no one spoke. One-Cip' paced. Finally he said, "I am going to the Sant-yagos."

"No," said Atl, defiant before he knew it. "I mean… we all go."

One-Cip' glared. "I must talk to them without distraction."

Atl stared at the ground, torn between his respect for One-Cip' and his fear for One-Cip's safety.

100

"We will not let them change us," said Deer of Stone. "Never."

One-Cip' inhaled deeply, then turned and began walking alone in the open. The soldiers coughed and held their stomachs. He was not in danger. He stopped and looked back at Atl.

"Me?" said Atl.

"Hurry."

Deer of Stone said to Atl, "We will not let them change us!"

Atl nodded, then ran quickly to One-Cip'. Then the two of them walked down the hill with dignity. The soldiers and porters were noisy and dusty and paid little attention.

One-Cip' found a lead Totonac guide. He grunted and the guide grunted and they stared at each other. "We are Totonacs," said One-Cip' finally, referring to himself, as he sometimes did, as part of the Totonac nation into which his father had been forced. "Our village was burned. We do not know who did it. Can you help us find our missing women?"

The man was short and thin. "I am Feathers on the Water. Do you have gold?"

"No." One-Cip's pain in saying it showed.

"Then why did you come to us?"

"We can work," said One-Cip'. "I know this land. I've traded here many times. These Sant-yagos have gained sway. Maybe you or they have seen something."

"Ask who you like," said Feathers on the Water.

Until Tonatiah had gone below the earth One-Cip' and Atl talked to any Totonac who would listen. Some Totonacs even asked Soldiers the questions, in their Sant-yago tongue. They learned nothing. Atl began to lose hope. At least some of his fear of the Sant-yagos left him. They did not have hating faces. They seemed more worried about their tired bones and their aching stomachs than about him or One-Cip'.

That night Feathers on the Water came to One-Cip' and said, "I have talked to the captains. They need more guides and porters. They will feed you and help you in your search if you will stay and work."

One-Cip' said, "Four more of our men wait in the woods."

"Have the gods given them health?"

"Yes, and made them willing workers."

"They may come as well."

Chapter 12

At the first misty light, the boy lay sleeping on his side, knees drawn up, one skinny forearm under his long narrow face, the other covering it. All but DeSparr and Beg gathered around him, rubbing their eyes and hands, tired and hungry.

"Who could even like… think about hurting that little boy?" said Zoe. "And like… why was he left with us? Who is he? Oh, the things he could tell us. You know, it's crazy, but last night I was able to get some of the Jaguar-people's talk. It's close to Nahuatl after all. It's a start."

Haughton-Alsef studied the boy. "Most likely he has been rebellious about some aspect of the tribe's customs, and has been exiled to us. We would be expected to adopt him or sacrifice him for some benefit to ourselves or to the gods or to the tribe, perhaps in return for the boots and clothes." He glanced at the log where Rachel had laid the knife. "Let's have a look at that magnificent piece, shall we?"

Howard and others gathered and studied the arrangement of attached teeth and eye-stones, as frightening as it was comical.

"Is it sharp?" said Crauder. He reached and felt its edge. A razor-thin line of red showed on his finger. "Dang."

"This is a highly crafted object of ceremony, a sign his people are civil. And they wouldn't have parted with it, perching it on his sternum, pointing it at his heart, unless their intentions for the boy were serious. The incident with the peccary only reinforces that conclusion." He placed the knife carefully back on the boy and knelt and posed seriously beside it. "Pryce, we need a shot of this."

Pryce held his hands out and shrugged ironically. "No camera."

"Bummer," said Haughton-Alsef. "But as I was saying, all of this points to a demand for some form of ritual human sacrifice. We know that this method of working out the inconsistencies of societal organization and survival has been known to blossom in the primeval springtime of many cultures. Even our Western cultural progenitors, the Greeks, have recently been found to have done it, and we've known all along about the Romans putting newborns in the wild to die, and…"

"Of course," said Zoe, "we won't like…"

"We hold to this boy's life just like our own," said Rachel.

"Try to stop and imagine," said Haughton-Alsef, pleasantly, "the shock and reverberations that could occur within the delicate social fabric of these happy people if we, who have invaded their world, were to deny them the appropriate outcome of their cherished rituals and ceremonies. We should ask: what is this boy's life now? He has been exiled by his own people. Unwanted. Can you imagine what that is like? And, if he was exiled for anti-social tendencies, as is likely, his own nature would only be a plague for him, a life of lonely terror. Would you force him to live with that?"

"Force him?" said Zoe. "How do you force him to live when he's like… already living?"

"I'm afraid there's another aspect to this," said Haughton-Alsef, avoiding Zoe's question. "If we as invaders do not comply, we will most likely bring down their wrath upon ourselves, possibly even death. You may have heard of the Elliot team killed by the Waodani in Ecuador. I've done considerable research on ancient Mesoamerican customs."

"So," said Crauder, "you're saying you're chicken."

"Not at all. Like any peoples, they feel compelled to express, to project, what seems normal, even beyond the ever-disintegrating boundaries of culture. And certainly, within their world-space, they have every right to expect compliance."

"Oh, so wonderfully said," said Mrs. Crauder, still favoring her sore rear-end.

"Chicken," said Crauder.

"Surely," said Haughton-Alsef, "our leader won't deny us a vote on the issue?"

"Well," said Smith, "possibly a study by a committee. But my vote would be against killing any innocent person." He appointed Haughton-Alsef, Dove-Ti, Blake, and Crauder to make a study.

"I can't believe this," said Zoe. "What are we like… doing?"

"Don't worry," said Crauder. "This bunch'll never vote for it."

"Let's open another bottle," said Beg, grinning.

Crauder glared at him. "Get a job." Then he knelt next to the boy. "Maybe this little jungle-jumper can help us find food." He lightly slapped the boy's face.

The boy's eyes quickly rounded. He rolled up on an elbow, scanned the area, and froze.

Dove-Ti bent over him and smiled and jabbed her finger in the middle of her bare chest and said, "I am Dove-Ti." He turned away.

Rachel reached slowly for his hand. He drew it back. She casually picked up a small rock and tossed it and watched it. He watched it, then watched her. She did it again, several times, then reached and lightly touched his hand. This time he let her. She gently turned her pale-white hand under his golden-brown one and lifted it and said softly, "Get up."

Dove-Ti also spoke in her usual soothing voice, but took too quick a step toward him. He jumped up, looked around desperately, and ran. Crauder and Blake ran after him. Crauder grabbed an arm, but the boy slipped away and ran to the edge of the woods, then stopped, skinny and awkward, arms folded.

"Let him go," said DeSparr. "Then we can disband our death committee."

"No," said Haughton-Alsef, quickly, almost dropping his pipe. "He's been given to us."

Rachel and Dove-Ti and Zoe smiled and called the boy again.

"Come back," said Rachel, motioning. "Come on." He crouched and glanced around nervously. Rachel signaled Crauder to back off and he did. She slowly crouched and duck-walked toward him, stopping often, talking softly, tossing little rocks.

Maria the translator joined the three. They squatted slowly and casually, not close together, avoiding sudden moves. Zoe talked softly, trying what she could of her language skills.

"Let the language people work," said Smith. "We'll meet again soon."

"But, what are we supposed to eat?" said Mrs. Crauder. "They took that piggary."

"Peccary," said Blake.

***

Rachel left the boy and walked back to Howard and L.P. at the hut. "A crowd scares him," she said. "And Zoe needs his full attention. She's already connected on several words. So, how's our hut?"

"All rented out," said Howard. "Demand's still high."

"So let's raise the rent," said L.P.

"How about a new wing?" said Rachel.

"A new wing," said Howard.

The three started framing a second room off one side of the hut, more posts, beams, and crooked purlins. They collected more bark-shingles and insect bites. They found more straight twig-nails and drove them through. Howard was able to drill holes with a stone he found and chipped to a fairly sharp, skinny point, inspired by the knife the Jaguar-people had left.

Once he reached under a shingle to adjust it and felt something warm, moist, and gritty. He jerked his hand away, then realized it was Rachel's finger. She jerked away too, and they laughed.

Beg fake-limped to the hut and watched them.

"Wanna help?" said L.P.

Beg held his stomach and groaned, "I just need a sip. Just a sip."

Crauder heard him. "You need something to do."

"But..."

"C'mere." Crauder walked Beg around to the back of the hut.

Howard and Rachel could still hear them.

"Get yourself together," said Crauder. "Find a job around here."

"I ain't able, y'know? I got this..."

"No excuses. Is this who you are?"

"I ain't a alky, really. Just a nip."

"You are an alky. Accept it. Forget the wine."

Howard noticed Maria the translator glance several times from the boy to L.P.

"L.P.," he said, "I think Maria likes you."

L.P. glanced at her. "I don't know."

Rachel said, "There's only one way to find out."

"Yeah?"

"Do something." She glanced at Howard.

Maria the cook came out of the woods with reeds and sticks loaded in her arms higher than her head. She plopped them all down next to the remains of the fire. She sat down, brushed the debris off her arms and breasts, picked up several reeds, and started weaving.

Crauder left Beg behind the hut. He saw Maria the cook's large reed mat, and laughed, hairy belly bouncing. "How do you do that?"

"Eh?" she said, squinting and frowning.

He held his hands out toward the mat. "How... do... that?"

They went on like that until she had him sitting and happily making mats with her.

DeSparr, still in pain, groaned and got up without stretching and walked uneasily to the ledge, tenderly holding his bandaged chest and arm. He watched the receding flood, privately.

***

"I'm going for more shingles," said L.P. He searched near the edge of the woods.

"Do you think they'll get together," said Rachel with her crinkled smile, "L.P. and Maria?"

"Who knows?" said Howard. "He's talked about her." He stopped. He was sharing confidential information about his old friend.

Rachel waited for more.

If he shared more, he would wish he hadn't later.

Finally she handed him another shingle and they nailed it. Again their hands touched, and she squeezed playfully and released quickly.

"Talk to me about the meeting again," She said.

"What meeting?"

"You know, in Tegucigalpa when they let Miss Margaret go."

"What about it?"

"How'd they decide? She's sixty-two, but she gets around."

"I don't think it was her age," said Howard.

"Then what?"

"Well, they said age, you know. But there were side comments. I don't think it was a coincidence the meeting was called when you and she were off to Copán."

"Side comments?"

"Dove-Ti was afraid Miss Margaret would try to 'convert the natives.'"

Rachel placed another shingle. "They dismissed her for that?"

"I was against it," said Howard. "But... Well, Haughton-Alsef said, 'She's an odd, unnatural woman, an unpredictable extremist,' and Smith said, 'We should release her from this for her own good.' And that's when Dr. DeSparr said, 'We should keep her for *our* own good.'"

"Dr. DeSparr sided with you?"

"He probably didn't know it was my side. I didn't say much."

"Then what happened?"

"Well, let's see… It was Dove-Ti who said, 'Let's not forget it was her choice not to submit her résumé.'"

"Wait a minute," said Rachel. "She didn't…?"

"On the form, all she filled in for credentials, was 'SaSi.'"

"Oh, yes. Sometimes she signed her letters that way."

"She is a little on the sassy side," said Howard.

"She didn't mean sassy. Her 'SaSi' stands for 'Saved Sinner.'"

"Oh. That's probably why Mrs. Crauder said she was afraid Miss Margaret would 'make us normal Christians look like a gospel sideshow.' Anyway, the way they stated it was, if I remember right, '…to lovingly release Miss Margaret with gratitude for her many accomplishments.' Crauder and DeSparr and I dissented."

"Everybody else voted against her?"

"L.P. was in his room, sick. Remember?"

"Yes. What about Zoe?"

"I think if you'd been there, she'd have kept her mouth shut. She said she liked Miss Margaret and all, but she wondered if it was wise to undertake a wilderness trip when our number was unlucky thirteen."

"But we had fourteen."

"Zoe told me later she forgot to count Beg. Nobody noticed. So in fact, Zoe actually helped achieve what she feared: unlucky thirteen."

Rachel sighed. "Miss Margaret did say if we found a tribe she wanted them to 'know about Jesus.'"

"Well, see, now right there, she was getting off-track with this expedition. No swaying their culture. They say, you know, that after any change, we'll no longer be able to look at them in their pure state."

"Pure?" she said. "Why do you always say, 'They?'"

"I…"

"Commit, Howard."

"Well, it's true Miss Margaret wasn't planning to do them any harm. They could decide for themselves."

"That's a big thing with her. No pressure or gimmicks."

"You and she were pretty good friends."

"Yeah. Did you know she lived in the Amazon basin for years? Way out in some village. A hut with a dirt floor. No running water. She'd have been apt to help us a lot right now."

"That I can picture," said Howard. "Shriveled-up-looking as she is, she wouldn't let anybody carry that huge travel-bag of hers. Not at the airport or the hotel or the bus."

"She's not shriveled-up. More like scrawny. Did you know she carries everything she owns in that bag? Literally?"

"You're kidding."

"Nope. She said once somebody in Recife gave her an expensive set of luggage. She sold it and bought some books for the kids in her school. Said she likes the kind of bag you have to tie together with rope because nobody will steal it. That's her."

"Ha," said Howard. "Yes."

"She was how I came to know about this trip," said Rachel. I actually met her five years ago in a book shop in Black Mountain. In North Carolina. That's where she went when she was on sabbatical. We kind of hit it off. She teaches little kids, like I do. But she had all ages, six to twelve, all in one room. She lives on about two thousand a year."

"Nah."

"It's true. She said she feels rich around the people where she ministers. They get about two hundred. I expect she knows as much as any outsider about the Amazon. I asked her if she would tell my kids about it. She did and they liked it, and so did I. Snakes, monkeys. After that she sent me letters and pictures. She keeps up with some of my kids, too, and their families. She came to see me when my mom died."

"Really?" said Howard, trying to picture ornery little Miss Margaret doing that.

Rachel nodded and touched the corner of her eye with the back of a finger, then smiled and picked up another shingle.

"Shriveled-up," said Howard.

"Scrawny."

***

Maria the cook got up and brought a long mat she had made and hung it from the open front of the first room of the hut. It made a partial privacy wall, a partial insect screen, and, if the sun would ever show again, a partial shade.

"Pat?" said Crauder to his wife. "Can you beat this?" He held up his first finished mat.

"Oh!" she said, and joined them and was soon making mats faster than he.

"Folks," said Smith to everybody. "The committee has come to a decision about the boy."

DeSparr turned from watching the receding flood. "The Death Committee! Is it thumbs up or thumbs down?"

Smith ignored the sarcasm and turned to Haughton-Alsef, who said, "The committee feels we can benefit from the boy. At least for information. They decided we let him live until events indicate a different course. I was out-voted, and I cannot guarantee we will be safe from the wrath of the Jaguar-people."

Howard looked at Rachel. "A vote about somebody's life."

"No vote would have changed my mind," she said, "Nothing happens to that boy."

"Well, back to work."

Howard and Rachel laid shingles and L.P. gathered more.

Maria the cook came from the stream with a basket she had woven, lined on the inside with a huge leaf, filled with a good pint of water. Pryce and the Crauders hung more big reed mats from the edges of the hut's roof, making it more enclosed.

Smith dragged a leafy branch to the hut and swept the dirt.

Crauder called it a "swoosh." He laid reed mats behind Smith.

Raul looked around. "Where is Pedro?"

Smith looked. "We made it very clear: no going off alone."

"God!" said Pryce. "Has he been kidnapped?"

Smith gritted his teeth. "We'll have to sit down and … No. Who will join me on a search?"

Blake, Raul, Pryce, Dove-Ti, and Haughton-Alsef volunteered and they all set out.

***

"Time for final inspection," said Howard about mid-afternoon. He and L.P. and Rachel stood back and admired the hut. The roof, now longer because of the extra room, was warped and shingly, like the wing of some huge bird lit there among the trees, or a part of the forest floor pried up for airing.

Footsteps squished in the woods. It was Pedro with a small dead rabbit in one hand. He stopped and held it up and grinned.

"Where've you been?" said Crauder.

"Eh?" said Pedro, still grinning.

"We have a rule."

Zoe looked up from the boy. "He's got food!"

"Get the fire going!" said Howard. He gathered the driest kindling from the hut.

"How'd you catch it?" said Crauder.

"Eh?" Pedro grinned again, then carried the rabbit to a flat rock next to the fire pit. He hurried to the stream to wash his hands, then came back and poked his finger into the rabbit. He pulled the skin off like a sock, exposing the pale meat.

He and Zoe talked in Spanish. Then she said to everyone, "He like... made a noose thingie out of the spare bootlaces the Jaguar-people missed, and put it on the end of a long stick. Then he found a hole and like... waited. He had to try several holes. Three rabbits got away. Trial and error kind of thing. It took a good part of the day, but – can you believe it? – it finally worked!"

Howard's mouth watered. He sterilized his chipped-stone knife on the fire and gave it to Pedro. Pedro carefully dug out the intestines and other unwanted parts, sterilized the knife again, and sliced the stringy-looking meat into twenty or so two-bite slivers.

Maria the cook stuck one of the slivers onto the end of a small stick and held it over the fire. The smell awakened in Howard cravings as strong as the peccary had.

Maria gave Zoe a sliver. Pedro grinned. "*¡Buen provecho!*"

Zoe nervously scanned the woods. "Where are the searchers?"

"Out looking for Pedro," said L.P., "who's standing right here."

***

Two hours later, Smith and Raul stood at the edge of the woods. It was still a surprise to see the team leader bare-foot in drawers and a straw hat, but worse, he looked beat. He was scratched and bruised all up and down one side. He stopped and stared at the team with a more burdened look of sadness than ever before.

"Pedro's right here!" said Zoe.

Smith looked and gave Pedro a slow nod.

Haughton-Alsef and Dove-Ti showed unscratched. Haughton-Alsef casually mouthed his pipe but Dove-Ti's eyes seemed to question seriously the air in front of her. Then Pryce showed, scratched and bruised like Smith, limping with an arm over Blake's shoulder. Zoe and Rachel hurried to them and helped walk Pryce to a point next to the fire where they helped him lie down.

The boy stood and watched.

"Dr. DeSparr?" said Zoe. "Could you take a look?"

DeSparr stood motionless.

Crauder said, "What happened?"

"Oh, god!" said Pryce.

"He had a rather rough little mishap," said Haughton-Alsef.

"He almost fell off a cliff," said Dove-Ti, blankly. "Uhm…"

Mrs. Crauder gasped.

"Dr. DeSparr," said Rachel, "Pryce needs help.".

Finally DeSparr knelt beside Pryce. "Where does it hurt?"

Pryce squeezed his eyes shut. "God! Where does it not?"

The boy also knelt beside Pryce and looked him over.

Haughton-Alsef stood with an elbow resting on his own bare stomach, holding the pipe at his ear. He said, "Pryce managed to hold to a tree limb. Quite heroically. Got a few leaf-burns."

"Leaf-burns!" said Pryce. "More than …"

"A miracle!" Haughton-Alsef quickly interrupted. "A miracle he was able to survive."

"Not a miracle!" said Pryce. "It was…"

"Now, I fear you have a little delirium."

"Don't do that!" said Pryce. "Don't do it. I'll tell about…"

"Dr. DeSparr," said Haughton-Alsef quickly, "How bad is it?"

DeSparr poked around and operated joints and asked Pryce each time if it hurt, and each time the answer came, 'Good god, yes.'

Finally the doctor said, "Scrapes. He's playing for attention."

"I'm not playing!" Pryce raised his head. "Ouch!"

Zoe smoothed his hair back. "What do we give him?"

DeSparr stood up, his face puffed and red. "Oh, just choose anything off the shelf."

Pryce rolled onto his side, away from DeSparr, grimacing. Most people went back to their rabbit-strips. Pryce cried out once or twice.

"One thing's gotta be said," said Crauder. "Pedro here shouldn't have gone off alone."

"He doesn't speak English," said Zoe.

"If he hadn't gone off, Pryce wouldn't be injured."

"Give him thirty lashes," said L.P. No one laughed.

"And," said Crauder, "what if Pryce hadn't held to that tree?"

"If he hadn't," said DeSparr, "we wouldn't have to haul him

111

around. And if we could have retrieved his body for…"

"Don't!" said Zoe.

"One rabbit a day," said DeSparr loudly, "isn't going to do it."

"We have plenty of water," she said. "We can last a long time."

Blake paced off distances and checked his safety perimeter markers. The Crauders got back to making mats, this time without Maria the cook, who was meeting off to one side with Smith and Pedro and Raul and Maria the translator. Smith talked to them in low, forceful tones while Zoe translated. Haughton-Alsef watched them intently. Howard and Rachel and L.P. watched from in the hut.

"He's letting 'em have it," said L.P.

Pedro took Smith's chastising patiently, but once Raul blurted in English, "We should all get out from this woods!"

Rachel said, "I'm curious about the knife. The one the Jaguar-men left us. I put it on that log over there. Now it's gone."

"Do you think the boy hid it?" said L.P.

"I don't think he's had a chance."

When it was dark, they were all able to get into the expanded hut and to sleep, fitfully.

***

The next morning Howard's bruises from the flood were better, but his head ached from lack of coffee.

The team met and Smith asked Raul and Pedro to help find food. Then he and Blake scoured nearby for dry firewood.

Raul and Pedro and Maria the cook stood apart, sulking.

"They didn't like it when Smith got after them," said Rachel.

"They'll get over it," said Howard.

Mrs. Crauder hung another reed mat, completing the screening.

Zoe and Dove-Ti sat with the boy. He squatted, hiney on his heels, and glanced around at the woods as if not interested in their talk. Zoe pointed at her hand and said, "Hand? Hand?" She also tried to dig word meanings out of him, pointing at his hand or foot and shrugging to show she didn't know the word for it.

He picked up a small weed and chewed on it. He picked things out of his hair and examined them. He wiped his face smoothly downward with one long skinny hand after the other. Now and then he said to no one in particular what sounded like, "Tee-week."

Beg watched them for a while, then got up and walked to the boy. "Ever get hurt playing ball?" he said, casually.

The boy seemed curious.

"I got this knee." Beg squatted like the boy, skinny knees at his ears, and chewed on a twig. "Hey, you ever heard o' joy-juice?"

Mrs. Crauder picked up an armload of leaves and grass she had brought from the woods, and said to everyone, "If you'll excuse me," and walked around behind the hut.

Howard and L.P. and Rachel touched up the hut.

Haughton-Alsef stood casually with the sulking guides and talked pleasantly. He pointed now and then at the woods.

Suddenly Zoe said loudly and excitedly, "I've got it! That word! It's his name! His name is Tee-week! Beg helped!"

Beg grinned and pointed proudly at the boy beside him.

Zoe and Beg repeated, "Tee-week! Tee-week!" and for the first time the boy laughed.

After that, no one could help but watch. Everything Zoe and Dove-Ti did regarding the boy, Beg approved with grins and nods.

Crauder beamed at Beg. "You're the man."

Tee-week's bare feet were, considering his squatting position, amazingly flat on the ground. His long skinny legs were folded like a grasshopper's. Sometimes he rocked back and forth between them as they gyrated each side of his shoulders. Other times he would bring them in, fit his armpits over his bony knees and lean forward. He would sweep a long arm and hand smoothly over the ground and some stick or small rock would disappear, then show up in his fingers. He would examine it then toss it as if disgusted.

Dove-Ti tried to talk. Once she tried to hug him but he pushed her away. He may have come to think of the team as harmlessly stupid. He began to talk more, and to point out things, apparently having decided it was he that was the teacher.

After Zoe had watched him for a while, she pointed at the ground and said to everyone, "The earth is 'ta-li.'" Then she pointed up and said, "A bird is 'toe-tote.' A flower is sho-cheet and that's what he's calling Dove-Ti. 'Sho-cheet.'"

He rocked back and forth, flicking a slender strand of tall grass. Now and then Dove-Ti would wince and scratch her forearm or side. Then he laughed when she realized he had been using the stiff grass to flick grains of sand at her.

113

Your punishment," she said, "is a hug." But he ducked and leaned away, waving his skinny arms for protection.

Mrs. Crauder appeared again and stood a little awkwardly, waiting for any comments about a sort of grass skirt and short top she had woven and put on.

"Dang, Pat!" said Crauder, still weaving reed mats.

"Oh, that's uhm, very nice," said Dove-Ti.

Mrs. Crauder blushed and said, "It itches a little."

Tee-week pointed at her and laughed. "Wee-peel," he said. When she was close enough, he reached his long skinny arm and smoothly patted the grassy blouse. His hands seemed to operate independently, as if not a part of him. "Mash-tee bung. Wee-peel."

Zoe watched and listened closely. "I've got it," she said. "'Wee-peel' is shirt. 'Mash-tee' is clothing." She kept repeating the words under her breath.

Suddenly Tee-week unfolded and walked quickly toward the woods. Howard and L.P. got up and ran after him, but he stopped at the edge. He reached down and pulled back big leaves and stalks and felt along their undersides, arms bending and rotating smoothly as if he were casting a spell. Eventually he came up with a huge grub. His hand passed by his mouth and one end of the grub, the head, Howard guessed, showed between his teeth. He spit it out as a smoker might spit the tip of a cigar. Then he squatted under a tree. His hands waved around in front of his mouth and the rest of the grub went in, part by part, as he chewed and swallowed. Howard watched dumbfounded. When the grub was gone, Tee-week got up and looked for another. He found one and offered it to Dove-Ti, who turned away quickly. He offered it to Howard, who also refused, hungry as he was.

Tee-week offered it to Beg, who took it and ate it, slowly, grimacing and grinning at everybody. "Aw, aw, aw…" When he finished, he said, as if he had earned it, "A touch o' red to top it off?"

"No way," said Crauder. "Don't lose your job."

Tee-week found yet another grub and ate it. Then he walked fast toward the stream. Howard, L.P., Rachel, Zoe, and Beg followed.

Tee-week picked up small rocks as he walked, and threw them ahead of him. They all landed in the roughly same spot next to the stream. Then he scooped them up in both arms and squatted next to a small side pool and waited silently, holding the pile of rocks against his chest. After about twenty long minutes, in which Howard got sore from

114

standing perfectly still, Tee-week tossed the rocks, spraying them in an arc across the main stream, moving nothing but his arms. Two small fish, guapotes, darted away from the rocks and into the side pool. He quickly bent down, his body amazingly twisted, and dammed the pool at its neck with a forearm. He waited silently again for several minutes. Then suddenly both hands shot into the water and trapped one of the guapotes. He stood and held it up proudly and exclaimed, "Teh-kwat!" He ignored the other teh-kwat as it got away.

"Wow!" said Howard.

"Good boy," said Beg, nodding happily. "Good boy."

"Get the fire going!" said Zoe. "We have like… food again!"

Before they got back to the camp, Tee-week pulled the fish's skin off and ate all but one sliver raw, including most of the bones, chomping proudly as they glumly watched. He gave the sliver to Beg.

Crauder said to Zoe, "Ask him if his tribe's gonna bug us again."

Zoe tried. He squatted and swayed and glanced around at the forest, proud and happy and full. He spoke now and then.

She shrugged. "I can't get it. He can't either." She used all sorts of body motions, saying over and over, "How long Tee-week here?"

Beg helped, motioning, repeating.

Suddenly Zoe said, "I got it! He said, 'Until I go.'"

"Until I go?" said Crauder. "That's a heap o' help."

"I know, but I got it! Know what I'm saying? And he did too!"

"Yeah," said Beg to Crauder, nodding, grinning. "See?"

"You got yourself a job," said Crauder to Beg. "Keep it."

Only Zoe and Beg had language success. Their efforts were strenuous and slow. Once Zoe said, "This little guy's smart." She and Beg somehow taught him several words, using repetition to drill them in. Tribe. Go. Come. Food. Kill. Eat. Day. More. Far. Good. Bad. And they learned more of his words.

Once Zoe looked up and said, "Something's happened between him and his tribe. A permanent separation. An exile, I think."

"I coulda told ya," said Crauder.

"It's dreadful," said Mrs. Crauder. "He's only a child."

"Dr. Haughton-Alsef," said Dove-Ti, "already guessed that."

Haughton-Alsef left the guides whom he had been huddling with and joined the discussion. "Well, I happened to have studied this area of anthropology. As I have mentioned, some Native American peoples are far ahead of us in handling individuals whose behavior differs with cultural standards. Simple exile, humane and just. They allow one to keep his freedom. We would do well to take note."

"Oh," said Mrs. Crauder, admiringly. "We can learn from them."

"My guess is," said Haughton-Alsef, "that he has repeatedly differed, in action, over some important tribal principle, and was finally judged incompatible."

"Could he be violent?" said Mrs. Crauder.

"Doubtful," said Haughton-Alsef. "We've seen no signs of it, and in such a society, where violence is not exercised by the authorities, it's rare among the people."

"They looked pretty violent when they stole our clothes," said Crauder. "Bows and arrows and spears and war paint."

Haughton-Alsef raised his eyebrows. "Ah, but research shows that there are long-standing customs among these kinds of tribes utilizing intimidation with no intent to commit real violence. It's mainly we who are the institutionalizers of violence."

"So why'd you let 'em take your stuff?"

Haughton-Alsef smiled. "Part of the game, you know."

"But look here," said Zoe, pointing at Tee-week. "How does a kid like this survive on his own? How does he find like... help?"

"He needs his family and friends," said Rachel.

"He would have known," said Haughton-Alsef, "that he was giving up those things when he repeatedly differed in action with the customs of his people. It was his own choice."

"You think he *wanted* to get away from them?" said Zoe.

"Every young boy's dream, eh? We can know something of his character: he doggedly pursues his dreams."

Crauder grunted. "Double-talk." He looked Tee-week over. "Reprobate."

Chapter 13

"Sleeping on the open ground is the same in the middle of the Sant-yagos as it is anywhere else," said Atl, when they woke. They got their few things together quickly as the soldiers heard their orders. Atl and Deer of Stone were assigned to carry weapons and armor on their backs for two different groups of swordsmen. One-Cip' was in front with the Totonac guides for he knew the land better than most of them. Two-Rabbit, Balanced Turtle, and A Fox is Mad were made to join the long line of porters following the army.

They spent most of the day crossing the plateau into blustering winds. The newness and oddness of it all helped keep Atl's mind off his fears and his earlier losses. He talked to a soldier named Alonso, who grinned and swaggered a lot. Alonso had big shoulders and a bulging stomach. He liked showing Atl the sharp edges of his sword, which he said was made of the world's hardest iron. His Nahuatl was bad but he helped Atl and Deer of Stone with his own language. He would point at a thing and grin and speak a Sant-yago word: "Falconet cannon. Capitán. Horse." He pointed at his red cloth hat and said, "Flemish." He turned his nose up at tortillas. "Spanish-speaking people eating such things!"

Before dark the army set up a torch-lit camp on the side of a small hill. The soldiers wrapped themselves in their metal cloth or armor, whatever they could find, and said a new Sant-yago word: "Cold." Even Atl and the mountain villagers were cold. The sleek Sant-yago dogs barked often. Finally all but the watchmen slept.

***

The next day the long lines stretched out again and the trudging was constant until Tonatiah was near his dropping ahead of them.

Orizaba was far behind. There was little to eat.

Atl and Deer of Stone learned more Sant-yago words. Once a soldier said a word and the others laughed and said Atl was too young. Sometimes they laughed at the way he said his new Sant-yago words.

He was surprised that the Sant-yagos could mark down their speaking on deerskin. He had seen the Aztecs do it with pictures but the Sant-yagos used a few simple marks which were easy to remember and stood for sounds instead of meanings. Deer of Stone saw it too, and they competed in learning. Once Atl marked Sant-yago sound-letters in the dirt to make the Nahuatl word 'tepe,' and though Alonso had never heard it, he was able to pronounce it just from looking at the marks. Atl pointed at the word, then at a mountain and said, "Tepe," and then the Sant-yagos knew the meaning.

Alonso was a swordsman and had a tall skinny friend named Gonzo, a pike man. His eyebrows were always high and his long nose ended in a ball. His iron hat sat too high on his skinny head. Gonzo said 'tepe' and pointed at Alonso's stomach and everybody laughed. Gonzo pushed Alonso who pushed back. Then they fought and made up and laughed.

Alonso and Gonzo taught Atl the Sant-yago word, 'friend.'

***

The next day's walking was the hardest yet. They climbed steep rocky slopes, dragged armor, and even carried the carts. By evening, they swarmed through a pass to a warmer land. There were scattered huts with squawking chickens and little yapping dogs. Food. But the friendly act of the people was false. At each hut Atl asked if anyone spoke Nahuatl. He wondered if several men gathering chickens held it against him that he walked with the Sant-yagos. He asked in Nahuatl, "Have you seen or heard of any Totonac girls taken from a burned village?"

They didn't seem to care about Atl's search. One swung his arm to the west. He spoke in Nahuatl. "Beyond these plains…" he glared at Atl to see if he understood and Atl nodded, "…there is the great city of Tlaxcala with tens of thousands of warriors. They are fierce." He pointed at the Sant-yagos nearby. "These are nothing, these are meat for Tlaxcalan stomachs. And beyond Tlaxcala are greater cities. Cholula and Tenochtitlán. And greater armies. The mighty Aztecs. You will all die."

Atl stopped asking questions in that region.

118

The army moved on, and the walking was easier, on flatter ground. They entered a neat, orderly town called Zocotlán. All the buildings, the temples, the great carved idols, the high palaces, defensive walls, and flat-roofed houses, were white.

"White Castle!" cried one of the soldiers. But the people were not friendly and the food was boring and sparse.

Atl convinced Alonso and Gonzo to walk with him and get closer to Cortés who was talking to a town leader.

The translating included Nahuatl. The Town Chief said to Cortés, "Motecuhzoma will not be pleased that you are here."

Atl was surprised by the answer from Cortes.

"We have come from far away under orders of Don Carlos our great emperor with many lords as his vassals. He commands that your great Motecuhzoma cease the sacrificing of his subjects, the robbing of his vassals, and the taking of lands."

It was the beginning of a prolonged speech. At one point his face was red and his neck throbbed. The chiefs listened politely but when he was finished they did not respond.

Atl and the two soldiers walked around a large temple and were stunned to see a huge pyramid of dry human skulls. Alonso counted and scratched numbers in the dirt and said, "Many thousands."

That night several Zocotlán leaders came with questions. Feathers on the Water described the might of Cortés, how he had defeated the Tabascans and arrested Aztec tax-collectors and gained the allegiance of the Totonacs. He advised the Zocotlán leaders to offer many gifts so the Sant-yagos would not be offended.

When Tonatiah finally climbed into the sky, the capitáns called the men together. The townspeople brought gold and cloth and two unhappy cooking-women. Cortés came from his tent and thanked them.

He mounted Rico, who turned around twice, snorted and kicked and raised his head and flashed his eyes as if filled with anger, or terror. Cortés' own face was calm. He turned to his troops. "We are in a hostile land." He pointed west. "Tlaxcala. Close formation. Eyes open."

***

Mendez caught up with Tomás, walking alongside the wagons. "Tomás," he said. "You know my heart."

"Only too well," said Tomás. "And you must know that

confessions to me do not count. I am not ordained."

"We are old friends. I know you are a man of integrity."

"So what do you want?" Tomás was sure it was, in the end, gold.

"Tomás! You must know how eagerly I have wanted to make up for all the wrong I did, to do something worthwhile in my life."

"So you joined this gold-seeking invasion."

"Tomás! I know some are greedy and power-hungry. But really, those things are part of my past now. I have this... this great desire to see the natives of this wondrous land exposed to the true cross."

The words, thought Tomás, were typical of the actor, the repeater of slogans. But just in case, it wouldn't hurt to suggest something that had been on his heart ever since coming to this land. "You were always better at the languages than any of us."

Mendez shrugged. "It is hard when you are poor, as I am."

Here it comes, thought Tomás.

"I understand the officers have collected large amounts of gold. And I wonder whether some tiny parts of that gold could be loaned out so that I could help the poor we encounter."

"I have no influence whatever. But..." Tomás decided to make Mendez prove his claims. "there is a way you could help these people."

"And what is that?"

"Well, I am told that you have learned the local Nahuatl well."

"Some learn it," said Mendez, "hoping to talk and find out where the gold is. But I only want to help these poor pagans."

"Wonderful!" said Tomás. The words, deceitful as they were, played to his goal. "The best thing you could do is translate the Vulgate into the language of these people."

"Tomás, I am sorry to tell you this, but these people do not read or write."

"Have you seen the two boys that joined us the other day?"

"I think so."

"Alonso tells me they are learning to read and write Spanish."

"Smart boys." Oddly, Mendez' face began to brighten.

Tomás had expected chagrin instead. But he went on. "They can learn to write their own language, using Latin letters."

"Tomás." Mendez smiled. "I will give it my best effort." And he thought: My mother did not see from heaven to deny me this open gift. The boys can be quite useful. And it is even sanctioned by Tomás.

Chapter 14

Howard and others kept their eyes on Tee-week. He seemed bored by the team, all but Beg, but not eager to run away.

Haughton-Alsef said to Zoe, "Ask him how far his tribe is."

"That won't be easy, but… Okay, let's see… Tee-week? Land of Jaguar-people? Where? We've got to learn some new words here. Okay…" She made hand motions and talked and carried on for some time. Occasionally Tee-week said something and raised a lazy arm, pointing roughly downstream, a little away from the river.

"How far?" said Haughton-Alsef, unusually impatient.

"I tried, but, distance, you know…"

"Can he show us?"

"First, I need to follow up on… he says there's somebody else, a like… grown man." Zoe talked to Tee-week some more, then said, "The man's like… out there. He's a thief. Wait a minute. The man – the thief – I believe he found something out there. A box."

"Really." Haughton-Alsef was intense. "What kind of box?"

"Wasn't Pryce's camera in a black waterproof case?" said Zoe. "It would have like… floated."

"A video camera," said Haughton-Alsef, "batteries charged."

Beg said, "Him show white man him tribe?" He pointed in the direction Tee-week had indicated earlier. "Huh? Him help white man?"

Tee-week obviously had no idea what Beg was saying, but jumped up and walked where Beg had pointed, along the ledge.

Haughton-Alsef and Zoe quickly followed, then Howard, L.P., Beg, Rachel, and Crauder, all bare-foot. After a winding downhill route, Tee-week pointed away from the river, across a gulch and up a rise, where three logs lay end to end on the side of the mountain.

"A boundary marker," said Haughton-Alsef. "Trust between

worlds. Zoe, can you find out if Tee-week's people have anything like, say, written documents?"

Zoe looked puzzled. "Written...?"

Crauder said, "These jungle-jumpers couldn't write an 'x' with a six-inch paintbrush."

"I wouldn't be so sure," said Haughton-Alsef.

They walked back to the camp and settled in. Tee-week rolled under the edge of one of the big logs. Beg joined him. Within minutes they were both asleep.

Pryce walked around holding his bruises. Haughton-Alsef took him aside and talked with even greater urgency than before. Pryce folded his arms and glared into the distance.

***

Blake and Smith came back with the few sticks of firewood they had scrounged. Zoe told Smith about the three logs and he chose her, Blake, L.P., Maria the translator, Rachel, and Howard to go and observe and keep their distance. "Take a couple of hours. Keep in touch."

When they reached a point near the three logs, Blake pointed. "Two watch the logs, two go back that way, and two over there."

Howard said to Rachel, "How about that grove of trees?"

She nodded. They crept and crouched where they could see and hopefully not be seen. Beyond them lay the gulch, then the three logs.

"My heart," she said, hand on her chest.

"Shh," he said.

"My mother said I kicked a lot when she was pregnant with me. Think about that. We were close even though she'd never seen me or talked to me."

"I can't imagine. Shh."

"Wait." Rachel touched Howard's arm. "Look."

Back in the old tall trees, downhill from the logs, stood a small man. Now it was Howard's heart pounding.

The man studied the logs, picked up a long bow and a small black box from the ground beside him, then sank behind underbrush.

"Must be the exiled man Tee-week mentioned," said Rachel.

"And that must be Pryce's camera box."

"His hair's peculiar," she whispered.

"Like purple plaster." Howard's voice shook with his heartbeat.

"Look on that middle log. Four arrows." They were thin and straight. Her arm pressed his and he could feel her pulse.

After about ten minutes, she whispered, "There he is."

The man slowly swung a foot out from the brush, still squatting, and set it forward silently. He froze, did the same with the other foot, then froze again, like a heron approaching a frog in a pond.

After several more steps, Rachel whispered, "He just wants his arrows." Then, "What's that?" Next to the arrows was a pair of boots, the same army-issue as the team's. "They weren't there a minute ago. Who put them?"

Howard tried to think.

"They're..." she whispered. "Remember? They're the ones Mrs. Crauder loaned me when we went to see the jaguar. I cleaned them and hid them. The Jaguar-men missed them when they raided us."

"Are you sure?"

"See that one boot with the white cloth stuffed in the laces?"

"The padding I gave you."

"That's it," she whispered. "So how'd they get out here?"

Purple-hair squat-walked from behind big rocks, his thick trunk straight up, elbows out for balance, the long bow in one hand. He took a few careful steps toward the boots, stopped, looked around, freezing after each short, quick jerk of his head, then took more steps. The black box hung from a cord at his waist.

"That's definitely Pryce's camera case," whispered Howard.

When he was near the boots, he untied the black box and set it on the end of the log. He took one duck-step toward the boots, but a sudden loud clattering came from behind the trees and rocks. He froze, then grabbed the box and the arrows, and was gone.

"What was that noise?" said Rachel.

"I don't know. It scared him. The boots are still there."

"But who...?"

Suddenly she pointed down river. "Look!" They stood.

Purple-hair ran in the level part of the river, away, under the trees, hopping left and right on rocks, arms out for balance, holding in one hand the long bow and the four arrows, and in the other, the black box by its string. You could hear his bare feet slapping the rocks even over the river's roar.

Rachel turned to the logs and said, once again, "Look!"

The boots were gone. Howard stared, dumbfounded.

Finally the two of them left the stake-out and joined the others, interrupting each other telling about Purple-hair and the arrows and the camera case and the boots. No one could explain it.

When they got back to the camp, Smith gathered everyone. Howard and Rachel told it all again.

"Strange," said Haughton-Alsef. "Strange indeed."

Zoe said, "The last time I saw those boots, they were like… under the overhang behind the hut. I remember. Here…" She went behind the hut and came back out with them in her hand. Rachel's mouth dropped. The wad of white cloth was still tucked into the laces.

"This is weird," said Howard. "Those are the boots we saw. Somebody put them out there, then brought them back here."

"It wasn't any of us stake-outers," said Zoe. "None of us has been like… behind that hut since we got back."

"It's quite doubtful it's the same pair," said Haughton-Alsef.

"It's the same pair," said Rachel. "The one we saw out there. That white padding was in the one boot just like it's been since I stuffed it in the other day."

"Oh, I'm sure it's hard to tell from a distance," said Haughton-Alsef, glancing pleasantly at Pryce. "And, not to cast doubt upon your powers of observation, but I think a bit of padding, a folded hanky, could be found in many a pair of boots in this jungle. These forest people are known to trade with fringe towns."

"It's the same pair," said Rachel again.

"Well," said Smith, "It's a little mystery for us to play with."

"Anything happen here at the camp?" said Zoe.

"Nothing," said Crauder, then turned to Haughton-Alsef. "Did you and Pryce see anything on your happy jaunt?"

"Oh," said Haughton-Alsef. "In that short time? Nothing."

"You were gone 'bout two hours," said Crauder.

Haughton-Alsef smiled pleasantly.

***

Tee-week stretched, sat up, rubbed his eyes, and duck-walked to the fire pit. Zoe talked to him again. Haughton-Alsef talked with Pryce and the guides, chuckling, puffing jovially on his unlit pipe.

L.P. said, "Haughton-Alsef's gettin' on the guides' good side after Smith blessed 'em out. He's cooking a plan. Trade those boots for that camera."

"He didn't ask the team's permission," said Howard. "That's why he tried to cover it up."

"At least the boots are back. Rachel, what was that sound that ran Purple-hair off?"

"I'd say it was like sticks hitting trees," she said.

"Haughton-Alsef," said L.P. "And maybe Pryce."

"To scare him just before he got the boots," said Howard, "hoping he'd leave the camera and the boots?"

"The noise came when he set the camera down," said Rachel.

"And before he picked up the boots," said Howard.

"Haughton-Alsef's no dummy," said L.P.

"But, he's always talking about never lying to the natives."

"If you lie," said L.P. "you talk a lot about how you don't lie."

"When Purple-hair ran away," said Rachel, "the way he ran, it seemed like something more sinister was going on than a failed trade."

"Like what?"

She shook her head. "I don't know."

One by one, the team curled up in the hut or around the fire.

***

Next morning most slept late. Howard got up and opened his book.

"Maria!" Shouted Mrs. Crauder, "Maria!"

Maria the translator stood leaning against a tree, shaking, breathing heavily, arms folded tightly in front of her, stunned.

L.P. ran to her. "Maria!"

Howard stuffed his book in its bag and ran to her. Rachel and Zoe and Tee-week joined them. Most of the sweaty, gritty team stood in their underwear around her, who couldn't speak for crying.

Rachel scanned the camp. "Where's Pryce? The guides?"

Maria started to fall, sobbing. L.P. tried to stop her, but knocked her down. She landed sitting up. She pointed into the woods.

"What is it?" said Rachel, helping to support her.

"*Los hombres locos*, they kill..." Maria fainted.

"Kill?" said Crauder. "What? Who?"

Rachel smoothed Maria's hair back. L.P. rubbed her arm. Mrs. Crauder and Zoe knelt beside her. Blake studied the woods.

Crauder gently patted her face. "Wake up! Killed who?"

"Let her rest," said Haughton-Alsef.

Crauder looked at Smith. "Why are they gone?"

"I'm afraid," said Smith, "they have gone without informing us."

Crauder said, "Maria, what…"

Let's not disturb her," said Haughton-Alsef, seriously.

But her eyes opened gradually. "They wish to kill…"

"That's alright," said Haughton-Alsef. "Don't talk. Rest."

She pointed again and cried weakly. "They are high in the mountain. Oh!" She folded her arms tightly. "I run to here."

"Who wishes to kill?" said Crauder. "Pedro?"

"No Pedro," said Maria. "*Los hombres del tigre…*"

"The Jaguar-men," said Zoe.

"Who do they want to kill?" said Crauder.

"They want to kill the one with the hair eh…" she looked at Zoe. "…*Morado.*"

"Purple-hair," said Zoe. "But why? I mean…"

"Why did you go up there?" said Crauder.

Maria glanced at Haughton-Alsef, then squeezed her eyes shut, sobbing. She said, "There is eh, *un arroyo* more high in the mountains."

"Are the others hurt?" said Rachel.

"I hope no. They try to stop the killing. They say me go back."

"Can you show us which way?" said Crauder.

"No! *¡Peligro!* They kill."

"Let her rest," said Haughton-Alsef quickly, but he leaned close and said, "Was Pryce hurt?" She only sobbed. He stroked her hair. "Was there anything like, say, a…" he shrugged and cocked his head as if thinking of possibilities. "Say… a box? A black box?"

She shook her head.

"Any, oh… say, writings? Anything like that?"

Again she shook her head.

"That's perfectly all right. Just rest now."

"Why do you keep asking about writings?" said Crauder.

"Just… you know, anything that might give us a clue."

Crauder patted Maria's cheek again. "Which way?"

She pointed into the woods. "You will find a path there."

"Enough of us and we'll scare 'em off," said Crauder.

"They are many," said Maria. "As when they came here."

"Come on," said Crauder to Blake. "They're scared of us."

126

"You're crazy!" said Zoe. "What if you like… don't come back?"

"We agreed," said Dove-Ti. "We don't push our values on others. We're civilized."

"We'll show 'em civilized," said Crauder.

"*Cuidado*," said Maria.

"Aw, we're just gonna find the guides. No trouble. Promise."

"Quietly," said Blake. He and L.P. joined Crauder, then Howard. Crauder called to Haughton-Alsef, "Coming?"

"We pledged not to interfere," said Haughton-Alsef.

Crauder stopped. "They've robbed us. They've killed somebody. Who knows what they'll do to Pryce? Our guides? If we don't act, we'll look even stupider and easier. Then we'll really be in danger."

"Dr. Smith!" said Dove-Ti.

"See you," said Crauder, and he and the others found the path. Smith said, "No unnecessary heroics, men. We need you here."

∗∗∗

Blake took the lead, looking for footprints on the rocky, uphill path. They stumbled often.

"Village should be in a high place," said Blake. "Near a stream."

Crauder dropped back, puffing, waving them on. Howard never let him out of sight. Blake stopped now and then to let him catch up.

The trail curved down into a wide, rocky stream.

"I was afraid of this," said Blake. They walked on rocks up the stream for another thirty minutes, checking the sides for a path or footprints out. Finally Blake said, "Take a break."

Crauder caught up and they each found a rock to sit on, amid thick undergrowth.

In a few minutes they heard the voice of a small child, easily distinguished from the other jungle noises, a two-syllable giggle.

Howard pointed farther upstream. "From there."

They got up slowly and crept on rocks, wading, crouching. Around a bend they came to huge, black, moss-covered logs jammed across the stream and jutting randomly into the spray. Water poured between them, carrying red and yellow leaves and slowing in green pools. High above them, bands of skewed light pierced the black tree canopy and divided the gray mist.

They crawled up the bank and knelt beside the huge roots of an old oak, breathing the cool spray. Through the mist and tangles of vines and branches around them, they could barely see, on the other side of the log jam, standing in a wide pool, about a dozen little red-gold boys and girls. Two young naked women squatted on the bank, elbows on their knees, palms on their temples, smiling now and then at a child.

Insects buzzed, birds squawked, monkeys chattered.

Now and then a child brushed away an insect. A boy pushed at another. A woman grunted and he stared at the water, hands clasped in front of his belly. Two girls sat in the pool talking softly and moving their fingers around on the surface of the water.

The women were not afraid. So there were probably guards. Howard felt a new kind of fear. Could they smell intruders? He didn't know if these people were connected with the thefts or the killing. He thought there were two things he was sure of: he and the others must get out, and they must not move. He began to shake.

Then he saw a guard, bits of him, through the leaves, squatting like Tee-week but tense and perfectly still, watching the children. He was thick and muscular, hair shiny and black, cropped all around. He held an incredibly long, tautly strung bow.

Howard whispered to L.P., "Don't move," even though L.P. was not even shaking, as Howard was. But at that, L.P. turned and one bare foot slipped and shot out like a European army goose step, and he went sliding down the rock, uttering a muffled but increasingly loud and shaky hum, into the stream. The splash was loud.

The women's voices had the sound of horror. The guard moved only slightly, leaning to see through the leaves, eyes round.

In an instant the women and children were gone. Two other guards showed and the three stood and drew their bows and barked.

Blake said, "C'mon," and the four of them didn't wait to see what the guards would do. They ran. Howard found new skills. His feet found the smooth sand or rocks under the water before his eyes spotted them. Blake loped like a deer. L.P. stumbled and stomped and splashed, his big stomach bouncing. Crauder puffed and grunted loudly. An arrow glanced off a tree and disappeared in some brush in front of them.

After fifteen minutes of scrambling over rocks and across logs, Crauder keeping up amazingly well, they ran across a pile of garbage just above a bank. Blake stopped. "There's DeSparr's black T-shirt," he said. They ducked and looked behind them. No one was following.

They searched through the garbage, breathing heavily, checking for the guards again and again. Piled among the rotting fruits and greasy animal parts were most of their clothes, less boots, soaked, heavy, and stinking. "Where's my pistol?" said Crauder. He found a long stick and started poking. Howard found his own pants. His knife was missing, but the boot-laces were still in the pocket. Finally they got Crauder to give up on the pistol, gathered big armloads, held them out as far from their noses as they could, and jogged back down the stream.

Blake pointed at a twisted tree. "That's where our trail came in."

Crauder gaped. "What's that?"

They looked. "A human hand," said Howard, dumbfounded.

Blake scanned the woods, then set his bundle of clothes on a rock. They all did the same and made their way to the hand. They saw, under the reflective surface, the rest of the body. The tall, purple hair had come undone and was spread out in the water.

"The guy you and Rachel saw?" said L.P.

Howard nodded.

"Was he here when we came up?" said L.P.

Blake shrugged. "I should've looked around better when we came by." He found a stick and pried up an arm. "They used knives." There were deep cuts in his side, and several bad bruises.

Blake pried the face up. It was badly disfigured. "And clubs."

L.P. pointed. "Look." Under some brush was the same pair of boots Rachel had stuffed padding into. "Those boots again!"

Blake thought, and said, "Nothing we can do. Get the clothes." They grabbed the bundles and the boots, and ran for camp.

Then L.P. stopped again. "Who's that? Pryce!"

Several yards from the path, lying against a tree, was Pryce, groaning and hollow-eyed.

He wouldn't talk. They lifted him and helped him walk.

✳✳✳

"Our clothes!" said Mrs. Crauder with glee, but drew back when she smelled them. Then she saw Pryce. "Oh! Pryce! Are you hurt again?"

Tee-week backed three or four steps away.

They sat Pryce down against a tree.

"He's a little loopy," said Crauder. "Needs the doc again."

DeSparr didn't move as the team waited.

"Doctor DeSparr," said Rachel, and the doctor finally checked

Pryce over. "Nothing new. Still fishing for attention."

Pryce only stared distantly.

Dove-Ti said to Blake, "We agreed, uhm… No going off…"

"Yes, but now we have our clothes back." Blake said it quickly and neatly, as if the raid had been carried out in the same way.

"And you're safe," said Mrs. Crauder.

"Where are the guides?" said Maria the translator, still worried.

"No sign of Maria the cook?" said Smith, "Or Raul? Or Pedro?"

"After we found Purple-hair knifed and clubbed," said Crauder, "we quit quick. Maria was right. He's dead."

Mrs. Crauder and Rachel covered their mouths. Pryce sank more loosely over his knees, arms hanging limp.

Finally Zoe said, "But, like… why? How could anybody…?"

"Probably they had a little much pulque," said Crauder. "They saw red when they saw purple in a guy's hair."

"We'll find the guides," said Smith. "Where were the clothes?"

Crauder pointed. "In a garbage pile. They kept the boots."

"Except these," said L.P. He held up the spare boots. "Again."

"What?" said Zoe. "Howard and Rachel were like… right."

Haughton-Alsef chuckled. "They do get around. Eh, Pryce?"

Pryce raised his head slowly and gazed blankly at the boots.

"Who…?" said Zoe. "Who is like… doing this?"

"Oh," said Haughton-Alsef, "someone must have taken them, maybe one of the guides, understandably, in case one of them needed them on their current jaunt."

"Then why weren't they wearing 'em?" said Crauder.

"Oh, who knows? Maybe they didn't fit, or started hurting."

"Okay," said Zoe, "but who like… killed Purple-hair?"

Pryce flinched.

"So much for somebody's crazy idea that they're not violent," said Crauder.

"God!" said Pryce, suddenly alert, still hollow-eyed. "Don't you see it? That's how they do it. Exiles can never come back. They…"

"We should," said Haughton-Alsef, interrupting, "reimagine this correctly. It's obvious this man 'Purple-hair' tried to return to his tribe for some inexplicable reason — and I'm convinced that happens quite rarely — and he met with the justice of his good people. I think we can say that we are witnessing, and may soon have the means to corroborate, what amounts to an extraordinary anthropological event."

Mrs. Crauder said, "Why would he want to return that badly?"

"If," said Rachel, "he had family in the tribe."

"He coulda made a new life," said Crauder.

DeSparr wheeled and glared at him. "You have no idea! You've never been alone!"

"Oh, yeah? I hiked Denali. Eight days and we never saw a soul."

"We?" said DeSparr.

"Quit whining, wimp," said Crauder. "You've got us."

DeSparr frowned deeply. "A person who sees the world as it is will always be alone." His voice trembled. "Even in a crowd."

"Well," said Haughton-Alsef, "I suppose we can agree that this killing, sobering as it may be to us, represents something of world-class note. We should assimilate what information we can."

DeSparr shouted, "He would have done anything to get home! And he was killed for it!" He turned away as if hopelessly surrounded by ignorance.

"Why," said L.P., "would they ditch the clothes after all that big to-do stealing 'em?"

"Maybe they felt bad about it," said Mrs. Crauder.

"They just wanted to go through the pockets," said Crauder.

"Why didn't they keep that pair of boots?" said L.P.

"Good question."

Haughton-Alsef leaned against a tree and drew a finger across his mouth and everybody waited. "We tend to assign to others, as we strain to see past the curtains of cultural consciousness, little more than the traits with which we are already familiar. And out of those we fabricate artificial, or perhaps real, universalities."

"Ooh," said Mrs. Crauder. "You put things so wonderfully."

"Double-talk," said Crauder.

"Well, it appears to me," said Dove-Ti, "from what researchers and scholars have been able to uhm, gather about these kinds of differently-focused people, whose realities are not necessarily the same as our realities, that it's quite possible they may have decided there were uhm, evil spirits in the clothes."

"Reality," said Crauder, "is reality, focus fouled up or not."

Haughton-Alsef smiled. "Don't be too sure. The untrue is true and the true is untrue."

"Oh!" Mrs. Crauder was overcome with awe and wonder.

"The clothes didn't fit," said Crauder. "Anyway, we've gotta find our cook and our so-called guides."

Rachel said to Howard. "I'm glad for the clothes, but you went against our rule."

"Just get your shirt on," he said.

Her face reddened and she glanced down at her scratched, bruised, vividly pale torso. "We have some washing to do," she said, and picked up a load of clothes and some of the bark-soap Blake had made, turned to Howard with head slightly cocked as if trying to understand him, then walked to the creek.

He followed her, hoping to find a way to make up. "Can I help?"

"Get a bundle."

So he went back to the ash pit and picked up another smelly bundle and brought it to the creek. "What do I do?"

"Just pull stuff out." She pointed to a side pool. "Put it there to soak. Then scrub. A lot. And then we can get our 'shirts' on."

"Sorry." He began dumping his load into the side pool. "I didn't mean the pun part of it. I'm not that clever."

"I know you're not that clever. But you did snap at me."

"Yes. I'm tired and sore and hungry. But so are you. So I mean it, I'm sorry."

She sighed. "Mainly I'm worried about the missing people."

"Me too," said Howard. "We didn't see a sign of them. We did see some kids bathing and a couple of mothers and some guards. The guards chased us away."

She shuddered, then began pushing the clothes under the water. "I wish Miss Margaret were here."

Dove-Ti and Maria the translator and L.P. came and helped. Another light rain began dropping out of the thick mist.

***

Then the scrubbers heard a happy squeal from Mrs. Crauder.

"What?" said L.P.

"Maria!" said Mrs. Crauder. "You're back!"

They left the scrubbing and ran to the ash pit as Raul and Pedro and Maria the cook stumbled into the clearing, tired and bruised. Smith had been about to organize another search for them.

"What happened?" said Mrs. Crauder.

Everyone gathered. Haughton-Alsef stood close to Raul.

132

"Pedro followed a bad path," said Raul.

"Mercy," said Mrs. Crauder. "Are you hurt?"

He shrugged. "Bumps." He pointed at Pedro.

Pedro showed his arm, which had a bad cut, but he acted like it was nothing. Zoe looked at it, then wrapped it in a newly cleaned shirt.

"What happened with Purple-hair?" said Crauder.

"It is very bad," said Raul. "We try to save him but the men they kill him."

"Who killed him?" said Haughton-Alsef, suddenly interrupting.

"The little men. They chase us away."

Haughton-Alsef glared. "Did you recognize any of them?"

"They were the many little men who stealed our clothes."

Haughton-Alsef opened his mouth, smiled pleasantly, and inserted the unlit pipe.

"We know about the killing," said Crauder. "We found him."

"You found him?" said Raul.

"We went to look for you. Now tell me this: why did you go?"

Raul glanced at Haughton-Alsef. "He…"

"I must confess," said Haughton-Alsef stepping in quickly, "I made a special request of our good guides." He slid a finger across his mouth. "Besides the great need we still have for our equipment and supplies, I didn't think any of us would want to feel responsible for the environmental damage that will likely be done by its scattering. I had a sense that the gentleman with the purple hair, the one reported to us by Rachel and Howard, might know where some of our things are, since he has apparently been observing us. The guides seemed to me the best qualified for finding him, and I asked them, along with Pryce here, to see if they could gather the pertinent information." He smiled sweetly at Smith. "I hope I haven't overstepped my bounds, or our rules." He gave everyone a pleasant, everything-is-now-cleared-up smile.

Raul added, soliciting his approval, "The camera – you say me the camera is the main thing."

Haughton-Alsef frowned briefly. "Well, all of it, you know."

"You're saying," said Crauder, pointing at the woods, "that without consulting any of us or our leader, you sent all our guides off beyond our safety perimeter which we all agreed was near-sacred, risking their lives and our chances of survival, and…?"

"My dear man," said Haughton-Alsef, pleasantly, "Had I known that my innocent efforts to improve our situation and protect the environment would become associated with such stressful situations for us and our good guides as have happened today by the unpredictable actions of our Jaguar-people, I would have never…"

"Unpredictable!" said Pryce. "They did exactly what you hoped."

"Now, now, Pryce. You're a little stressed, understandably."

"So how," said Crauder, "did Mr. Purple-hair get into the Jaguar-people's territory?"

"Oh," said Raul proudly. "That was the place to look for him."

"How'd you know?"

"Mr…" Raul pointed at Haughton-Alsef. "He say…"

"This is most likely a tragic misunderstanding," said Haughton-Alsef. "Language, you know."

"No," said Raul, trying to be helpful. "You say in that place. Use the boots. Make him cross the line. You remember, eh?"

"Ah, so that explains the boots," said Haughton-Alsef quickly. "Our good guides thought I had asked them to take them."

Rachel leaned close to Howard. "So Purple-hair wasn't only trying to go home."

"Looks like he was lured," said Howard.

"Let Raul talk," said Crauder. "Tell me this, Raul: how did you guides get separated from Maria the translator, and from Pryce?"

"We say, 'Maria! Go back to here,'" said Raul. "Pryce, he run."

"God!" said Pryce. "They were killing the man!"

"Perfectly understandable," said Haughton-Alsef, smiling knowingly at Pryce. He sucked on his pipe. "But now we can know that we have seen proof of a long-standing system of local justice."

Zoe said, "I'm going like… huh? I'm scared. You know?"

"But such fear is a detached fear," said Haughton-Alsef, "a discovery of something internal to the tribe, not likely a threat to us."

"I'm scared," said Zoe. "And it's a like… a-ttached scared."

"Not to diminish the man's suffering," said Dove-Ti, "but I hope we can understand that what we see as theft, they see as sharing, and what we see as murder, they see as justice." She bowed her head. "May we have a heightened awareness of the customs of these people."

"The noble savage!" said DeSparr, loudly and facetiously.

"Trust is all-important," said Haughton-Alsef.

"Anyway," said Smith, "we've found them."

"You mean," said Crauder, chuckling. "They've found us."

Chapter 15

"We are respected now," said Atl. "They have at last let us pull these carts."

"Atl," said Deer of Stone, "that is called, 'making us do their work.'"

"But look how easily and smoothly the circles move across these ruts, even when the carts are full." Atl turned his cart side to side. He knelt and studied the circle and felt around it with both hands. "We can make them when we get back home and..." Suddenly he stopped and looked down, his face sad and angry. "I... I did not forget..."

"I will never forget," said Deer of Stone, glaring.

"It is just that home is still in me," said Atl.

Deer of Stone kicked a big rock fiercely. "And in me. Always."

Atl noticed a tall, friendly-looking Sant-yago watching them.

Deer of Stone said, "I will be nice to the Sant-yagos while I have to, but I will not like them. They are less like us than the Aztecs, and I believe we will in the end hate them more."

"Remember what your father says. 'Hate hurts most the hater.'"

"Wheel," said the tall friendly Sant-yago, pointing at Atl's cart, and smiled as he passed.

"Respect," said Atl, and Deer of Stone shrugged.

"Wheel," echoed Alonso, ambling up to them, pointing at one of the circles. He stood with a hand on a hip, grinning and pointing at other parts. "Axle," he said. "Load."

Deer of Stone set his handle down to rest his arms, but the cart rolled backwards and he had to run to catch it. Alonso and Atl laughed.

"Pull!" shouted an officer harshly from the soldiers coming up.

They both pulled again quickly, then for a long time, mostly uphill. By the time Tonatiah was straight-up their muscles ached.

"Respect?" said Deer of Stone. Atl shrugged.

"At least you and I are together," said Atl.

"Try saying that in the Sant-yago tongue," said Deer of Stone.

Atl brightened in spite of his aching. He was able to get the word 'together,' but not the words 'at least.'

Then Deer of Stone said all of it, and gloated. "If we know their tongue," he said, "we can better find the killers. And get back at them."

"But how to know who they are. And how to fight."

"We will learn."

Deer of Stone pronounced the Sant-yago word for 'how,' and Atl quickly said the word for 'know,' and Deer of Stone said the word for 'fight.' And they competed like that, in the Sant-yago tongue, as they pulled the carts.

***

Finally Tonatiah rested and the long line of soldiers stopped for the night.

"He watched us today," said Atl. He pointed at the tall Sant-yago. "I have seen him before. In Cempoala. Yes, he is the one who translated for…" Atl bit his lip.

"I remember," said Deer of Stone. "When Dahlia told the woman she liked her dress."

"We will find Dahlia," said Atl.

That night Two-Rabbit came. "Good news. The Sant-yagos have decided to let us all sleep together."

"Who decided?" said Deer of stone as they laid out bedding.

Two-Rabbit pointed at the tall Sant-yago. "He helped us talk, and worked it out for us."

The man saw them looking at him and walked to them smiling. His deep-set eyes twinkled. His manner was gracious and engaging.

At the same time, One-Cip' and the others joined them, with Feathers on the Water.

The Sant-yago said, in good Nahuatl, "Two-Rabbit told me of your tragedy. I have not heard of missing women, but I want to help."

Atl said aside to Deer of Stone, "He takes time with us. He has say with the soldiers. He has manners and poise. He speaks Nahuatl better than the other Sant-yagos. We have luck."

Deer of Stone said, frowning, "The Aztecs in the High Valley had 'manners and poise.'"

"Why," said One-Cip' to the tall Sant-yago, bruskly. Atl winced. One-Cip's tone was suspicious.

"A people in distress?" said the tall one. He bowed, eyes rounded. "Anyone would help."

One-Cip' grunted and looked to one side, and for the first time Atl was disappointed in his old mentor who seemed crude next to the courteous Sant-yago.

***

Four Sant-yago messengers came running and shouting to Cortés and his officers. They talked seriously and fast. Feathers on the Water said, "Cortés sent these messengers earlier to tell the Tlaxcalan war chief Xicotenga that he wishes to pass through in peace, and..." He suddenly turned, glared at the woods, pointed, and shouted, "Warriors! Tlaxcalans!"

All the soldiers looked and crouched and steadied their feet. Officers stared stiffly.

About thirty men and boys crouched behind trees and rocks, in brightly colored cloth or animal skins, quilted padding, and tall feathers. Some looked like skinny jaguars. They held spears and bows.

The courteous Sant-yago said to Atl and the group, "Follow me to a safe place."

Atl looked back, stretching his neck. Eight Sant-yagos rode out on the beasts, stopping when they were near the Tlaxcalans. They made hand signals. Suddenly there was angry shouting, and many Sant-yago soldiers shouted back and broke ranks and chased the few Tlaxcalans into the woods. Even some of the Totonacs joined the chase.

Atl and the others crouched behind carts and watched.

Deer of Stone looked at Atl. "You are shaking."

"I cannot stop it," said Atl. "So are you. But look!"

The attacking Sant-yago soldiers reached the woods and stopped. Arrows and stones flew out at them, then hundreds of Tlaxcalans ran out shouting and waving clubs.

"It was a trap!" said One-Cip'.

All the Sant-yagos but the tall courteous one joined the battle. Iron sticks popped and threw out fire and smoke. Clouds of dust rose. Iron swords swung back and forth. Atl winced when he saw the first red gash.

"This is what the Sant-yagos are like," said Deer of Stone, as if he knew. "No ceremony. Do you remember the war-stories in the High Valley? How clear and clean?"

"You hate the Aztecs."

"Yes, but they follow the code. And so do these Tlaxcalans."

"In their stories," said Atl, "they follow the code."

A Tlaxcalan fell to the ground, his side gashed. Atl hid his eyes.

"The code," said Deer of Stone, "requires only the bravest …"

"I know, I know," said Atl, glancing and looking away quickly.

"Look," said Deer of Stone. "Tlaxcalans are falling."

"The Sant-yagos run around crazy," said Atl. "No capturing."

The whole struggling mass of men moved slowly back into the woods and the noise lessened and the Tlaxcalan cries grew more distant.

"Look how tired the Sant-yagos are," said Deer of Stone. The soldiers stood for a long time, then finally returned to the trail and trudged once again, helping each other.

Atl passed Tlaxcalans lying bloody, not moving.

Several soldiers walked among the bodies and chose and dragged two fat bloody ones.

"They are bringing them to us!" said Atl.

Deer of Stone stepped back, his fear showing for the first time.

The soldiers threw one body into each boy's cart.

Atl held his stomach. "I will pull without looking."

"Try to think of it as… peccary meat," said Deer of Stone.

"I have tried," said Atl, "but I can only think of it as what it is."

That night they made camp on a wooded hillside.

Soldiers guarded three live Tlaxcalans wrapped in fishing nets.

Two-Rabbit and A Fox is Mad brought clay bowls of stew, and they all sat down to eat.

Two hurt Sant-yagos came. "Where are the dead Indians?"

Deer of Stone pointed at the carts, and the soldiers drew iron knives and cut out body fat and rubbed it on their own wounds.

Atl decided not to eat.

"These new soldiers," said One-Cip', "are well-armed and do not give up. Cortés easily makes allies." He rubbed his knee. "But there are tens of thousands more of Tlaxcalans we have not yet seen. And the armies of Motecuhzoma are even greater."

"But," said Atl, "do they not have a way about them?"

"They can be cruel," said One-Cip'. "We cannot trust them."

"They are not cruel to each other," said Atl. "Only to enemies."

"Enemies!" said One-Cip. "It is their doing to come into this land. They create their enemies. This killing would not have happened if they had not come. They have come for power and gold! That talk about a better god is only an excuse."

"Is that not the way of the Aztecs as well?" said Atl.

One-Cip's face grew red. "I am going to the stream to wash."

***

An officer came to Atl and Deer of Stone. "You are needed."

"By whom?" said Deer of Stone.

"By Capitán de Alvarado, now."

They followed the officer. So far they had known de Alvarado to be jovial and confident. But now he was angry. And Atl was surprised to see, standing there in chains, the tall soldier who had helped them.

De Alvarado was translated. "Do you know this man?"

Atl and Deer of Stone looked at each other. "Yes," said Atl.

"Where was he during the battle?"

"With us," said Atl. "He kept us out of the soldiers' way."

"Can you testify to his character?"

They looked at each other again. "Yes, truly," said Atl.

De Alvarado glared at the tall soldier, then reluctantly signaled the guard and the chains were removed.

The tall one walked back with them. "Thank you for telling the truth. To explain what happened, I must tell you that I was unjustly charged with cowardice by jealous soldiers."

"Jealous?" said Deer of Stone.

"They thought I used you to make myself look good by shielding young porters not trained for battle. And to avoid fighting."

Atl was glad they had been able to return his kindness and trust.

"What is your name?" said Deer of Stone.

"I am called Ramiro Mendez."

Chapter 16

"They have raided us," said Smith to the gathered team. He was obviously frustrated. "They have abandoned this boy, and they have killed one of their own."

"They're crude ," said Zoe, "and like... unpredictable."

"In fact," said Haughton-Alsef, "to them, we seem crude. And unpredictable."

Crauder defended Zoe. "They don't think our boots are so crude! Or our gifts!"

"And now," said DeSparr, who had not moved for some time and seemed a part of the mud and brush and thick mist as if having evolved up out of the earth, "the plague of ignorance spreads among us."

"Oh, Mr. Crauder's right," said Zoe. "Their behavior is like... totally unacceptable. Anyone would agree. You don't find us sneaking around stealing."

"That's because," said DeSparr. "We sneak better. We never do it in the open."

"One might even say it is precisely in 'the open' that we steal," said Haughton-Alsef, egging DeSparr on. "Their land, their lumber, their labor."

"How about invasion of privacy by photographers and thrill-seekers?" said DeSparr. "How about sloppy summaries of their ways? How about misleading the world about them just to build our own artificial — and financially lucrative — reputations?

There was a sudden dour silence. Haughton-Alsef forced a condescending smile.

The red color of Zoe's face deepened, and the skin puffed with visible anger. "How can you," she said to DeSparr, "with your like...

nowhere personality, stand there and criticize us?" Then she shut her mouth suddenly, as if afraid she had gone too far.

DeSparr opened his mouth with forced calm, and spoke in a carefully paced monotone. "Would you please explain to me the meaning of 'nowhere personality?'"

Crauder chortled. "When your mouth is smarter than your brain!"

"Jud!" said Mrs. Crauder.

DeSparr's stone-white face became bright red. "Brain! Personality! It might interest you to know that none of you exercises his brain enough to see that there is nothing there but tissue, and that nothing you say matters," the voice grew steadily louder, with a paced rapidity and a tone of final triumph, "because the only difference in a human brain and the brain of any animal or snake or bug in the ground is the shape and size and number of convolutions and those are no more than small quantitative differences that leave no qualitative basis for defining or assessing or even acknowledging personality — personality of the 'nowhere' variety or any other — and therefore," his voice grew louder, "there is no such thing as personality! There is only the atom, no, the quark! The Higgs-boson!"

After a silence, Crauder pretended curiosity. "So you're saying you're smarter than a bug?" There were chuckles.

"Smarter," said the mouth. "And I am smarter than a horse or a porpoise and I am smarter than you, but it means nothing because there is nothing to mean! And it's too bad your simple mind can't see that!" DeSparr had lost his cool and seemed almost comical. His face grew even redder, his mouth more distorted, and his voice louder. "But you ask me and I tell you without hesitation or qualification, you jut-jawed Neanderthal, that — yes! — I, who see this fact in far more complex variations than any of you, with your limited set of convolutions, am smarter than a bug!"

The echo came from the mountain. "A bug!"

"I knew it!" Crauder grinned proudly. "I knew you were!"

The laughing was unavoidable and prolonged and unkind. Howard laughed. Even Smith chuckled, amicably. Rachel did not laugh, but went back to scrubbing clothes at the stream.

"Anyway," said Zoe, "while you guys were out there like… stalking around, I was under that tree talking with Tee-week."

"Did you get anywhere?" said Mrs. Crauder.

141

"Well…" Zoe looked around at each person, serious. "I've found out something new."

"What?"

"Tee-week mentioned another tribe."

"Mercy."

Haughton-Alsef stepped closer, face intent.

"And he's afraid of them. His whole tribe is afraid of them."

"The Jaggies are afraid of somebody?" said L.P.

"He says they wear clothes."

"Dark green clothes?" said Howard.

"You guessed it. The ones we saw when the pilot's body like… disappeared. I was right. They're a completely different tribe."

Haughton-Alsef was frozen, listening.

"The Greenshirts," said L.P. "That'd be the Greenshirts."

"Does he give them a real name?" said Smith.

"Yes," said Zoe. "Are you ready? I don't have it exactly, but it's something like the 'People of… like… Sacrificing.'"

"Oh!" said Mrs. Crauder.

"God!" said Pryce. "They'll sacrifice that pilot. Who's next?"

Haughton-Alsef almost dropped his pipe. "Does Tee-week know if these people can read and write?"

"Read and write?" said Mrs. Crauder. "Cannibals?"

Zoe shook her head. "Don't know yet."

Zoe went back to Tee-week. "I'm asking him where those people live."

Everybody watched. Tee-week laughed and looked around as if not interested.

She repeated the question, using different Nahuatl words, then again and again, getting closer to him and speaking louder, until finally he frowned and said something and nodded and held his long arm out and pointed a couple of times up the side stream, toward the mountains. He stopped his chewing and grimaced and brought his other hand down across his face.

Then she said to the team, "He says they stay to themselves, and if you ask me we shouldn't go like… tramping around."

Rachel came back from the stream. "We have clothes, cleaned and ready."

"Oh!" said Mrs. Crauder. "Wonderful."

"And wet. But whoever wants them can put them on."

142

Most of the women followed Rachel. They were gone for a while, then came back bathed and fully clothed and still soaking wet in the rain. Then the men, except DeSparr, took their turn. When they were back, DeSparr strode to the stream, then showed again in his black pants, black T-shirt, and black jacket.

Haughton-Alsef smiled, "Au naturel no more."

DeSparr looked up through the trees. The whites of his eyes glimmered in the dark hollows of his otherwise pale, just-washed face. His red mouth cracked and his teeth glistened through the black beard. "Nature is all we are. We will rot with it."

"Dang," said Crauder. "Any other happy thoughts?"

"You will learn to take me seriously."

A bird cackled loudly. Monkey-whoops spread through the trees.

The team decided to divide the nights into two watches, to reduce the amount of lost sleep. That night Howard was on the first watch with three others, tired and sore and barely able to stay awake until they were relieved. Then he was barely able to sleep the rest of the night, bunched with the others in the hut.

In those moments between sleeping and waking he dreamed of the lonely old jaguar. Tee-week duck-walked beside it, carrying a large dinner plate of rabbit intestines. The jaguar turned to Howard, its head now as big as the hut, and opened its mouth and inhaled calmly and steadily, never stopping to exhale. The nose and eyes sat imbedded in a mass of muscles, red and stringy, and out of them sprang yellow-white teeth. Tee-week squatted and offered the plate, now dream-transformed to a great dinner table, and Howard climbed onto it.

The mouth opened wider behind the teeth, and far into the great black void of it were tiny lights, like stars. Suddenly hundreds of men in loafers and cardigans and women waving credit cards stampeded across the dinner table where Howard sat. They shouted, "The only escape from the jaguar is into its mouth!" and they ran into the void, magically suspended, and flung their arms and shouted, "In is out!" and "Void is solid!" And Howard wondered who they were, and they noticed his question, and explained in ways that made perfect dream-sense, "We are who we are!" and he and Tee-week nodded to show each other they understood it all. And as the people-who-were-the-people-they-were rushed in, they grew bigger and became smoky and faded into the darkness as more thousands of people came, and Howard was drawn inward with them and grew large and smoky with them. Nothing seemed more natural. And he freely waved his hands and feet, and dearly loved the freedom, but no matter how long his arms and legs became, even when he knew he was larger than the entire universe, he could never find anything to touch, and that became a horror worse than teeth. He awoke sweating, grasping the air, slapping the ground, craving solidity, even pain, anything he could fling himself against.

He shook off the fear of something lurking in the thick, after-rain fog.

The team met again and Dove-Ti had the them draw straws for who would search for firewood. DeSparr and Howard lost. Not again, thought Howard.

Blake gave him two yellow candles. "You can mark trees with these."

He put them in his soggy pocket. DeSparr didn't move.

"You have to go, doctor," said Crauder. "We drew straws. Chance is the fairest way."

"Any 'way' we use is chance," said DeSparr. "The most careful planning, like the cleverest ridiculing of me, is no more than a chance dancing of the molecules of your simple brains."

"No weird-talk," said Crauder. "You're doing what's right."

"I will do what I want and it's neither right nor wrong."

"I'll go," said Rachel.

"Thank you, Rachel" said Dove-Ti.

Going on a search with Rachel wouldn't be as trying as with DeSparr, but Howard would be careful, would not reveal too much.

"Rachel," said Smith. "Howard." His moist blue eyes sagged. "Don't forget: we depend on you to respect the safety perimeter. Stay within ear-shot. Never separate. We need each of you. We're in no shape to handle a search, or injuries, or the burden if we have to travel."

Howard nodded, and he and Rachel began walking uphill. They stopped at one of the salvaged yellow ribbons Blake had tied to trees to mark the safety perimeter.

"The limit," she said.

He studied the rocks and brush where they rose into a tangle of vines and huge old trees and disappeared into darkening clouds. None of the team had been farther up that mountain. "What we have is soaked," he said. "We keep looking." He stepped past the ribbon.

"We all agreed," she said.

He pointed casually in several directions. "It's arbitrary. Blake could have put it over there, or up there." He picked up several sticks.

She said, "Those are just as wet as these," and threw hers down. Her ghostly pale skin, along with her baggy shirt and pants, which she had washed to white perfection that morning, seemed, in contrast with the dark, sodden woods, to glow. "If one of us gets hurt, it's a huge problem for the rest."

He admitted to himself that he was afraid of going on alone. He didn't want to admit that he was drawn by the way her curves disturbed the flow of her loose cotton. A plan formed. He would force her to choose. She could overstep the safety perimeter with him or leave a search partner alone in those unmapped woods. Either way she would violate a team rule. To think of her in violation of anything had a certain dark appeal. "You can go on back." He was sure she wouldn't.

"The rules." She frowned. Her voice shook. "We all agreed."

"Then choose your rule to break."

She inhaled loudly. "What's wrong with you?" But she followed.

He thought: I am amazing. He pulled a yellow crayon from a pocket and marked trees, several strokes on the damp bark. He walked faster, pushing through bushes, jumping little streams. She kept up, set-jawed, flushed, and silent.

The foggy day-darkness hid unknowns but seemed also to shield him and her from both danger and disclosure.

He reached a thinning of clouds and finally stumbled into clear air on a rocky, treeless divide dotted with scrub bushes. She followed.

Below, the clouds spread like a boiling white sea, making dark, blue-gray islands of the other mountaintops. Above, a vast, lumpy cloud-ceiling dropped streams of mist like gentle fingers into the coves on the sides of the mountain-islands.

Birds and monkeys chattered from below.

"It's unreal," he said of the view.

"But it's real," she said, which he took as correcting him.

"I just meant that as an expression." He breathed deeply in a fresh breeze. He felt enriched blood flow into his arms and legs. He saw more vividly, heard more clearly, smelled more richly.

She brushed back her hair, blown in her face by the breeze, and gazed at the clouds and mountains. "How did it happen?"

"It just happened," he said.

"Not 'just.'"

"Just?" he said. It was not the first time she had used one word in a way that seemed too plain, or too deep, or both.

She nodded. "Not 'just.'" Fog slid up and across the divide and wafted between them. Big black rocks, faceted like huge broken gems, glistened wet behind her.

"What did you mean the other day," he said, "by 'Cost?'"

"What?"

"DeSparr asked if anything mattered. Just after the flood."

"Oh. I don't know. It just came out."

"But... what did you mean?"

She thought and said, "Well, if you give up something and it helps somebody — I mean, when it doesn't help you — that's cost. And that's what I think matters."

"Doesn't make sense. Anything we do is to help ourselves first, even if it's just to make us feel good about ourselves."

"It makes better company. Company matters. You were pretty clever getting me up here."

"Me?" He felt his face flush, but stood straighter. "Clever?"

She smiled. "I just meant that as an expression." She turned and walked toward the far end of the divide where there was a thick wood. She glanced back at him, and now it was he following her. When she came to skewed slippery rocks, she reached for his hand. Her grip was firm and warm and she spread her fingers so that his slid easily between them and when they had passed the rocks she let go just as easily.

"Oh," she said, stopping where charred bones and dry, rotting skin were scattered on the ground. "Somebody ate big animals here."

"Maybe somebody sacrificed humans," he said, though he couldn't tell by the bones. "Maybe the people Tee-week told us about. The People of... what did Zoe say? ...of Sacrificing."

"I doubt that."

"I don't. The Aztecs did it to appease their gods. Zoe says isolated groups of Aztecs are still around."

She stopped walking again and faced him. "Howard, I... I'd like to ask you something."

He did not want personal questions from her. And he did want them. "What?"

She put her fingertips together lightly in front of her. Strands of light brown hair blew across her face. Her eyes rounded. She cleared her throat lightly. "Do you remember Dr. DeSparr yesterday, saying you can

146

feel lonely even when a lot of people are around?"

"I'm sure he does, the jerk."

"Well, I just wondered... do you ever feel that way? Do you know what I mean?"

The shiny wetness of the narrow divide now vanished into a new white fog coming up and filling the vast, once-clear air. It all seemed both confining and infinite, momentary and eternal, as if she and he and the glistening rocks on which they stood were afloat in space, being driven across worlds. He took a deep, fog-drenched breath. "Yeah."

"Is that 'yeah' you know what I mean, or 'yeah' you feel lonely sometimes?"

A kind of noise grew in his blood. "Both." He was surprised that he wanted to touch, just lightly, the slight hollow of her cheek with the backs of his fingers. There had to be a reason to do such a thing. But no words came equal to the gesture. Her hair lifted again in a breeze. Her neck was thin and smooth and he could see blue veins throbbing. Her attention altered, without connecting wires or tubes, his mental and physical state. He had never understood how that could happen.

Since eighth-grade science he had built his incomplete view of the world. Nature. Technology. Sex. But he saw now, and just now, that there was something in her that was not curves or movement or words. Something new. Not new, exactly, newly sensed. And not sensed by senses, for it was not a thing having shape or sound or smell. Sensed now in spite of the vast gray sky and the jutting black crags around them, sensed in spite of the huge complexity and baffling order of all the world, in spite of the seeming effort of all matter to upstage that which was in her, by inside-out imitation, but which it could not be, and which it was for.

A breeze dropped from the high wood, blowing fog away and carrying its odorous mix of growing things and rotting things. She and he turned and walked again toward it, picking a route through big rocks and slender hip-high brush.

"So that's pretty top-priority?" He said as her words came back to him. "Company?" His own talk of self-first and god-appeasement was fading like the mist. The noise in his blood seemed to become tuned.

"Well, sure it is," she said.

"You mean ... love, right?" It was a hard word to pronounce.

She thought and said, "I would say, 'love-love.'"

It sounded like little-girl-to-grandmother talk. "What?"

147

"Not just 'love,'" she said. "Costly love."

They walked again. The trees in the high wood rose from thick undergrowth. She found an opening and stood in it facing him. Shadows deepened behind her. Slender trunks sprang from the matting of wet leaves and moss pressed down over the lacework of thin roots and fungi, which he could barely see but which he knew lay under everything, delicate and vulnerable and necessary.

His breathing had become deep and heavy, and hers too. A pure white mist blew down from above the trees and glanced off them, toward the camp.

He began to see in himself something like what he had come to see in her, and it too was not a sensible thing, and whatever it was, he had for most of his life unknowingly hidden and protected and ignored it, as a brittle shell surrounds its yolk, or as a guard stands in the snow at the gate of a castle whose fire-lit interior he has never seen.

And he thought: there is nothing humans do as impractical as a kiss. They work, they eat, they sleep. All for reasons. What is the logic, pressing two faces together? Two mouths? And it was hard for him to bend his neck, and it seemed hard for her as well.

Her hair had the smell of new woods growth. The angle of her head adjusted imperfectly to each increasing level of embrace. Their noses got in the way. Their lips were softer and fuller than he had expected, and warmer. Their arms held their bodies tightly, and it wasn't clear which heartbeat was hers, which his. Their responses were bold and untimed now, as if the ideas of giving and receiving had lost their distinction. Rather than using or owning or enjoying each other, they became, more in the yielding than in the taking, one.

The parting of lips was slow and focused. She did not, as others had, swing her hair and look up at the sky and laugh. She didn't even smile, or wait cow-eyed for more.

A thought, new to him, came suddenly, that for her, he would do or give anything. But he did not say it, for he was sure that, with her, there was nothing in just the words that would prove them.

***

Her eyes darted and her body became suddenly taut, as if she had heard a stirring in the brush. She let go and ran back onto the divide, looking back in quick, sharp, focused glances, confusing him. He

148

ran to her and reached for her waist.

She swirled behind a young, twisted tree. She curled her fingers around a slender vertical branch. Her body and arm made an arch with the branch, ready to pull away. She held her breath, mouth relaxed, face down slightly, eyes round and direct to his, searingly alert. No part of her moved. The end of the branch quivered.

Finally her breath came in words. "Can't you talk?" The edges of her mouth went down and up, making, then stopping, frowns. "What's wrong with you?"

"Nothing," he said, to avoid taking the time to figure out what she meant.

"What will you do?" Finally her frown stuck and she stood balanced on both feet as if ready to run, and when he advanced she jumped to one side, then the other. He quickly reached through the scraggly little branches and took her arm again and held tightly and stepped around the tree and took her other wrist with his other hand and let the first go and wrapped his arm around her waist and drew her to him. She was firm and thin and light and he could feel the trembling in her bones, and could tell that, in the light of their new, natural strength and fear and expectation, the sense of oneness, which he was sure he and she had shared equally, was leaving him and her, as if dismissed without notice like an unpaid, unappreciated servant, and there was in its place a tyranny of unthinking impulses.

He turned, and she turned, beside the twisted tree, breathing deeply and shaking in his and her natural strength and otherwise silent. He looked into the dark grove, the hall of a hundred tree-trunks, where the wild and natural smells of life and death seemed rich and good, and the world could not see in nor he or she out. And he stepped, and she did, her waist taut but unresisting in his arm, through the long streams of mist snaking up from the fog-sea below and the high pure mist still winging down, stepped toward and through the opening into the grove, into its shadowy darkness, hesitantly, almost reverently, as if it had been silently declared his and her own ritual chamber.

***

His eyes adjusted and he could see, on the rocky, eroding face of the dark cove opposite them, under ancient leaning trees, hundreds of winding, twisting roots imbedded in little cracks. The whole formation opened to him and her, shadowy and soggy. A huge dead oak, still clinging to its thousands of brown leaves, stood guard. He let go of her waist to be sure any decision would be hers as well as his. Another breeze came, a horizontal one with a strong smell like that of large animals which made him stop under a fat old branch of the oak. She stopped there too. He moved only his eyes and saw nothing, but the animal smell was stronger with each breath.

Then came a blur, big and black and tan, from behind the walled corner of rock, swift and silent, turning, leaving the ground in a long arch, stretched and soaring with easy power, and Rachel looked up and inhaled deeply, and Howard did, and as suddenly as it had started, it stopped, settling softly and systematically on the fat dead branch above the two, nearly hidden in the brown leaves, ears perked, nose moist, breath heavy.

Howard's once-brimming blood iced. The canines in the open mouth were like thick, yellow-white knives. Insects quickly found the round, squinting eyes, which seemed more to look than to see. The ancient body with its fading black rosette-spots slumped over the great oak branch like a thick smelly rug on a porch rail. The hind legs dug detachedly. The mid-section rose and fell with deep, deliberate breaths, the throat too old to hide the sound of them.

It had, Howard thought, one purpose. And soon. Any move could trigger it. Rachel's face glowed, a deep pink, as if fighting an urge to scream. And the focus of that morning's new strength had shifted once again, this time to paralyzing fear, the moment of bold adventure on entering the wood having become as vague and elusive now as the earlier moment of oneness or the mindless blood-tension when he snared her waist.

An ear twitched. Rachel's throat squeaked. Its eyes shot in her direction. If it attacks, Howard thought, either he or she is done for. So one should leave now, get a head start. No sense both dying. Rachel had bugged him, tried to change him. Now he had the unconsidered thought that if she were dead he wouldn't want to live.

"Run," he whispered, his voice annoyingly shaky.

"What?" she whispered, too loudly, but the cat didn't move.

"Run!" he said, more strongly this time. "As fast as you can. I know what to do." It wasn't a lie because he knew she didn't believe it.

The beast adjusted its weight on the limb, raised and twisted its head to one side, cough-growled, almost as a yawn, then settled again into the slumped position. It looked away as if bored, then looked back as if only casually interested. It cocked its head like a pet might, and Howard suddenly saw it as strangely attractive, almost mesmerizing. Its eyes quit squinting and grew bigger, he thought, than they could have been, and round, even soft, and his and Rachel's second-by-second survival in the closeness was as exhilarating as it was frightening.

Then she said, "Hold my hand," and Howard felt her fingers on the back of his hand.

"Not now." He pushed her hand away, staring in fear and delight at the cat's big soft eyes, then in spite of the immediacy of the danger, felt a quick painful regret, and remembered her question about loneliness. He started to turn to her, but at his first movement, el tigre's ears flattened outward and back, and the meaning was unmistakable.

Howard whisper-shouted, "Get going!" and as he motioned with his hand as if to push Rachel to safety, the whole cat became bigger, the mouth wider and darker, yellow-white teeth lining the black and red cavern, and it seemed to inhale the forest and the mountain into an inner blackness, and there was a slowing of time, as in a dream, and the cat's perfect movement seemed armed with power beyond itself, as if it were a sleek sculpture picked up and thrown with practiced might, and the forelegs reached and wrinkles formed in the fur of the shoulders like the imprints of giant fingers, and the eyes were clear, not soft now, not anything, something like the lens of a scanning camera, and the cat was as real as all nature and hugged him, and he pushed and hit at the neck with his fists and felt how little relative strength he had.

And then he and it were on the ground and his body or maybe just his head felt a brief numbness as if struck hard. His mind sped but the cat was faster, like light, and big, and the hot odors choked Howard, and all the trees and sky and mountain seemed to melt into warm slobber, and he felt fear and stress and defiance, but no pain, and there seemed to exist nothing but the cat and him and the unseen Rachel, and then there was another thud, and he smelled her hair like new forest growth. In all that turmoil he smelled her hair. And in the twisting of bodies, three bodies now, he felt the softness of her curves. The great toothed head suddenly jerked and growled and chomped, and the clawed paws raised and lowered as if petting, over and over, and then it was as if the universe receded and the cat, able but unwilling maybe to take on two, was up in the reappearing air of the earth, floating casually away, a few steps on the wet forest floor, stopping and standing, the large, thick neck-head hanging between bone-shoulders, red stains on the scruffy fur about the knife-mouth, tongue hanging, back sagging between short, thick club-legs, the scanner-eyes looking casually at the two as if nothing had happened.

Howard knew that Rachel was lying beside him but he couldn't take his eyes off the cat. He had brought her, tricked her against her will, against the team rules, and on purpose. He began to feel a large cooling and stinging on his neck and arm, but still didn't look. The cat turned and walked away, crouching under thick brush, then crawled into a small hole in the wet, crumbling stone.

Howard was cold all over now, and shaking. Finally he looked at his shoulder and chest. They were covered with blood. He felt weak.

He looked at Rachel, what was left of her. She did not move.

***

L.P.'s voice was like distant echoes in the night.

"Howie? Howie?"

"What's wrong," said Howard.

"How do you feel?"

"Fine. Not fine." His head was heavy. His skin stung.

"You had a run-in with an animal. Was it a tiger?"

Howard tried to sit up, tried to think. "It was in the tree."

"Easy, Howie." L.P. turned. "Less, did you hear that?"

Howard turned his head and pain shot through his neck. He barely saw, near him in the dark, DeSparr and Dove-Ti on their knees next to a large white bundle, working.

"It's no good," said the doctor.

"Shut up," said L.P. "It's fine, Howie."

"Yeah," said DeSparr, "Just fine. Except she may live."

Howard got to his elbows with some pain. His neck was stiff. He lightly touched his aching right shoulder and arm. They were wrapped.

"Where's Rachel?"

"She's sleeping. You need sleep, too."

"I've got to see her. The cat jumped us. She's…"

"She can't be disturbed."

"Can't…?" Howard sat up. "Okay, L.P. Let's hear it."

L.P. lit a match. Team members lying in the hut turned to avoid the light. Howard glimpsed a face, Zoe's, staring back at him, eyes

152

rounded in silent horror. DeSparr, exhausted, quit working on the white bundle and lay down next to it.

L.P. held the match to the candle, cupping both hands. He sat slumped, legs crossed. "You should hear it from DeSparr, Howie. Except he needs sleep right now."

"From you."

"I won't jerk you around."

"Give it to me straight."

"She's in a coma."

"Coma."

"She's... not supposed to make it." The match almost burned L.P.'s hand, and he dropped it and everything went black.

"Rachel," whispered Howard.

L.P. struck another match and this time lit the candle. "You're not too bad off," he said. "Cuts and scratches." He cleared his throat. The shadows of the candle trembled under his eyes. "Even if she does make it... Well, DeSparr used the word paralysis. He won't say how bad." L.P.'s eyes rounded. "Deep cuts... Howie, are you sure?"

"Speak."

"Deep cuts on her neck and the side of her head. I heard him say something about – this was just mentioned as a possibility, okay? – but something about brain damage." L.P.'s voice stopped quickly, as if he had said too much, as if Howard might hit him.

Howard nodded, pretending he could take it. "She can be fixed."

"Well, you know, no supplies or medicine. It's up to DeSparr."

Howard had made Rachel go. He acted against his and her and the team's solemn vows. He even enjoyed making her break those vows. He had recklessly risked, and probably lost, his new, most surprisingly precious hope. None of it could be erased. And after all that, nothing could be called bad news except, "It's up to DeSparr."

He said, "I've got to see her."

"He only lets Zoe near her," said L.P. "And Dove-Ti."

"Has she said anything?"

"She comes out of her coma now and then. Well, sort of semi-conscious. Doesn't talk. Doubtful she knows what's happened. Whoever's watching shoves water in her. Zoe got a piece of mango in her once. It's been like this since we brought you both back last night."

"She could wake up." Howard tried to get up. His shoulder gave way and he groaned. Several people groaned and turned over. He managed to get on his hands and knees. One arm worked. He crawled to her. She was like a mummy in the wrappings. "Rachel?"

Dove-Ti's voice came, groggy. "No... disturb. Uhm..."

He lightly touched the wrappings with his bad hand. One of her arms was not wrapped and seemed to glow red even in the dark. He could feel the heat before he touched it.

Just yesterday she could still hear and speak. Just yesterday he let such little things bug him as her digging into his personal life, as her trying to change him. Now he was changed. Not the way she must have intended. And not just guilt-feelings. Guilt. An awareness of its reality.

She had suffered horribly and was on the verge of death. He squeezed between her and Dove-Ti and turned onto his back. His bad arm pressed Rachel's bare arm. Surely she had sensed the oneness. "Rachel," he said to no answer. He pressed against her, as if pressing long enough and hard enough would erase the wrong. But it only made her almost unbearably hot arm even hotter.

"Just FYI," said Dove-Ti, "I have a low threshold of uhm, harassment awareness..."

Chapter 17

Again the soldiers and guides and porters and allied warriors trudged with the long lines on a new, sunny morning through wide fields and scattered groves of trees. They passed more cave-dwellings in the sides of hills, and men stood outside them, leaning on coas and watching as if they knew something was about to happen.

And again shouts came from across a field, and Tlaxcalans, more this time than before, rushed from the trees in battle dress, shaking fists, prancing, throwing stones, shooting arrows. They wore red and white feathers and waved red and white banners.

"The colors of Chief Xicotenga," said Feathers on the Water.

And again there was a trap, then a battle, bigger and more bloody than the first. Again the Sant-yagos drove the Tlaxcalans back, but lost one of the riding beasts, and were barely able to rescue its rider. Again the friendly Mendez crouched with Atl behind his cart.

The Sant-yagos were too tired to chase the fleeing Tlaxcalans.

Again a dead fat Tlaxcalan was loaded into Atl's cart. He had seen that men could kill without regret, and he imagined that he could do it. He thought of the swarm of fierce faces and was sure that when they came again, he would fight them off.

He said to Deer of Stone and One-Cip', "They stand over the bodies and laugh. They are not only strong but good-natured."

One-Cip' said, "I have talked to Totonacs who say Xicotenga has held back his main force. It is near Tlaxcala itself. The cruelty of the Sant-yagos may catch up to them yet."

Atl was becoming disappointed in One-Cip'. He was of the old, stern, worn-out ways.

There was a sudden commotion, and shouts. "Gibraltar was a fine mare!" Capitán de Alvarado stormed around, orange hair flowing, face bright pink. He stepped up on a large rock. "We started with sixteen mounts. The commander's chestnut died in Cempoala. We're down to fourteen. We made mistakes today. Only by the grace of God did we prevail! Tomorrow we go over the new tactics." The soldiers stood tired and serious.

"They do not revel in their win," said Deer of Stone, "but talk of mistakes."

"They want to correct them next time," said One-Cip'. "That is how they win."

De Alvarado jumped off the rock and turned to leave, then shouted back over his shoulder. "Double the guard! Day and night!"

***

The next two days were spent making arrows, cleaning equipment, dressing wounds, and marching closer to Tlaxcala. Several times the officers stopped the long lines and lectured on battle tactics. "Close lines, soldier-to-soldier cooperation, standard formations." Each day the officers sent out scouts, then soldiers to seize nearby villagers and bring them for questioning.

After more marching, the officers shouted, and again the long lines came to a noisy halt. Several Tlaxcalans showed on the trail ahead, not in war dress. They began handing out tortillas and several fat gobbling turkeys to the soldiers.

Atl said to One-Cip', "Are they making peace?"

"It does not look that way to me. We are near Tlaxcala. Watch."

Then one of the Tlaxcalans shouted many words, and a translator shouted, "We have come to fatten you Sant-yagos! This is the reply of Xicotenga to the mad Cortés! We shall eat Sant-yago arms and legs! We shall eat the meat of your riding beasts! Our women are at this moment preparing corn and tomatoes and beans and chili peppers for stew of Sant-yago hearts!"

Cortés and his officers accepted the food seriously, without comment, then dismissed the Tlaxcalans. Cortés shouted orders and several officers heard them and turned and shouted to the men and all of them took weapons from carts, ran to their units, and formed lines and groups. An officer called One-Cip', Two-Rabbit, Balanced Turtle, and A Fox is Mad to join them. The soldiers began a short march up to the edge of a wood facing a wide valley and moved the supplies and battle gear into place there.

"It is all right," said Ramiro Mendez, appearing with turkey meat he had hidden in an empty wooden box.

"Thank you, of course," said Atl and Deer of Stone at the same time, awkwardly trying to mimic the courteous style as they began eating.

"I am happy to help." Mendez' Nahuatl was perfect.

"We are happy to thank," said Atl.

"By the way," said Mendez, "There is an informer. I may be able to find out who your killers of your people are."

"You mean..." said Deer of Stone, suddenly interested.

"Yes. But the informer needs gold."

"Gold?" said Atl.

Mendez smiled. "That is always the way, is it not?"

"But we have none. How..."

"Luckily," said Mendez. "I happen to know a source. But I need your help."

"Our help?" said Deer of Stone. "What can we do?"

Mendez winked. "Tonight I will show you. Quiet for now."

When the soldiers began to settle, Atl noticed some going to a quiet place and kneeling before one of the brown-robed men. They bowed their heads and mumbled. He decided they were asking help from whatever special god they intended to honor with their killing.

Finally all but the watches were asleep.

"Come with me," whispered Mendez from the blackness. Atl and Deer of Stone followed him to low ground behind the officers' camp. Guards stood near rows of carts with wood boxes. He showed them a note in the Sant-yago tongue. "De Alvarado," he whispered, "would like me to make a gift of a small gold ring to one of the cooks."

"He would?"

"She does amazing things with dog." Mendez smiled. "But this is the lucky thing: the cook knows about the killers you are after. As the gift-bearer, I should be able to get the story."

"Where is the ring?" said Deer of Stone.

"Shh," whispered Mendez. "The guard will demand a bribe if we ask him to get the ring himself. De Alvarado never admits that he offers bribes, so he did not give me extra for that. You can go in and get the ring while I talk with the guard."

"Is this stealing?" said Deer of Stone.

"No, no." Mendez smiled. "The gold belongs to De Alvarado.

He asked me to deliver it to the cook. It is just that the guard does not know. I did not trouble the capitán for a pass note. That would be making a mountain of a mole hill. I just told him I would get it done. I knew I could depend on you two."

"Ah, yes," whispered Atl, pretending to understand.

"Where is it?" said Deer of Stone. "The ring?"

"It is in the third box from this end, in a gray cloth bag with a brown pull-string. Bring the whole bag. All of it, whatever else may be in it. I will return the rest later. And do not forget: the officers need their rest. How quiet can you be?

"Like death," whispered Deer of Stone, "if we are to learn of the killers."

"Good. Do not forget: it is our secret." Mendez approached the guard, began talking with him, and glanced back, giving the go-ahead.

The boys found the box, silently opened it, squinted in the dark, and found the gray bag with the brown string. It was very big. In it was a huge ring, and many shiny emblems.

"I am afraid," whispered Atl, reaching in for the ring.

"The whole bag," whispered Deer of Stone. "Mendez said 'the whole bag.'"

It did not make sense to Atl, but he put the ring back.

The two of them stood looking at each other in the dark.

"It will help us find the killers," whispered Deer of Stone.

Atl tied the string and picked up the bag. It was much heavier than he expected.

"Mendez is smart," whispered Deer of Stone. "We have luck."

When they returned, Mendez smiled and went through the contents of the bag. "Yes. This is the one. I will take it to the cook."

"But there are other things in the bag," said Atl.

"Oh," said Mendez as he left. "It is all right. I will return them."

"When will you tell us about the killers?" said Deer of Stone.

"After I talk to the cook tonight. I will tell you tomorrow."

"The cook is that way," said Deer of Stone, pointing opposite Mendez' direction.

"Yes. You are right. I... I have a small matter to see to first." Mendez crept away silently.

Atl said, "This is like a gift from the gods."

Chapter 18

S leep came mercifully, and lasted even through the mountain roosters. But loud bird calls and monkey whoops and first light waked Howard. He rolled over slowly and painfully, and the delight of some fleeting dream about uninhibited answers to unnamed questions back in Georgia faded before the returning memory of el tigre's work.

The gray morning seeped into the hut and spread across the white mummy. She lay on a stack of the Crauders' woven mats. There were two small openings in the wrappings at the slight bump of her nose, and one at her mouth. Only a glint of a tooth showed. Her chin was raised, as if she were conscious and listening for news of the tribe. A few strands of her light brown hair lay matted on the cotton at the side of her head. The only other part of her he could see was the red swollen arm, still radiating heat.

Her breathing was hoarse and irregular. When it stopped, his stopped too, and did not begin again until hers did. He pressed his mouth against the wrappings at her mouth, so unlike the warm, responsive lips of yesterday, and tried to speed her breathing.

Nothing changed for an hour. He shook DeSparr, who had been sleeping beside him, and exaggerated. "She's not breathing."

DeSparr opened his eyes slowly and stared at the roof of the hut. "If she quits breathing that'll mean she's dead. If she breathes again, she'll die later. Let nature take its course, and me sleep."

"But," said Howard, "she tended you when you were hurt." He knew it wouldn't help. When she would stop breathing, he would try to stop until she began again, but his body was his master and he would finally gasp. He stroked her hot arm and spoke softly into her wrapped ear. "Rachel." He whispered so others wouldn't hear. "I'm sorry. I broke the rule. Only me."

DeSparr sighed sarcastically and turned over.

Howard studied the mummy-wrappings, trying to recall the look of her sleek, pale softness, the line of her nose or forehead or lips, but the only images that came were those of her mangled body on the divide, quickly receding into the spreading blood. Just yesterday she could hear and speak. What tiny nonsense he had let it bug him that she tried to change him.

Dove-Ti sat up and touched his arm. "Here…" She handed him a small, damp wad of paper. "It was in Rachel's pocket," she said, "before we tore her clothes for bandages."

He opened it. It was Rachel's mother's note about the necklace, now stained with dried blood. He smoothed it and folded it carefully.

Finally he crawled outside with pain and effort, and stood in another cool, calm mist. He found his book in its plastic bag and slipped the note in with it.

L.P. stood waiting, his bare belly poking out where more of his shirt had been torn off. His sleeves were gone.

"I've got to talk to DeSparr," said Howard.

"He was way into the night doctoring. Better let him sleep."

Howard sighed. "I made her violate the safety perimeter."

"Don't…"

"Worse," said Howard, "I pushed her hand away. I did it just before the attack."

"Don't worry about that. It's her life now…" L.P. stopped as if he had said too much.

Zoe woke up and rubbed her fingers through her hair, shaking it. Her sleeves were gone, too, and more of the bottom half of her shirt. She looked at Howard. "Oh, Howard." She turned and walked down to the stream to help Dove-Ti wash bandages.

Howard knelt next to Rachel and stroked her arm.

Dove-Ti and Zoe came back with armfuls of clean, wet rags. They looked Rachel over, then stretched the rags across a stick-frame above the fire. Howard helped.

Zoe said, "We scrubbed these as hard as Rachel would have. It's so important now, around her, to avoid any more like… infection. Oh, I'm so sorry, Howard, it's so hard to like… know what to say. I felt so close to her, you know. Oh, Howard, how are you?"

"I can't get her to wake up."

"Oh, if anything happens to her… There are things I need to

160

like... talk to her about... She's been so... She bugged Blake and me about, you know, but now that she's... Oh, Howard, what like... happened?"

Her words, her focused attention, got Howard choked up. But he said, "A jaguar..."

"Yes. I heard. It's so like... awful! I thought jaguars didn't..."

"This one did. It jumped up in a tree and then jumped on us."

"Oh, I can't stand it. Doctor DeSparr won't say anything." She rolled her eyes.

Just then DeSparr got up and walked to the stream. Howard followed. The doctor scrubbed his hands over and over, using some of Blake's bark-soap.

"Less," said Howard, surprising himself using the doctor's first name. "How is she?"

DeSparr rose and strode back up and joined Zoe and Dove-Ti in the hut.

Howard followed. "Less! How is she?" He leaned in to watch.

DeSparr said, "Stand back. We need the light."

Howard stood back. "Can I help?"

"We're crowded as it is."

After about an hour in which the three of them seemed to deliberately block his view, Dove-Ti came out with the old stained, smelly bandages Zoe had taken off. She handed them to Howard, motioning to the stream. But he waited, hoping to see or hear any news. She took the dried rags from the fire back to Zoe, then carried two water-leaf-baskets to the stream, filled them, brought them back, and gave them to Zoe.

Howard assumed they were washing and re-wrapping Rachel.

Finally DeSparr stepped out and walked again to the stream. Howard followed, carrying the bundle of stained bandages. DeSparr found an exposed root under a huge tree, out of sight of the others, and sat straight up as if posing for a serious photograph.

Howard brushed off another root and sat on it, holding the rags. The stream raged hollowly against the rocks. "When will she...?"

"Comas," said DeSparr to the trees, "are unpredictable. True, she is strong."

"So you're saying she may..."

"All we can do — we have no medicine — is let the body undergo whatever chemical processes of resistance it can muster."

161

"So you think she may…"

"In this case, there's virtually no chance of survival."

Clouds hung heavy except for a tiny break to the south.

Did the doctor enjoy inflicting misery? Could vengeance spill over to Rachel as a way of getting back at Howard for the ants, for the ruining of the grandeur of the self-drowning attempt in the flood, for hearing the confessions afterward?

"But what," said Howard, trying to keep it technical, "is the damage?"

"The others have been told. The skin of one side of the head was hanging loose. A canine pierced the skull, and may have entered the brain."

The canines were big, Howard remembered.

"There is probably a loss of the use of the left eye. What bone fragments could be found have been picked out, and all of it sewn up."

"With what?" Howard didn't care what, just needed any information.

"Threads from a torn shirt. Mrs. Crauder washed them and twisted them." Now DeSparr could abandon the loud superior act. His medical skills, along with the facts themselves, were all he needed to establish what seemed a long-sought sadistic power over Howard. "Raul found a maguey leaf and made a needle from it. It's not curved, so the skin had to be pooched up for sewing. The work could only be crude. Her neck and the side of her head will never look the same."

"She'll have scars?" said Howard.

"Scars? She'll be lucky if she lives. No. She'll be lucky if she doesn't live."

Howard kept reminding himself that at least she was alive now. Something, an unusual movement in the woods beyond the stream distracted him for a second. He picked up one of the rags and scrubbed, hard, as if to destroy it. "She can be fixed back in Atlanta," he said.

"There was a great loss of blood," said DeSparr. "The coma itself could be permanent. Again, there was probably brain damage. Paralysis is likely. Partial, total…"

Howard had trouble listening. He tried to picture brain damage, paralysis, deformity. If she lived, would he recognize her? Would she recognize him? Would she even remember him?

"No medicine," said DeSparr. "Plenty of infection."

Again there was an unusual movement of leaves at a distance.

162

"You can at least minimize the scars," said Howard.

"If you want to remember the look," said DeSparr, "take good care of any photos."

Howard wanted no more. He studied the woods. Now the lack of the odd movement of leaves, along with the fresh woods smell, made memories come, of the quiet before el tigre, of the smell of her hair.

"She jumped in," he said, lapsing into his own confessing mode.

"She what?" said DeSparr.

"I was attacked first. Rachel jumped in."

"Why would she do that?"

"I don't know. To stop the attack."

Only DeSparr's eyes betrayed a hesitant belief. "No one risks their life for someone else. Survival is the raison d'être of the human animal."

"Survive only to survive?" said Howard, belying his earlier argument with Rachel. "That's pointless."

"You got it, Howie." The eyes were triumphant. "Everything is pointless."

The clouds loosened to the south.

DeSparr's face went gradually and oddly limp. Finally the head turned and motioned behind Howard, toward the camp and the team. "They're debating whether to keep her alive."

Howard squawked, "What?"

"The body will slow us badly when it's time to move on. There's precious little time for even basic needs, let alone tending to a hopeless case. They're…"

"Hopeless!?" said Howard.

"They're asking where the greater good lies."

"That's crazy!" Howard pictured a meeting like the dismissal of Miss Margaret.

The forming of DeSparr's words was slow and dramatic. "I – am – not – crazy."

"Not you," said Howard. Then he thought: you are crazy, you are suicidal, you can't connect, you unwittingly highlight your feelings of inferiority with your pretensions of superiority. You deny the supreme value of human life, the very basis of your profession. You are crazy. But he said, "I meant the idea. The idea is crazy."

***

Footsteps behind them were Smith's. He was visibly shaken, the old burdened look of his eyes had spread to his entire face. He almost stumbled a couple of times before sitting down on a root. He glanced at Howard, then leaned forward and folded his arms on his knees. Finally he said, "Howard, I wish there was something I could ..."

"We have to save her," said Howard. "Is it true that some are talking about...?"

"I feel awful," said Smith, seeming to have resigned himself to forces beyond his control.

"It was not her fault," said Howard, trying to build a case, quite honestly, that was sympathetic to her. "It was my fault. I made her go beyond the perimeter."

Smith said, sadly, automatically, "It's in God's hands now."

"Now?" said DeSparr. He opened both hands, palms up, and studied them. "Who's hands was it in before?"

"You can do it," said Howard. "You're a doctor."

"Boil one of these roots," said DeSparr. "Feed her the juices."

But Howard thought he heard in the sarcasm a crying out, a hope that things were not hopeless. "Let's," he said, "do what we can."

Rachel had mentioned prayer once. If Smith, the church leader, were to pray for her, he would be more inclined to keep her alive. "We could," said Howard, artfully, "pray."

Smith rubbed his face, as if trying to sort it all out. "Religion would have us save Rachel," he mumbled. "But religion would also have us save the largest number."

"So," said DeSparr, facetiously, "adjust your religion to the situation."

"It's a complex issue."

"But," said Howard, "to save her and all of us, that would be the largest number."

"I wonder," mumbled Smith, with a slump-shouldered tone of giving up everything he ever loved, "if religion can even save itself."

And before Howard could think of an answer he saw, far beyond the stream, in contrast with the gray mist, in the same casual way you might become aware of any stranger in any public place, what had caused the earlier leaf-movements: a man in long, loose shirt and pants, dark green, standing now in the open.

Howard's heart thumped. "The Sacrificing People."

Smith looked. "I thought things couldn't get worse."

***

The little man found a place not only to stand and watch them, but to make himself obvious in spite of fifty yards of trees and vines. He was somewhere between thirty and fifty, round-faced, reddish-brown, with short, black hair. He looked like the Jaguar-people, but no weapons or war paint. And his bearing was different, a restrained curiosity, energy, even authority. He stood alert, feet apart, head cocked to one side. His elbows stuck out, as if he were ready to wrestle. He leaned to one side, as if having to look around obstacles.

He stretched his arms upward, then slowly lowered them.

"They sacrifice humans," said DeSparr. "He knows we have a dying body. We can…"

"Don't even think about it," said Howard.

"Who's that?" whispered L.P., sneaking up behind them.

"Get Tee-week," whispered Smith.

"Right." L.P. crept back toward the camp.

The little man started walking toward them, dodging tree limbs, staring straight at them. Once he tripped and caught himself awkwardly. Two more figures showed behind him, a man and a woman, also in the course dark green top and bottom, barefooted. Then three more.

"I'm glad that stream's there," whispered Howard.

"But it's easy to cross," whispered Smith.

"At least they're not carrying weapons."

"No face paint. No jewelry. They're actually quite plain."

They stopped at the stream.

L.P. sneaked back again. "Nobody can find Tee-week."

"What?" said Smith and Howard at the same time.

"They're all looking."

The little man spoke and made hand signals across the stream. He stood with his feet apart and knees bent as if ready to jump, leaning to one side then the other.

"The Greenshirts," said L.P.

"The People Who Sacrifice Humans," said DeSparr.

"Yeah, but 'Greenshirts' is easier to say."

"Either way," said DeSparr, "we're in danger."

"Let's show numbers." L.P. turned to the camp. "Hey! We need people! Now!"

Crauder was already coming.

"Who's watching Rachel?" said Howard.

"My wife," said Crauder.

Howard began to sense in the little man's hand-signals a reference to a hurt person. "He's talking about Rachel."

"How could he know?" said L.P.

"I don't know. But we're not going to let him have her."

Dove-Ti and Zoe and Blake joined them

L.P. asked them, "Still no Tee-week?"

At that the little man suddenly looked at L.P., raised an arm, and said clearly, "Tee-Week!" The boy appeared behind him, fully clothed in the dark green.

Howard and the rest stared dumbfounded.

Finally Zoe called to him. "Tee-week!"

He hid behind the others.

"He's probably told them how stupid we are," said DeSparr.

"Maybe they want to uhm, help," said Dove-Ti.

"If they offer help," said DeSparr. "it will be to set us up. Tee-week probably told them we have a body. That's what they want."

"Why take just one body," said Crauder, "and it messed-up? They could take us all back to the wives and kids, tie us to the trees. We'd keep 'em in protein for months."

Zoe listened carefully to the little man. "Same language as the Jaguar-people." She got his attention and said, slowly, first in English. "We come in peace. Who are you?" Then she tried Tee-week's Nahuatl.

Haughton-Alsef arrived.

Zoe watched and listened to the little man's authoritative hand and body motions.

Finally she whispered, "I believe his name is like... Tetl."

"Well," said Smith, "we came to make contact. Ask what they call themselves."

Zoe tried and Tetl watched and listened intently. Finally he repeated a phrase several times, pointing to himself and his comrades.

"It's them," she said. "This, like... Mr. Tetl didn't make any bones about it. They're called 'The People of the First Sacrifice.'"

"Oh great," said L.P. "Straight from the original Aztecs, eh?"

"They took the pilot," said DeSparr. "Now they're after..."

"They won't get her," said Howard.

Tetl made motions as if he were about to cross the stream. "Don't let him," said DeSparr.

Crauder said, "He coulda crossed already. They're afraid of us." Tetl was insistent, and finally Smith said, "Tell him 'only him.'"

She motioned and talked and finally Tetl seemed to get it and stepped quickly and lightly across on rocks. Most of the team took several steps back. Smith and Zoe kept their distance, but Zoe talked.

Zoe said, "Can I like... help you?" Then she used Nahuatl and hand motions.

He spoke and pointed up toward the hut where Rachel lay. "Wait," said Howard.

"It's okay," said Zoe. "He just wants to see. One man."

"What if they want her?"

Smith said, "We'll watch him like hawks."

They all followed, nervously. They pulled back the hanging mat-screen. Tetl seemed surprised at the wrappings. He looked up at Smith.

"Her name is Rachel," said Smith.

Tetl cocked his head, curious.

"Rachel," said Zoe, pointing at Rachel. She pointed at Tetl and said, "Tetl. Tetl." Then she pointed at Rachel again. "Rachel. Rachel."

"Ra-chul," said Tetl. He held a hand over her. He raised his eyebrows as if to ask permission.

Smith looked at DeSparr. DeSparr pushed in front of Tetl and carefully pulled back some of the wrappings from the side of her head. Her hoarse breathing was more exposed now, louder. The light brown hair was the only thing Howard could identify, the rest was red and black lumps and rhythmic, blood-soaked stitches going in several directions. He had a half-second memory of her soft pale face, her direct look, her crinkled smile, but he couldn't hold it. He looked away quickly.

DeSparr put the wrappings back. Tetl turned and pointed down across the stream, to the other Greenshirts. He motioned and talked to Smith and Zoe.

"The others?" said Smith, bowing and smiling. "No. Only you this side."

Tetl talked and pointed again at the stream and the other Greenshirts, and at Rachel.

"He's like... using the word for 'give,'" said Zoe.

"We have nothing to give them," said Smith.

"Not Rachel," said Howard, "for sure."

"He may want to like… give us something," said Zoe. "Does that make sense?"

"They didn't go to all this trouble to give us something," said DeSparr.

"He may be offering this spot," said Haughton-Alsef, "saying we can stay. Many aboriginals consider the land to belong to everyone."

"Then how can he offer it," said Crauder, "if it's not his?"

"He is probably telling us that his people would like to be friends, since we're neighbors now. But they will, if we insist, stay on their side of the stream."

"How do you know all this?" said Crauder.

"Zoe has interpreted excellently and I can combine her reports with our body of knowledge about the cultural systems of primitive Mesoamerican peoples."

DeSparr sneered. "You think they're nice, but they'll kill you."

"Doubtful. But they may expect some small reciprocation."

"For what?" said Crauder. "For not killing us? Most people call that a protection racket!"

Tetl studied Rachel's wrappings, bending left and right, and frowning. Then he smoothed the air a foot above her, palms down, and chanted. His voice was overly nasal, and startlingly uninhibited.

DeSparr said, "Telling his gods there's a new sacrifice coming."

"Not happening," said Howard. He looked away, up, at the roof Rachel helped build. Pagan rites wouldn't affect her. They wouldn't.

Tetl knelt beside her, giving her bandaged shape, which was slightly arched as if striving to escape, a kind of momentous presence. He rotated his upper body, still chanting.

The team watched in the way a crowd might watch a crazed man writhing on a sidewalk.

Finally he got up and brushed the dark green cotton at his knees. He talked to Zoe, motioning with his hands toward the river.

"What's he saying?" said Howard.

"He's saying," said Zoe, "Don't make camp on sand."

"They've been watching us," said Howard, deflecting attention from his own hasty decision to set up the first camp on the silt bar.

"Rain will come," said Zoe, translating, "and the water will rise and wash it all away."

"Okay, okay. Let's take him back down to the stream."

Smith agreed, and they walked Tetl back.

"Perhaps some token gift would be in order," said Haughton-Alsef when they stood again at the stream.

A dozen People of the First Sacrifice, the Greenshirts as L.P. nicknamed them, watched from the other side.

"But what do we have?" said Dove-Ti.

Smith took off his straw hat, looked at it, and offered it to Tetl.

"Oh," said Dove-Ti, "that's a wonderful gesture. Uhm…"

Tetl took it, bowed, asked something, then offered it back.

Zoe studied him, then said, "I think he asked, 'May we?'"

"May they what?" said Smith, taking the hat back.

"Probably stay and get to know us," said Haughton-Alsef. "A subtle way of assuring themselves we are not a danger to them."

"Oh, the simple uhm, humanity," said Dove-Ti, "untouched by greed."

"Humanity is greed," said DeSparr. "Greed and hate and death. What they want is to make sacrifices to their crazy gods. If there's a sick body, that's the easiest way."

"My dear man," said Haughton-Alsef, "for that, they wouldn't have to ask."

"Any idiot," said DeSparr, "would know to ask first! It's easier. Don't be a fool."

Haughton-Alsef forced an uneasy smile. "If you're right…" He motioned toward the hut. "…then one of us can be the salvation of the rest of us."

"Nothing happens to Rachel," said Howard.

Haughton-Alsef puffed thoughtfully on the pipe. The empty bowl whistled. "No need to worry. Just pacifying the doctor there."

"You're pathetic," said DeSparr.

"Nothing happens to Rachel!" said Howard again. But DeSparr and Haughton-Alsef seemed more obsessed with their private fight than his frustration.

Smith held up a hand and turned to Zoe. "Can we try again?

He and she sat on tree roots with Tetl and talked haltingly for about a half an hour while the team and the Greenshirts watched.

Howard paced back and forth between the stream and the hut, making sure Rachel was not disturbed.

169

Finally Smith said, "It appears they would like to camp there, on their side of the stream."

"We're in trouble," said DeSparr. "And there's nothing we can do about it."

"They've uhm, greeted us with civility." said Dove-Ti.

"Civility!" said DeSparr. "What else? They're at home here! They're used to killing. They do it in ceremonies for their gods. Then here you come, seduced by the jungle, pregnant with your now-burdensome jaguar victim. They can't believe their good luck. They'll greet you the way smiling abortionists greet scared mothers. Why wouldn't they be civil?"

Dove-Ti bristled. "I hardly think that analogy…"

"We can avoid offending them," said Haughton-Alsef, "by honoring their request to camp nearby. I so move."

Crauder laughed. "What else can we do? Tell them to get lost?"

Smith wiped his glasses. "Any discussion?"

"Nooo," said Crauder. "Just be sure they stay over there."

"Addendum:" said Howard, "nothing happens to Rachel."

"Any opposed?" said Smith without Howard's addendum. "Nooo."

"Then so ordered." Smith bowed briefly to Tetl. "Yes, yes, thank you. By all means." He pointed at the other Greenshirts across the stream, held his palms up to them like a gentle cop stopping traffic, and said, "We thank you for staying on the other side." Zoe tried to translate. Then Smith took his hat off and swung it to indicate the stretch of ground from the stream up to the hut. "And we'll stay here."

When Zoe had finished translating, she said, "I think he got it."

Tetl bowed and, with his odd mix of authority and humility, raised his hands once again toward what was for Howard an increasingly strange, myth-filled Honduran sky. Then he turned and talked to the other Greenshirts. He swung his arms toward their camp, then swung them up toward the hut where Rachel lay. He did the same in reverse. He went through the cycle several times, talking as he did.

"I think he's saying," said Dove-Ti, "that they stay there, and we stay here."

When Tetl had finished, Tee-week and two others ran off into the woods. Tetl crossed to the other side, then turned back to Zoe. She and the team bowed and smiled. He bowed, and they did again, and he cut it off with an authoritative wave of his hand. He directed the

Greenshirts in their camp-making, though they seemed to know what to do anyway.

Watching them, Howard thought they seemed more disciplined, devoted, and dangerous than the Jaguar-people.

"Well," said Smith. "We'll have to sit down and discuss these new developments." He found a rock to sit on, about halfway between the stream and the hut where Rachel lay. Others found places to sit or stand. He fidgeted uncomfortably, then looked at DeSparr. "First, just how bad is Rachel?"

DeSparr raised his head and opened his mouth importantly. "Coma. Probable brain damage. Likely paralysis. Head, neck, and shoulder badly disfigured. She'll probably die."

"No," said Howard.

Zoe put her head in her hands.

"We'd better do something," said Crauder. "Those people are camped right in front of us. And the chicken Jaguar-people got my gun."

"God!" said Pryce. "Isn't anyone scared? They could kill us all tonight!"

"Actually," said Dove-Ti, "they have behaved uhm, civilly."

"I think," said Haughton-Alsef, smiling pleasantly, "that there's something in what Dove-Ti says. While it's likely they practice human sacrifices, as we've been told, they would do it, judging by their manner and dress, with well-planned ceremonial order. It won't happen today or tomorrow. And I doubt seriously they would be inclined to go through the ceremony with more than one honoree at a time. So we…"

"Honoree?" said Crauder.

"The person they sacrifice would be highly honored. Studies have shown that these are not happenstance events. A high degree of preparation is as important as the ceremony itself. So, as I was saying, we have time to negotiate. Quite seriously, there's much they could do for us. That is, if they were, shall we say, properly compensated."

"We couldn't cough up a crumb," said Crauder, "for a cat."

"Ah, but we can demonstrate," said Haughton-Alsef, "tolerance of their practices."

"They don't give a pig's lip if we're tolerant."

"If our beloved Rachel were to be pronounced unable to recover…"

"No more!" said Zoe. "No more of that!"

"Forget it," said Howard, shaking. "You won't get past me."

171

Haughton-Alsef lowered his head and raised his eyebrows. He smiled pleasantly and naturally as if Howard's outburst were a mental collapse as amusing as it was embarrassing.

"What if," said Dove-Ti, soothingly, "none of that works? I uhm, heard of these people, they were stranded on a mountain after a plane wreck. No food. And one of them had died..."

"No!" said Zoe. "We're not even going to talk about that."

"I can see you feel very strongly," said Dove-Ti, soothingly. "And thank you for sharing your feelings. But at the same time, certainly, we should have the uhm, open-mindedness to consider rational options even when they may lie beyond our own limited cultural experience. Of course nothing extreme should be done until absolutely uhm, necessary." She smiled. "And I believe we have another what if. What if the weather improves and we are able to find our way out of here? As much as we all love Rachel..."

"We carry her with us," said Zoe.

"No question," said Howard.

Zoe said, "I'm really like... surprised at you, Dove-Ti. You've been to seminary kind of thing."

Dove-Ti smiled calmingly. "Actually, I'm glad you mentioned seminary. It was at New Heritage that I learned how a concept of the precious sacredness of life may be seen to include extraordinary and — allow me to emphasize — compassionate protection of life from harm."

"Exactly," said Howard.

"Wait a minute, Howard," said Crauder. "I don't think she's saying what you think she's saying." He glared at Dove-Ti. "What in blazes are you talking about?"

"Well, someone whose uhm, future may be filled with pain and agony, and whose sense of self-worth is totally compromised by their unwanted, or burdensome dependence on others, or by their disabilities or deformities, may be compassionately relieved, their life made more 'sacred,' if you will, by letting them, or even helping them, pass on out without having to face the debilitating deterioration and misery. In a very literal way, it's a means of accomplishing nothing less than a miracle cure. When you think of it, it's like a wonderful dream, the end, and the prevention, of suffering. In many ways, this is not about old uhm, fears and dogmas, but about aesthetics and sensitivity."

Crauder squinted at her. "'Pass on out'?"

"Die," said DeSparr as if explaining the obvious to the ignorant.

Mrs. Crauder sucked a long, loud breath.

"Well, that's a new one," said Crauder. "Got a problem? Just die. End of problem."

"Dove-Ti is quite right in this," said Haughton-Alsef. "After all, it is the 21st century."

"Who can make a judgment like that?" said Zoe.

"Well," said Dove-Ti, soothingly, "the answer that comes to mind is, 'loved ones in consultation with a caring doctor.'"

Everyone looked at Doctor DeSparr. He said, "Sugar words."

"We keep her alive at all costs," said Howard, jaw trembling.

"Another way to put the question," said Dove-Ti, even more soothingly, "might be, 'Who has the right to decide that a person must live a life of pain and misery?'"

"How do you 'decide' she'll live," said Crauder, "when she's already living?"

"You don't," said Zoe. "You're not talking about deciding she'll live. You're talking about deciding she'll like... die. Who can predict how like... painful or miserable she may or may not be kind of thing. Or even if she would want to brave the problems anyway? Only God."

"I think," said Dove-Ti, calmingly, sounding as if she were reading from a book, "that God would want us to welcome the continuing uhm, evolution of our thinking, and to heighten our awareness of the needs of others, to overcome traditions that may cause unnecessary and unintended suffering, to see such a decision not as a challenge to outmoded beliefs, but as an act of kindness and beauty. Can you not envision the gentle, intimate beauty, however tearful, in the witnessing of the death of a suffering person? It's uhm, revelational. One thing I believe we can all agree upon as Americans is our inherent rights and freedoms. And certainly the flip side of each person's right to a meaningful life is the right to be free from a life deprived of any meaningful qualities. Clearly we shouldn't presume to deny anyone."

"What do you mean," said Crauder, "by 'meaningful?'"

"Well, meaningful means, uhm... Of course it means just what it says. Meaningful."

"You got that stuff at New Heritage?" said Crauder.

"Well, I hardly think 'stuff...'"

Haughton-Alsef smiled reassuringly. "We have with us a qualified doctor." He turned to DeSparr. "You, good doctor," he said, "have the credentials. Certainly you, like the rest of us, want the best for

173

Rachel. So, let's get to the heart of the matter. What meaning would you say her life has at this point?" He smiled pleasantly, put the pipe in his mouth, raised his chin, and waited for the answer.

"The word 'meaning,'" said DeSparr, "in itself, has no meaning."

"We need facts," said Smith.

"This crowd wouldn't recognize a fact," said Crauder, "if it sat in front of us like a donkey on a dinner table."

Haughton-Alsef lowered his chin and looked at DeSparr, still smiling pleasantly. "Put it this way: wouldn't you say that her life has been rendered meaningless?"

"No!" said Zoe and Howard at the same time.

And Howard would have preferred a loud "no" from the doctor too, but he only said, slowly and pointedly as if for fools, "The word 'meaningless' is meaningless."

Smith studied his hat. "Now, on another subject, what thoughts do we have about food?" He looked at Blake.

"Well, I…"

"None of us knows how to like… find food here," said Zoe.

"There's plenty," said Blake. "Unfortunately, hard to get."

"Maybe we can discuss these things better after a good night's sleep," said Smith.

The Greenshirts had become amazingly silent.

Howard and L.P. were assigned watches opposite the camp from the stream, if the word "watch" applied when not even a star was visible. Blake and Crauder were assigned other spots.

L.P. slept immediately. Howard tied the bag with his book and Rachel's mother's note to a belt loop. He was tired, and sick of the team's desperate discussions. He was unable to stay awake.

***

He half-woke just before dawn and started to stretch. The pain in his shoulder hit and he squawked and crouched and grabbed his arm.

"Hang in there." said L.P. "Rain's stopped. Fog's lifting. River's down."

Howard stood. "I'm checking on Rachel."

L.P. followed.

"Do you think they're up?" said Howard.

"The tribe guys? Haven't heard 'em. Maybe they've left."

"Left? They wouldn't just leave." Howard looked at L.P. "Would they?"

L.P. shrugged.

"Did you get any of that hand-signing last night, back and forth across the creek?"

L.P. shrugged. "Nahuatl to me. Nobody understands anybody."

"It was Tee-week told us about the human sacrifices. Now he's joined them."

L.P. spit. "Smart-mouth little brat."

"But why would he join up with those people? Especially as dangerous as they are? I mean, he knows they're the 'People of the First Sacrifice.'"

"Maybe he thought they'd give him something for telling 'em about Rachel."

"You think?" said Howard. They both started running.

When they reached the hut they found only the straw bedding, no Rachel. Beside the straw was Beg, curled up, asleep.

"Rachel!" shouted Howard. "Beg!"

Beg opened his eyes.

"Where's Rachel?"

Beg raised his head and squinted at the empty straw. "She up?"

Others awoke. Howard ran around the hut, then to the edge of the woods. "Rachel!"

Blake and Crauder hurried in from their watches. Smith and others showed.

"I coulda told ya," said Crauder. He whirled. "Where's my pistol?" Then he threw his hands up, remembering.

Smith put the hat on. "We need to sit down and…"

"We need to find her!" said Howard. He and several others spread out, pulling back brush, shouting. "Rachel!"

"Down here!" shouted Blake from the stream.

All but DeSparr hurried to the stream, then stopped, dumbfounded and silent except for Mrs. Crauder's gasps, staring where the People of the First Sacrifice had camped, where all traces of them were now gone, where red butterflies fluttered up into the mist.

Chapter 19

Tonatiah lay ready to break into Tezcatlipoca's night-smoke. There was not a sound in the world. Tlaloc had emptied no jars in those days and the streams ran small and smooth and silent. The great birds stood on the tops of the clouds. The small birds crouched in the gray mist in the tops of the trees. The insects waited under the leaves, in silence not to wake the small birds. Peccaries stood tight together and breathed slowly and carefully. The jaguar sniffed the last of the night air.

The first man-sound came with the first dim light, from the hills to the west, bold and drawn out, as if in great need, "Shee-ee-ah-waah-toong!" Its quick lustful answer was thrown back by other hills, "…aah-toong!" Then came the drums, slow, "Bm… bm… bm."

Atl sat up. The air did not move. There were no smells of cooking, no groans of waking. Hazy outlines of Sant-yagos moved silently in the fog, one here, three there, a wide, round eye shining now and then from under a helmet. Hands felt the ground, picking up swords and armor and arrows.

Deer of Stone sat up. He and Atl rose and walked softly to a slight rise but could see little in the fog. Around them more Sant-yagos grouped and whispered and held quietly to their spears and cross-bows and iron sticks. Even the beast-whinnies from deep in the trees seemed muffled. The drums far away kept up the slow rhythm.

"What is wrong?" said Atl.

"They are out there," said Deer of Stone. "The Tlaxcalans. Thousands."

"How do you know?"

"I know."

They both strained to see. The fog slowly thinned. A long green valley dropped away, heavy with dew. Far across it, fog-grayed men and boys showed, shoulder to shoulder, masses, swaying slowly and heavily side to side, walking, stirring up insects and grass and leaves, bows and spears and clubs in hand, skin painted or wearing skins, heads painted or wearing animal heads, arms or legs feathered. He could not see their faces, but could sense the dark fixing of their eyes forward, and the readiness of every muscle as if at the point of kill on a hunt.

More distant men and boys showed on a farther hillside, then more on another. Banners of red and white began to show through the mist, and more men and boys on a fourth hillside, with other banners of other colors, and Atl knew Deer of Stone was right. There were thousands, tens of thousands, shifting slowly on their feet, coming down the hills, shoulder to shoulder, flashing their blood-hunger.

"Shee-ee-ah-waah-toong!" came the cry again, and its answer, and from many places now the drums, faster, "Bm… d-bm… d-bm."

Suddenly, from the trees near Atl, two Sant-yago officers ran far out onto the field, fast even in the iron armor. Three soldiers rushed to catch up. They stopped so far out that they seemed small and almost as gray in the mist as the oncoming masses, who now raised bows and shouted and chanted. The officers studied the land and pointed and talked, paying no mind to the arrows falling short in front of them.

Then they turned and ran back to their soldiers in the trees and shouted. All the officers gathered with them and talked and made shapes in the air with their hands and drew pictures in the dirt and pointed at the Tlaxcalans and argued and finally separated and stood back from the lines and began shouting, with translations for the Totonacs, "All men! At the ready! Now!"

The soldiers ran out from the trees and lined up side by side facing the officers, and in a short time all were in groups of thirty or forty. Even bandaged soldiers stood with them. And behind each group sixty or seventy Totonacs lined up as ordered.

One officer turned and glared at Atl. "Every man!"

Atl looked at Deer of Stone. "They think we are men."

"We are," said Deer of Stone.

"Where do we go?" said Atl.

"I do not know, but we had better go somewhere."

They walked toward a group of soldiers, staring across the fields at the tens of thousands. "Remember the nest of yellow jackets we kicked up last year?" said Deer of Stone.

"Yes. Where is Mendez?"

"He has the gold we got for him," said Deer of Stone.

"And no answer about the killers of our village."

"Bring cart!" shouted an officer to Atl in poor Nahuatl. "Now!"

Atl stiffened. He saw a cart in the trees and ran to it. It had a thick cloth cover. It was heavier than the earlier carts. Deer of Stone helped him get it started, and he pulled it over the rough ground.

Deer of Stone was called to another group. He glanced back at Atl. Then Atl heard One-Cip' shout, "Capitán de Escalante, hear me!"

De Escalante turned to him.

"There is a pass, a fine one, that I have traveled before. I can show you. Your whole army can escape through it if you move now."

De Escalante smiled. "There will be no escaping."

"But," said One-Cip', "you will be overrun. You know that the Aztecs themselves have not been able to defeat the Tlaxcalans."

"You need not fight, old man. Go to the trees and wait."

One-Cip' looked around and when he saw Atl he said sadly, "Take good care. Very good care."

"Yes," said Atl. "What will you do?"

"I will urge another capitán." He left, searching the lines.

Suddenly, the ground shook. Atl jumped. Eleven beasts and iron-covered riders stormed out of the trees behind him. He ran to one side. They galloped around big rocks and up the rise, ducking their huge heads and snorting, in line with the soldiers. They pranced nervously. He could feel their heat and the wetness of the air around them. One of them glared at him with a feverish eye, and the top of its front leg quivered. The riders folded down the flaps of their iron helmets. They held out long, pointed poles. Swords hung at their sides. They beat their shoulders and chests. Even their hands and fingers were covered with iron. One beast snorted and pranced. Another reared and turned five times before its rider could bring him under control.

Then Atl heard shouts from officers far down the line, and de Escalante stood in front of his soldiers. "Form the squares!"

The soldiers moved around quickly until they formed what, if seen from high in a tree, would have the same shape as the square stones in the Aztec cities.

"Hurry!" shouted de Escalante to Atl, pointing to the square.

"I…" said Atl. "I…"

"In the middle!" shouted de Escalante. His eyes drilled into Atl's. "Now!"

178

Atl strained at the heavy cart and finally pulled it between two soldiers and into the square. De Escalante walked with him and when they were in the middle he reached for the cart's cloth cover and pulled it back. Swords and spears and shields shone in Tonatiah's new light. Soldiers came quickly, grabbed weapons, and returned to their places.

"Stand here," said de Escalante to Atl. "You and the cart stay with me where ever I go." He leaned and looked down into Atl's wide eyes and drew his long shiny two-edged sword. "If you do not do just what I tell you, as soon as I tell you, I will run you through with this." He leaned closer. "Do you know what I have said? Do you see?"

"Yes," said Atl. His voice squeaked. He tried not to think what the sword would feel like going through his stomach. From across the fields, he could hear the murmuring drums and screams, closer and louder. He felt again the drawing from deep within himself, the snarling faces and teeth and horns waiting just beyond the trees. He raised his head to defy them, and stood ready.

He heard a voice. "Hey." He looked around. It was Alonso, in his red Flemish hat, part of the same square. He ran to Atl, gave him an animal-skin vest, and jumped back to his place. The vest was torn and stiff and smelled like the Sant-yagos, but Atl put it on. Alonso grinned. "It will be all right." That did not calm Atl. He wished for Mendez.

De Escalante barked a loud order and all the men on each of the four sides turned outward, so that Atl could see only their backs. The capitán barked more orders and walked around briskly inside the square. The soldiers drew their swords, raised them, lowered them, turned and faced all the same way and walked and stopped and faced outward again. They were like a flock of birds, or a school of fish, moving suddenly in the same direction at the same time, stopping all at once, waiting. Wherever the square moved, Atl stayed in the center. The cart was lighter and easier to pull now. He learned fast.

Then de Escalante put a hand on Atl's shoulder, climbed onto the cart, and looked beyond the square to other Sant-yago formations. Atl could see that some of them were shaped like squares, some like arrowheads, some like circles, and some in straight lines.

Atl heard noises to one side. Four iron logs were pushed to a line, side by side. "Falconets," whispered Alonso loudly to Atl. An officer shouted at the struggling men and they stuffed cloth and black powder and river rocks into the hollow ends of the iron logs, using long sticks. Then a group of soldiers in an arrowhead-shaped group pointed iron sticks toward the field. "Harquebuses," said Alonso. Another group brought up long rods with sharp metal blades on the ends, and formed a line next to the men with the iron sticks. "Halberdiers," said Alonso.

Then more Sant-yagos shouted orders down the line, and their own drums began a rapid staccato, the first loud noises from their side of the field. The Tlaxcalans shouted back louder and beat their drums faster. De Escalante raised his sword and pointed it toward the field and shouted, "Forward!" All the soldiers kept the form of the square and walked toward the jumping, shouting tens of thousands. The square moved left and right, and even rotated, as the capitán shouted.

The Tlaxcalans came closer, slow-dancing, tall feathers swaying. Atl could see their dress. Quilted cotton wrappings, thickly woven basket-coverings, big feathers on their arms, as if winged, or tall feathers or leaves front to back across the tops of their heads, all decorated with rhythmic lines and colored shapes.

The nearest and biggest mass of Tlaxcalans flew red and white colors. And they were close enough now that Atl saw in front of them the most fearsome sight he had ever seen. A jaguar danced on its rear legs. On its head was a huge fan of tall, blue-green quetzal feathers shaking in quick, perfect rhythm with each firm, slow step forward. Inside its open jaws was the living head of a man, a chief, glaring fiercely from between the teeth. The jaguar's knees bent and its head went back and its front legs raised high and inside the jaguar's jaws the man's mouth opened and the cry came again, harsh and piercing, "Shee-ee-ah-waah-toong!" and the answers were thrown back from the hills, "...aah-toong!"

Suddenly Atl was almost knocked down by quick blasts of air, harsh booms to his left, and looked, and saw great clouds of blue-white smoke pouring from one hollow iron log after another, then drifting up. Many Tlaxcalans in the front line fell. Others stopped, but lurched forward again, pushed from behind by more waves of warriors, stepping around the fallen bodies.

The jaguar stepped higher on its rear legs and raised its front legs higher and wider and the man-head in its mouth screamed louder. All the Tlaxcalans raised their spears and shouted, "Pigs in iron!" and raised bows and arrows and obsidian clubs and bags of darts and slings and stones. They held shields in the shapes of the heads and shoulders of warriors to make their numbers seem even greater. "Silly hats!" they shouted. "Come near!" They screeched and made shrill whistles and long howling blasts from conchs and pounded the drums fast now, "D-bm-t-k... d-bm-t-k." "Sant-yago meat!" they shouted, "Tasty!"

The red and white warriors came straight for Atl's square. "Beast-meat!" they shouted. "Stew-filler! Come near!"

A distant cry came from far down the line of Sant-yagos, and de Escalante raised his sword again, and all the Sant-yagos shouted and raised their weapons and walked faster toward the Tlaxcalans, keeping the formations. They echoed together the cry as if it were the one great and final command: "Sant Iago! And at them!"

"Pick up any weapon that falls," said de Escalante to Atl, "and carry it back to the soldier. He cannot leave his place in the line. If he does not want it, put it in your cart."

"If I can't get to them," said Atl "what...?"

De Escalante glared at him and patted his sword.

"Yes," said Atl. "Yes."

The square to Atl's left stopped and he looked and saw them hold up small heavy bows mounted on heavy sticks for aiming. "Crossbows," said Alonso. They let go swarms of short, heavy arrows which flew faster than hunting arrows, soared farther, and thumped many in the middle of the Tlaxcalans, knocking them down. The crossbow men walked forward again, pulling back the bows and fixing new fat arrows in them.

Then again loud booms came from the iron logs, and blue smoke flew out across the field and more Tlaxcalans fell, but others quickly filled the gaps. Sharp cracks and smoke came from the iron sticks, and more Tlaxcalans fell.

Then Atl noticed that some of the divisions of Tlaxcalans had stopped and were dancing and shouting where they stood.

Eight of the beasts and iron-hatted Sant-yago riders rode fast onto the field, holding their lances out and forward, shouting. They galloped straight into the red and white Tlaxcalans who stepped back to avoid the lances. Then the riders dropped their lances and drew swords and hacked and slashed. The beasts reared and kicked with their stone-hard feet. Arrows and sling-stones rained on them, bouncing off the iron. The Tlaxcalans near them backed off, ducking the flying beast-feet and their own spears and arrows. In time the whole mass of them was stopped, and the riders jumped off their beasts and quickly picked up their lances and got back on and turned and rode toward another mass coming forward down a hillside. But the Tlaxcalans they left only

181

laughed, and the jaguar pranced bigger and shouted louder, and the red and white mass moved forward again, madder.

De Escalante shouted more orders and the square turned and moved at an angle from the Red and Whites, then the capitán shouted again and the men turned straight at the Red and Whites, drew swords, walked faster with the strange rhythm of clattering iron and thumping animal-skin, and shouted again, "Sant Iago!" Atl could see, through the spaces between the soldiers, the eyes of the Red and Whites, wide, as if in a spell, and fixed, as if upon himself. At another order, the square turned at another angle, then turned back straight.

Alonso looked over his shoulder at Atl and grinned. "This confuses them." But to Atl they did not seem confused.

Then arrows and stones rained down on the square. Atl ducked and cringed, but was more afraid of de Escalante than the arrows and stayed close and listened for orders. Then something hit his chest and he felt the jolt of it in his bones and it threw him off balance and he saw the face of Dahlia flash in the air as he fell. "Get up!" shouted the capitán, reaching and jerking an arrow out of Atl's animal-skin vest and throwing it back at the Red and Whites. Atl jumped back up and looked and saw that the vest had stopped the arrow and he was only scratched.

"E-eh?" said Alonso, grinning and looking back at him.

There were so many arrows that, wherever the square marched, it seemed to leave a trail of straw. One soldier laughed at the way the arrows bounced off the iron. Some who did not have iron helmets, like Alonso, held shields or iron-covered arms above their heads. Atl held a bare arm above his own head and pulled the cart with the other. At times he was hit, but only with glances.

The men of another square to his right held long iron-tipped spears straight up, as high as three men. "Pike men!" shouted Alonso, grinning. "They will trap the enemy and direct them to us!" Atl did not know why Alonso was happy about that.

Atl's square was so close to the Tlaxcalans now that he could feel their heat and sweat, and hear the desire in each scream and see the blood-lust in each eye. He could not stop shaking and sweating and he wondered how Alonso could stay calm. Forty men in their square against thousands. He could not get enough breath, and the air was filled with dust and body-odors.

Then he saw the pike men's square again. This time it turned toward the Red and Whites and shouted, "Sant Iago!"

"And at them!" shouted the men of Atl's square in answer. Then, one side of the square of pike men stopped in place as other sides kept moving, so that they separated, unfolding the square until it became a long straight line facing along one side of the Red and Whites. It was like magic! The soldiers lowered their pikes and the points bristled far in front of them and they walked steadily forward, shoulder to shoulder. The Red and Whites laughed at them and jeered and threw rocks and shot arrows, but backed off slowly, turning, as Alonso had said they would, toward Atl's square. One of the pike men was tall and skinny and his helmet rocked on his skinny head. "Gonzo!" whispered Atl.

Then Atl saw a mass of Tlaxcalan blues running down from a hill behind the pike men, and he cried out, "Gonzo!" The men of de Escalante's square cried out with warnings, and the capitán of the pike men shouted orders and every other pike man raised his pike straight up, so that half were still pointed at the Red and Whites, and half at the sky. It looked like the ribs of a fish. Then those with raised pikes turned about and lowered them and held off the attack from the rear. The blues finally turned and slowly backed away.

Then Atl noticed that the blues and all the Tlaxcalans except the Red and Whites were now waiting on the hillsides, as if to see how it went with Xicotenga their ally before coming down again to fight beside him.

***

But the Red and Whites were still thousands and they were close now, and the jaguar pranced mightily and the man's face in its mouth screamed and Atl felt the intense heat and noise and smell. When the two armies collided, the noises changed. Screams gave way to grunts and curses and cries of pain, whizzing of stones and arrows to slaps and thumps of hand-to-hand fighting. The rhythmic marching gave way to the clash of iron and wood and flesh and bone, the smell of trampled weeds and grass to that of hot breath and sweat.

Atl's arms and shoulders were bruised. He could see Tlaxcalan eyes, and to him it seemed they wanted to kill him for helping the Santyagos. They were stopped only by the shoulder-to-shoulder lines.

The old wild horned faces began to rise from the battle and to draw him from himself and he feared that he would be killed before he

183

settled anything about Dahlia or his people or his life.

The capitán glanced at him less often now, and kept shouting to the men, "Shoulder to shoulder! Hold to the line!"

Three Tlaxcalans came running for the square locked arm-in-arm and hit a soldier all at once. He gave way and they crashed through, suddenly doubling in size. One tripped on the fallen soldier, one's arm was grabbed by another soldier, but the third came straight for Atl. Atl jumped behind the cart and hid his eyes and heard a loud clattering against its side. Finally he looked, and saw the capitán pull his sword out of the warrior's chest, then run fiercely for the other two, where he helped kill them and lift the fallen Sant-yago back to his place in line. Some of the men who saw it cheered.

"Left!" shouted de Escalante, and all the soldiers stepped to the left. Atl saw a fallen sword and ran to pick it up — it was heavy — and returned it to its owner. "Forward!" shouted de Escalante, and Atl hurried to drag the cart and keep it in the center, and one corner of the square moved into the mass of Tlaxcalans like an arrowhead. "Halt!" Atl stopped the cart and the soldiers on the point swung iron swords in front of them, fast and furious like the teeth of many jaguars, and the sky flashed from their edges. Pieces of wooden Tlaxcalan swords flew about. Some Tlaxcalans kept a good distance, some jumped at the shoulder to shoulder lines and quickly back, others came too close and were cut to pieces. Sad to Atl, the bravest were the most quickly killed. Still they danced and screamed and swung their clubs and wooden swords. The grass and weeds grew red with blood.

De Escalante shouted another order and the men in the square moved, making the square a circle, fighting as they went, rotating the circle halfway, then formed a square again. "Forward!" shouted the capitán, and a new corner of the square, an arrowhead of two fresh sides faced the warriors and the two tired sides got their breath.

Atl dragged the cart once more. He tried to step around the fallen Tlaxcalan bodies, but the capitán glanced again, and Atl held his breath and pulled the cart over a body. Another sword fell and when he turned to pick it up he saw that it was stuck in a dead Tlaxcalan's arm. He closed his eyes and pulled it out and tossed it quickly, hilt first, to its owner. Injured Sant-yagos kept their places in line with the help of their comrades on each side.

Once when the square turned, a corner soldier was knocked forward and down, and left stranded. The soldiers each side of him cried to him as they closed the gap, but he could not get up before two Tlaxcalans rushed and pulled off his helmet and grabbed his hair. Suddenly hundreds of the enemy stopped to watch, which gave the square a chance to advance faster, stepping over Tlaxcalan bodies. Atl watched as the two Tlaxcalans dragged the unlucky soldier to an open part of the field and laid him on a large rock and with quick ritual honors tore part of his bloody insides, his heart, from his chest. The Tlaxcalan masses watched reverently as they retreated.

As the square moved deeper into them, Tlaxcalans began to circle it, and the tired soldiers on the two rear lines were more exposed. De Escalante shouted and the square parted at the rear, and the lines swung open as the pike men's square had done, and with effort pushed the Tlaxcalans back into a flat front. At that point the soldiers formed a long straight line and Atl and the capitán had no protection to their rear.

Atl felt something brush his foot and looked down. A wounded, bloody-faced Tlaxcalan lay there. He grabbed Atl's ankle. Atl jumped but it was too late. He could not break the tight, one-handed grip. Then the warrior's other hand showed with a bone knife, and blindly swung it at Atl's legs, missing. Then, still awkwardly holding Atl's ankle, he rolled over and jumped to his feet, making Atl fall. Atl clawed at the ground as he was dragged away. He grabbed and hugged the neck of a dead body for an anchor, terrified as his face pressed the lifeless face. His ankle would not come free. It would only rotate, slipping in the sweat. He rolled and twisted, avoiding the knife. He yelled. Two other Tlaxcalans made it around one end of the soldier's lines and came running to help his captor. The square kept moving forward, away from him, now closing again, without him.

Who would care? His mother! But she was dead. One-Cip' and Deer of Stone were nowhere near. Again he saw a flash of Dahlia. Was she even alive? He screeched and cackled loudly as he had on the mountain hunt. As long as he rolled and twisted, the warrior had to think more about holding than stabbing. Atl tried to trip him with his free foot, but it only made him madder and stab more wildly. The knife hit his legs several times. The two other warriors jumped over Atl and reached for his arms.

There was a sudden darkening. A body flew over Atl and hit the wounded warrior in the middle with a thump and a loud grunt. The warrior let go of the ankle, and Alonso's red hat landed on Atl's stomach. The other two warriors stepped back, then ran for Alonso. Atl scrambled up quickly and, before he could stop himself, kicked dirt in the downed warrior's bloody face. Alonso stood to defend himself, but the Tlaxcalans overpowered him and started dragging him away. Atl screamed for help, but the square had tightened its lines.

"Get back in the square!" shouted Alonso.

"No!" Atl could not leave Alonso who had saved him. What could he do? He looked in his hands. He had only the red cloth hat.

With effort, Alonso drew his sword. The Tlaxcalans holding his arms swung their clubs, hitting him once on the back of his bare head. He fell forward, but when they let go of him he caught himself and started running back toward his place in the lines. They laughed as his armor slowed him, clattering noisily, and they began to catch up.

"The cart!" shouted Alonso to Atl. "You can't help me!"

Atl had not stayed in the High Valley long enough to be well-trained in fighting. But he ran to a spot between Alonso and the chasers. "No!" shouted Alonso. All Atl had to fight with was the red hat. It was soft and harmless, but he threw it at them.

And to his surprise, they stopped to grab it and fight over it. Quickly he turned and ran with Alonso and they were able to make it back to the square. The soldiers let them through. The capitán was mad, pointing at Atl with his sword and shouting, "To your duties!" Atl saw two fallen swords and picked them up and returned them as soon as their owners could turn and signal him. He noticed bloody cuts on his arms and legs, but none were deep.

***

The day dimmed and quieted. None of the masses on the hillsides had come back onto the field to help the Red and Whites, who began to stand in place without dancing or shouting or waving their weapons, without the sounds of the drums behind them. The jaguar-man was nowhere to be seen. Sant-yago commands echoed from tired throats. "At ease," said de Escalante to his men, just loud enough. The Tlaxcalans began searching through the bodies and pulling them off the field, glancing up at the Sant-yagos now and then. The Sant-yagos counted and called out names. Finally, one by one, they sat down and dressed their wounds. As far as Atl could tell, few of them had been killed, though many were wounded, and the field was littered with dead Tlaxcalans. He feared that Deer of Stone could be hurt, or others of his

186

people, or Mendez. He wished he knew where they were, which parts of the battle they had fought in.

The Tlaxcalans had made at least one ritual sacrifice of a Sant-yago. The Sant-yagos, even though they had made no ritual sacrifice, seemed to think themselves the victors. The square, slow and tired, made camp and posted watches. Atl lay down. In the new calm, he slept as he never had, without a thought of Ixtilton.

Early the next morning, just as the soldiers were rising and groaning, six Tlaxcalans stood at a distance without weapons or paint, bowing. De Escalante sent six soldiers out, with drawn swords held low at their sides. They walked slowly and carefully. Finally they met the Tlaxcalans, who gave them a small piece of animal skin and turned and left. The soldiers brought it back. Pictures had been burned onto it. The capitán called for an interpreter.

"'Welcome to you, warriors of Don Carlos,'" said the interpreter, reading the pictures, "'welcome as honored guests, into the great city of Tlaxcala.'" The interpreter looked up at the capitán. "It is said to be from Chief Xicotenga."

"Quickly," said de Escalante. "Take it to Cortés."

Chapter 20

"Rachel!" shouted Howard, scanning the woods where the Greenshirts had disappeared. "Rachel!" He looked at the other team members. "We've got to find her. Spread out."

Smith stared sadly at the stream where he and Zoe had tried to hand-sign with Tetl. He proclaimed with slow sobriety, "They have deceived us." He looked at Howard. "How long have they been gone?"

"The longer," said Howard, "the farther away."

"And the smaller chance of tracking them," said Blake.

"Tracking them?" said Zoe. "You're not like…"

"Blake!" Howard pointed across the stream. "do you see a trail?"

"Maybe."

"I'm gone," said Howard, and ran to cross. Blake ran with him.

"Boys!" said Smith, oddly.

They slipped several times but didn't fall.

"Blake!" shouted Zoe. "Howard! Don't let him!"

Howard said to Blake, "They need you here."

"They're safer here than Rachel is there," said Blake. "And you can't find trails."

"Wait!" said L.P. behind them. He slipped and fell in the stream.

"Stay here!" said Howard as he and Blake scrambled up the opposite bank. "We can't risk it!" He was annoyed. His shoulder hurt.

"Risk what?" said L.P.

"Your… clumsiness!" said Howard to his truest friend.

L.P. slipped awkwardly and fell again.

"This way," said Blake. They ran into an open muddy area. "Look." He pointed at two parallel sets of prints. "These are deeper."

"So…"

"So they're carrying something."

Their bare feet patted wet sticks and leaves for an hour. The ground was rocky here, soft there, sometimes muddy, mostly uphill. They ducked tree limbs, skirted underbrush, splashed through streams, fell, got up. Howard took the falls and the fire in his shoulder as a welcome distraction, a blurring of the shock and fear of Rachel's disappearance.

Blake said, between huffs, "They didn't cover their tracks."

Howard thought about that. "So it could be a trap."

"Maybe."

They crossed a break in a ridge and ran beside a wide, swift stream. They reached a point where the stream crashed from around a mountain, then barely saw on its other side, high on a rock out-cropping, textured and colored like the woods, a basket-style hut.

They slowed. More huts. Then in the dark shadows of the trees Howard saw a young man in the dark green cotton of the People of the First Sacrifice, sullen and resigned, maybe contemptuous, his posture like the beggars of Atlanta.

Then they were surprised to see, ahead on the trail, a dozen Greenshirts and their leader Tetl.

Howard shouted, "Rachel! Where is Rachel?" He frantically swept his hands across in front of himself to mean a prone body. He put his palms together and leaned his cheek against them to mean sleeping. He raised his hands and eyebrows to mean a question.

Tetl was a foot shorter, but seemed taller. He cocked his head as if he had to look around something to see Howard. "Ra-chul," he said, and pointed across the stream, at the huts on the mountainside. Then he motioned for everybody to follow him.

"Hey," came L.P.'s voice from far behind.

Howard looked. L.P. was stumbling, panting.

"How'd you get here?" said Howard.

L.P. motioned as if to say keep going. When he caught up, he said to Blake, "What do they want with us?"

But Howard answered. "Tetl says Rachel's over there, on the other side of the stream."

L.P. said, "Did we catch the fabled People of the First Sacrifice in a moment of niceness? They're gonna show us Rachel before they..." He stopped himself.

"We're three more for their gods," said Blake.

L.P. backed up. "Let's find her, but... let's keep our distance."

Howard ran ahead and asked Tetl again, "Where is Rachel?" Tetl motioned Howard back.

Howard knew he had hurt L.P.'s feelings. He dropped back beside him and said to the woods ahead, "I guess I'm sor... uh... ry. About... you know... saying what I said."

Suddenly L.P. pointed up into a tree, and Howard looked and tripped on a huge root, which L.P. carefully avoided. Howard landed in a black, gritty puddle. L.P. walked on without looking. Tetl turned to watch Howard but kept walking, backwards. The others glanced and laughed. Blake offered to help, but Howard waved him off and got up in two tries, his bare feet slipping, the pain shooting through his shoulder.

Howard caught up, annoyed. "What'd you point at?"

L.P. looked him up and down, at his ragged, wet, muddy cotton. "I believe you were saying something earlier about me being clumsy?"

Howard brushed his shirt and scanned the mountainside. "You are clumsy."

They followed the trail and the stream around the mountain and saw, in the thick woods on its slopes, more huts.

They came to a narrower part of the stream where it had cut a craggy bed about thirty feet deep. Two pine logs lay across it, side by side, the large end of one next to the small end of the other, making a bridge of about twenty feet. The logs were not roped together and sagged unevenly in the center. The bark was worn away along their walking surfaces, so that they were slick with mist from the violent splashing against the jagged rocks below. Tetl shouted over the noise of the stream, his voice thin against the roar, motioning for them all to walk across.

L.P. stepped back and shouted over the roar, "No way!"

Howard, and even Blake, refused. Tetl pointed across the stream. "Ra-chul." He walked out on the logs, about six feet, turned, held his arms straight out on each side of him, and with a certain authority, ran in place. The logs bounced alternately under him.

"No way!" shouted L.P. again, looking away. "No way!"

Then Tetl turned and ran all the way across, arms outstretched. The logs bounced so much that he had to bend his knees almost to his chest with each step. He actually hopped once or twice. His bare feet turned outward and wrapped over the tops of the logs. Then he turned and bounded back across in the same way.

"That mountain's like an island!" shouted L.P. "Looks like this stream goes almost all the way around. If we cross, we'll be trapped!"

Tetl shouted something and one Greenshirt lay on his back in front of him. Tetl and another Greenshirt picked him up, one by his feet, the other by his shoulders, and they carried him, bouncing and swaying, across.

Then, still on the other side, Tetl shouted, "Mosh!"

The sullen young man Howard had seen earlier showed.

Tetl motioned for Mosh to come down to the stream. Mosh slowly obeyed. He stood at the ends of the logs as Tetl high-stepped back across them and held out his arms as if to say, "Who's first?"

Howard tried to focus. He had always stuck with commitments. His dad had built that into him. That was why he rarely committed. But Rachel was over there. He had only known her for a few months. The kiss on the divide, the everlasting half-minute of oneness, her jumping in against the cat, leaving him only injured and herself near death, moved him to speak. "I'll go."

Tetl barked again at Mosh, who bent slowly and put his hands on the ends of the logs, steadying them with his body weight. Then Tetl motioned for Howard to turn his back to him. Howard did and Tetl grabbed him and pulled him back and caught him under the arms. The fire shot through his shoulder. He squinted and gritted his teeth and said, "Rachel." He closed his eyes. Someone else picked up his feet. The crossing was thankfully less animated than Tetl's earlier ones. They put him down gently on his feet, and his knees gave way, but he caught himself awkwardly before he hit the ground. The Greenshirts laughed as if he had intended to fall as a joke.

He couldn't see much in the thick woods rising into the village.

Tetl and the other carrier bounced back across the logs and brought Blake in the same way, then L.P., moaning loudly.

Blake said, "If we have to get out, I think we could hug those logs and crawl back across."

"With Rachel?" said L.P. "You're crazy."

"Other thought," said Blake, "that stream can't go all the way around the mountain."

"You're saying there's a back door somewhere?"

"Should be."

"Rachel," said Howard to Tetl.

Tetl began walking toward the village. Everybody followed, up the mountain path between big trees and rocks and into the village.

The huts were well-camouflaged and far apart. Howard couldn't see more than six or eight of them from any one place. It occurred to him that none of it could be seen from the sky, even on a clear day. Most were basket-style huts, like the one Howard and Rachel and L.P. built, but better, with vines woven tightly between thin vertical poles driven into the ground. Other huts were made of stacked blocks of earth. Most doors and windows were hung on the inside with gray or green cloth. Some roofs were covered with big leathery leaves in different shades of brown, lapped like shingles. Others were of thatched grass. The walls of two long huts followed the curves of the rock outcroppings they were built on. At several huts, men were climbing on them, repairing the roof or adding a room.

Then, ahead of them, next to one of the huts, stood Tee-week, dressed like the Greenshirts.

"Tee-week!" said Howard.

Tee-week looked away quickly, but joined the procession.

"Tee-week," said Howard again. "Where's Rachel?"

Tee-week avoided eye contact and shrugged.

"These people don't act like they sacrifice humans," said L.P.

"What I've read..." said Howard. "Human sacrifices were done decently and in order, so to speak."

"Good. That's just the way I want them to cut my heart out."

"I don't know about these people," said Howard. "But the Aztecs were well organized: commerce, schools, world-class art, architecture. They did human sacrifices like going to a ball game. Crowds cheered. Getting the victims ready was a big thing. They even honored them."

"Could these people be some kind of Aztecs?"

"Who knows?" said Howard. "Let's just get Rachel out."

The trail through the village was long and rocky. The Greenshirts seemed weightless, walking little ridges and gullies easily. Tetl tripped a couple of times, distracted by dignity-maintenance.

Finally they reached a small clearing where tortillas and beans and avocadoes were laid out in clay dishes on a reed mat. There were several plump papayas. Tetl poured water from a large clay bowl into a smaller one. In it, he and the others scrubbed their hands.

"Mm, finger bowls," said L.P. wiggling his fingers daintily.

Tetl motioned for Howard and Blake and L.P. to do the same, and they did. Tetl raised his arms, said something, lowered them, and held them out, toward the spread.

L.P. grinned. "We get to eat?" Then his face dropped. "They're fattening us up." But he dropped to his knees and dug in, then Blake and Howard. All the food was fresh. The only seasoning was chili peppers, too much for Howard, but bearable. There were cloths for wiping fingers.

When they had their fill, Tetl got up and led them all, including Tee-week, back to the trail and farther up the mountain. They came to a wide, flat area. The path joined several other paths passing around a ring of small, loose stones piled about a foot high. Inside the ring was smoothed sand about twenty feet across.

Tetl stopped just outside the ring and stood, feet apart, where all of them could see him. He bent his knees and adjusted his elbows and feet. He cocked his head and turned it up to look at Howard. He spoke forcefully, with dramatic gestures, sometimes hitting his palm with his fist. When he stopped, he glared at them.

Howard had the sudden, frightening thought that Tetl was answering, with hand motions, his earlier questions about Rachel, that she had been sacrificed there. He felt the blood drain from his face.

Then Tetl pushed at the air with both hands, grunting and shaking his head. "Nok!"

He spoke to Tee-week, who looked at Howard, pointed at the ring, and said clearly in English, "No."

L.P. whispered, "Tee-week remembers an English word."

"But," whispered Howard, "No… what?"

"Probably 'no, you better not do anything wrong around here.'"

It was true, Tetl's demeanor, as well as the general orderliness of the village, implied a serious code of conduct, and if so, even though it might include violence, it would not be arbitrary. There would be, most likely, as they had hoped, rules. Sacrifices would be ceremonial, which would give them time to respond, or to debate if debate was possible, or to plan a way to get Rachel out, if she were there, and if she were still alive, and if escape were possible.

"Rachel," said Howard to Tetl.

Tetl stared at him, then drew back, turned, and walked up another rough trail, head forward. Once he stopped and pointed back at the ring of stones and said firmly, "Nok!"

Blake said, as they stared, "I don't like that place."

"That place is Trouble with a big 'T,'" said L.P.

"Have you guys ever heard of stoning?" said Blake.

"Oh, c'mon," said Howard.

L.P. said, "Don't get in trouble with the law. Big-'T' Trouble."

They saw women for the first time. Several were gathered around a young, attentive girl. They seemed to instruct her, seriously.

"Pretty low student-teacher ratio," said L.P.

Sometimes eyes peered out of hut windows. The smell of small fires reminded Howard of family camping trips when he was a kid. Did Rachel's family camp? Her image came and went.

Then Tetl stopped in front of a number of scattered stone markers, like a graveyard. The stones were not carved, but rounded and smooth, like river-rocks. He held a hand out to one of the markers and the newly filled dirt beside it and looked at Howard. Howard saw that, tucked under the stone was a piece of yellow cloth.

Tetl lifted the rock and pulled out a pair of broken earphones.

"The pilot!" said L.P. "They've buried him."

They stared at the grave, then Howard said, "You don't think they found him still breathing, and carried him up here so they could sacrifice him?"

"That's it," said L.P. "That's it."

"He should've at least had a Christian burial," said Blake.

"If he was a Christian," said L.P.

"He was Honduran." Blake closed his eyes. "Our Father who art in heaven…" Howard and L.P. joined in, mangling the few parts they could remember from Sunday School.

Tetl waited until they opened their eyes, then led them again up the slope. "Ra-chul."

"A mountain can only be so high," said Blake.

Suddenly a shout came from one side of them and tree branches bent and leaves whipped and there was what seemed a large animal but was actually a human in animal skins swinging toward them, vine to vine, howling like a monkey. The howls echoed from the mountains. L.P. and Blake and Howard hit the ground at the same time. The man swung over their heads on a long springy vine, with a large dipping rhythm, screeching, glaring, disappearing into the brush beyond, leaving an acrid after-odor.

Tee-week seemed as puzzled as the three. One of the Greenshirts watched his reaction and laughed so hard he started hitting the sides of his head. Others laughed as well.

Tetl didn't laugh. He seemed annoyed. He said, "Kee-ah!" with disgust. He put a hand over his mouth and nose and looked at the other Greenshirts. One mumbled, "Sho-lo-peet," and they all laughed again.

"Sensitive soul," said L.P., staring after the sho-lo-peet.

Tetl led them to a curving hut with a few stone steps. In front of it, hanging by its trigger guard from a tree limb, was Crauder's pistol.

They stared open-mouthed. L.P. said, "How did...?"

Tetl smiled and nodded as if proud of it.

"Okay," said L.P. "The Jaguar-people took the pistol from Crauder. So it had to come from them to here. So, obviously, there's a connection between these tribes."

Blake shook his head. "Not a close one, I think."

"Tee-week came from the Jaguar-people." said Howard.

"But," said L.P., "the Jaguar-people left Tee-week with us when they took the pistol. He didn't have it. So how'd it get here?"

No answer. The stream roared far below. Gray smoke from a wood fire drifted up and was lost in all the rising mist. Beyond the pistol Howard noticed, through a few small openings in the trees, miles of rising forests and distant blue ridges, possibly forming the edge of the wilderness. And he made out a gap.

"Blake," he said, studying the gap. "How far is that ridge?"

Blake shrugged. "Ten, twelve miles."

Tetl led them all into the hut, talking importantly.

It was dark, but Howard made out a young woman on her knees. He had a fleeting thought that it could be Rachel, but as his eyes adjusted, he saw that her hair shone softly black. And she was pregnant. She had a wet cloth and was gently wiping something – a red arm, the only bare skin showing out of a lumpy mass of clean green cotton in the shape of a woman, lying on a stuffed, mattress-like bag of the same green cotton.

Howard wanted it not to be Rachel still in that deathly condition and wanted to have found her. He said, "Rachel?"

Tetl held both hands out toward the prone body. "Ra-chul."

***

Howard's knees gave way and hammered the stone floor. His eyes stung, staring at the wrapped head, the tuft of light brown hair, the nose and mouth holes, the glint of a tooth. He leaned over and assured himself there was breathing. He saw the old scar on the back of the swollen wrist. Then he was overcome, and wept.

Someone blocked the light at the door. It was Tee-week. He walked straight to the opposite side of the hut and knelt. Howard heard a groan from there, and saw another green mass of cloth and a black-haired woman lying in it, turning.

It seemed they were in a primitive hospital. There was no furniture. The floor was the slightly curved top of the stone outcropping on which the hut was built. Everything was clean, even a bright green grasshopper on a window ledge.

Blake turned and walked softly to the door and stood facing out.

Howard touched Rachel's shoulder wrappings, then the bare, hot skin of her now-clean arm. No response.

He felt his old urge to run, in its most physical sense.

The young woman dipped the cloth in a clay pot of water.

Rachel's chin pointed up, as if straining against the air while fighting a painful, motionless battle inside herself. Her breathing was still hoarse, but less labored than before. Was that a sign of strengthening or weakening? He wondered if she had any idea that she was in the village of the People of the First Sacrifice, who may sacrifice her. Could he save her as effectively as she had saved him? Would she ever again have a thought or a memory of him?

He lightly rubbed water onto her arm. He lifted the maddeningly small tuft of her hair. It had been washed. It embarrassed him to speak her name in front of the others who must have known it was pointless.

The oneness he had discovered between them on the divide had struck him as something new and important, even as it caved so easily under the pressure of more natural impulses. And he wondered again whether she had sensed it, and if she had doubted, as he had, that it was anything more than a dream-wish. A painful throbbing went down his spine and through his body, so painful that tears came. He wrapped his arms around himself, not caring that the physical pain hit his shoulder again, or that another pain was now in his knees where they had slammed against the stone floor.

The nurse's eyes rounded. She lightly touched his forearm. She seemed to know his feelings. He wished she could explain them to him.

Did he love Rachel? Had Rachel loved him? What was love? On the divide he chased her even though she resisted. Then she stopped resisting. Were those things love? What was her 'costly love,' her 'love-

love?"

She jumped in when el tigre attacked. She could have run away. No one would have faulted her. But, knowing her, she would have probably done it for anyone. So had there been anything at all special?

When he got up the nurse smiled and said softly, "Ra-chul." Her chubby, red-gold face was smooth and calm. She was neither aggressive nor shy, ready to serve but not servile.

Finally he got up and he and L.P. walked to the door where Blake stood studying the pistol still hanging from the limb. Several Greenshirts stood outside.

"Four chambers are empty," said Blake.

"Crauder always kept it fully loaded," said L.P. "He showed me."

"None of us ever fired it," said Howard.

It hung by a twisted cotton string, perfectly still, pointing down.

"So how'd it get from the Jaggies to here?" said L.P.

Blake shrugged. "And why?"

"Maybe they think it's magic," said Howard.

Blake nodded.

"Anyway," said L.P., "how do we get out?"

Howard pointed through the mist. "Maybe that gap."

Blake studied it, then glanced at Rachel's hut. "It's not just the mountains holding us."

"We could take her with us," said Howard. "They carried her some distance and she survived it."

Blake pointed at a couple of sticks he had stuck into the ground, leaning against each other. "My 'sextant.' That gap's west. At minimum, a long, hard day walking."

"Tegucigalpa's west, isn't it?" said Howard.

"The mountains and rivers get rougher that way. And, no maps."

L.P. said, "Somebody's got to let the team know where we are."

"Do you think they'll come?" said Howard. "DeSparr? Haughton-Alsef? The Crauders? And will these people take them in?"

About that time Tetl and Tee-week stepped out of the hut.

"Let's ask," said L.P.

First Howard used the few words he had learned and lots of hand motions to try to ask Tetl what they planned to do with Rachel, but Tee-week didn't get it. Then he tried to get Tetl's okay for the rest of the team to come and stay, and after Tee-week helped translate, Tetl agreed, holding his arms out toward the village as an invitation.

"I'll go," said Blake, "But the team will want to know, and I need an answer. Just how hostile are these Greenshirts?"

"Tell 'em anything," said L.P. "We need numbers. Tell 'em they're not very hostile so far. That's not a lie."

The limb in front of them moved in a breeze and the pistol flashed bits of misty skylight and swung back and forth against the glimpse of the far gap.

Tetl insisted they all follow him down to the stream, where they watched Blake cross the logs slowly and carefully, arms out, with a Greenshirt girl in front and a boy behind, spotting him.

"Do you think he'll come back?" said L.P.

"Blake's good for his word," said Howard. "But the others…?"

"They'll come for the food if nothing else."

Blake waved from the other side, then walked briskly off into the woods.

Tetl walked back up the trail into the village. One boy, about nine or ten, chubby except for his skinny head and huge ears straight out, stayed and watched Howard and L.P. with folded arms, as if sizing them up. He grinned proudly and pointed at his tummy. "Peets."

After an awkward silence, Howard echoed, "Peets."

Peets grinned, then slapped Howard's stomach and laughed and leaned back and stared at him as if he had asked a question and was proud to listen for the answer.

"Howard." Such familiar bravado in a kid annoyed Howard.

"Hyde," said Peets, grinning. Then he slapped L.P.'s stomach.

L.P. frowned. "L.P."

"Ebbee," he said. He started back up the trail with a sort of swagger, then stopped. "Hyde, Ebbee."

It was late, and cooler in those higher mountains than it had been for them yet. Several villagers put on light quilted vests.

"Do you think these people can support us?" said L.P. "Our whole team?"

"Probably," said Howard. "I don't know whether I should be glad to have the extra numbers, or afraid Crauder or DeSparr or somebody will do something to make them mad." He looked back up the mountain. "I want to go back and check on Rachel."

The two men who had stayed with them started to walk up the trail, and Peets motioned with his hand for Howard and L.P. to follow. They led them toward Rachel's hut, but stopped at a vacant hut just downhill from hers. It was dark inside, but Howard could see two clean stuffed bag-mattresses like the ones in her hut, and two neatly hand-sewn cotton quilts.

The two men held their hands out as an invitation, then left. "This must be our room," said Howard.

"Not bad." L.P. lay on one of the mattresses. "Considering." "Not bad at all," said Howard, but L.P. was already snoring.

Howard sat on the other bag. How would the other team members behave here? What chances did Rachel have against not only her injuries, but the People of the First Sacrifice? How much time did she have? Was the pilot still alive when the Greenshirts found him? Did they sacrifice him? Eat him? Why else would they bring him?

He crept to the door. It was completely dark, no lights inside or outside the huts. Here and there a star blinked between black leaves. In one direction he could see all the way to the stream far below, where stars were reflected. He made out the silhouette of a man standing as a guard, not moving, but seeming to move against the flow.

Then he heard a soft murmuring from some of the huts. He crept back in and lay on the bag-mattress and felt a relief in his back. He listened. The murmuring became a sound strange for that black night. Singing. It started in one hut, then spread, with a simple harmony. Some voices were smooth, some coarse, most nasal. Men and women and children. It was not based on the eight-note scale. Five, maybe. He would have been fascinated were he not disgusted by their peaceful sound, who sacrificed humans. Nazis ordered the killings of millions of innocent people and sang of civil pride. Marxists ordered the killings of millions of innocent people and sang of sharing.

The singing grew stronger and more in concert. He was glad L.P. was asleep because he began to weep. Not just for Rachel, or for his sense of loss. And not just for the way the singing almost made the People of the First Sacrifice seem gentle. But because it gave him a sense of some great lack, maybe internal, maybe universal. He pulled his quilt up. Though he wept, he didn't want the singing to stop. When it did, he was asleep.

Chapter 21

"The Cholulans are friends of the Aztecs," said Atl. The army's long line stretched up from the river, where they had forded, to the high ground just outside Cholula.

"So I have heard," said Deer of Stone.

They walked with the others from their village, happy that they had all survived the great Sant-yago-Tlaxcalan battle.

On the other side of the trail were green fields of maize, and beyond them, blue-green valleys and gray-blue forests where gentle winds spread waves across the tree-tops, and beyond all that rose blue mountains, and the white peaks of Popocatepetl and Ixtaccihuatl shone like unmoving clouds. And on the other side of them, they all knew, lay the High Valley, and the city of the Aztecs, and its upside-down twin in its wide blue lake.

"Out there," said Balanced Turtle, "is a clear, cool stream."

"I wish that were all we had to think of," said one-Cip'.

Cortés led the Sant-yago and Totonac lines into the city. The two thousand Tlaxcalan warriors remained outside the walls.

"The Tlaxcalans and Cholulans are old enemies," said One-Cip'.

"Will there be another battle?" Atl could learn fighting skills and some day use them against the killers of his mother.

One-Cip' frowned. "We will leave all this when we can."

"But where will we go?"

"First, we can go to what is left of our village. Then to a land I know of, where there are no battles or sacrifices or gods."

"What is this Cholula town like?"

"They pay regular tribute to Motecuhzoma."

"Will it not anger Motecuhzoma that they have welcomed the Sant-yagos? You have said that Cortés wants to fight the Aztecs."

One-Cip' ducked as they squeezed through the gate. "Maybe. But if Cortés doesn't fight the empire down, he may talk it down."

Feathers on the Water said to de Escalante nearby, "It is a trap. Inside the town walls they can slaughter you. They have separated you from the Tlaxcalans to weaken you."

"Cortés knows of this possibility. We will be ready."

"Also, there are often many Aztec warriors camped nearby."

"We know."

Then Atl saw the avenue, like Cempoala's, with stone buildings and pyramids lining each side. The people stood along the avenue and on the tops of the buildings, watching. The line of soldiers ahead turned into an opening between two buildings.

"Look," he said to Deer of Stone. Cholulan men with bright feathers and gold and silver bracelets bowed pleasantly and pointed the way into a great paved court wide enough for thousands of people, enclosed on all sides by stone buildings.

Boys and girls came out among the soldiers with clay dishes stacked high with tortillas and fish and papayas and beans and tomatoes. They even served Atl and Deer of Stone as if they were as important as the soldiers.

"I like the way they pepper it," said Balanced Turtle.

"This," said Deer of Stone, "is the best meal we have had since… In a long time."

"Be watchful," said One-Cip'. "Much of this is like the treatment of captives who are to be sacrificed."

"But we are not captives," said Atl.

"Listen," And they listened and could hear, over the clattering and talking of the soldiers, from several directions beyond the walls and buildings around them, the regular digging and scraping of earth and chopping of wood.

Beyond the west walls, as Tonatiah sank, Atl could see the pink snow of Popocatepetl, and the orange smoke darkening upward to gray.

Even the stone floor of the court let them sleep well, and another rich meal the next morning strengthened them. When they rose and began gathering and stacking and arranging supplies and equipment as the Sant-yagos directed, they saw town leaders and priests pass on their way to and from a room on the far side of the court. Twice, when the door was opened, they saw Doña Marina inside, and once Cortés.

About noon Capitán de Escalante came out of the room with a

Cholulan man and a boy about Atl's age and called for three Totonac volunteers. When he got them he also volunteered Atl. "Go out with these men to the Tlaxcalans." He gave the oldest Totonac a note. "Find Mangetl and give him this. Each of you bring back two bags of harquebus balls." He pointed at three carts. "And bring those back full of cross-bow arrows."

Atl felt a chill. He glanced back but could not see One-Cip'.

The oldest of the Totonacs asked, "Will there be a battle?"

"Precautions only," said de Escalante. "But keep the arrows covered, out of sight."

"But where… how do we…?"

De Escalante pointed at the Cholulan man and boy. "These will show the way. They have a pass. Act as if you are only carting straw and firewood." He put his hand on his sword and glared at Atl the way he did in the Great Battle. "Do not tell anyone anything. Clear?"

"Yes."

The boy quickly lifted a handle of one of the carts with one hand, holding his other behind his back. Atl took the other handle. "I'll help you," he said in Nahuatl. "Do you know Nahuatl?"

"Yes."

Two of the Totonacs pulled the other two carts, and they all left the court and followed the Cholulan man along a narrow, winding route through the town, avoiding the main avenues and plazas.

"What is your name?" said the boy.

"Atl. What is yours?"

"Tree. I fish with the net."

"So? I use only the spear. The spear is better."

"I like the spear, but…" Tree grinned, "I get more with the net."

"Yes," said Atl. "No doubt. But the net makes it too easy."

"So?" said Tree, and they both laughed.

"I was in the Great Battle," said Atl, " between the Sant-yagos and the Tlaxcalans."

"Sant-yagos? These iron-hats? The men of 'Don Carlos?'"

"In battle they shout…" Atl was suddenly embarrassed to claim to repeat such brave words. He made a funny face and wagged his head, "Sant! Yago!" They laughed again.

"What was it like?" said Tree.

Atl grinned sheepishly. "I was scared." Secretly he felt that Tree must have been impressed.

"I would have been scared too," said Tree.

They walked out onto a narrow trail between maize fields. "Have you been to the High Valley?" said Atl. "For training?"

"Tenochtitlán? No."

"I have," said Atl, surprised at feeling proud of what had been a true horror.

Tree held out his left arm, the one that had been behind his back, showing Atl that it was shriveled. "They didn't want me."

Atl was shocked. He stared. "You would have done better than I," he said. "I almost got killed."

"I am glad you did not," said Tree. "Be watchful and careful. I hear people talk. They think the iron-hats do not fight fair. They think the iron-hats deserve to be slaughtered like animals, as they have slaughtered others, rather than be honored in a captive-battle."

Atl felt less sure of the day.

The Cholulan man led them into the Tlaxcalan camp. He shouted, "Where is Mangetl? We have a message from the iron-hats!"

A man came and they talked, then directed Atl and Tree loading bundles of thick, heavy arrows into the cart.

"For these," said Atl, "the Sant-yagos use bows mounted on big sticks. They aim better that way, and shoot farther."

Tree seemed impressed. The Cholulan man mumbled as they started back to the town, "Mangetl says that my town is planning a trap. But I am sure they are not."

"Yesterday," said Atl, proud to add important facts, "I heard Totonacs warning the Sant-yagos of a trap in the town."

"Rumors. The Cholulans will not harm them."

"They said there are many Aztecs outside the walls," said Atl, "ready to help in the trap."

"Sometimes the Aztecs camp nearby. But not today."

"Anyway," said Atl, feeling important talking of such things with a man of this great city, "the Sant-yagos say they are ready for any Aztecs and any Cholulans. That is what these weapons are for."

Then something in the man's face caused Atl to suddenly fear he had talked too much, had given away secrets. If the Cholulans were planning a trap, Atl should reveal nothing of what the Sant-yagos knew or said. He hardly knew these Cholulans. Feathers on the Water and the officer had trusted him enough not to hide their talk from him. Now he had betrayed their trust. But maybe it was common information. Maybe it did not matter.

"Here!" shouted One-Cip' across the court to Atl when he was back and had turned his cart and bags of harquebus balls over to de Escalante. Atl went to him as the capitán sent Tree and the Cholulan man to the far side of the court.

"Stay away from battles," said Tree, waving with his good hand as they parted. "I hope to see you again."

Atl waved. "Me too," he said, and thought: a new friend is a good thing. He said, "Do not eat all the fish you catch with your net."

Tree said, "Do not starve for so few catches with your spear!"

They both laughed.

Two Sant-yago officers stood with One-Cip'.

"What did you hear?" said One-Cip', tired and worried.

Atl knew what that meant, but he needed to think. "Hear?"

"From the Cholulans," said One-Cip'. "Cortés fears a trap. What do you know?"

If Atl told, he would feel better about having talked too much. "I… They… The man said the talk of a trap is not true."

"He talked of a trap? What brought it up?"

"I don't know. Oh, he said the Tlaxcalans mentioned it."

"We know this," said one of the officers.

"What else?" said One-Cip'.

"That the Cholulans want us out," said Atl, "but will not hurt us. That there are no Aztecs camped outside the town at this time."

"Is that all?"

"Yes."

The officers turned and talked to each other heatedly.

One-Cip' leaned close to Atl. "They are looking for facts," he said. "And this next question is important. Did you say anything?"

"About… About <u>what</u>?"

"Did you say anything about what you have heard, anything that would let the Cholulans know the Sant-yagos expect a trap?"

"I… No!" he lied. "Why would I…"

"Good," said One-Cip', believing Atl without pause, Atl who had never lied to his mentor who had taught him the value of honesty from his earliest memory.

The officers turned to One-Cip'. "Did the boy say anything?"

Cold chills ran down Atl's back as he heard his own lie repeated from honest One-Cip's mouth. "Not a word."

"Are you certain? Do you put your life on it?"

A painful chill swept over Atl.

"I am Certain," said One-Cip' with no doubt of Atl's word.

Bright red heat flashed across Atl's face and his knees gave way and he fell and tried to get up. "Find a quiet place," said One-Cip'. He helped Atl up. "The trip was hard on you."

The officers left quickly and went to the room of Cortés.

Atl could not get his mouth to speak. One-Cip' walked with him to the shadow of a wall where Deer of Stone and A Fox is Mad and Two-Rabbit stood talking. Atl could not look them in the eyes after such a cowardly lie as he had told and caused his mentor to put his own life in danger by repeating. If Deer of Stone, One-Cip's son, knew, it would be the end of their old friendship. Could they see his lie in his eyes?

"Bad chicle," said A Fox is Mad, spitting. "The Sant-yagos are easily cheated at market."

"What does the chicle tell you?" said Two-Rabbit.

"Bad time coming. Bad for many. A tragedy among us."

"Do not scare us old man," said One-Cip'. "Not today."

Atl sat against the wall in pain. He thought that he should confess to One-Cip'. But how could he tell him he lied to him and worse, stood by when he put his life on it.

Maybe it was because Atl did not take A Fox is Mad's prediction seriously, or because he thought One-Cip' was always able to handle anything, but he said nothing. And he saw again the fierce swarm of faces glaring at him from the air around him, taking away from him, and not being real but seeming real and coming closer, and he could not sleep but he could not think about any one thing either and could not remember, when morning came, what he had thought about through the night, but he knew that he had hardly slept at all and that when he did sleep he had horrible dreams in which he was always in the middle of the swarm of faces and even he himself had fierce greedy eyes as they did and his mouth breathed out hot choking smoke with words that said he himself would be the cause of a horrible thing about to happen.

***

"This food is not so good," said Deer of Stone as the Cholulans served a meal the next morning.

"Not like what they gave us before," said A Fox is Mad.

205

"And the boys and girls do not smile today," said Two-Rabbit.

"We are past our welcome," said One-Cip'.

Atl stared at the ground, afraid to look up at One-Cip'.

A soldier near them threw down his dish. "Rotten!" he said. Others grumbled and did not eat.

Then the shout came from across the court, "A trap!"

Others shouted, "When? How?"

"At today's banquet!" came the answers.

Soldier-messengers ran through the crowds. "The Cholulans will lock the gates! They will slaughter us like rabbits in a pen! They have hidden weapons in these buildings!"

"The digging and chopping you heard!" shouted the messengers. "Barriers in the roads! Pits covered with leaves, big enough for even our horses! Spikes inside!"

"Lying Cholulan devils!" shouted a soldier.

"I have seen their skulking eyes!" shouted another.

"Sacrifices were made last night to their war god!" shouted a messenger. "Motecuhzoma has sent armies to the outskirts!"

"But Cortés has a plan!" shouted another messenger. "We will turn it around on them!"

"Hide near the gate! Prepare crossbows! Spears! Harquebuses! Cannons! Bring the horses."

"Let them in! Then lock and man the gates!"

"Shoot from the rooftops! Stab them at hand! Give them what they plan to give us!"

Deer of Stone said to Atl, "They will turn it around on them. The kind of thing we have dreamed of for the killers of our people!"

Atl's blood stirred, afraid and tired as he was, hearing the brave, shouting Sant-yagos.

"We can learn from this," said Deer of Stone.

"Mendez!" said Atl, suddenly relieved to see their tall friend.

Mendez had two iron knives. "Don't worry. I will teach you."

"Where have you been?" said Atl.

"Important business," said Mendez. "But bring these knives and follow me." He led them to a row of animal skins hanging between posts. Soldiers were stabbing at them, making holes. "Try your hand at these skins. Think of them as the killers of your village."

"Did you get the news of them?" said Atl.

"Later. Now you must practice."

206

Suddenly Deer of Stone thrust his knife into a skin and it broke through. Atl did the same, but not as eagerly or quickly, and the skin moved back and was only scratched.

"Harder!" said Mendez. "Faster! Kill!"

"Yes! Kill!" shouted Deer of Stone, stabbing again.

Atl tried again, harder, grunting, and his knife broke through.

"Your killers!" said Mendez. "Give them back what they did!"

Atl and Deer of Stone stabbed many times until the skin was shredded. Twice Atl's hand hit a post and once hit Deer of Stone's knife and he saw his own blood come, and he knew that revenge held danger, and the pain of injury gave him a kind of release from the guilt of having betrayed One-Cip'. He was gaining the skills of the Sant-yagos. He was even able to hold back his fear of harming a man if the man was the killer of innocent people.

One-Cip' watched. He seemed both sad and curious. He did not seem to know of Atl's lie, though he still stood in danger of it should the Sant-yagos find out.

The Cholulan man had tricked Atl, used his friendship with Tree. Stopping the Cholulans from killing the Sant-yagos would stop the danger to One-Cip' and ease Atl's guilt. He stabbed again and again. If Tree could see him now, bold and sure like the Sant-yagos.

And, what Dahlia would think if she could see, if she were alive!

The shouting began across the court, "Sant Iago! Sant Iago!"

An officer stood on a bench. "Quiet!" Every Sant-yago obeyed. Amazing, thought Atl. Brave warriors act together. He stood as taut as a drawn bow, and as ready.

***

The main gate was opened and all eyes turned to it. Still the soldiers strictly obeyed the order for silence. Two Cholulan men stepped through and raised conch shells and blew long notes as they walked. Solemn blackened priests and town chiefs in bright colors followed. They stopped and loudly announced across the court to Cortés, in Nahuatl, "We have brought you the armed warriors you requested. They will accompany you to Tenochtitlán." Behind them stood long lines of men and boys with weapons and warrior paint and padding.

"Make way!" shouted an officer, and the soldiers stood back and watched as many hundreds of Cholulans paraded into the great court.

Young Cholulans smirked, and young Sant-yagos smirked back.

When all the Cholulans were in, the gate was quietly closed by two of them, and by two of the Sant-yagos, and there was silence.

Atl had seen the Sant-yagos win and not be hurt. And now he had gained some of their skills.

The priests and town chiefs made their way to the corner where Cortés waited. Cortés sat forward on his beast and faced eastward. Atl could see the snow of Popocatepetl hanging above and far behind him. His eyes darted in his fixed, frowning face. One hand held the beast-ropes and scratched his black beard, the other rested on the hilt of his sword. Doña Marina stood beside him. He glanced at the closed gates.

Atl felt strong, alert, excited. He felt his sweat and his tight muscles and his wanting to show his new skill.

Rico swung his head and snorted and pounded the stone pavers with his hard feet. Cortés sat straight. He spoke sternly and loudly, and the translators Aguilar and Doña Marina spoke. "We have done you no harm! Why do you wish to kill us?"

The Cholulan priests seemed dumbfounded, unable to answer.

"We have done nothing to you," said Cortés, "but warn you of your wrongs: your idol-worship, your sacrificing of innocent men, your eating of human flesh. These warnings are only for your good." Cortés sat straighter. "Why have you barricaded the streets?"

Suddenly one priest started to leave, but the others caught his arm and held him.

"Why have you dug pits in the main roads? The only roads we can take to leave your city? Why spikes in them? Why have you sent your women and children away?"

The Cholulans gaped at him.

"You say, 'We have no more maize,' yet you deliver great quantities to Aztec warriors waiting outside your city." Cortés led Rico a few steps toward the priests who stepped back, surprised. A Sant-yago stood near Cortés making marks on a small skin in his hands. Aguilar and Doña Marina motioned and talked beside him. "This is your thanks after we have come like brothers to tell you of our Lord God and the orders of our great Don Carlos. Instead you plot against us!"

Cortés took his hand off his sword and pointed. "You have sacrificed seven of your children in hope of victory in this treachery, and all in vain! Your false gods are evil and have no power over us." At that, the priests seemed shocked, but now the young Cholulans laughed, as if

Cortés were crazy. Cortés put his hand back on his sword.

Suddenly a priest looked frantically around, then at Cortés. Other priests tried to stop him. "We would never..."

"Your treason against Don Carlos," said Cortés, "will not go unpunished. Let this be a lesson for all who disobey the orders of our king!" Cortés pointed to an harquebusier on a roof who raised his weapon, then made it pop. A Cholulan fell.

"I see the devil himself!" shouted a soldier, pointing aghast at another Cholulan.

The soldiers drew swords and knives and aimed shoulder-guns and crossbows. The priests ducked and tried to hide behind each other. The Cholulan warriors raised their bows and arrows, their wooden knives and clubs. Suddenly the whole court was mad.

Iron splintered wood. Spaniards grunted and howled and thrust their knives. Cholulans fell one after the other. Some even jumped into the air as if to escape into the sky. At Tlaxcala Atl had not known until it was over who would prevail. Here he knew it would be the Sant-yagos. And he could see the Cholulans falling everywhere.

"Go!" shouted Mendez to Atl and Deer of Stone. "At them!"

Atl stepped forward, then back, then forward again.

"Swing your knife!" said Mendez. "This way!" He thrust his sword forward as if stabbing an enemy. "As I taught you!"

Atl thrust his knife at the air.

"At them!" shouted Mendez, who himself stood back.

Hundreds of Cholulans lay bleeding and groaning, the blackened priests with the rest. Some Sant-yago soldiers even laughed.

The fear in the Cholulans gave their faces the look, to Atl, of evil cowardice. He took a step forward, and this time, another, then looked back at Mendez, who pointed at a fallen Cholulan still moving. It would be easy. The greater the defeat of these people the surer was One-Cip's safety from Atl's lie, and the lesser his own guilt in it. He ran for the struggling body, but he was knocked down by another Cholulan, and he saw the wooden knife come at him and he rolled to one side and saw the desire to kill in the man's eyes. Atl stopped for just a moment, overcome with horror, that anyone would want to kill him whose mother had loved him, who had not yet found her killers, who had never spoken to Dahlia of his hope to spend his life with her. He dodged another thrust of the man's knife, then roared with madness.

He got to his feet and dodged the swinging knife until he could rare back and swing his own. It passed short, and before he knew it, a Sant-yago struck down the Cholulan and stood above him laughing, hands on his hips.

Atl turned once more to see what Mendez would advise, but he only saw his back, disappearing into the door to the room where the weapons and the officers' valuables were stored.

Atl turned but his feet got tangled in the legs of a fallen body and he fell toward another that was lying on its stomach, moving, still acting out, Atl thought, its hated, cowardly nature as if it thought it deserved to live, and he raised his knife quickly and aimed it at the back, the skin like a hairless animal's, and he brought the knife down with both hands and the body rolled over onto its back but Atl was quick, and followed its movement, and kept his aim, and put all his own weight into the aiming. Time slowed greatly and he made out the lines of the ribs and turned the knife as needed so that it would pass between them and just before it struck he saw the hand come up to block it, the withered hand, and saw the eyes wide and heard the mouth cry, "Atl!" and his weight would not stop, and he felt the knife break through the skin and the ribs and the deep flesh, and saw the eyes stare in terrified unbelief, then fade and lose focus.

At first Atl tried to jump back up as if to start over and stop himself sooner, but as he tried to pull the knife he stumbled and fell back onto the body, his own chest pushing the knife deeper. "Tree!" he shrieked over and over. He shook the body, trying to make it move again, avoiding looking at the open, unseeing eyes, finding movement only in the blood spilling and soaking into the cracks between the stone pavers. "Tree-ee!" Tree had been full of life and hope and questions and energy and caring. He had been, in such a short time, Atl's new, good friend. How could he not move, not even breathe?

Atl raised his knife and struck it against the stones, raging, where it would not enter but only chink and spray dust, striking over and over as if it would reverse the entering into Tree's body, but Tree's blood flowed and absorbed the dust Atl's knife made, and darkened. And Atl's eyes darkened and his strength left him and finally he dropped and lay across the body and his insides quit hurting and went to nothing, and he thought maybe his life was going into Tree, or Tree's death was coming into him, as it should, as he deserved it to do.

Chapter 22

Howard woke staring into lumps of daylight diffused around the woven vines of the walls of the hut, hearing a hundred birds seeming to complain and question and greet the day all at once. L.P. still slept, silently now. Howard got up and stretched and walked outside. The fog was thick, creating a sense of isolation and serenity, as in snow.

In the door of a nearby hut, barely visible, a thin, middle-aged woman in a dark green tunic and skirt stood watching him. She held a roll of sticks and colored strings under one arm, the only other color, dim in the gray-green mist. When their eyes met, she smiled shyly, looked down, then walked to a spot next to a tree and let the sticks roll out in front of her. He had already guessed they made up a loom. She pulled a strap from it over her head and around her waist, and looped a small rope from the other end around the trunk of the tree. Then she sat on a short log and her hands began moving deftly.

Howard faced in the direction of the far gap, hidden now by fog. He felt the urge in his feet, and ran in place. In the freshness of the morning, he was confident he could steal Rachel away, though he didn't know how.

L.P. staggered out, rubbing his eyes. "How's Rachel?"

"C'mon," said Howard.

The pregnant nurse from the day before was just back, relieving the night nurse. She smiled. Howard knelt. The wrappings were fresh. Rachel's breathing was still raspy and labored, her arm still swollen and red and hot, her profile still seeming to strain upward.

He pointed at the clay bowl of water, then at Rachel's mouth, and raised his eyebrows, asking the nurse. She nodded, cheered at the successful communication. She leaned forward and lifted Rachel's head. He picked up the bowl and held it to Rachel's mouth opening. He let a few tiny drops fall and nothing happened. He poured a few more, and there was a slight smack from deep in the throat and the nurse sat back and smiled at him. He kept it up, slowly, more troubled by the sickly sounds than relieved.

He looked at the nurse and repeatedly moved his hand out from his mouth and said, "Bah bah bah," to indicate words, and pointed at Rachel and looked at the nurse again, as a question.

The nurse shook her head and made a sad face.

Then came the voice of an old man from the door, startling Howard. "Hyde? Ebbee?"

Howard looked around quickly, and stood up.

The man stood silhouetted in the door, short, stooped, breathing noisily, bent a little to one side as if favoring a leg. Peets must have told him their names.

"Taht-lee," said the nurse, standing. The old man stepped with a painful limp. He patted her pregnant stomach and they hugged briefly.

Howard thought 'Taht-lee' must mean 'father,' or 'uncle.'

The man's clothes fit badly, probably because of his contorted shape. His face was deeply wrinkled. He had no teeth. His eyes were deep-set and alert, brown in pinkish white, and moist, possibly from pain, and rounded when he looked away from the nurse and up at Howard, whom he studied seriously, almost affectionately, as a grandfather might study his tall grandson.

He directed Howard's attention to Rachel and said, "Ra-chul."

Howard was surprised at his pronunciation. "Yes." He feared the man knew he cared for Rachel, who was about to be sacrificed, and wanted to help him understand what an honor it was to be.

"You Ra-chul want... be good?"

"Yes," said Howard, surprised at the English. "I want her to be well. You speak Engl... my language?"

"Eh?"

"You speak like me?"

"Spea...?"

"Talk. Say. Tell. Like me?"

"Tee-week me... tell," he said, haltingly, then bowed, with apparent pain. "Ebbee. Hyde." He pointed at his stomach and said, "Ehec," and bowed again. Howard and L.P. returned the bows awkwardly. He pointed at the nurse and said, "Chal-chee."

Chal-chee giggled and pointed at her face. "Chal-chee." Then

212

she pointed at her stomach and shrugged, grinning. No baby name yet.

Ehec leaned to one side and barely lifted a foot and set it down, paused, then took another short step. After four more, he slowly and carefully knelt on both knees beside Rachel, holding Chal-chee's hand for balance. Howard helped hesitantly at an elbow. Brownie points might help in the future. Ehec studied the wrappings, touching them. Finally he looked up and raised his hands and gently spoke what seemed a petition to a god. Chal-chee seemed pensive.

Appearing at the door was the fat little silhouette of Peets. "Ebbee! Hyde!" he said, and motioned for them to follow him and was off. Howard looked at Chal-chee, who was helping Ehec up. Howard reached for his arm and L.P. did too, making too many helpers. Chal-chee smiled and nodded toward the door. They should go with Peets.

Outside, Peets stood sideways in the fog, waiting.

"Ridiculous," said Howard.

"Do we have to humor them?" said L.P.

"Til we can make plans for getting Rachel out."

L.P. looked back. "Do you think it's okay to leave her?"

"I'm sure they'll make a big to-do before they try anything."

Peets led them past huts and intersecting paths, winding through the village. It was impossible to make a reliable mental map.

All the trails seemed to pass or start at the ring of stones.

L.P. put a foot in the sand inside the ring and wiggled his toes.

"Nok!" shouted Peets.

Several villagers rushed from nowhere, shouting, "Nok! Nok!"

L.P. jerked his foot back. One villager quickly brought a straw broom and, reaching from outside the ring, swept L.P.'s print smooth.

Peets signaled and led them up the trail.

"Something about that place," said Howard.

"It's Trouble with a big 'T,'" said L.P. "I told you."

"Yeah. Good thing I've got you, with all your knowledge."

"I'm telling you, keep the law… whatever the law is."

Peets led them to a pool in a stream and handed L.P. a broken piece of a kind of soap and pointed to the pool. Several men had just bathed and were getting dressed.

"Bath time," said L.P. "They want us fat and clean."

They stripped and got in. The water was cold. They scrubbed with soapy fingers for a long time. A lot of dirty water rinsed out of their matted hair and stubby beards.

"Hyde! Ebbee!" said Peets. He held up, in both hands, clean sets of dark green clothing like the villagers wore. He handed them loincloths, and they couldn't figure out how to put them on. Peets tried to show them, pointing and trying not to laugh. Howard had to favor his right arm. They finally made do.

"Good thing these people like their clothes baggy," said L.P. as they pulled the pants on. They were roomy enough but short, coming to just below their knees. The shirts were also baggy but short. Peets gave them each a little bag with strings. "Fanny packs," said L.P.

Howard opened his. Inside was the plastic bag with his book and Rachel's mother's note.

"Look," said L.P., opening his bag. "The airport photos."

Peets pointed at the photos and grinned, as if complimenting L.P. on their quality. Then he led them to a hut, where a woman invited them in. He stepped in and pointed at the walls. Several rough but cheery paintings of people and animals were colored with simple, vivid, unifying themes, boldly and thoughtfully composed, bright and cheery.

"Wow," said Howard. He and L.P. studied them for a while.

Then Peets took L.P.'s photos and talked instructively, as if making suggestions.

"He thinks these are paintings," said L.P. "Smart-mouth kid. No better'n Tee-week."

They walked on and passed four women with waist-strap looms. Howard was sure two of them giggled when they passed, and he was immediately self-conscious about the bad-fitting clothes.

The fresh, smoky smell of corn roasting in shucks wafted in the fog. Several women rolled and beat out tortillas on flat rocks. One flopped a fish on a heated rock, where it sizzled.

"Corn, cotton," said Howard. "There must be open fields."

They passed Mosh, leaning against a tree. He smirked like a kid watching a classmate being led by the ear to the principal's office.

"Look at that!" said L.P. as they rounded a curve.

Again a chill went through Howard. Four boys, or young men, in the baggy green clothes walked down toward them carrying long bows and spears. One held a heavy pointed stick. Two had quivers full of arrows on their backs. They passed, poking at Peets, teasing him. He kept his head up. Then they ran on down the trail, jumping roots and rocks, holding their bows and spears out for balance, crossed the log-bridge and disappeared into the woods.

"And who would they be?" said L.P. "Warriors?"

Howard shrugged. "Hunters, maybe. Fishers, maybe."

Several men and women with long, sharp sticks passed them.

"I know what those are," said Howard. "Coas. For digging."

"Are they about to put in a street?"

"Farmers, my guess."

"Rush hour. Everybody's going to work."

"Speaking of work," said Howard. He pointed at a crew of men and women weaving vines through skinny vertical poles, making a new basket-house. Two women wove, one on each side of the row of poles, passing the vine back and forth. Three men knelt on the stone floor laboriously sawing lengths of raw vines with crude stone knives like the one the Jaguar-people had left with Tee-week, but without the eye and tooth decorations.

"These people aren't dumb," said L.P.

"They could use better tools," said Howard.

Peets led them into a big hut. Eight men and women sat on the stone floor around a wide cloth with clay dishes piled with cooked fish and sliced papayas. Some nodded as an invitation.

Tetl was there, and offered Howard and L.P. places next to him.

L.P. said, "I haven't seen any human meat yet..."

No one got it, but when Howard said, "Shh!" they all looked.

"They don't know what I said," said L.P.

"I don't care. Just... don't say stuff like that. Be polite."

"Yes, Ma."

Tetl offered them the washing bowl and offered food.

The man sitting beside Howard seemed to want to talk, but only smiled. He was taller and thinner than the others, about Howard's age.

Tetl said something to Peets, who bowed slightly, and left.

Howard saw Tee-week sitting behind two men. He nudged L.P., then said aloud, "Hi, Tee-week."

Tee-week held his head up and looked proudly around the room. But Howard couldn't catch his eye.

L.P. whispered to Howard, "Brat."

"C'mon, L.P. I mean it."

"He ratted." L.P. leaned closer. "Got Rachel kidnapped!"

"We don't know for sure. Just play it safe. And don't forget: he learned a good bit of English from Zoe. We're going to need him."

Tee-week finally looked at Howard. "Zoe... come here?"

"Maybe," said Howard.

Tee-week pointed at his own thumb, then Howard, then at his first finger, then L.P., then he straightened all the fingers of both hands, closed them, held up seven fingers, then dropped his hands to his lap. He stared at Howard as if asking a question.

Howard showed Tee-week his own fingers. "Seventeen in all."

Then Tee-week and Tetl talked again.

The man beside Howard said, "Sho-lo-peet?" He laughed and pointed outside, nodding and grinning.

"Yes," said Howard, smiling hesitantly. "Sho-lo-peet."

Others laughed, nodding at each other, remembering. It was genuine, contagious laughter. Howard and L.P. joined in.

Then Tetl said something and everybody quieted. He raised his hands and spoke seriously. Then he held his hands out to the dishes.

The man next to Howard looked at him and pointed at his stomach and smiled. "Zomatl."

Howard pointed at himself. "Howard." Then at L.P. "L.P."

"Hyde," said Zomatl, nodding and smiling. "Ebbee." Then he pointed roughly in the direction of the hut where Rachel lay, and clasped his hands together and said, "Chal-chee, Zomatl..." It became obvious he was the husband of Rachel's nurse, Chal-chee.

Howard laid his hand on his own chest. "Rachel."

Then old Ehec stood at the door, bent, steadying himself.

Zomatl stood. Ehec walked carefully to Zomatl's spot. Howard stood and Ehec shook his head and motioned for him to sit back down, but he and Zomatl helped Ehec to the floor.

"So, if I have it right," Howard said to L.P., "Zomatl's Ehec's son-in-law."

Three people let Zomatl squeeze in on Ehec's other side.

When Zomatl sat down, his knee accidentally hit Ehec's arm. Ehec winced, then hit Zomatl's leg with the back of his hand. It wasn't a hard hit, but Zomatl was embarrassed, and moved a little farther away.

Ehec raised his hands in the same way Tetl had done. It seemed to hurt his shoulders. He opened his mouth, then stopped, lowered his hands, and stared at the wall. The skin hung heavy below his eyes as if he had been overcome by a sense of irony and loss. Then his face softened and there was a brief, moist sadness which reminded Howard of Smith. Then there came a small, bright, humble smile. His sagging shoulders lifted. He put his hand on Zomatl's shoulder and spoke softly.

It was obviously an apology. Zomatl listened seriously, then smiled and nodded. Ehec glanced down thoughtfully at the spread, spoke to Zomatl again, and they both chuckled. Then Ehec raised his hands, spoke, and everybody went back to eating.

After breakfast, Peets came and led L.P. and Howard to new huts being built. Tetl was there and made it clear they were to help.

"So before they eat us," said L.P., "they enslave us."

"I don't mind," said Howard. "Hopefully we'll have time to learn these paths, maybe find that 'back door.'"

A ring of bare vertical poles about six inches apart and about six feet high, were stuck in the ground around the sides of a wide flat rock. The rock was obviously the future floor. Three men squatted in the middle, cutting lengths of vine with the stone knives. They had to stop often to chip and sharpen the knives.

Tetl pointed at another hut nearby, almost finished, indicating that Howard and L.P. should learn from the two women weaving vines into a similar set of poles. They had almost reached the top. They hung on the sides as they worked, one hand holding to a secure vine, toes worked in where they could. There were three window openings and one door. Peets and others brought stacks of large leathery leaves.

"Roofing," said Howard.

He and L.P. stepped up closer to the two women and watched. The women smiled and worked more slowly, and leaned their heads to one side, so not to block the view.

"You ready?" said Howard to L.P.

They picked up one of the vines the men had cut.

"You know what?" said L.P. "We can show 'em how fast Americans get things done."

"Let's do it."

L.P. stood on one side of the wall and Howard on the other. They passed the vine back and forth, weaving it. Howard tried not to lift his right arm too high, though the shoulder was feeling better. The vine didn't bend easily, and had bumps and snags, and after weaving it through about ten poles, it was obvious it wasn't going to pull up tight.

What do we do?" said L.P.

"We admit defeat and ask the women," said Howard.

They stopped and asked the women, with hand signals, what to do. It took a while, but finally the women showed them how to twist the vine as they went, accommodating the snags, and pulling tight at each

217

pole rather than every few. So Howard and L.P. pulled their failed vine back out and started over, this time in less of a hurry. One of the men cutting vines next to them laughed good-naturedly as if they had done it wrong on purpose to make a joke.

They developed a rhythm.

Suddenly L.P. yelped. "Hey!"

Howard looked down. He had somehow caught L.P.'s green pants leg between a vine and a post. The other men nodded and laughed again to show they caught on to that joke, too.

Howard and L.P. had to redo the weaving through about six poles. Finally they wove their way all the way around to the other side of the door. By then the women had done three more of their courses.

Peets showed again with roofing leaves. He looked at the work, then kicked it, testing it.

"Hey!" said L.P., but it held just fine and Peets grinned.

Howard stood and stretched, careful of his shoulder. As he did, something small but bright red caught the corner of his eye in the crotch of a tree. It was his pocket knife, unopened.

"Look at that!" he said.

L.P.'s mouth dropped. "How'd they…?"

"It was in my pants when the Jaguar-guys took them. And it wasn't in them when we found them in that garbage pile."

"So the Jaggies had it," said L.P. "How'd it get here?"

"They must have traded it for something." Howard picked it up. Peets and Tetl watched. Howard held it toward Tetl. Howard took Tetl's blank stare for permission. There was dirt in the grooves but he was able to open it. Peets stepped back surprised when the shiny stainless steel blade appeared. Tetl studied it seriously. All the Greenshirts watched. Howard wiped the blade with his shirt tail, making it even shinier. For the first time he felt he had something on them.

***

He reached up with his left hand, still protecting his right shoulder, and cut a small branch off the tree with one easy slice. He looked at Tetl, whose open mouth snapped shut. Then Howard walked to the vine-cutting operation. Several Greenshirts stepped back as he passed. Only the too-small clothes kept him humble. He picked up a vine and measured and cut several short pieces quickly and easily. Tetl was dumbfounded.

He offered it, handle first, to one of the men who had been cutting vines. The man stepped back, then, as Howard insisted, took it and started rubbing the blade lightly against a vine. Howard showed him how to push down and slice at an angle along the grain, which the man did, and the vine parted easily. He tried again, but used the wrong side of the blade. Howard showed him the difference by lightly touching each side to the man's finger. "Sharp," he said. "Dull. Sharp. Dull." The man grinned and nodded knowingly and measured and easily cut several more lengths.

Tetl finally straightened and motioned with his hands for everyone to get back to work.

L.P. and Howard picked up one of the now fast-growing number of newly-cut vines and started a second course.

In less than an hour, the vine-cutters had finished all the pieces needed for both huts. One of them tapped Howard on the arm and smiled and returned the knife.

Howard smiled, surprised. "They gave it back," he said to L.P. The blade had dulled. He found a good stone and started rubbing it against it. The vine-cutters watched. He slid the sides of the blade on his nose to pick up oil, and two men jumped to stop him, but calmed when it was clear he wasn't mutilating himself. They did not laugh.

L.P. said, "They want your body whole."

"Not funny." Howard dropped the knife in his fanny-pack.

Finally Tetl led Howard and L.P. back toward Rachel's hut.

"Something's happened to her," said Howard.

"Nah," said L.P. "He just knows we wanta see her."

They stepped into the hut, and as Howard's eyes adjusted to the darkness he saw not Rachel, but the other sick woman lying on the mat. He cried out, "Where is she?"

Tetl quickly pointed at the mummy-wrapped Rachel lying now where the other woman had been.

"They've moved her!" said Howard.

"Probably to prevent bed sores," said L.P.

A new nurse pushed corn-meal into the mouth-opening of Rachel's wrappings. Two or three times Howard heard a weak gulp from her throat. But when he knelt beside her and tried to talk and touch her, there was no response of any kind.

He caressed her bare arm. He had led her into el tigre's wood.

219

He had pushed her hand away.

He stood and stepped to a window and pulled the green curtain aside. In a dark, shaded grove Zomatl knelt before Chal-chee. He delicately touched her huge belly. He held his ear to it, and her hand caressed the back of his head. Howard looked away.

Tetl came and led him and L.P. back to the job site. A man brought food similar to what they had had for breakfast.

"Lunch," said L.P. They ate on the spot, and went back to work.

That night Howard and L.P. ate again with Tetl, Peets, Zomatl, Ehec, and the others, this time with new, vine-weaving blisters.

Howard wiped his pocket knife on his shirt, washed it in water with his fingers, and sliced one of the little tomatoes into his bowl of beans. Everybody stopped and watched the knife slide easily through the plump red flesh. He sliced some dried pimentos and added them.

L.P. said, "Do you think they'll put us in a pot with tomatoes?"

"Shh. When Zoe comes, she'll talk and find out."

L.P. picked up a papaya. "Maybe they'd rather hold us as slaves."

"On the other hand," said Howard, "Are they holding us at all?"

"They're not dumb. They know we'll stay for Rachel."

***

The next morning, under a dull gray sky, after they had bathed and eaten and visited Rachel, who was the same, and worked a couple of hours on the hut, they heard a commotion in the area of the log bridge. Tetl got up from his work and craned his neck, then everybody followed paths down through the village.

At the stream, they saw Blake on the other side. Crauder and Smith and Zoe huddled with others, peeking from behind trees.

Blake shouted. "They don't want to cross!" Only the thinnest tones made it across the roar of the stream. "How's Rachel?"

"The same!" said Howard. "Send DeSparr!"

Blake glanced back into the trees and shook his head. He tested the bridge with a foot. Two older boys quickly showed and helped him cross, one boy in front, walking backwards, the other behind.

"Is it the bridge they're scared of?" said Howard.

"Partly. But the rumors, too."

"There's plenty of food."

"Even for food… they won't cross."

Haughton-Alsef, holding his pipe to his mouth, and Dove-Ti, her head ducked, both stepped out into the clear. Then Raul and Pedro and Maria the translator. Shuffling directly behind Dove-Ti was Beg, also ducking and peering around her head, swaying left and right. They were all grimy and dirty in the ragged remains of their clothes.

Then from behind Howard came one of the young Greenshirts, running. He ran out onto the bridge, arms out for balance, shouting and grinning, bouncing deeply with the logs. Before he made it all the way across, the team had vanished again into the woods. The boy stopped, still balancing himself on the bridge, staring at the empty clearing.

Tee-week showed. "Tee-week!" shouted Blake, pointing across the bridge. "Can you go talk to Zoe?" Tee-week walked to the bridge, where two Greenshirts helped him cross.

Zoe stepped out of the woods and approached Tee-week. She eyed him suspiciously, then talked, eyes round, hand and body movements urgent. Eventually Haughton-Alsef sauntered over to join them, then Dove-Ti, then Beg.

"I'm getting an idea," said L.P. as they watched. "The team can just stay on that side of the stream. Camp out there."

"And?"

"And maybe we can get the Greenshirts to take 'em food. Or maybe they'll give it to you and Blake to take to them. They won't starve. And they won't have to cross the bridge. And, they won't feel trapped. They'll have their own — what? 'Burb.' Yeah."

"Let's go," said Blake.

"Good as the Greenshirts are with huts, they could build a better bridge," said Howard as they crossed with two boys helping.

"Slows attackers down," said Blake.

They joined Zoe and Tee-week. Smith stepped out from behind a tree. The Crauders joined them. Then DeSparr, glaring angrily.

Smith said, apologetically, "So glad you found Rachel, Howard. How is she? Is she better?"

Zoe turned from Tee-week, to hear the answer.

Howard shook his head. "She needs DeSparr. These people are trying to look after her. I don't know for what purpose later on."

"I'm trying to get like… info about her," said Zoe, and turned back to Tee-week.

"But, remember," said Smith, "we voted not to split up. That's still important. If we stick together, we may still be able to observe and make notes and somehow get out safely."

"But Rachel is over there," said Howard.

"I know," he said. "I know."

"The Greenshirts have been decent so far."

"That's what Blake told us, but you know what Dr. Haughton-Alsef has pointed out, that people who are used to a kind of organized violence can be quite civil otherwise."

Howard pointed across the stream. "L.P. has an idea."

"The 'Burb!'" shouted L.P. "Build the 'Burb!'"

Howard explained the idea about the team camping where they were, with food deliveries.

Tetl walked toward them on the bridge, slowly, not to scare the team. Most scattered anyway. Zoe and Smith did not flee, and Howard introduced them to Tetl. Zoe's attempts to talk with Tetl and Tee-week were spotty and halting and as usual involved a lot of hand motions.

Finally she said, "Tetl insists nothing be built out here in the like... open. We can build back there in the woods. But only with certain materials and colors kind of thing. He showed me like... small logs and sticks, green, brown, gray."

"Their building code," said Howard. "Neighborhood covenant."

Others began coming back out of the woods, curious.

"Also," said Zoe, "he offered us like... food, from their village."

"So L.P.'s idea will work," said Howard.

"What are they gonna do," said Crauder, "bring it to us?"

"I offered L.P. and Howard," said Zoe, "as delivery boys. Okay, Howard?"

"I will. And maybe Blake. But L.P.'s afraid of the bridge. Ask Mr. Tetl about Rachel. What exactly do they plan to do with her?"

"He recognized her name," she said. "But, I don't know."

"Keep trying. Every time you get a chance, okay?"

"Okay."

Tetl talked to the four young Greenshirts at length, instructively. He indicated to the team that the four would stay and help. Then he left.

"Okay," said Blake, pointing into the woods, "the 'Burb.'"

"Yeah." Crauder rubbed his hands together. "Tool time."

Howard pointed out sites back under the trees, on flat rocks this time, and they began building.

After some time, Zoe said to the team as they worked on huts, "I've found out some pretty uncool stuff. It's like... true about the human sacrifices. I triple-checked."

Howard had nursed a tiny hope that it wasn't true. Old Ehec, Chal-chee, Tetl. They didn't seem the type. But it was true that civility, at least on the surface, could flourish amidst institutionalized violence.

Zoe went on. "Tee-week says the sacrifices happen maybe like... one every few 'moons.' But it's actually not quite that bad. Well, I mean, I know it sounds bad... and, like... it really is bad and everything, but you get advance notice kind of thing, before they get you ready. Their tradition is that they like... help you get better. Then when you're better, they... Do you see what I'm saying?"

"What do they do?" said Mrs. Crauder.

"Dang, Pat," said her husband. "They say, 'So sorry. Bye-bye.'"

"It's more meaningful to everyone," said Haughton-Alsef, "if the one being sacrificed can consciously experience the ritual with them."

"Ugh," said Zoe. "But that fits what Tee-week said. And he told me that Tetl says they give you instructions and stuff. And then do it."

"How long do the 'instructions' take?" said Crauder.

"I don't know. And I know this is weird, but you're glad to be sacrificed kind of thing."

"Well, what if I'm dang well not glad?" said Crauder.

"Bodily sacrifice," said Haughton-Alsef, "is part of many primitive religions, not only acceptable, but highly honored. So preparation and ceremony are of course established values."

"One every few moons'll wipe 'em out," said Crauder. "That's several a year."

"He says it's mostly people from outside," said Zoe. "Now and then somebody from their own tribe, but mostly outsiders."

"Mercy!" said Mrs. Crauder. "We're outsiders! And... Oh, no!"

"What?" said her husband.

"The pilot! The helicopter pilot! They did that to him!"

"Didn't Blake tell you?" said Howard. "He's buried up there."

"Like the ancient Aztecs," said Haughton-Alsef, "it's a way to give back to their gods."

"And," said Zoe, "Tee-week says children. Their own children. I couldn't believe it."

"Sacrificed?" said Mrs. Crauder. "Mercy! Why?"

Haughton-Alsef rubbed a finger across his lips. "Some number of sacrifices can be quite necessary in a society like this. Fewer hungry mouths, you know. Less demand on the gods who gave the children and who must maintain the environment that nourishes them. We have a rare opportunity to gain a heightened awareness of our wider world."

"I get 'em already," said Crauder. "They're cock-eyed crazy."

"I think," said Smith, "that we can sit down and discuss this."

"Would you go across?" said Howard to Smith. "If I took you?"

Smith looked across again, at the few visible huts and people in green. "I have so looked forward to seeing them, to studying them. But maybe later. I need more information. Do you think it's possible they could show us how to get to Tegucigalpa or some highway?"

"I don't know." Howard turned to DeSparr. "Dr. DeSparr? Rachel needs you."

"Is there no witch-doctor?"

"Come on, man," said Howard. "She needs a good doctor."

"You think I'm 'good?'" The question was not about DeSparr's own skill, but about Howard's ability to assess it.

"Of course," said Howard. "But this is about her, not you."

DeSparr looked at him as if analyzing the reaction of the human to the removal of hope. "The best doctors in the best hospitals could do nothing now. Here, dirty room, tropical heat, humidity, unknown micro-organisms. Witch doctors. Human sacrifice."

"Actually, the room is surprisingly clean."

"There's not even an aspirin in a hundred miles."

"But you know things, Less." Howard reminded himself that Rachel was the only team member who had been openly conversant with DeSparr. He said, "It's Rachel, Less. Rachel!"

That seemed, at least for a moment, to shake DeSparr from his detached posturing. He looked finally down, at the log bridge.

"Those logs aren't so bad," said Howard. He pointed at the two young Greenshirts standing at the bridge. "They'll carry you."

"Shut up."

Howard shut up.

Finally DeSparr raised one foot, mechanically, and stepped to the edge. He stood for another minute, then collapsed, flopping oddly to the ground, face to the sky, eyes distant, unmoving, ready to be carried.

***

After a long, hushed half an hour beside Rachel on her mat, DeSparr leaned back, in the kneeling position. "No good signs."

Chal-chee was busy tending the other woman.

"But," said Howard, "at least she's still breathing."

"Breathing means nothing." DeSparr was less loud, but still stage-like, still detached, still lecturing some imaginary gathering of unthinking admirers. "Infection goes on destroying. Even if death is defied against all odds, there was a great loss of blood. There have likely been strokes." He rose to his feet and turned to an open window and studied the dimming light between the black trees. Howard barely heard the self-congratulatory words, mumbled as if to some imaginary being, "My stitches survived the transport."

"Well, what do you suggest?" said Howard. "With no medicine?"

DeSparr jerked, turned, stepped stiffly toward the door, then stopped. "Let the witch-doctors work." The tone implied Howard was too late begging. He glanced at him as if to assess the level of inflicted shock and misery, then passed through the door and away.

Howard got up and walked to the window. He had no reasonable case against DeSparr's diagnosis. He fixed his eyes in the direction of the far gap, not visible now in the growing darkness. Beyond it was maybe a town, or at least a road. He could run and bring back help or medicine for Rachel. It would justify his violation, once again, of the team rules. The tribe would probably not offer her up to their gods in the couple of days it would take.

Chapter 23

Tomás reached to comfort the little girl, but she shuddered and ran and left him holding his hand out uselessly.

Fernando said, "The Cholulans were not completely innocent."

All but one of the dead or wounded warriors had been taken from the court. Next to the one body was a boy, about twelve, soaking several large cotton rags in a wide clay bowl of water, dropping them on the stones, and scrubbing. Other children scrubbed other stones.

"They did not start this," said Tomás.

"We heard rumors," said Fernando.

"Rumors. Who saw Aztecas waiting outside the town?"

"The barricades and pits and spikes were real enough."

"Even so, does that prove they meant to slaughter us?"

"Groups of our soldiers are searching the town right now," said Fernando, "sending back reports of more evidence of a Cholulan plot. If they meant to slaughter us, they will never forget this lesson."

Tomás spoke softly. "The dead have already forgotten."

The girl swabbed stones nearby. She had a rag and two bowls.

"Tomás, I promise, I did not know… Only a few officers…"

"Was it for 'Crown?'"

"I was not in on it."

"Or was it for Christ?"

Fernando stiffened. "Enough. A good cause requires sacrifice."

"Sacrifice of others?"

The boy molded a human shape out of clay and blood.

"Such a practice is not without precedent."

"So, armed with 'precedent,' we subvert our stated cause."

"They sacrifice others," said Fernando angrily, "for their causes. What do you recommend? Sermons? Cortés tried that."

The girl went for a bowl of fresh water.

"So slaughter is the only alternative to bad sermons?"

"At least after this," said Fernando, "they will listen."

"Will they? Will they heed with their hearts who speaks with his sword?"

"As a matter of fact, Tomás, the sword is all they understand."

"'Understand,'" said Tomás. "Law, medicine. These we 'understand,' or try to. The sword we comply with, or resist, or die by, but we do not 'understand' it."

"Words!" said Fernando. "I prefer action. And good actions require courage."

Tomás picked up one of the rags soaked with blood and sweat and grime. "'Good actions.'" He threw it down.

"Then I suppose you will say, 'love your enemies.' Be sweet."

Tomás started to walk away in anger, but stopped. "Fernando. 'Love your enemies' means more than sweetness. It means that having faith in the utterer of those words is of the heart and mind, not of the sword. It means giving yourself to a good purpose. It is personal, not institutional. It builds people up rather than destroying them."

"Enemies destroy those who love them," said Fernando.

"Maybe. But were these our enemies before we invaded?"

"Tomás, you have to see this as… as a holy war."

"A holy war?"

"Yes, like the great Reconquest of our beloved Spain." Fernando straightened proudly.

The girl returned with the fresh water.

"Fernando. No matter what the outcome, a 'holy war' can never succeed for Christians. It is self-contradictory and self-destructive. I am telling you, faith cannot be forced. A man can be forced to say anything, but never can he be forced to mean it."

"Half of Spain converted to Christ under the sword."

"No. Those people identified with religion under the sword."

"Oh, come now, Tomás! You are splitting hairs."

"Am I?" said Tomás, calming himself. "Do you remember, at the university, how old Rodrigo frowned when we made jokes about the inquisitions? Why do you think they were sanctioned in the first place? Because the forced 'conversions' were no good! And the inquisition our majesties impose today is failing because it is doing the same thing!"

Fernando's face reddened. "It is approved by Leo the Vicar of

Christ. Would that I were one of those whom he allows to kiss his feet."

"Christ washed the feet of his followers." Tomás dropped to his knees and crawled gently toward the girl and picked up one of her rags.

She moved away, afraid.

"Our Giovanni de Medici," said Tomás from his knees, "has created cardinalates for his nephews, has made the sale of indulgences official." He dipped water from the girl's bowl. "Forgiveness for a price." He scrubbed stones, hard. "He acts as though his office is a gift from God for his family's personal enjoyment."

Fernando moved away from him.

"Call it splitting hairs," said Tomás. "But religion and faith in God are not the same."

Fernando was aghast. "The church, Tomás!"

"God save the church!" said Tomás loudly, voice cracking, arms straight to the stones, one hand squeezing the bloody rag, head raised, eyes shut tight, tears flowing. Then he remembered the children and tried to smile at them, but they moved farther away, one by one, with their bowls and rags, glancing back with questioning, childlike disgust.

Fernando took a deep breath. "Tomás, Tomás."

"It is all right. I am… I will be all right."

"Tomás. You have kept up your studies, it is true. But I have learned useful skills, too. Practical things, while you pondered."

"You have," said Tomás. "And any of the padres could argue me into the ground. So here we are. Two old friends acting as if we know what we are talking about!"

They both smiled, then laughed, and laughed louder. Tears ran down their faces and fell on the stones and diluted puddles of blood.

The boys and girls stared at them, frightened.

The sound of a footstep came from behind a column. Padre Díaz stood there. He smiled and bowed slightly and left.

Tomás and Fernando looked at each other and tried to remember all they had said. Heresy was punishable by death. Tomás held the bloody rag tightly under his chin and whispered a prayer.

***

New maps hung on the stone walls, over native paintings. Padre Olmedo looked up seriously and thoughtfully from his writing. "You know the name John Huss?"

"Yes," said Tomás. "University of Prague. Against simony. Against priest-initiated forgiveness. Scriptures the source of understanding. The highest loyalty of a Christian is to Christ, not to Crown or Church. All that. Burned a hundred years ago."

"A hundred and four. You read this fellow Erasmus, do you?"

"Yes. You know how I feel about these things."

"I do. I have enjoyed our discussions. And I do not dispute your feelings. But, Tomás, you must not incite officers against their capitáns."

"Have I?"

"You and I know you have been talking to Fernando Serra."

"Fernando is more loyal to Cortés than any officer on this expedition. We are old friends. We talk, just as you and I talk. Has someone listened in? Díaz?"

"Díaz just happened to pass. It is all right. I listened to him, but since he tried his little mutiny over the sunken ships, he has no sway with Cortés. Just remember that I do."

"I will, Padre."

Olmedo pointed at the huge Vulgate in its wooden covers lying open on his table. "The church does uphold the Scriptures, you know."

"I know. I am no radical, padre. Well, not…"

Olmedo sat back and gazed at the bit of sky visible through the small hole in the wall. "Those Cholulans out there, killed in the court. Just boys. Heartbreaking. This day will be told to generations."

"What have we taught them, killing while proclaiming Christ?"

"Believe me, Tomás, I talk to Cortés. He is not a great listener, having the king's ear. His theology is odd, but sometimes he makes a good point. You have to agree things are more complex these days. New trade routes, technology, weapons. I still don't know how that compass thing works! New races of peoples, the growing power and wealth of our king. Ideas of right and wrong are not so clear as they used to be."

"The Scriptures have not changed. You can show Cortés."

Olmedo's eyes grew round and wet. "I am trying, Tomás."

"I will pray for your efforts."

***

"I was just looking at it," said Ramiro Mendez as he opened his palm. The tiny gold ring shone in the middle. "That is all."

"Come with me," said the guard.

"Would you like it?" Mendez held his hand out to distract the guard from his other hand and the cloth bag of gold coins and emblems, which he let slide into his trousers.

The guard took the ring. "You are not allowed in an officer's room."

"This? An officer's room? I didn't know. It is so small, you see."

"Come with me."

"But..." said Mendez. "The ring. I let you have it."

Now his mother was starting the punishment. Now she was standing on the walls of heaven, talking in her persuasive way to the angels, having them send a guard who would take a bribe from him and still do nothing for him in return.

The guard took him to a sealed, windowless room and chained him to an iron loop anchored in the stone floor. But he failed to search Mendez. The first flaw in his mother's plans. But no, she would have thought of letting her son keep the bag of gold as long as he was chained. Gold was no good in itself. The freedom it would buy was his one hope through his trapped, tormented years.

"I want to see Tomás de Santillana," he said.

"Pfft!" said the guard.

"I am serious. You are religious. I want to repent."

The guard closed the door and slid the iron bar across it.

"Repentance!" shouted Mendez as he took the bag from his trousers, picked out a gold coin, and tapped it against the door. "Repentance!" In the silence he hid the bag well behind one of many loose stones in the walls. He tapped the coin again.

Finally the iron bar scraped again and the door cracked open.

Mendez held the coin out to catch the light.

The guard said, "Would any padre do?"

"Only Tomás. And send a needle and thread. My clothes need work. Your help will give me a generous spirit."

Later that day another guard brought needle and thread. Mendez hinted at gold. The guard set up a candle on the stone floor and lit it. After he left, Mendez studied the walls. They were well built and thick. No physical escape. No one to talk to. No one interesting enough, or intelligent enough. Only vague adversaries on the fringe. He lay on the floor and stared at the flame.

A moth circled close to the flame. "The tiny light opens to all the world, eh?" said Mendez. Once it flew too close and fell to the floor.

It fluttered weakly and moved only a fraction of an inch at a time. "You lost your freedom trying for a forgery," he said. "And ended up burned. Surviving the fire is worse than dying in it, eh?"

The next morning the guard let Tomás into Mendez' cell, then, after Mendez gave him the promised coin, locked the door.

"You know I am not ordained," said Tomás.

Mendez shrugged as if generously granting to Tomás that his lack of ordination did not matter. "I hope the Cholulans and Tlaxcalans have settled down, my brother."

Tomás said nothing, annoyed that Mendez called him 'brother.'

"I did not participate in the massacre, you know," said Mendez. "A matter of conscience. A 'holy war' can never succeed for Christians."

"So Padre Díaz was not the only eaves-dropper in the court."

"You know I will not report you, my brother."

"You cannot blackmail me, Ramiro. Olmedo already knows of my opinions."

"You know I would not do that, Tomás. I bring it up only because I must talk about my sins. I am having this difficulty." He pointed at the stone walls. "I need your help."

"If you are convicted of this theft, the penalty will be death."

"Oh, they will not convict when they see the lack of evidence."

Tomás was disgusted. "Why did you do this, Ramiro?"

"You know me too well, my brother. I happened to be in the room, looking for a Bible, you know, and saw the ring. It did not seem like much. I did not even mean to take it, just happened to be looking at it when the guard showed up. Perhaps I was tempted. You do not know how hard it is for those of us who have so little, especially when we have decided we want to always do the right thing."

Typical Mendez, thought Tomás. Completely missing the fact that he was talking to a man who owned nothing but a cheap brown robe and cast-off sandals. "Do not make excuses, Ramiro."

"You are right. And I want to repent. Will you forgive me?"

"It is not for me to do."

"But I need to hear it from you. I know I have been wrong."

Tomás felt sick. How different was this cowardly liar from the childhood hero he had looked up to in the university years ago.

"Anyway, Tomás, there is just one thing."

"And what is that, Ramiro?"

"If I could sit one last time on the side of a hill, see God's marvelous creation. If I could hear your voice, Tomás, my old friend, talking to me about the things of God. I do not ask you to be my advocate with the officer. I do not even ask for freedom. But if I could repair at least my friendship with you, before I die. On the side of a hill."

Tomás said, "You want me to get you out of here?"

"Just for an hour. One hour. It is not unusual. The army moves prisoners often."

"I do not have the authority."

Mendez leaned close, as if sharing a secret. "I need God."

Tomás sighed. "And how do I know you are sincere?"

Mendez held up a hand. "It is all right. If you do not trust me, I understand. Nothing lost. I am not asking for more than this one thing. If you cannot do it, then leave me. I will not trouble you again."

"Then God be with you," said Tomás, and turned to go.

"We can bring the guards with us," said Mendez, quickly. "They can chain me to a tree." He shrugged as if to say that it was that simple.

"And then what?" said Tomás.

"The holy Bible. Padre Olmedo's. Could we take it with us?"

"Olmedo keeps that book guarded."

"But you can…"

"I am sorry."

"Then I guess I will never be able to start the translation."

"Translation?"

"Tomás, I have heard you mention the need for it. I am ready."

"Ramiro, you may not be acquitted."

"Then forget it."

Again Tomás turned to go. He thought: if he does not protest my leaving, he could be sincere. He knows Latin, Greek and Hebrew, if his learning has not expired over his years of corrupt living. And he knows Nahuatl better than any Spaniard. He could translate it. And it is even conceivable that he could get himself acquitted.

Tomás called for the guard, who opened the door for him. He left, and heard no protest from within.

***

"Hello again," said Olmedo, sitting back. "What is on your mind, Tomás?"

"Padre. The man Mendez is in prison again. Theft of officer's

232

gold. He is sure to hang this time.

"And he has made some sort of last request of you."

"How did you know?"

"That is what prisoners to be hanged do. Does it involve me?"

"Well, he wants to borrow your Bible."

"My Bible? There are other Bibles."

"He insists on yours, with all your notes. He wants to translate."

"Translate? He will be hanged before he can write 'In the beginning God...'"

"I know. But on the slight chance he could be acquitted, and the slight chance he is sincere, it seems worth it to help him with meanings."

"You know what he is doing. He is trying to get a reprieve."

"I know."

"And he will not get it."

"But what could it hurt?"

"Tomás, you are naïve. But take it. Teach. Then bring it back."

Tomás picked it up, regarding again the thick wooden covers delicately carved like a church facade. "Thank you, Padre. Pray for me."

"I will."

He found Mendez' guards and explained the request to them.

They went with Tomás to their capitán and said to the capitán, "Mendez is no trouble."

The capitán said, "Nevertheless watch him more closely than other prisoners. Chain him to a tree. Never let him out of your sight."

***

Tomás had been to the spot before. It faced a grassy slope to the west, then maize fields, then vast dark forests, then jagged blue-black mountains against an orange sky. Two cones of snow made pink by the reflected sky hung vaguely in the orange. It was late in the afternoon.

The guards ran a chain through Mendez' iron anklets and around a large pine tree and attached a lock.

Tomás sat beside him.

Mendez rubbed his hands together happily, as if receiving gifts. "Something from Matthew," he said, "please."

"As I remember," said Tomás, lifting the wooden cover, "you were good at Latin."

"The best in my class. The best in Latin, Greek, and Hebrew."

233

It still amazed Tomás that Mendez had thrown out the excellent education he had earned with such distinction at Salamanca and chosen a life of greed. It was a shame that such talent would be lost on the gallows. But he remembered his own cowardice abandoning Rosa when she was under attack, and he knew he could have been another Mendez were it not for having been captured by Christ. He deeply wished for Mendez' awakening. "Your talents," said Tomás. "could have been used for good."

"I suppose they could be used for many things," said Mendez.

The guards stood at a grove of trees, facing the long view.

Tomás turned a number of pages and cleared his throat and read: "Jesus said, 'Whoever finds his life will lose it.'"

"Tomás," said Mendez, jovially, "that makes about as much sense as mud."

"Let me finish," said Tomás. "Then Jesus said, 'Whoever loses his life for my sake will find it.'"

Mendez only smiled and shook his head. "Mud."

"Ramiro, do you think you can translate this book?"

"Oh…" Mendez suddenly looked serious. "Of course."

Tomás would play along. The slightest chance the Aztecs could have the Bible was worth it. "Ramiro, if you do this, and do it right, it will serve Christ better than anything I have done or ever will do."

"I could never equal your achievements, Tomás."

"But," said Tomás, "to do it right, there are certain things — meanings — that you must understand."

"I know that, Tomás. I will have to develop symbols to represent the sounds of Nahuatl. I have decided it will be best to teach them our own Latin symbols. I will need the help of the Totonac porter-boys whose trust I have already earned."

"Yes, you will have to carefully develop writing. But the meanings… I cannot tell you how to choose each word, but if you know what the Bible is getting at, the main message throughout, it will help you more than anything else. Do you know it?"

"To do good?"

"No. Deeper. You were told all your life to do good, right?"

"Yes, and yet I did not. I see your meaning. So then, what is the main message?"

"All right. Look…" Tomás picked up the Vulgate. "Here is the book of Deuteronomy. Let us see. Here, in the early pages, the Shema.

Listen: 'Hear, O Israel: the Lord our God, the Lord is one. You shall love the Lord your God with all your heart and with all your soul and with all your might.'"

"I have heard that before."

"Yes. It is the most important command in the Bible."

"More important than 'You shall not kill?' I would never kill."

"Mendez. Listen. 'You shall not kill' is a big one, but look." Tomás found a page in the Gospel of Mark. "All right. This is when a religious scribe — a man who really knew the Bible — asked Jesus, 'which commandment is the most important of all?' Jesus quoted what I just read you. See? There. But he said there was a second most important command. It is also from Deuteronomy: 'Love your neighbor as yourself.' Look at the Ten Commandments: the first few have to do with loving God, and the rest with loving people. This will help you understand the meanings, help you translate well."

Mendez said, "Those two commands trump all others?"

"Jesus put it like this: 'All the law and the prophets hang on these two commandments.' Love God. Love others."

"Thank you, Tomás. If you can vouch for me that I will…"

"No deals, Ramiro. Remember? You just wanted to sit on the side of a hill and…"

"Yes, fine, I just thought … But if you do not want to help…"

"Ramiro."

"Yes."

Tomás turned to another page. "Those are the foundation for all that the Bible tells us to do. There is also the most important fact. It is called the *evangel.*"

"From the Greek," said Mendez. 'Good message.'"

"Yes. Now here, in Paul's letter to the Romans…"

"Let me see that," said Mendez, crawling behind Tomás, looking over his shoulder, pulling at the chains.

Tomás read, "For even though we sinned against him, Christ gave his life for us." He looked back at Mendez. "You see, the evangel is…"

Then it seemed to Tomás that Mendez lost his balance and bumped Tomás's back and pulled on his shirt, and he suddenly had an odd feeling inside his chest and had to cough. His head became light. He cried out but his cry had a strange gurgling sound, and he could not give it force. The pink snow cap of the volcano started turning and rising but never moving from its place. He tried to concentrate and make it stop. The hillside and the grass turned and twisted and came up to him and stopped when it was against the side of his head and then the whole view spun again, faster and faster, and sucked him into it and he began falling through the funnel of it, through the sky also spinning, out and up, and there was a kind of distant glow.

***

Now, thought Mendez, rising from the bodies of Tomás and the two guards, the Bible. The guards had been easy, believing he would share the gold and take them with him after they unchained him. Stabbing them was tricky, but he prevailed. Now he dug the gold rings back out of their clothing and returned them to the bag he brought from the cell, still hidden in his trousers. He left the bodies behind the rock where they would likely not be found until morning.

The Bible lay on the ground half-open. The wooden covers were intricately carved, valuable in themselves. The pages were decorated with swirling colors. People would believe him, even respect him. Anyone who would carry so large, so heavy, a Bible. Even the heathen would be moved by its beauty. And they would pay much for it.

He looked around and saw no one, then suddenly froze. Did Tomás move? Cough? He looked. The brown robe lay perfectly still. He would wash it of its blood later, take it quickly now and leave the body. The night would give him cover until he was well away. Come day he would use the sun to navigate to the coast. He would swing far to the south, where no one would look for him. His wit and language skills and the gold and the image the Bible provided, these would get him through, get him to a ship back to Cuba, then to Spain, or France, or even the new riches of Florence.

They did not know how much gold he had stolen. Only his mother in heaven could know. He thought he would like to shout up at her in defiance. But no need angering her. He had stolen it bit by bit. The two porter-boys had helped quite well, unwittingly. He had hoped for even more, but things got tense. He had more now than ten farmers or tanners or builders or weavers of Europe would earn in a lifetime.

He closed the Bible, stuffed it under an arm, grabbed the bag of gold and Tomás's robe and the knife, and ran, stumbling at first under the load. Miles from the army, exhausted, he found a hiding place under an overhanging rock. He rested, breathing hard.

Then, by moonlight, he began carving into the inside of the Bible's wooden back cover. He gutted it, and held it level on his lap and dumped all the little gold pieces into the depression and spread them around. He scanned with eyes and fingers the ground on each side of him. No gold had been dropped. He tore out the thick last page and covered the depression, forcing the edges down into the thin grooves he had carved around it. He closed the book and strapped it shut. He washed Tomás's plain brown robe and took off his old clothes and put the robe on wet. He tied the bag of his own clothes and the Bible, with its gold, on his back and stuffed the knife into his waist-rope. It was working. He was glad he was as strong physically as he was mentally. And he chuckled to himself, thinking how strange he, Ramiro Mendez, soon to be fully and finally free, must have looked walking and skipping through the forest with a bag and a big book, in a long brown robe.

Chapter 24

The next morning Howard and L.P. looked in on Rachel again, and again there was no change. Peets came for them for breakfast, and afterwards Tetl sent them across to the team's 'burb' with baskets of fruits and tortillas donated by villagers. L.P. finally agreed to cross again, carried by two big boys, squeezing his eyes shut and holding tightly his two baskets loaded with food as if they would save him if he fell.

"I believe," said Smith, as the team met, "that we had best discuss our situation."

"Let's just finish the huts," said Crauder.

Howard said, "I think we can finish them by tonight."

"By the way," said L.P., "Crauder's pistol is up there."

"What?" said Crauder, dumbstruck.

"It's hanging in front of the hospital, where they have Rachel. We don't know how it got here."

"And..." Howard held up his pocket knife. "This, too."

"No doubt there's been trading," said Crauder.

Smith said, "Zoe? Can you and I get some kind of dialogue going with these people?"

"The word 'dialogue,' might be optimistic. But, yes. We'll try."

Suddenly Tetl, Peets, and two more Greenshirts came bounding across the bridge. Tetl walked around surveying the work. He tapped his finger against a purlin sticking out, then pointed up. He spoke, repeating himself twice, changing his foot positions and head angles each time as if that would help communicate, which it didn't.

"It's like... sticking out from the trees," said Zoe. "That's what he's telling us."

"He's afraid somebody'll spot us from the sky," said Crauder. "They must've seen airplanes and helicopters lots of times."

"Oh, if somebody would spot us," said Mrs. Crauder.

Howard cut at the offending purlin with his knife. The freshly cut end had a bright cream color. Tetl searched the ground, picked up a handful of brown dirt, and rubbed it onto the end.

Zoe said, "Mr. Tetl?"

He stared at her, curious, head cocked and rotated up at her.

"Tee-week?" she said.

Peets turned and ran to the bridge and crossed it, arms out, shouting, "Tee-week!"

"Folks," said Smith. "Better get back to work."

Howard and others started gathering large sticks.

Smith stayed with Zoe and Tetl, and the three were joined, a few minutes later, by Peets and Tee-week, all trying to talk and understand.

After about an hour Smith announced, "Mr. Tetl says they know the woods, apparently for miles out. But this village is isolated, and they want it to stay that way. But don't worry. We will find a way out."

***

Everyone worked at his or her job, translators, builders, stand-and-watchers, stand-apart-and-thinkers, until late afternoon, when Howard put the last shingle on the roof.

Howard looked at L.P. "You ready?" The two crossed again, with help. Peets had organized a food donation center.

"We've gone from being guests to being on welfare," said L.P.

"Maybe our slave-labor will compensate," said Howard.

L.P. started packing baskets. "Go ahead. Check on Rachel. I'll finish this up."

Chal-chee greeted Howard as usual with a smile. He knelt beside Rachel and her fresh wrappings. He lightly rubbed her hair. He took water from the bowl and cooled her hot, red arm. He could stay with her, unable to help, or he could run, find help, and come back.

If there was a town just beyond the gap, and if everything went well, he could make it in one day, then back the next. Two days. Maybe Tee-week would guide him. There was no guarantee the gap would lead to anything. But neither did staying guarantee anything. True, he would want to be there in case she didn't make it. But that wasn't as important as even a remote chance of finding help that could save her.

He would have to do it secretly. His running would be viewed as desertion. But many of the team had in effect deserted Rachel when they talked about letting her "pass on out," or even be sacrificed, as if she were a suffering wounded animal, or a broken piece of furniture.

He would listen carefully to what Smith and Zoe learned.

He joined L.P. who had finished gathering baskets of food and they took them to the Burb. The team sat in a circle in the clearing and ate, tired and quiet. The Greenshirts had made it clear there were to be no outside fires after dark.

When Zoe sat down, Howard blurted, "What'd you find out?"

"A lot," she said. "Tee-week was helpful. Arrogant, but helpful."

"What'll they do with Rachel?"

"Well, Tetl said to wait and he would take us to an old man tomorrow who'll tell us more about their like... religious practices kind of thing. We did learn a few things. The pilot was alive when they found him on the chopper blade. Unconscious but alive. Tetl said they brought him here and he 'gave himself.'"

"Mercy!" said Mrs. Crauder.

"'Gave himself?'" said Howard. "For sacrifice?"

"Presumably. And he's like... buried in that cemetery you saw up there. Also, there's another sick woman besides Rachel."

"Yes," said Howard. "We've seen her. She's in the same hut."

"Do you know who she is?"

"No."

"Are you ready? She's like... Tee-week's mother."

"Tee-week's from the Jaguar-guys," said Crauder. "How'd his mamma get here?"

"Okay," said Zoe. "Reverend Smith, make sure I get it right."

Smith smiled shyly. "You got it better than I did."

"I need to back up a little," she said. "This is really complicated. Okay. I'm talking to Tee-week, and I go like... 'How'd you get here?' And Tee-week goes, 'My mother,' And I'm like... 'Wha-a-at?' and Tetl looks at Tee-week and Tee-week tells him what we're talking about and Tetl says stuff to Tee-week, and Tee-week goes, 'My people...' His people are the Jaguar-people, you know, not the Greenshirts. And he goes, 'My people found out about Rachel and...' Don't worry. His people, the Jaguar-people, they don't have any say here. So he goes, 'My people found out about Rachel and they want her to...' Well, what he said was, 'They want her to like... die.'"

Mrs. Crauder gasped.

"They?" said Howard. "They don't even know her."

"Well, they know of her," said Zoe. "Word gets around. But I was like… 'Hu-u-uh?' So I had to go over it with Tee-week and Tetl several times. Tetl's like… This is Tetl talking now, Tee-week translating. Tetl says, 'We don't believe this, but the Jaguar-people believe that a person's life can go into another person."

Howard said, "Okay, but, why do they want her to…?"

"Bottom line, they think Tee-week's mother won't die if Rachel's life like… goes into her kind of thing. Do you see what I'm saying?"

"That," said Mrs. Crauder. "Is just ignorant."

"So," said L.P., "if Rachel's life went into her, that would make Rachel, uh…?"

"Dead," said Blake, and Zoe nodded, biting her lip.

Then Mrs. Crauder smiled. "Or, the mother's life could go into Rachel!"

"Dang, Pat!" said her husband.

"I don't get it," said L.P. "If they believe that, why wouldn't they just sneak into Rachel's hut when the Greenshirts aren't looking and… you know… uh…?"

"It doesn't work if it's murder."

"That little stipulation," said Haughton-Alsef, "would have evolved along with the rest of the belief. Imagine the motivations otherwise."

And also," said Zoe, "they don't want to offend the Greenshirts. Tee-week said that. The two tribes don't get along, but there's some kind of like… stand-off agreement."

"How," said Dove-Ti, "did the midland forest persons find out Rachel was here?

"The who?" said Crauder.

"She means the Jaggies," said L.P. "But what I don't get is, what's in all this for the Greenshirts? Why would they go to all this trouble? There has to be an angle. And I'm wondering this: why isn't Tee-week afraid for his mother? The Greenshirts could sacrifice her. She's prime material. Sick. Captured."

"I asked Tee-week that," said Zoe. "He said his people, the Jaguar-people, brought her to be helped. And the Greenshirts agreed. There are several possible reasons I'll get to in a minute. But it looks like the Greenshirts are known for like… cures. And you know what? Something else. Tetl told me Tee-week was considered a problem kid by the Jaguar-people. And they get rid of problem kids. They like… banish them."

"So that's why they dumped him on us," said Crauder.

"Pretending it was a gift," said L.P.

"They probably dumped Mosh on the Greenshirts," said Howard. "That sullen kid."

"Yes, yes," said Zoe. "They told me he was a Jaguar-guy misfit."

L.P. nodded, "Just wait til he gets sick. Then, hel-loo, Mosh."

"And that 'Sho-lo-peet you guys saw?'" said Zoe. "Nobody knows where he came from."

"I doubt they can help him," said L.P. "He's probably acting crazy so they won't think he's cured and ready to be sacrificed."

"So, anyway," said Dove-Ti, "You're saying Tee-week ran away from us knowing the Greenshirts would take him?"

"That's what it looks like," said Zoe.

"But wasn't he afraid they'd sacrifice him?" said Howard. "He's an outsider."

"Well, he made some kind of like… deal. I suspect it was something like… 'Help my ma and I'll tell you about a sick woman.' See what I'm saying? And that may tell us something about the Greenshirts' intentions for Rachel."

"Not gonna happen," said Howard.

"But," said Mrs. Crauder, "Why would Tee-week want to live with them instead of us?"

"Yeah," said her husband. "Why would he want good food, dry shelter, intelligent people, all that, instead of us poor lost idiots?"

Zoe nodded. "He does think we're stupid."

"We're college-educated!" said Mrs. Crauder.

"How'd my pistol get up there in their village?" said Crauder. "Did you ask 'im that?"

"Yes! Oh. yes, the pistol!" said Zoe. "Now. Okay. That's another reason the Greenshirts are helping Tee-week's mom. And you're not going to believe this part. The pistol — get ready — that's how Tee-week's mother got hurt. See, according to Tee-week — and I hope I got this right — I had to figure out the half I didn't get from the half I did get — but, after the Jaguar-people took the pistol, you know, when they raided us and took our clothes and all, they like… went back to their village, wherever that is. Then there was this like… dance. Something to do with Tee-week's exile, you know. They had just given him to us. The dance was centered around his mother. Maybe it was like… to comfort her for losing Tee-week, come to think of it. Tee-week found all this out later, from her. He said they like… waved the pistol around like a sort of trophy thingie, you know, and it 'popped.' Just, 'Pop!' You know? They got excited and made it pop again. And again. Then, he said, 'the spirit of it reached out.' See what I'm saying? And that's just when his mother like… cried out and grabbed her leg with both hands, and they looked and found a small hole on each side of her thigh. Get it? Then later, a fever came, see, and by that time they had found out that these people here, the Greenshirts, these People of the First Sacrifice, had a sick woman, you know, which was Rachel. So they like… brought Tee-week's mother here, with the pistol as a gift, hoping she could get the life from Rachel when Rachel was, you know, sacrificed kind of thing. That's pretty much what Tee-week told me."

"I never…!" said Mrs. Crauder.

"That pistol belongs to me," said Crauder.

"So," said L.P. "Tee-week's mother is not to be sacrificed?"

"Not if the Greenshirts want to keep the peace," said Zoe.

"What do the Greenshirts get for all that?"

"They think they're gonna get my pistol!" said Crauder.

"Primitive cultures practice reciprocity," said Haughton-Alsef. "It's quite important to them. Gifts must be rewarded, wrongs must be righted."

"Tee-week did say the Jaguar-people, not the Greenshirts, want the pistol close by her," said Zoe. "For its magic, if you see what I'm saying."

"So," said L.P., "the pistol toggles between hurting and helping."

"But," said Mrs. Crauder, "don't they think it's evil?"

"They don't seem to think good or evil," said Zoe, "just magic."

"So," said L.P., "the Jaguar-people get Tee-week's mother healed, and the Greenshirts get a really cool-looking piece of shiny metal they don't know is a pistol…"

"Ah," said Haughton-Alsef, holding up a finger, "but the pistol has a spirit."

"Yeah, okay, so they get the cool shiny piece of metal with a spirit. And back when the Jaggies raided us, they got rid of Tee-week making like he was a gift to us so they could justify stealing our boots. And they luck up and get this shiny pistol to boot. Oops, bad pun."

"They have the advantages of generations of accumulated

243

experience with this concept of reciprocity," said Haughton-Alsef.

"Yeah," said Crauder. "They've learned how to cheat."

"And Tee-week," said L.P., "gets a nice town to live in instead of our dump, and protection from the sacrifices along with it."

"That little jungle-jumper's no dummy," said Crauder.

"So who are the big losers in all this?" said L.P., rhetorically.

Haughton-Alsef held up a hand. "Not too fast. It isn't necessarily we who are the losers. So far, possibly only Rachel, unfortunately, qualifies for that. We still have our..."

"If it's Rachel, it's us," said Howard.

L.P. nodded, agreeing.

"Everyone to their choice," said Haughton-Alsef. "But as I was saying, we still have our freedom and our opportunities to observe."

"God! You call this freedom?" said Pryce. "Opportunity? What are those Sacrifice People going to do to us? Make us their food? I'm sick of this."

L.P. said, "The Greenshirts have plenty of food."

DeSparr gazed up through the trees. "Their gods don't."

Howard didn't sleep well that night.

***

Next morning the team gathered in the mist. DeSparr stood apart again, but within earshot.

"You're learning the language," said Mrs. Crauder to Zoe, as Howard and L.P. brought breakfast across the bridge.

"A lot of stuff's not clear. Tee-week thinks we have like... peas for brains. His thing is mischief. He got Peets to dance across that bridge, and almost seemed disappointed when he didn't fall off."

"So," said Crauder, "you've got yourself a juvenile delinquent for a translator."

"Tetl tries to help, too, but he's usually like... ordering people around. There's an old man. Ehec. You should have seen him cross the bridge. Slow, but like... no problem. He wants to learn English. He's got Tee-week like... teaching him."

"I know Ehec," said Howard. "Anything about Rachel?"

"No. But Ehec told me something else last night."

"What?" said Crauder.

"Well, the first people we saw were the like... Jaguar-people.

244

Then Tetl and these Greenshirts. And now…"

"And now what?" said Crauder. "Another tribe?"

"'Ya-si.'"

"'Ya-si?' Who are they? A tribe of vampires? Huh?"

"A person," she said. "He's like… high chief or something. They call him 'Ya-si.'"

"Is he a bigger wheel than Tetl?" said Crauder.

"Tetl's like… in awe of him."

"Was it Ya-si's idea for them to kidnap Rachel?" said Howard.

"Could be."

"Uhm," said Dove-Ti. "Can we meet this Ya-si and establish a dialogue?"

Zoe shrugged. "I don't know where he is or anything yet."

DeSparr spoke to some distant audience. "Finally, you see it. With a high chief, a justifier, sacrifices can be done 'decently and in good order,' just as your churches over the centuries have justified slavery and segregation and abortion."

"Zoe," said Crauder. "What about the Jaguar-guys? Do they have this same high chief? This Ya-whoever?"

Zoe shook her head. "This Ya-si is part of the Greenshirts' own like… religious beliefs."

"It's quite surprising," said Haughton-Alsef while sucking the empty pipe, "to find a smorgasbord of religions in such a sparse population." He waved the pipe. "And in such a remote location."

"They told me more stuff," said Zoe. "There's supposed to be this like… important ceremony this afternoon. And we can watch."

Smith stopped spinning his hat and said to everybody, "Watch and remember everything you see and hear."

"What will you 'civilized' people do," said DeSparr to the trees, "if they start to cut out someone's heart? Maybe 'nice' old Ehec will do it. Will you stand by?"

"Don't forget," said Dove-Ti, calmingly, "we are the intruders. We must find it in ourselves to respect their normal customs just as we uhm, expect them to respect ours."

"But wait," said Zoe. "Are we being honest here? If they kill an innocent person… I mean, can we really call that a 'normal custom?'"

"Oh, lord!" said Mrs. Crauder, suddenly. "What if it's Rachel?" She put her hands over her mouth and looked at Howard.

Howard thought: oh, lord.

Smith, Zoe, and Crauder sat with Howard and L.P. at the circle of stones in the village. Tee-week was there to help translate.

Old Ehec looked up from his wrinkled face as if some invisible weight were pulling his neck down. He gave Howard a slight smile of recognition. He seemed even smaller, next to the tall Smith, than when Howard had first seen him silhouetted in the door of the hut where his daughter cared for Rachel. His feet were separated widely. His hand gripped the gnarled top of a walking stick. He talked to Zoe, mixing some English words with his own language.

"The ceremony will be farther up," said Zoe, translating. She pointed toward a pool in a small stream just below a rocky waterfall. "And like... soon."

"Does it have anything to do with Rachel?" said Howard.

Zoe talked to Ehec, then said, "No."

"Ask Ehec what they want Rachel for."

She asked, and Ehec said, "Take ..." Then he said, "Ya-si coco-lees-tee tweek yee-ollo."

"He said, 'Ya-si wants to 'take the sickness from her.'"

"Will they make her 'life' go into Tee-week's mother?" said Howard.

She talked again. Sometimes Ehec, with Tee-week coaching, clearly repeated her English words, adjusting his grip on the walking stick as if it helped the pronunciation.

She said, "Ehec says, 'Only the Jaguar-people believe that.'"

Howard said, "Ask him if he can talk to Ya-si."

She asked and Ehec said in English, "Yes."

"Where is Ya-si now?" said Howard.

Ehec spread his arms to indicate the whole area. "Here," he said.

"I believe it must be a god," said Smith. "Not a real chief."

"But," said Howard, "what does Ya-si want after Rachel's sickness is taken from her?"

Zoe talked with Ehec for a long time. Finally she said, "Well, when she is awake, Ehec says that Ya-si wants her to like... well, to give up her life."

"I coulda told ya," said Crauder, stopping and glaring at Ehec.

"Yep," said Howard. "And why just her?"

Zoe tried, then said, "Ya-si wants us to give ourselves as well."

"Oh, right," said Crauder. "Wipe out the whole human race."

Howard looked at L.P. "The Aztecs did it to thousands."

"We need to get out of here," said L.P.

"Are we sure of your translation, Zoe?" said Smith. "I know you're doing the best you can, and we certainly appreciate it. But this is so important…"

She talked some more to Ehec, then said, "I'm sure."

"Can you find out," said Smith. "Where Ya-si is? How does Ehec find out what Ya-si wants? And can we talk to Ya-si ourselves?"

She talked again for a long time, with a lot of gesturing, asking the question in several different ways. Ehec set his walking stick down against a log and talked and often punched the palm of one hand with the knuckles of the other. She finally shrugged and said, "He's trying to tell me, but I don't get it. Something about 'writings.'"

"Writings!" said Smith, surprised and delighted. "They can read and write. Dr. Haughton-Alsef was right."

"What if we just took Rachel and left?" said Howard.

She talked to Ehec again, and he called Tee-week and sent him off. Soon he came back with Tetl.

Zoe used the simplest words and phrases. After another ten or fifteen minutes, she finally said, "They thought we like… agreed."

"Agreed to let them kidnap her?" said Crauder. "Is he kidding?"

"Remember the day Tetl first came to our camp? He stood at the stream and kept going like…?" She swept her hands back and forth.

"I remember," said Smith.

"He thought we agreed to let them take her and make her better kind of thing. He was just letting us know how they would like… get her out, across that little stream. They took her early the next morning."

"They've got plans for her," said Crauder. "Trust me. Why would they go to all that trouble? Come out of nowhere and ask us? Carry her way up here? Just to care for her, who they don't even know?"

Howard said, "We're taking her out of here."

"We'll have to sit down and talk about that," said Smith.

Zoe said, "I think Ehec is sure we won't try that. This like… terrain. Also, let's don't ask any more questions for a while, okay?"

Tetl pointed at the ring of stones and looked at Howard. "You tell?"

"Tell?" said Howard.

Old Ehec picked up a stone from outside the ring and made throwing motions, frowning and wincing at a pain in his arm.

Zoe took a deep breath and sighed and talked to him again, for a while, working out word meanings, then finally said, "If you like... break the rules here, you can be put in there. See? Wait." She talked to him some more and said, "I don't think you're going to believe this, but, oh my god, I don't think I believe it, but he says people throw stones at you, and they, well... they throw them until you're... like... dead."

"I coulda told ya," said Crauder.

"I'm out of here," said L.P., taking a couple of steps back. "I told you. It's Trouble with a big 'T,'." Everyone stared at the circle, the unspotted, smooth-swept sand in it.

"They keep it pretty darn clean," said Crauder, "to be killing people in it!"

"I'll bet they cover up all the blood and stuff," said L.P. "That's what that sand's for. That's why they don't want it messed with."

"Oh, please," said Zoe. She turned to talk to Ehec again, nervously. After some time, with a lot of back-and-forth questioning, she calmed, and finally said, "Wait. It's not that bad. I mean, it is bad and all, it's not like... you know, perfect or anything, but he said that, if you don't know a rule, you won't get like... stoned for breaking it."

"If you're bad," said L.P., "the Jaggies get rid of you. These people: they stone you."

"Keeps 'em in line," said Crauder. "We need one of those in Georgia."

"No wonder they act so decent," said Howard.

"Just in case," said L.P., "I'd be interested to, uh... to know what those rules are." Then he held a hand up. "But don't let them know I know."

Chapter 25

Atl had to work to lift his feet. His neck would not turn to look back at Cholula. He had not cared when One-Cip' gave the word and they were able to sneak away from the Sant-yagos. He could not bear to be who he was. To think of his own name made him feel sick.

What would be done with Tree? Did the Cholulans use carved death-arcs? What was Tree's last thought of Atl as he watched him push the knife into his heart?

Atl had asked for punishment. One-Cip' had said, "You have hurt enough. This kind of thing has happened to others." It did not help. The picture of Tree in his pool of blood would trap his inner eye again and again. The hanging faces came, leering, showing their teeth.

He stumbled and fell and wanted to lie there until his whole body withered like Tree's arm. He only got up, slowly, to keep Deer of Stone from helping.

One-Cip' and the others turned to an old narrow path ahead. They stopped at a stream. One-Cip' and Deer of Stone and A Fox is Mad fished. Balanced Turtle lay down.

After some time One-Cip' got up and walked to Balanced Turtle. "Here is a clear stream," he said. Then he felt Balanced Turtle's brow and neck and shoulders.

Balanced Turtle seemed not to notice the stream.

"Your skin is hot," said One-Cip'.

"My head hurts," said Balanced Turtle. "And my back."

Atl sat and would not eat.

"You must come," said One-Cip' to Atl as they packed the fish and got ready to leave the stream. "We need you."

"Go without me." It did not bother Atl now to defy One-Cip'.

"Some of the women may be back at the village," said One-Cip'.

249

"Why would they go there? It is burned. Anyway, they must never know how evil I have become. If you saw Tree's eyes…"

"A good friend like Tree would want you to get over this."

"As you have said, a snake sheds his skin, but he is still a snake."

"Come."

Atl got up slowly.

They walked six days, stopping only to fish and sleep. Once they caught a turkey, and twice killed rabbits. They saw the last of Popocatepetl, and passed snow-topped Orizaba. The others took turns helping One-Cip' whose knee was weak and hurting, or carrying Balanced Turtle who was weaker and hotter and vomited often, and finally Atl helped, and looked up more often, and finally fished, and even ate, far now from the horror of Cholula and the evil he had done to Tree. It helped to think of the kind Mendez, who did not kill, who helped others instead.

He said to Deer of Stone, "The Sant-yagos are to blame."

"So now you are speaking," said Deer of Stone.

"They came and caused all this."

"The Aztecs were first to blame," said Deer of Stone.

"Anyone who is not of our village is evil."

"Now you see it."

"Except Mendez," said Atl.

"Mendez is a Sant-yago. He urged us to kill."

"But it was to help us save ourselves. He did not kill."

"That was because he was a coward," said Deer of Stone.

It was the middle of a morning when they reached the village. There was no sign of life. The maize still lay in the bins. The tops of the graves had sunk. On one was a tiny sprig with a leaf. Atl kicked it and let it fall into the ashes. What was left of the small flowers in the chinampa was smothered in weeds. Someone or some animal had taken vegetables. He could see the broken stems. Thoughts of his mother overcame him, but he recovered. He did not hope for Dahlia, so that he would not be disappointed when he did not find her. But he was disappointed. The sky was mottled and dark. The morning was like evening.

One-Cip' called Atl and two others to help put fresh dirt on the graves and pack it down with their feet. When they were done, Atl stood and looked around. He felt hatred for the stories of the old time, of the men and women who had cleared and settled the village, who had built up skills and taught each other. He hated the memories of the rich cloth colors and patterns invented by the women and sold in far places. He hated the stories of the men who hunted and plowed and reaped.

He hated the memory of the big fight he had seen between Two-Rabbit and Marigold. Everybody had watched, and old Brown Rose had been called. Brown Rose had said that Two-Rabbit should not trade for silly things. He had abided by her ruling ever since, even though Brown Rose died the next year. He said that Marigold was worth giving up his silly wishes. But now Marigold was gone. A hateful story.

Atl hated the memory of the thrill when the elders let him and Deer of Stone stake out the swamp east of the village, and build the long chinampa island, and plant willows on the edges, and drag waterways for the dugouts. The grain and beans and squash and the thousands of flowers should have died in the ground before the killers came.

In the ashes where a cooking hole had been they built a fire and cooked fish and sat in a circle and said nothing until finally One-Cip' spoke. "I was wrong about the Sant-yagos," he said. "I think they will succeed. They will destroy the Aztec ways."

"They do not honor those they kill," said Deer of Stone.

"If I were to die," said Balanced Turtle, straining against his worsening sickness, "I would at least want a time of honoring."

Atl was afraid to speak for he might cause the others to show their disgust with what he had done. Two-Rabbit lay silent.

"We were lucky to get out of Cholula," said Deer of Stone. "We are more worthy than a people who wait for others to come and take them and their children for sacrifices or come and destroy their villages."

Atl thought: Deer of Stone is already thinking of the day when he will take his father's place as the leader.

***

"We must go," said One-Cip'.

"Go where?" said A Fox is Mad.

"South. I know a forest where there are no Aztecs and no sacrifices."

"And no Sant-yagos," said Deer of Stone. "And no gold."

"We can start a new village," said One-Cip'.

Balanced Turtle held his sides. He spoke weakly. "Will there be a clear stream?" Little red spots covered his face and arms.

"Will the gods follow with us?" said Two-Rabbit, sadly.

251

"I overheard two Aztec priests," said One-Cip'. "They came to Cholula from the High Valley, where men and children were being given to the gods in hope of stopping the Sant-yagos. After they watched the killing of the Cholulans, one of them said, 'The gods have left.'"

Two Rabbit said, "We have no women." He looked at One-Cip'. "You, old man. You have learned to live without a woman, and maybe we all can, but... What is the reason to build a village?"

"It will only be half a village," said Balanced Turtle in his pain.

"There are villages on the way," said One-Cip'. "We may find women. We will stay here nine days. We will pack down the graves and get ready to travel." He looked at Two-Rabbit. "I remember that Marigold's loom was not burned."

Two-Rabbit shrugged. "Someone has taken it."

"Still there are things we can trade," said One-Cip'. "I found two good copper hoes."

Atl had the idea that he could begin to make up for his evil. "I can make a cart." He had thought of doing it before. "I can make wood circles for legs."

The others seemed to wonder whether he still had his mind.

"Like the Sant-yagos," he said. "To carry things when we travel."

It was the first time any of them had laughed since before Cholula.

But he would do it anyway, at his secret hut. Was it still there? He would finish the roof, and fight off the memories of Dahlia.

When the meeting broke up, they spread to the woods to scout.

Atl ran straight for his hut. It seemed less far now, after all the travels. When he saw it through the leaves, he stopped. It looked plain and sad. He waded to it, and looked up. The old repair Dahlia had made had lasted after all. He stopped thoughts of her.

He climbed from the stream to the entrance. He was surprised to see, in the darkness, Marigold's loom. Clothes hung on a wall. Something moved and he stepped back. There was bedding, and a baby, two babies, asleep, breathing!

He looked around at the forest, saw no one. He crept inside, quietly, and smelled the bedding. It was vaguely familiar. Thoughtful Rose. But she had not been pregnant. He scanned the forest. Did the old stone jaguar, held by the roots of the old acorn tree, know anything? No. "The gods have left." He glanced back at the peaceful babies, then climbed down to the stream and waded to the stone face. Above him

Tonatiah slowly drew the clouds aside and reached through and touched the rocks and ground, and moved gently across the jaguar's huge face, along the curves of her nose, her cheek, her frowning eyes, her lips, her teeth. The smooth stone seem to breathe in the changing light, to swell against the tightening roots. He sensed a personal presence.

He looked around again. The stream dropped steeply beyond that place and allowed a view, and he was surprised to see that, if he were to stand directly in front of the jaguar, with his back to her, he could see what she could see: the white peak of Orizaba, which his mother had shown him from another place years before.

He crossed the stream and climbed toward the face. He had never touched her.

As he drew closer, the sense of a personal presence became stronger. He stopped, afraid. The huge thick acorn-tree towered above him. It held her with its roots. Light, high breezes drifted, and tall slender trees swayed gently, together. The air was fresh. A lizard ran silently down the trunk, under a root, and into an ear. She was only stone. He reached out, hesitated, stared into the deep hollows of her eyes, then reached closer. He could not deny the strong sense of life. He boldly, but lightly, touched the tip of her nose.

Suddenly the forest darkened. His hair stood up. His body froze. Dark, writhing forms darted from above and behind the huge head, in blurry silhouettes against the sky. They made garbled, shrieking sounds. One of them landed on him, then another. They were slimy and crawly. He could not move or resist. Parts of them swarmed over his face and covered his eyes. He and they tumbled down the bank, wrapped together. His arms and legs were caught up in them and he could not stop the falling. They landed in the water, his head under. It was suddenly cold. The forms struggled, holding him. He coughed bubbles and breathed water. They let go and splashed around him, still shrieking. He raised up, coughing. They rushed behind him, splashing. If he turned, they darted behind him, always behind him. Now the air was cold. He rubbed the water out of his eyes.

One of the garbled voices spoke in his tongue. "Do not look! Do not look!"

"What?"

Another shrieked, "Close your eyes!"

The voice was unmistakable. "Dahlia?" he shouted! "Is it you?"

"Yes! And Thoughtful Rose, and Pink." He almost looked. "No!

253

We are naked!"

She was alive! And the others! Again he turned.

"No!" Her voice shrieked again. "Where is Daddy?"

"At the village. He is alright. So is Deer of Stone."

"Stay," she said. "We are going to the hut."

He looked up again at the jaguar. Their feet splashed behind him. "We were bathing," she said. "We heard your steps and hid behind the tree." The splashing on smooth rocks came from farther away, and so did her voice, which was the same but different. "When you touched the jaguar we thought you were going to climb the bank."

He peeked. Their golden forms twisted as they ran. Dahlia looked back and picked up a handful of rocks and threw them at him.

He waited in the cold water. Finally Dahlia shouted, "Now!"

He got up and turned. She stood in the door of the hut in a white cotton tunic, in the sunlight and dancing shadows of the tall swaying trees. How rich her red-gold skin looked against the white! She seemed stronger, more confident. The babies cried behind her.

He ran up the bank toward her, tripping twice. She watched him and smiled as if his tripping had been a clever entertainment for her.

Then, in front of his no-longer-secret hut, in the late summer of the year One-Reed, Atl put his arms awkwardly around Dahlia's waist. Her arms were tight around his neck, her cheek tight to his. Thoughts of the village's destruction and of his mother's death, which Dahlia knew about, and of the Aztecs and the Sant-yagos and their battles, and of his killing of Tree and his creeping despair, which she did not know about, seemed to empty and flow between them, as if they had each picked up an end of a great log which the other had been carrying alone.

Thoughtful Rose joined the hugging. Pink wanted to know if he had presents for her. Both babies howled.

***

When they had faced the Aztec tribute-takers in Cempoala, Atl remembered, One-Cip' had been alert, and on edge. When they had found the village burned and destroyed, and the women dead or gone, the strong old man had been stern and hard. When the Sant-yago battles had been fought against the Tlaxcalans, and the dead lay all around, he had been bitter. When they left the slaughter in Cholula, he had seemed to despair. Today, when Dahlia his daughter in her white tunic walked from the woods into the burned-out clearing, tears poured from his reddened eye, and he hugged her unmercifully.

And when Two-Rabbit saw his daughters, he became new.

As Atl watched Dahlia, he was once again glad for the stories of the old time, of the men and women who had cleared and settled the village, who had built up skills and taught each other. He loved the memories of the rich cloth colors and patterns invented by the women and sold in far places. He loved the stories of the men who hunted and plowed and reaped. And he was glad for the chinampa skills he and Deer of Stone had brought to their people.

Finally they all sat down and Dahlia told the story of herself and the girls. Pink kept interrupting, but no one minded bad manners that day. The girls had been away, bathing the babies for their mother, when the village had been destroyed. When they came back, well after mid-day, and the village men were still away on the hunt, they were horrified. They leaned on each other and cried and cried. Then they thought they could be in danger themselves, so they ran, still crying, with the babies whose mother had been killed, into the forest, into Atl's hut where they had hidden and lived ever since. After several days they sneaked into the burned village at night and were able to find plenty of maize in the bins and to pick vegetables in the chinampa.

"Where is Shy Petals?" said Two-Rabbit.

"We have not seen her," said Dahlia. "Alive or…"

"She was close to having her baby," said A Fox is Mad.

"We can search for her," said Two-Rabbit.

"And we have much else to do," said One-Cip'.

Dahlia directed Thoughtful Rose and Pink, and they gathered what maize and other vegetables and fruit they could find in the bins and the chinampas, and began the drying and packing of most of it and cooked the rest, and repaired clothing.

Again Deer of Stone and Two Rabbit scouted, this time looking for Shy Petals, and Atl went to his hut and began to plan his cart. One-Cip' and A Fox is Mad gathered more maize from the chinampa and began to make new basket packs with sturdy head-straps. Balanced Turtle picked up some straw to help them, stared at it in his lap, then lay down and slept. He had many red spots on his chest, back, and legs. Dahlia looked in on him often.

"No Shy Petals?" said One-Cip' as they gathered that night.

"No," said Deer of Stone.

Dahlia said to Thoughtful Rose, "Go ahead."

Thoughtful Rose said, "What?"

"Tell them the poem you told to me."

Thoughtful Rose reddened and cleared her throat softly. "There was nothing," she said, "Into nothing came Coatlicue. The gods twisted her and broke her. She became the earth and the sky. There was food and life. The earth and the sky became her. She twisted the gods. The gods left. There was nothing."

Everyone thought in silence.

Then One-Cip' said, "In time we will go to another land. It is my hope that we will find more than 'nothing' there."

Balanced Turtle's eyes opened. Red spots covered his body. "I hope we find peace there," he said, painfully, "and a clear stream." He was in more pain each day. Some of his red spots became blisters. He tried to help in the work, but his joints and muscles ached.

The babies cried and cried. Dahlia stirred water and maize. Atl found honey near his hut. Dahlia stirred it in. Sometimes the babies swallowed the mixture, but they were losing weight.

Atl worked for days on his cart using his stone tools. It was crude, heavy, and stiff. One of the wood circles kept coming off, and both of them had the outline of a potato, which gave the whole thing a hobbling motion when he pulled it, and he knew it would make the others laugh. He tried reshaping the circles, but that only made smaller potato-shapes.

After the nine days of preparation, each had a full Basket-pack. They strapped one of the babies, Seven-House, to Dahlia's back, and the other, Rose Blue, to Thoughtful Rose. When Atl brought up his cart, it pitched from side to side as it rolled. Everyone laughed, as he knew they would. And he laughed. "But it will work," he said, and put tools, extra clothing, maize, and dried fruits in it.

Both babies cried weakly.

When they were ready, One-Cip said, "We will go out of the empire and keep going. We will go through Chiapa, through the land of the bats, around the Maya of Copán, beyond the silver hills, beyond any of the powers."

"I wish Mendez were with us," said Atl, "in case we meet Aztecs or Sant-yagos."

"I want nothing of them, not even him," said Deer of Stone.

Atl studied the ruins as they left. "It is no longer our village."

Deer of Stone pointed at his own head. "We will take the real one with us." He picked up a small, charred stick and put it in his basket-pack. "We will never forget."

"No," said Atl. But it was easy to leave.

The air was sweeter the farther they walked from the burned village. Both babies tired themselves crying, yet slept poorly.

Dahlia walked with Atl. Seven House rocked gently on her back.

He stared at the path ahead. "We have left our ways. Only your father knows what it's like beyond the next village."

"He says we are leaving the killing. The 'bad-spirit' of it."

"I think he is right. There is much we will have to learn."

"We have at least one big problem." She looked straight at Atl. "No woman has a man. No man has a woman. What is our future?"

"We have two babies. And your father said there are villages. We may find women as we go."

Dahlia looked away. "Like breeding dogs."

"Breeding dogs? Do you think we could do that?"

She stared at him again, then looked away. "Forget it."

Atl said, "I am glad the babies stopped crying."

Dahlia kicked a pebble. "Seven House. Rose Blue. They need energy. The more starved they are, the less they eat. We can barely get water in them. They need their real mother. And she was killed."

Cracking noises came from the trees. Then silence. Everyone stopped. More cracks, like footsteps. Then a human voice. A dirty, scratched woman in a torn skirt peered around a bush. She cried out loudly as soon as she saw them.

"Shy Petals!" cried Dahlia.

Shy Petals made her way out of the brush. Her great stomach had shrunk. Her breasts were bigger than ever, swinging side to side. Dahlia ran to her and hugged her and calmed her. Thoughtful Rose leaned against her and patted her arm.

Everyone listened to Shy Petals's story. Like the girls, she had been away from the village when the killers came and, like the girls, saw, and was afraid to go back. She ran and walked far away, finally stopping in a deep ravine. She ate berries. Her baby came, a boy. Where was he now? He was sleeping in the ravine, wrapped in cloth and branches. When she saw One-Cip' and the others on the trail, she cried for joy.

But when they told her they had not seen her husband since the killings, she cried for sadness. She took them to her hiding place in the

257

ravine, and showed them her fat, sleeping baby. They all gently stroked him and passed him around. He smiled when they touched his cheek. Once he even laughed.

A Fox is Mad built a fire and they all sat around it, silent, listening to the cooing of the three babies as they sucked in turn from Shy Petal's rich supply.

Finally they walked again, and that night made camp outside Cuetlachtlan.

The next day they went into Cuetlachtlan and met a man named Ocelot, a traveling trader like One-Cip'. One-Cip' told him of the burning of his village and the murders of the women. Ocelot exploded with anger. One-Cip' explained that they did not know who the killers were, but Ocelot seemed ready to kill them on the spot, whoever they were. But even with his quick temper, everyone liked him.

***

After four days in Cuetlachtlan, the group packed and set out again. Only One-Cip' had ever been that far south. Ocelot joined them, along with his wife Temple Tree and their little boy Monkey Laughs. Temple Tree introduced One-Cip' to her friend the widow Morning Glory. Her only child, a boy, had been taken in one of the Flower Wars for the sacrifices. One-Cip' seemed to take a special interest in her.

As they walked, Dahlia said to Atl, "Monkey Laughs is cute."

"I am glad Ocelot came," said Atl. "He was a warrior and can teach us."

"And Temple Tree," said Dahlia. "Now we have a married man and woman."

"We have had good luck since Shy Petals found us."

"Even that was good luck," said Dahlia. "She is talented. After she started spinning, hers was the only cotton thread your mother would use." She caught herself. "Oh. I am sorry."

"It's alright. I can put it out of my mind."

"You can? How?"

"I think of the killers, of making them wish they never had…"

"I thought Cholula was enough for you. I thought it cured you."

"I thought so too, but the hatred comes back."

"Don't let it. We are gone from all that now."

Atl shook his head. "Someday I will find them."

Dahlia pointed ahead. "Who's that?"

A tall, bearded man in a brown robe stood beside the trail facing away from them, shoulders slumped. A large bag lay at his side.

"Looks Sant-yago to me," said Atl.

When the man turned and saw them, he picked up his bag, which seemed heavy, and ran into the trees. Leaves and twigs popped and shuffled. He fell and got up twice.

Atl smiled at Deer of Stone. "Noisy runner."

Deer of Stone did not seem to hear, but glared, with Ocelot, at the woods where the Sant-yago had run. Suddenly he and Ocelot dropped their basket-packs and ran after him. Their feet did not make a sound. Two-Rabbit quickly joined them. Atl started to follow, but One-Cip' stopped him.

Finally the three came back, leading the Sant-yago and carrying his heavy pack. They brought him to One-Cip'. He was a head taller than any of them.

"Tongue?" One-Cip' said in Nahuatl.

The scratched, sweating, bearded face looked vaguely familiar.

"Nahuatl, if you please," the Sant-yago said, his eyes round and innocent. He scratched his beard, then bowed twice and said, "I am travelling to the endless waters."

"Why did you run from us?"

"I was afraid. I do not know the ways here."

"Good reason," said One-Cip'. "Some people here would kill any Sant-yago."

"And I thank you for your kindness," said the man. He spoke Nahuatl very well. His voice was familiar.

"Are you a Sant-yago priest?"

"Why... yes. I urge peace." He glanced at Dahlia. "Could you help me find my way?"

"First answer. How are you priests different from the soldiers?"

The tall Sant-yago looked One-Cip' up and down. "We believe in helping the Totonacas. We try to keep the soldiers peaceful."

"Why do you do this?"

"I... we... have seen what fine people you are."

"Mendez!" shouted Atl, happily. "You are Ramiro Mendez!"

Mendez smiled, hesitated, then boldly said, "Why yes, I am."

"Don't you remember us? Your friends?"

"Ah! Of course. And Deer of Dirt, and let us see..."

"Stone," said Deer of Stone, "Deer of Stone."

Atl said, "Why are you wearing the robe? You're not a priest!"

"Became one," he said quickly. He brushed his lips with his fingers. "I want to help others, as I helped you, you remember. That is what priests do. So I became one."

One-Cip' said, "What is in your pack that is so heavy?"

"Oh, my study papers. Some bedding. My book of the priests."

"Show us."

It bothered Atl that One-Cip' was so harsh with the well-mannered Mendez.

He hesitated again, then said, "Alright. Here…" He laid down his bag and pulled out thin deerskins stacked between plates of wood. He pulled up one of the wooden plates, and Atl saw marks on the skins like the talk-marks of the Sant-yagos. Mendez flipped through many, many skins covered with the marks. "Priest words."

Atl looked closely. He knew to follow the marks from left to right. He pronounced them, though he did not know their meaning.

Mendez smiled, hesitantly. "Very good."

"But I do not know the meaning," said Atl.

"The tongue is called Latin. It is for us priests."

Deer of Stone couldn't resist. He pronounced several words.

One-Cip' was surprised at the boys' reading. But he seemed even more wary of Mendez than before. Dahlia also seemed wary, and shy about his glances.

Finally One-Cip' straightened and said to Mendez, "You may travel with us. You must do as I say. In two days you will see a path to the road that leads to the endless waters."

***

That night they made a fire and sat around it.

"I am going to scout the trail," said One-Cip'.

"I will go with you," said Atl.

"No," said One-Cip'. "Stay together. I know the trail." He glanced at Mendez. "Stranger, you must sit where you are and obey the others. I put Ocelot in charge."

After One-Cip' left, Atl sat next to Dahlia.

She said, "How do you know the Sant-yago?"

"Mendez? He helped us in the battles. He is smart and strong and caring."

"He should learn to run more quietly in the woods," she said. Atl laughed. "At least he is well-mannered."

"Have you noticed? He stays away from Balanced Turtle."

"Now that you say it."

"Poor Balanced Turtle," she said. "Covered with blisters. He can hardly move. He is miserable. He does not speak any longer."

"I am glad he is small," said Atl, "and easy to carry."

"Look. Thoughtful Rose and Pink are with their father now." Atl looked. "Two-Rabbit is happy."

A Fox is Mad threw more kindling on the fire.

Shy Petals said, "What will tomorrow bring?"

"I wonder," said Two-Rabbit. "We have left our village behind."

"Our village," said Deer of Stone, "but not our ways."

"We should be ready," said Two-Rabbit, "to learn new things."

"We will never change," said Deer of Stone. "No Aztecs now."

"The Sant-yagos could change the Aztecs," said Two-Rabbit.

"They will not change us," said Deer of Stone.

Two-Rabbit studied Mendez and his stack of deer skins in the wooden plates. He said, "What do your markings say?"

Mendez looked surprised. "These? Ah." He lifted a wooden cover. "They say, 'Peace,' and, 'Love the stranger ...'"

Atl's back went cold as he saw, falling from a small hole in the raised plate, one of his mother's wooden ear-spools. It rolled in the dirt. Mendez reached for it quickly.

Atl gasped. His eyes burned and tears flowed suddenly. He could not stop the memories. The tiny metal beads embedded in the spools. The warmth and the sureness of all things. He had been able so far to stop the thoughts. His mother, who loved him and wanted everyone to be happy, was made to suffer great pain, the sweet life he knew through her eyes and her touch, destroyed. No more would her delicate work, her rare talent, delight the world. Worst of all, she was taken from him. "Oh!" he said, loudly.

"What?" said Dahlia.

Atl pointed at the spool as Mendez tried to hide it. Atl thought for a moment he looked guilty. Not him! Our one helping friend!

Atl felt a presence above him: the old swarm of faces.

Dahlia knew the spool, too. "Your mother's...!"

Deer of Stone said to Mendez, "How did you get that?"

"This?" Mendez tried to slide the spool back into the hole. "I found it. Is it yours?"

"Where did you find it?" said Deer of Stone. "What else do you have in that wood plate?"

"Nothing." Mendez slid a hand over the cover and lowered it.

"Why do you hide it?" said Deer of Stone. "Let us see."

"Oh, it is nothing. Would you like the spool? You can have it."

"You are hiding something." Deer of Stone stood, angry.

"Oh, no," said Mendez. "No." He slid it all behind him.

Deer of Stone boldly stepped behind Mendez. "What is this?" He pulled off the inside cover and pieces of gold and silver fell to the ground. Among them was the other ear-spool.

"Give me that sack," said Deer of Stone. He picked up Mendez' big carry-sack.

"No!" shouted Mendez quickly. "That is for me only!"

Deer of Stone opened it and reached in and pulled out a folded piece of cloth. No one but Atl's mother ever put the colors together that way. He unfolded it. "No burn marks! You took this before...!"

"I found those things on the road." Mendez tried to smile.

"Such fine cloth lying on a road? What road? Where?"

"I do not know the names of places." He pointed. "Back that way. After the fire."

"How did you know about a fire?"

"I... I did not. You said something about burn marks."

"You said, 'After the fire.' How did you know when it was?"

Mendez thought fast. "It, eh... It is a story told..."

"Who told you?"

"I... I do not remember. It..."

"What is the story?"

"A village was burned and... and..."

"Village? How did you know it was a village?"

"It is told."

"Who burned it?"

"Soldiers. No." He laughed lamely. "No. Natives. I mean Aztecs. Yes, the Aztecs whom you hate. They did it."

"The Aztecs never do that." Deer of Stone reached in the bag again and pulled out several pieces of Sant-yago style clothing. Then he pulled out a small animal skin bag with Sant-yago markings on it. He loosened its pull-string and turned it up. Out of it fell jewelry, familiar pieces that had been worn by Atl's mother and Two-Rabbit's wife Marigold and Two-House's wife.

Ocelot stepped up beside Mendez, glaring at him.

"Where did you get these?" said Deer of Stone.

"I told you. I found them."

"In this bag?"

"Yes. I found the bag and its contents and hope I can return them to their owner."

"It is a Sant-yago bag."

"The bag is not mine. I found it." Mendez looked around, seeming about to run.

"What are the marks?"

"They say, eh, 'Sant-yago bag.'" Mendez took a step, but Ocelot blocked his way.

Atl looked at the marks, then pronounced them. "Ra-mi-ro Men-dez." Suddenly rage pushed his sorrow back. Mendez had won their trust, knowing all along that they were the very people whose village he had destroyed, whose loved ones he had burned and killed. Killed Atl's mother! The hanging swarm of faces laughed and drooled.

Deer of Stone straightened. "Does anyone doubt?"

"He is the one," said Atl, tears streaming.

Mendez grabbed what he could and turned to run, but Ocelot and Deer of Stone grabbed his arms. "No," he said, struggling.

"Is he the killer you have spoken of?" said Ocelot.

"The gods have given him to us," said Deer of Stone.

They both held Mendez who seemed to shrivel into himself.

Atl felt suddenly ashamed for having thought his people, and especially his honest, caring mentor One-Cip', were simple and backwards before this man of fake manners.

"Kill him," said A Fox is Mad.

"Too easy," said Deer of Stone. "Too quick. Burn him. Slowly. As he did our..."

"Burn, yes!" said Ocelot, whose eyes glared with rage.

A Fox is Mad grabbed more wood and put it on the fire.

Now Mendez tried to smile. "You must understand..."

"We understand," said Deer of Stone.

The flames grew higher. Two-Rabbit picked up a heavy stick and held it to the flames. "My sweet Marigold," he said.

"Others did it," said Mendez, sweating. "I tried to stop them."

"You have already lied to us," said Deer of Stone.

The coals glowed brightly. Sparks popped and spewed.

"You... you are right. I should not have lied. It was my bag, but I was afraid you would think it was I that burned the village, so I... You must know that one man could not burn so many huts. I..."

"Many huts?" said Deer of Stone. "How did you know it was many? If you only tried to stop the killers, why did you never tell us before, back in the army, when you knew how badly we needed to know?"

"Oh... I..."

Suddenly Two-Rabbit swung the flaming stick, screaming. He hit Mendez in the side, making him cry out and bend over.

"Wait!" said Deer of Stone.

Two-Rabbit hit Mendez again.

"Wait!" Deer of Stone held up a hand, and his expression promised a better revenge. Two-Rabbit bit his lip and stopped.

"Take his carry-sack," said Deer of Stone as Mendez tried to get his breath. "We will make him suffer as he made our people suffer, by taking all he has, and by burning him to death. Atl, take the stack of skins and the wooden plates and the gold. We will keep them for ourselves."

Mendez could hardly breathe for the fear.

Atl didn't mind Deer of Stone's acting as leader in his father's absence and Ocelot's rage. No one minded. They all, even the women, wanted the same thing, the slow torturing of Mendez. The same lust was in their eyes that was in the hanging faces, and Atl felt it in himself. He could not wait to see Mendez' horrible pain and screaming.

"Don't let him die too soon," he said.

Chapter 26

Haughton-Alsef's and Dove-Ti's curiosity about the coming ceremony overcame their fear, and they let the village boys carry them across the logs and up past the ring of stones to the pool where the others waited. Blake watched the "hospital" where Rachel lay, ready to alert Howard and L.P., even though Ehec said she would not be part of the ceremony.

Tetl directed everyone to keep a space open in the middle, even though each villager seemed to know where to stand, apparently having come together like that often.

And in that space stood the girl, the one Howard had seen the first day being instructed by the women, in a plain long gown of the dark green cotton, her red-gold skin clear and clean.

The villagers smiled briefly at each other, from otherwise serious faces. They watched the girl with quiet awe, the way people approach a silenced birth-room, or a funeral.

The girl stared thoughtfully at the ground, through it. She seemed wise beyond her years.

On one side of her was a small pile of clothes and two clay dolls, and on the other, tiers of big rocks, like over-sized steps, backing steeply up the mountain slope for about fifty feet. Behind her were the trickling falls, where the little creek widened into the pool, which was three or four feet deep. A tall tree, deathly white, hung over it, leafless except for a few green shoots struggling toward light from its gnarled base.

Old Ehec stood beside her, feet well apart, leaning on his stick.

A young man began walking back and forth in the open space. Another walked out with a drum and thumped loudly and pushed his neck forward and back, like a walking chicken. The sound and sight of it were annoying. The first man hopped whimsically and ridiculously on his toes. He threw his arms about as if disjointed, sometimes crouching and grinning distantly. Another joined him, and hopped in the same senseless way, not in time with the thumping drum, grinning falsely and mindlessly at the people he passed.

Howard hadn't expected an attempt at entertainment. The antics were showy and self-centered. A woman joined them, then another, twisting with the same self-engrossed bad taste. No one objected. If anything, the crowd seemed sympathetic.

Suddenly there was a rustling in the trees and most of the team ducked as the sho-lo-peet swung out across the clearing on a vine, barking and laughing wildly, and disappeared on the other side. He left an odor trail. Several villagers looked at each other and held back giggles.

Then a dancer ran from one side of the clearing to the other, arms outstretched, then to another, then another, as if chasing some vague elusive thing. Others did the same, randomly, some hopping on their toes, some crouching and bouncing, some on their bellies, snaking back and forth through the clearing, all waving their arms in poor time with the drum's non-rhythm. Howard felt bad for them.

Oddly, the girl in the center seemed thoughtfully obsessed with their bad dancing.

Then the first dancer suddenly stopped and crouched and looked up as if he had seen something fearsome, or beautiful, in the trees. It made Howard look, but he saw nothing. Then another dancer looked up, then others, and they began standing and raising their arms.

Their movements and the drum slowed and became regular. A young woman threw her arms out as if discarding things, and spun gracefully. She raised her arms thoughtfully as if reaching for something, then opened them as if receiving. That slowed her spinning. She brought her hands to her face. The other dancers, one by one, did the same.

She turned and toe-stepped smoothly onto the first rock tier, then sideways across it, arms and head raised again, followed by other young men and women, arms and heads raised. Then she led them up to the next higher tier and back across, then another, in switchbacks, and so on, all of them becoming more rhythmic and coordinated, lifting knees high now, passing each other on alternating levels like slowly streaming ribbons in Asian dances, until the young woman reached the top, and the long line, in its upward spiral of about twenty tiers, stopped.

At that moment the lowest dancer crouched and held his arms over his head, palms together, like the point of a flame. He stood again, slowly, lifted one knee, then spread his hands and lowered them and his knee, and the next did the same after him, and the next, all of it making a sort of wave of rising and spreading and falling arms and knees, as if a flame were passing along the spiral of bodies, left and right and up until it reached the young woman at the top where it seemed to pass through her body to her raised arms and out of her open vibrating fingers. They repeated the wave again, smiling now and rocking their heads, and again and again. They began to sing softly, in rhythm with their body movements and with the now syncopated drum, faster, each person's arms rising gracefully higher with each repetition, as a sweet undulation, faces smiling happily at each other and the crowd, and all the intertwining movements made them appear to be one living body, given being and life and movement by the seeming flame flowing harmoniously through them. Then at once the drum stopped, and they stopped, arms and heads raised, only the open hands of the young woman at the top still vibrating, and in the eerie silence that followed, the team, and all the villagers, finally exhaled.

Dove-Ti started clapping, and Haughton-Alsef joined her, throwing his head back with a congratulatory grin, then a couple of other team members joined in, but they all quit when they realized that none of the villagers clapped. Smith held a finger to his mouth.

The dancers didn't lower their arms or their eyes, but began singing again, softly, and this time all the villagers joined in. Their simple unusual harmony carried a sense of both foreboding and wonder. The very range of tone qualities, from nasal and thin to resonant and warm, like the range of skin color and style of movement, only served to underscore a sense of depth, not so much of space or sound, but of oneness of spirit, and Howard did not feel entertained, but thought how there are times when you see and hear something you have never imagined, a wonder, from fellow humans, as if you were in a dream from which fear and inhibition had been removed and only a certain openness, devoid of malice or envy, remained.

He was amazed they could achieve an effect so intense that it would cross over to him an outsider, and even remind him, oddly, of the oneness he had felt with Rachel on the divide, and in spite of his fears he had an urge to join in and sing with them.

But he also knew there was, in the wonder of the dance and the singing, a sense of foreboding, a sense of a looming alteration of one's life, and he could see how it was true that by art and emotion, people could be made to face and accept almost anything, even a drowning, and his head got the better of his heart and he was able to hold back.

The singing stopped and as the dancers stood panting deeply, Chal-chee appeared, carefully carrying in front of her, in her hands on top of her pregnant stomach, a stack of what looked like dried animal skins, each about a foot and a half square.

Haughton-Alsef was suddenly beside himself. He dropped his pipe, stood on his toes, and stared at the parchments, mouth open. Then he stepped forward, actually pushing several people, to get a better look.

Chal-chee held the parchments nervously, as if they might come to pieces any minute.

"Latin alphabet," said Haughton-Alsef, still on his toes.

Chal-chee stood, with the writings, next to Ehec and the girl.

Now and then a dancer would rest his or her arms for a minute.

Ehec took the top sheet and held it out on shaking, upturned palms. He squinted, then read slowly.

"They can read," whispered Haughton-Alsef in awe. It sounded like the Nahuatl Ehec had spoken with Zoe.

Ehec said the word "Ya-si" a couple of times in the reading. He looked up often, as if he had it memorized.

The villagers listened not so much to be entertained, but to hear what they had heard before, to grasp once again, together, the meaning.

"'Death,'" whispered Zoe. "I heard the word 'death.'"

"Oh boy," whispered L.P.

When Ehec stopped reading, the girl picked up the pile of clothes and dolls. She carried them to a spot in front of the tiers of dancers and set them down.

"And," whispered Zoe, "I heard the word 'sacrifice.'"

Howard said, "I thought they only did this to really sick people."

"Maybe she was sick," said Zoe. "and now they've like… gotten her well, ready for this."

The dancers sang again, softly, then finally lowered their arms and watched. There was only the sound of the falls. The girl stepped back from the clothes to her position beside Ehec.

Howard would have to decide again, as he had when DeSparr walked into the river, or when the Jaguar-guys turned to him after drowning the peccary, or when the old man laid the knife on Tee-week's chest. There were lots of people. He would not be able to save the girl, but only turn her sacrifice into a disrupted one instead of a beautiful one. He was surprised that the beauty of the singing and the dancing and even Ehec's reading reduced the sense of horror, even in himself.

Ehec handed Tetl the page and motioned for the girl to turn and step into the pool. Howard's throat tightened and before he knew it he had taken a step forward.

A man and woman, the girl's parents, he thought, came solemnly forward holding a large earthen jar with a wide mouth. They handed it to Ehec, who placed it under the little falls where it began to fill.

Then he carefully stepped into the pool beside the girl and put his hand on her shoulder. Howard took one more step forward, and Smith motioned for him to stop. Haughton-Alsef worked his way closer to Tetl who was now holding the parchments.

Ehec didn't seem strong enough to push the girl down unless she were willing. So far she had seemed willing. But Howard was sure she would struggle when her lungs began to hurt. He remembered the flood, the impersonal way in which the water invaded his body. He looked around. There was a kind of social inertia. The villagers had seen this before.

He got Smith's attention. "We can't let…"

"Shh," said Dove-Ti.

The villagers didn't seem to notice, so he went on. "We can't let them do it."

Smith held a palm out and down.

Dove-Ti nodded and whispered, "We must respect all…"

"Baloney," whispered Crauder.

Maybe, thought Howard, Crauder would side with him. But he didn't want sides. He just couldn't stand the thought of her being drowned.

Ehec, still holding the girl's shoulder, said something to Chalchee and she handed Tetl another page and Ehec laid a finger on it and nodded and Tetl began reading. Again Howard heard the word, "Ya-si." He took another step.

"We have no right to interfere," whispered Dove-Ti. "We are the intruders."

He glanced at her and was surprised at how pale she was and how fearfully she stared at the girl. He sensed no dark side to anyone's motives, no desire to witness the pain of another.

"She…" was all he could think to say. He was amazed how little thought he had given his own moral principles, and how shallow was any thought-foundation within him by which those principles might be justified or given unity or integrity.

Tetl stopped reading and Ehec pushed lightly downward on the girl's shoulder. She hesitated. Tears showed on her cheeks.

Howard took another step, and so did Crauder.

Smith and Haughton-Alsef and Dove-Ti all said to them at the same time, "No!"

The sense of urgency in Howard grew stronger as it was opposed. Was it conscience or defiance? He would be overpowered, could be stoned. He didn't even know the girl. She was cute. What would he feel if she were ugly? Deformed? Retarded? Where must he draw the line, stop giving in? Innocent human life seemed a good place, and that thought stirred him, but it was as deep as he could think, and not deep enough, because when the girl's knees began to bend and Ehec's hand kept pressing her shoulder and Howard saw how many and how devoted were the villagers and how lonely was his cause, he waited.

She was in to her chest. She closed her eyes tight. Ehec picked up the big jar from under the fall, now full. He raised it, struggling under its weight, awkward on his feet, then emptied it, drenching her head and shoulders. He set the jar down again, knelt beside her, and pressed her shoulder again. She bent at the waist, then went under.

Howard could almost feel it himself, the being under, as if he were in the flood again. Did he see her eyes, so full of her unusual child's wisdom, looking up at him through the water? The air rushed into his throat and his foot shot forward, but then she came up, and he lost his balance in his stopping, and Smith and L.P. had to reach and grab his arm to keep him from falling. Ehec and several villagers glanced at them. Then Tetl held the pages out in front of him again, and read.

Howard whispered to Zoe. "What's he reading?"

"Something about cleansing," she said. "A parent. A child. Some kind of spirit. Obedience. Training... I don't know."

Then the girl and Ehec rose.

Howard kept shaking. He whispered to L.P., joking to cover his tension, "I thought it would be the old drowning thing."

L.P. whispered, "Just a watered-down version."

The girl stepped to dry ground. The wet green gown clung to her form and the expression on her face made all of her seem to glow in the crowd like sun through leaves. She wiped the water from her face and hair, crying.

Howard said, "I guess their sacrificing doesn't include girls."

"Just outsiders," said L.P., "like Zoe said."

Haughton-Alsef and Zoe talked.

"I want," said Haughton-Alsef, "to get a good look at those parchments. We need to know what language they are written in."

"Probably Nahuatl," said Zoe.

"Do you realize how significant this is? Nahuatl in Latin characters? It's huge. When can we get another look?"

"That won't be like... easy. The best I can tell, those writings are majorly valuable to Ehec and the tribe, and they're kept carefully hidden for like... safekeeping kind of thing."

Haughton-Alsef said, "Will they be brought out again soon?"

"Just for ceremonies, I think."

"Like, if they decide to do something with Rachel?"

"I hope they don't. But that would be the kind of thing."

"Well, I think we would do well to encourage them to move on to the next sacrifice. It's an opportunity to witness the way they apply their beliefs, and to see again those super-important 'writings.'"

"Nothing happens to Rachel," said Howard, interrupting.

Most of the team crossed the stream, with help, to the Burb.

Howard and L.P. stayed in the village and slept again in their hut next to Rachel's.

***

When Howard got up the next morning it was still dark. He dressed and looked in on Rachel, who was no better. His urge to run was strong, though not aimed. He began following a trail in the woods on the back side of the mountain, toward the possible 'back door' he and L.P. and Blake had wondered about. The trail was steep, leading upward around the mountain to the south and east faces. There were no huts on that side.

When light began to show, he found an opening in the pines that led to a flat-topped rock projecting over the cliff's edge like the front half of a rowboat. There was about a two hundred foot drop straight down, and below that a tumbling slope of jagged rocks. A gust of wind made him step back.

If he could just have fifteen minutes to talk to Rachel, to tell her what he had held back in three months of opportunities. What he would

271

give! All he owned. His right arm. She saved his life.

But of course that was all academic. Who would want his right arm? Maybe cannibals. He chuckled ironically. But even digesting his right arm, they could do nothing to heal her.

Far beyond him, silhouetted against the newly glowing eastern sky, lay another range of mountains, their tumbling ridges heaved up like great ancient knuckles, throwing a gray-green darkness back across the valley. A white waterfall slid down a smooth gray rock face, seemingly motionless in its distance. Two specks, which he could tell were large birds, circled in front of it, brightly sunlit against the shadowed slopes.

Thick trees of a thousand shades of green clamored for light on the mountainsides. Their tops followed and revealed the cascading flow of ridges. Here and there maverick limbs reached above the canopy like deft bony fingers, leaf-clusters arching across their tips like cards being shuffled. A dead tree, stark yellow-white and unmoving, contrasted the swaying waves of living leaves.

At the valley bottom, several segments of the river barely showed through breaks in the trees, the river on which they had come, which had flooded and nearly drowned Howard and DeSparr and taken, then sent, them all to a new and different world. He could barely hear the roar of its rapids. Two visible parts of it were in direct line with the low sun, reflecting it as if another sun were glaring with fierce little eyes from inside the earth. The water had the look of molten silver, shedding a thin mist upward to hang above the trees like a wispy, ragged curtain, giving away, even where the river itself was not visible, its snaking route.

The rising sun hung in the silver-blue sky with such brightness that it seemed to burn a hole there. Its reflections from the still-dewed leaves of the mountain ridges were searing and precise, forcing Howard to shift his gaze downward, where the soft darkness of the deep shadows were interrupted only by the two brightly lit birds, still circling.

Rachel, worth living for, was dying because she jumped in on el tigre for him. She was being punished for his forcing her to follow him. Each day of her not waking decreased what little hope he had.

He looked down. Two hundred feet. Objects having mass attract. He had, in common with the earth, gravity. He had been accidentally born, designed by genes. He was no more than what he ate. What could he do? Nothing.

Pray.

Why did he think of that? Rachel had used the word once or

twice. It was what you did when there was no hope. You didn't expect an answer, but it would make you feel better.

Pray to what? Could there be anything out there that could hear and help? Why would it, or he, or she, or they, listen to Howard who had hardly given it-him-her-them a thought before?

He could invent a god, tailor-made to his needs. But that would only work when it didn't matter. Now he had a real need, and only a real god could do anything about that, assuming it existed and assuming it cared to bother, and assuming he hadn't run it off or disgusted it.

It, he thought. If there was a god, he hoped it wasn't an it. People of old prayed to the earth, the sun, fire. Those things would only stare back. No, they wouldn't even stare. They were as sightless as they were mindless. And it was the earth and the sun and fire, infection and heat and rot, that were mindlessly killing Rachel. Talk to an it and it hears nothing and knows nothing and does nothing.

Know. A thought almost came, but passed.

There have been gods that were brilliant ideas. But an idea was just an it, too. The universe, the sum of all nature and all ideas. That great system was, like a true work of art, so much more than the sum of its parts. But like a painting or a symphony, it couldn't hear or think or respond. The sum of all its was just a greater, more dazzling it.

Rachel was about to die. And if a god was what was needed, it would have to be real, would have to be a thinking, caring, acting god, and he didn't really know a god, thinking or not. He never really knew the Sunday School one. Nor the Greeks' gods. Nor the Hindus'. Nor the Greenshirts'. So there was nothing. Untold numbers of people, many good people, had in the history of the world cried out to a god in time of danger, then suffered indescribable pain and loss. So why should a caring god suddenly be trotted out for him like a genie, ready to serve?

***

"Hyde," came a voice from behind, startling him. He turned.

"Mister Ehec," he said, and his neck stiffened.

Ehec stepped onto the rock with Howard and stood facing the valley, toothless mouth panting, feet apart, knees bent for balance in the gusting wind, soft eyes studying Howard. "See much here."

Howard looked out again. The two birds soared higher, lit by the sun. Howard could see now that they were huge harpy's eagles.

"Yes," said Howard, forming his bare feet to the rock, steadying himself in the gusts. "It's scary."

Ehec smiled. "To see scares."

Something moved to the east. Howard and Ehec turned at the same time. It was one of the eagles, gliding toward them, higher now, the sun behind it in the clear sky. Howard squinted. It rode the wind in place, suddenly up a little, down a little. The long wings made a thin line, angled slightly from level. The head rode small and shrewd between them. Its eyes would focus on a rat in a field, a monkey in a tree, a fish in a stream, the one chosen doomed.

Howard blurted, "I want to save Rachel."

Ehec looked at him. "You see her much."

"I love…" No word seemed right. It seemed pretentious in front of Ehec to use the vague word love, which Howard had so casually thrown about in the past. "I care…"

"You will give?" said Ehec. "For her?"

Howard could tell it was simple curiosity, not an offer, but he said, "Anything."

"She gave?" said Ehec. "For you?"

"Yes. You know?"

"Zoe tell." Ehec raised his hands as he had before and looked up and spoke. "Ya-si good. Ya-si give. Ehec need Ya-si."

Was he trying to summon his Ya-si out of the air? He did it with such confidence that Howard began to fear it could actually happen. But he said, "I don't see Ya-si."

"Not see," said Ehec, glancing at Howard, still holding his hands high. "Know." Ehec looked up again, and his voice was softer. "Ya-si, may you help Hyde."

It touched Howard that Ehec prayed for him. But he knew better than to hope. It had become obvious their god was tailor-made to justify their deadly practices.

"Can you ask Ya-si to let Rachel live?" Ehec's answer could reveal his motives.

"You," said Ehec. "You ask. You say, 'Ya-si, may Rachel live.'"

Howard looked up. He couldn't do it. It wasn't him. "You ask."

Again Ehec raised his hands and spoke, first in his own language, then in English, "Ya-si good. Ya-si, may Ra-chul live." He looked at Howard.

"Now what?" said Howard.

"Eh?"

"What will Ya-si do now?"

"Up to him."

"So much for Ya-si," said Howard, sarcastically.

"Eh?"

"I don't know," he said. "I don't know how I got into this. I came here for I don't know what reason, probably to run, run, run... no, to find something, I don't know what, and I met her, and she bugged me, and I held back and never talked to her — well, talked, but not talk-talked — and she cared for me — I could tell she did — and I would give anything for her now, but ... I want out of here. I want to run. But I don't want to leave her. I'm..."

"You tied up?"

"Yes. Good one, Mr. Ehec. I'm all tied up."

Suddenly the eagle came again, out of the sun, and Howard and Ehec turned to look, and he almost reached for it, irrationally, but held back. Then he thought, in his desperation, that it was coming to him, and he could pray to it. At least it was alive. Its stern face seemed wise. It was free to soar higher than anything. It could know things and have powers. Of course that was crazy. He turned instead to his easy, familiar, stress-avoiding approach to any problem, extreme analysis. He unsquinted and saw the eagles' eyes, fierce, sharp, large, sensing, better eyes, he had heard, than human, and if he had it right, the muscles of its eyeballs, like those of his own, changed the shapes of the eyeballs as needed in order to throw the rays of light coming through their appropriately contoured lenses onto their retinas in the precise arrangement needed to trigger complex but unified and accurate signals, which were sent from there through innumerable tiny nerves to the brain, the muscles and the lens and the retina and the nerves and the brain knowing nothing of each other, or of anything, but operating in ways he had heard were the result of a great genetic non-design developed by and bound to nothing more than the lucky or unlucky falling together of atoms over billions of years, the same thing that caused his own eye and his brain to receive and record the images of the coming eagle, like a digital mechanism, and none of it knew anything, none of it was connected to anything by any means other than lifeless, thoughtless chance. None of that could receive a prayer.

Then suddenly, the eagle's mate appeared, and the two came on, riding the wind with a purpose and harmony born of their company, riding with sudden risings and bankings, as if they were one, their route and goal directed by the most subtle twisting of their spreading end-feathers, a little here, a little there.

"The bird free," said Ehec. "Give self, be free."

Howard shook his head at the contradiction.

"Give self to way of sky, wind. If not..." Ehec raised his hands, swooped them down, twisted his fingers together as a bird crashing to the ground, and said, gutturally, "Kee-ah!" He smiled and looked at Howard.

Howard wanted to admire, even envy, the great eagle, and not to think it had to "give self" to anything. But the oneness of the two birds as they circled, like that he had shared with Rachel on the divide, required a certain giving of self. Ehec's new thought was scary, the strange irony in which the eagle, by enslaving itself to the laws of flight, not even understanding them, had gained a freedom far in excess of that which it would have had had it followed the first freedom-loving impulses to defy and reject those laws, to play in and around what seemed to it the whole world, the nest.

And Howard had a sudden, overwhelming sense of the presence of laws about which he must decide, laws not of science or of civilization, but of love and the living of life, free from which he would never know freedom.

He didn't know those laws of love and life. Worse, they probably had to do with Ehec's brand of giving — human sacrifices — and that revived in him the urge to run. He almost lost his balance in a gust.

Ehec's selflessness was okay. He could be like that if he wanted. But the fearsome connotations of his religion were not. His talk was both personal and alien, both attractive and terrifying, like the jaguar he saw in the shadows just before the flood, and again on the divide, and like, yes, Rachel.

The eagles brought their wings down powerfully, banked away from Howard and Ehec and swept out over the dark valley, bright in the sun, gliding away along the mountain slopes.

"You knife?" said Ehec.

Howard fumbled in his fanny-pack for the knife, then showed it. Ehec studied it. "What for? What knife for?"

"For cutting," said Howard. He opened the blade.

"Knife for cut," said Ehec. "But in bag... not cut?"

"Well, obviously, somebody has to pick it up and use it."

"What you for, Hyde?"

That was sudden and, Howard thought, unfair. But he would not say to this primitive villager, that he, from the land of great medical and commercial and engineering feats, did not have an answer. So what was he 'for?' Then he felt a sudden chill. Was he supposed to prove he should not be sacrificed?

He would not let himself look stupid. If he couldn't answer that question, of all questions, he could rightly be thought stupid. So what answer? The knife. It was of his great civilization. It had impressed the villagers. It was well-designed, well-made, functional, solid, flashing skylight. It told Howard nothing.

"I design. I plan good ways to make, uh, huts." But whether designing buildings was a good reason for existing or not, Howard knew it was not enough to be what he was 'for.'

"I am not for just one thing," he said. "I am for many things."

Ehec nodded. "What are the things?" He was relentless.

Howard had never let his formal education be a matter of pride, but it did leave a gap between him and Ehec. How do you talk to a man caught up in a primitive religion? How do you tell him that you try to see things objectively, scientifically, without prejudice? And suddenly that thought generated an outpouring of newly exposed prejudices from his own education, few of which said that Rachel's life, or his own, had a high or sacred value apart from artificial rationalizations, but rather that life and the universe were formed by a series of unthinking accidents, that humans are no more than smart kinds of animals, fleshy machines, that there is no good or bad, no guilt apart from the ever-changing system of laws, that reason and the senses are the only means of knowing truth, which probably doesn't exist, and even that the word prejudice itself only stands for that which differs with those prejudices.

He was amazed that any answer seemed false or shallow. Worse, he couldn't deny that the question was of supreme importance. Why had he hardly considered it in all his twenty-nine years? What was he for?

A new, faint possibility refused to go away, that Ehec had something, that his Ya-si was real, that his prayer for Rachel could actually change things. But he wouldn't let himself hope.

His feet began, before he was aware of it, to step lightly in place. When you're running, people don't ask you abstract questions. "I have to go," he said.

Ehec smiled and bowed. Howard bowed and stepped back from

the ledge, then turned and walked quickly, then ran, back toward the village, and was struck with a new fear, that his running had failed to avoid a decision because avoiding a decision was in itself a decision.

***

The next morning Howard crossed over and joined the team, all but DeSparr, who were gathered for the morning meeting in the 'Burb.'

"These people," said Haughton-Alsef, "are experiencing the primeval Springtime of culture. Their intentions regarding us, and our dear Rachel, provide us with an ace up our sleeve, so to speak."

"Out of the question," said Howard.

"She's not recovering. It's obvious, sorry to say, that she'll never regain a meaningful life. We can't see her or talk to her. We don't really know her any more. Supporting her sacrifice will alleviate what has become, let's admit it, a burden for us. And observing it will add immeasurably to our body of information about these people. And they can help us find our way out. It's a win-win situation."

"Monkey manure," said Crauder.

Howard excused himself, crossed back over, climbed to Rachel's hospital hut, and was surprised to find DeSparr there. He caressed her wrappings. No response. "How is she?"

"Nearer her god to him."

Howard dismissed the crude sarcasm. "At least the Greenshirts want her well, even if it's just so she'll make a proper sacrifice."

DeSparr suddenly glared at Howard. "I do not want her to die. You may remember: there are no antibiotics."

"I didn't mean you," said Howard, not completely truthfully, but he was glad to hear the denial, and surprised that DeSparr bothered to explain his own feelings. "I'm glad you care."

"I didn't say..." DeSparr clapped his mouth shut.

Howard stood and walked to the door. It was pointless talking to DeSparr. Antibiotics were the key. The Greenshirts were reluctant to go far from their village. If Howard could get beyond their limit, wherever that was, he could find a town and antibiotics. Could he? There was nothing else. If he failed, he failed.

Would she last until he got back? Hopefully. But even if she didn't, his staying wouldn't change that.

He would get some sleep, then go for the gap before sunup. Run

278

when he could, walk when he had to, rest when it was too dark to see his way. Water would be easy to find. He could go days without food. If he ran across a ripe mango or two, so much the better.

Maybe there would be a hospital, or a drug store. He imagined people in flowery shirts. A shack. A roadside telephone. A road.

***

"He fall!" It was Raul's voice from the log bridge. "He fall!" Howard ran quickly. Others gathered at the stream.

"Who!" said Crauder. "Where?"

"The Beggar! He fall."

"Is he hurt?" said Crauder.

"He is eh, death."

"No!"

"Si. He try the bridge. I come too late to him."

"Where?"

Raul pointed over the edge, into the stream. "He is there!"

They all looked. Beg's deformed body lay over rocks, head under water, blood flowing. Crauder and Howard and several Greenshirts climbed down and scrambled on the slippery rocks trying to pull him up.

L.P. shouted, "What's that?" He pointed at several pieces of broken green glass wedged between two rocks.

"I..." Dove-Ti was distraught. "I didn't mean for him to drink the whole bottle."

After they handed the body up the bank, one man to the next, the Greenshirts insisted he be buried immediately.

Smith organized and led the service as the team and several Greenshirts stood in a circle. Dove-Ti wasn't able to participate for her desperate crying. Crauder sat with his head in his hands. When Smith was done, Ehec and Tetl raised their hands and spoke in their language.

"That coulda been me," said Crauder when it was over.

"What?" said Dove-Ti.

"I was a drunk." Crauder looked at his wife. "Pat knew it. Boy did she. I lost three jobs. If she hadn't kept after me, stuck with me..." He stared at Beg's grave and blubbered.

Chapter 27

Mendez tried to jerk loose, but the four hands of Ocelot and Deer of Stone held like death grips.

"The robe," said Atl.

"Take it off," said Deer of Stone.

As they stripped him, Mendez was sure his mother was delighted to see him lowered to the level of the natives. She was always the cleverest in the end. She had seen all he had done after all. She always waited until he thought he was free. She would be smiling now as she always did when he was about to be whipped by the priests.

He had learned to take it, to make an iron face and never show his fear or pain when they hit him. But these people were talking about fire. Hell could come now. He began to shake violently. He cried out, "Please! No!" He remembered the women in the village, crying out the same thing, and how it had done them no good because he had not cared about their suffering, had even enjoyed it. "You have the wrong man!" he cried. He forced a straight face, his best innocent, helpless eyes. "Honest."

They got four ropes from their supplies and tied one to each wrist and ankle.

Mendez tried once more to break free, with all his strength, and was able to tear his arm away from Two-Rabbit, but not from Deer of Stone's iron grip. Immediately Two-Rabbit and Atl and Dahlia and Shy Petals jumped on him, grabbing an arm and a leg and the loose ropes, and brought him down.

They carried him to a spot between two trees about three man-lengths apart. They looped the four ropes around four tree-branches and pulled them, raising him spread-eagle, belly down, in the air. They tied the ropes tightly. Mendez turned his head up and saw in their eyes that

280

they would not stop until he had suffered the most horrible levels of pain, as the village women had at his own hands, and finally death.

Deer of Stone pointed at the ground beneath Mendez. "Build a new fire here."

"No!" said Mendez, jerking and pulling uselessly at the ropes, wrenching at the pain in his side where the sticks had hit him, clinging to every precious last moment of his long hope for wealth and freedom. "No! Please!" It could not be over. He had always been able to make a deal. "I will do anything!" he said. "The gold! The silver! You may have it all! Anything!"

"It is ours already," said Deer of Stone.

A Fox is Mad laid kindling under him.

"Under his face," said Deer of Stone.

A Fox is Mad moved the kindling to a spot under Mendez' face and lit it with a flaming stick from the first fire. Then he carefully set larger pieces together above it.

Smoke rose. Mendez turned his head to one side. The ropes cut into his wrists and ankles. His shoulders and hips began to ache. Quick. Think. He should have known these savages would not make a deal. Who would? "Mother!" he shouted. He raised his head. It was harder to hold it up in the awkward position. "Do not let them…" She never listened before. Why now? The smoke entered his lungs as he breathed again to speak. "No! Please!" He choked and coughed. Each new breath drew in more smoke. Water poured from his eyes.

He heard Deer of Stone say, "I am glad to finally see this."

His mother would not make a deal. Would God? Forgiveness was part of all that business. There was no priest. But God should be impressed if he sounded sincere and humble. How would Tomás have done it? Mendez prayed out loud, in Latin, "God. I have sinned. I mean it humbly. Forgive my poor, humble soul."

He choked and coughed, worse this time. Then he began pulling and pushing violently, turning his head greatly for air, twisting his body unnaturally, and jerking his wrists and ankles painfully against the ropes. The shaking made the tree-branches wave unnaturally. They returned the shaking as if mocking.

God was not listening. He must get God's attention. Gold had always bought God's favor. "Gold," he prayed in Latin. "I will give all the gold to a church. All of it."

The fire grew. A quick, searing burn hit his shoulder, another his

281

cheek. Then a more general, oppressive heat. A suffocating thinness and hotness of air. Deer of Stone and the others prodded him with sticks and mocked him.

God! The pain! The gold wasn't working. The Natives have it now, anyway. What else? The natives. Mendez' disdain for them had grown to fearful hatred now. But Tomás had said that God cared about them. Was there a deal in that?

"God," said his thinning voice, "I will do something for these people. Something very, very good. Just free me and I promise to… to… what?" Atl stopped poking to move the Vulgate away from the fire. "Yes, God!" he prayed. "I will give them your book!"

Atl picked up a heavy stick and hit Mendez' back with it.

As Mendez breathed in for the next words, the long, thin upper length of the flame snaked into his mouth and throat. He tried to scream but failed. He tried to swallow but all his spit was burnt away and there was only a dry rasp and a searing internal pain. He turned as far as he could to one side, and felt the flame on his cheek, but was able to keep his mouth away. "God!" he cried with unstoppable hoarseness. God was not dealing. "The pain! Please!" He jerked against the ropes, wanting to curl up like a baby, but the ropes held him straight out over the flames. "God! What more?" If he could only die now, it would be over. But he was not dying. Something was wrong with his offer to God. "Oh!" he suddenly thought. "They cannot read!" He thought fast. Tomás wanted the Vulgate translated into the natives' language. "I will… I will give them writing! Teach them to read! Yes! God! I will translate your book. I will…"

***

Arms wrapped his waist and pulled him from the fire. The arms of God? Had God acted? Was he saved? The pain was still intense.

"You are what?" said a loud voice.

"Burning him!" said Deer of Stone.

"Who said to do this?" It was the voice of One-Cip'

"I did."

"Stop now!"

Billows of white smoke rose past Mendez as the fire was kicked out. He coughed again, drily, and his throat burned horribly. "Please God!" he cried hoarsely and thinly. "Now heal this pain!" Instead, the pain increased, and blackness came all around him.

"Cut him down." One-Cip' turned slowly, pressing a hand against his knee, and set his carry-sack against a tree.

Deer of Stone and Atl and Two-Rabbit cut the ropes and carried the now unconscious Mendez aside and lowered him to the grass, on his unburned back, gently, as they knew One-Cip' expected. Layers of skin peeled back on the neck and shoulder.

"There will be no more of this," said One-Cip'. "Look at him. How could you?"

"You would have done it too, father," said Deer of Stone, "if you knew…"

"Knew what?"

Deer of Stone picked up the little bag with Mendez' name on it and pulled Atl's mother's ear-spools out. "He is the one who burned our village and killed our people."

One-Cip's face dropped. "How do you know he didn't find these, or trade for them?"

"We questioned him," said Deer of Stone. "There is no doubt."

Atl and the others nodded. "It is true." They explained the lies.

After a long silence, One-Cip' said, "Still, we cannot become like he is, and do what he does."

"But…" said Deer of Stone. "He killed our…"

"I know. And I feel the hate for him as well. And I want him to suffer, to balance it all. But haven't we learned that no good comes from killing and torturing?"

"What would you do?"

One-Cip' thought for some time. He stepped aside and sat on the root of a tree and put his head in his hands and thought and thought. Everyone waited. Finally he got up and said, "If he survives this, we will make him our slave."

"I cannot look at him without hitting him," said Deer of Stone.

"Then hit him wisely."

"I… don't know what you mean."

"Hit him when he is not obedient. Get much work out of him."

"As long as he lives," said Atl and Deer of Stone together.

"And may he live long," said One-Cip'. "We can use a slave."

Deer of Stone pointed at the wooden plates. "There is much gold." Atl opened the plates and pulled back the deerskin Mendez had pushed into the grooves around the hollowed-out chamber. The gold fell out. One-Cip' asked for a cloth and spread it, and they gathered the gold and blew out the leaves and dust and put it on the cloth.

"What is it worth?" said Deer of Stone.

One-Cip' tied the cloth as a bag around the gold. "Nothing."

"What of Mendez' other things?" said Two-Rabbit.

One-Cip' said, "He may keep his clothing if he wants. The talk-symbols on the deerskins show much work and, it seems, much thought, and someone who knows the meanings may find it useful. If Mendez lives, we will make him carry all these things as we travel." One-Cip' picked up the bag of gold and carried it into the woods.

"Where are you going?" said Atl.

"I'll be back. I'll tell you then."

"But…"

Ocelot ran after One-Cip'. "You aren't leaving us?"

"No," said One-Cip'. "Wait here."

Ocelot turned to the others. "Will he take the gold and run?"

"No," said Atl and Deer of Stone at the same time. "Never."

That night One-Cip' showed again at the edge of the trees, tired and scratched. "The gold is buried," he said.

"Where?" said Deer of Stone.

"No one will ever know."

"But…" said Ocelot. "We could have used that…"

"Mendez desired it. He stole it. We must not desire it. When I gave my tiny bag of gold for Dahlia in Cempoala, the gold I had added to and guarded for years, I felt much lighter."

"Why did you not tell us you were burying it?"

"So you would not have the burden of knowing where it is."

"It was not yours to hide."

"It was not yours. It was not Mendez'. It was the Sant-yagos' and the Aztecs', but we will not go back to them. We have seen what their love of gold caused."

"We lived all our days," said Deer of Stone. "without the love of gold. And it was not even Father's gold that saved Dahlia in Cempoala."

"The luck saved her," said Atl. "And Cortés' desire for power."

"And Father's wisdom," said Dahlia.

"So," said Ocelot, "on what do we depend?"

"Our ways," said Deer of Stone. "We will never change."

"Father's wisdom," said Dahlia.

"All of our wisdom," said One-Cip'. "And our courage."

The next day, Mendez still lived but Balanced Turtle died. They carved a wooden death-arc for him, and could not make it look as good as the ones he carved, but they laid it around his head where they buried him on a ridge away from the road, high above a clear stream.

Then for two days they travelled, passing the turn to the road that led to the endless waters, not even pointing it out to Mendez. And even though he was in great pain from the burns and could only walk in short steps, as his ankles were tied to the ends of a short rope, they made him carry loads on his unburned back, strapped over his burned shoulders, including the deerskins with their talk-symbols. Once when he asked, in his wheezy voice, to rest, Atl and Deer of Stone hit him with heavy sticks and gave him more to carry.

"Wise hits," said Deer of Stone, smiling.

Atl knew it was not what One-Cip' meant by hitting wisely, but in spite of the lesson of Cholula, he began again to think of ways to get back. It was easy now. And each deserved hit pointed to Mendez' brutality and away from his own against Tree, at least for a moment.

They all made Mendez serve as they travelled. They kept him roped to one of them, though he never tried to escape, scarred and sickly, afraid now of the unknown, knowing they would easily hunt him down, having nothing to take with him. They did not let him complain or even talk of anything apart from his work for them. After many days of travel, on a long, rainy day, One-Cip' found a spot, and said they would settle and build their new village.

"It is far away from the land of the Aztecs and the Sant-yagos."

"But there is no swamp," said Deer of Stone, "for a chinampa."

One-Cip' thought and said, "You are right. The chinampa you and Atl built was of benefit. We will keep looking."

After two more days of walking, they found a site high above a stream and a wide swamp.

"Balanced Turtle would have liked this spot," said Dahlia.

"We can build two chinampas here," said Atl.

"Yes, two," said Deer of Stone, "now that we have slave help."

They began to lay out their village the very next day. Deer of Stone insisted they plan it as much like their old one as they could. It was clear he felt he would one day follow his father as the village leader.

In the following days, they built their huts and set up the maize-bins and dug in the swamp to make a new chinampa. They worked hard all day, each day. They began living by the same rules and worked in much the same way as they had always done.

They worked Mendez in every way they could, making him learn what he didn't know about their kinds of huts and gardens. They watched him, and tied a rope to him and to a tree when he was not working. They were not used to holding a slave, and were surprised that, now and then, when they accidentally forgot to tie him or watch him, he did not try to run away. He worked hard.

"He is trained now," said Deer of Stone, "like an animal."

Atl let the ugliness and slow healing of the burn-marks mask what seemed to be changes for the better. He would not forget what the man had done to his village and his mother. Mendez accepted the hating and the work and the beatings without complaint. He rarely talked, except to ask about meanings of words he had not yet learned.

***

When the building was mostly done, everything was clean and neat. Atl and everyone, even Mendez, seemed pleased. They all knew what their chores were and began working at them. After this, there was not as much work for Mendez, and when he was not working and serving, he cut squares from new animal skins left from the hunts and the feasting and the sewing, soaked and scraped and stretched and dried them. At times he studied the animal skins he had brought with him, then made marks on the new skins with a feather split on the end and some water he had mixed with crushed oak galls and boiled with sap from pine trees.

Sometimes he kneeled and closed his eyes and talked softly in his thin, hoarse, troubled voice.

Deer of Stone never talked to him, but one day Atl could no longer put aside his curiosity and demanded to know from him what he was doing when he kneeled and talked, and Mendez said that he asked his god to heal him of his burns. He said that he was doing a work for his god in return, and one day he would show it to Atl.

Now that Atl talked with him, he began asking about the sounds of Nahuatl, and listened carefully to the answers. He worked with it, and the Sant-yago tongue, and the tongue of the marks on his stack of old skins. He said his healing would take many years because the work would take many years. How well he was healed would depend on how well he did the work. He said he had to rebuild in his mind many things he had learned in his training long ago in his own land.

Sometimes he made separate Nahuatl marks to show Atl, and explained them. "The tree is tall. Today it will rain." At first Atl did not want to think that anything from Mendez was worth his time, but he was drawn more and more to the marks, remembering what he had learned from Alonso and Gonzo. Still treating Mendez harshly, he began to learn more of the words, and their sounds. One day he made marks for words himself, and showed them to Dahlia and Deer of Stone, and they learned them as well.

Mendez described sheep to Atl and asked him if he knew of animals like them. Atl didn't, so Mendez explained what they were and what a shepherd was.

Atl worked in the chinampa and learned words in his spare time through the dry, cool season, and after one more rain-time and one more dry season, and three times trading with travelers passing through, he began to ease his hatred of Mendez, and to read.

***

When the next rain-time began, and the new village was almost two years old, three visitors came. One of them wore a brown robe like the one Mendez had worn when they discovered him on the trail, the other two wore the clothes of the Sant-yago warriors.

The one in the robe stepped forward. He did not smile or frown. He was skinny and his ears stuck out and his eyes were soft.

"Nahuatl?" he said.

One-Cip' nodded.

"I am Tomás. These are Juan and Emilio. We are looking for a man of our company. His name is Ramiro Mendez."

Mendez crouched behind a tree, but the visitors saw him.

"Ramiro?" said Tomás. "Is that you?"

Mendez straightened and wheezed, "How did you…?"

"Traders talk."

Tomás said to One-Cip', "May I talk with him?"

One-Cip' nodded. He said to the villagers, "Let them talk," and to the other two visitors, "Do you know chinampas?"

287

"We have seen chinampas in Mexico," said one.

"Then help." One-Cip' turned to the villagers. "Back to work."

Tomás turned again to Mendez. He spoke sharply now. "I have some nice scars on my back."

Mendez looked down. "I am sorry, I…"

"I thought I was dead. But you missed the vital organs."

"Thank God."

"But the two guards died. Ramiro, you are wanted for murder, attempted murder, theft of the King's property, theft of officer's property, direct disobedience, cowardice, desertion. And more."

"You are arresting me."

"I have no authority. Ramiro. Look at you. You have changed."

"I am a slave here."

"Your face. You have burns and bruises."

Mendez had to clear his throat often. "They beat me. I work. They burned me years ago. They hate me. They have good reason."

"Do you remember when I was gone for days with two of the disgruntled sailors? We said we had been kidnapped by natives?"

"De Alvarado set up a whole new policy about leaving."

"We were not kidnapped."

"Ramiro, you do not have to tell me."

"I had talked the sailors into going with me to find Indian gold on our own. They were fed up with Cortés and de Alvarado. I had seen this Indian, this one here, One-Cip', offer gold to save his daughter from the Aztec tribute-takers in Cempoala. I asked around and found out where he lived. We met some stray Indians on the way and promised them gold. When we found the village, the men were not there, only women and children. We were ecstatic. We tore down several huts looking for treasures. When we found none, we got out of control."

"Ramiro…"

"No. I will tell all. It gets worse. Without gold, our plans were ruined. And the villagers would get out the word of our raid. I told the sailors I saw the devil in the women, and we killed them and the children and burned them in their huts…"

"Ramiro, this is worse than… It is beyond…"

"I know."

"You know I will have to report this and tell your whereabouts."

"I am ready for full justice. After that I killed my Indian helpers, the ones who didn't leave me, to silence them."

"Are you threatening me?"

"No. I would not be able to carry through. All I ever wanted was to be free," said Mendez. "Now look at me." He sighed, hung his head, and mumbled, "I stole officers' gold, bit by bit. I hid it in the wood covers of Padre Olmedo's Vulgate and carried it away."

"You have it?" said Tomás. "The Vulgate?"

"It is in my hut."

"Where is the gold?"

"The Indian here, One-Cip', hid it far away. Only he knows."

"The officers are desperate to find you. Search parties are out. There are no more battles to take up their time. The High Valley has been taken and the Aztec empire belongs to Cortés. They want you dead or alive, but much more bounty is placed upon the gold."

"Cortés has succeeded?"

The old Mendez would have first asked about his own chances, and made up lies and excuses to win sympathy. Tomás was shocked at the list of crimes, the treachery, but also shocked at Mendez' endurance under the harshness of the villagers' treatment. "Cortés has set the empire up as a colony for Don Carlos, and is to be its governor."

"He has realized his dream."

"At great expense to the natives. He charmed and intimidated Motecuhzoma and marched right into Tenochtitlán, in the High Valley. Governor Velasquez of Cuba, who has been angry at him since he sailed against his orders, sent an expedition to capture him, but Cortés led part of his own troops from the High Valley and defeated them in Cempoala. And the survivors of the expedition? What do you think he did? He talked most of them into joining his own army."

"That is his way."

"Yes. On his way back to the High Valley, he took local Indian families from Cempoala, then abandoned them when they were too slow. They were found and massacred by maverick Aztec warriors. When he returned to Tenochtitlán, he found that his army had been pushed out of the city after his officers had ordered a massacre of Aztec priests. None of the officers has Cortés' sense of diplomacy. So this time he had to use force to take the city back. That took a couple of years. Motecuhzoma is dead, and Cortés rules. It is amazing how quickly the organization of the Aztecs, and their way of life, is falling apart."

Tomás surprised himself talking so openly to the seemingly new Mendez, even revealing his feelings. "None of this had to happen."

289

"Has he been as cruel as I?"

"Not with such cowardice and hate. But cruel, yes. He has had success in his goals. He reports directly to Don Carlos the king now."

Mendez slumped. "You are right. I am a cruel, hating coward, and a failure. And I deserve no sympathy." He opened his mouth and pointed into his burned throat. "I deserve this."

"It has changed your voice."

"It has changed more than that."

"What do you mean?"

"Like Cortés, going directly to the King, I went over everyone's head and made a deal with God. He will heal me if I will translate the Vulgate into the language of these people."

"You? You really intend to translate the Bible?"

"That is the deal."

Tomás was happy to hear that, but had to be honest. "Ramiro, you cannot make a deal with God."

"When I made my offer, God stopped them from torturing me."

Theologically muddled as Mendez was, he was the most capable on the expedition of learning and using languages. It is what Tomás had wanted for the Indians ever since Cuba. But Mendez was also the most capable of sounding sincere when he was lying.

"That is a lot of translating."

"I have already assigned symbols to the sounds. One of the boys helps me with the word meanings. Would you like to see the three pages I have translated so far?"

"All right. But, really, Ramiro, you have to understand the larger meaning as well as the words. You, with your past and your…"

"Christ's willing death in my place." Mendez wheezed. "His conquering of death. The gospel, the 'eu-angelion.' These make you able to know God, his goodness, to be in company with him. Love God with all you have. Love your neighbor. Make it purposeful love, sacrificial if necessary, like Christ's."

Tomás blushed. "I think you have it better than I told you."

"I have prayed and read, prayed and read." Mendez got up and asked One-Cip's permission to bring the entire Latin Bible to Tomás.

One-Cip' nodded. Mendez got it from his hut. Tomás smiled. "It is true. This is Padre Olmedo's Vulgate."

"I brought it for selfish reasons. I used the wooden covers to carry the gold. And I thought I could sell the Bible when I reached

Spain. But I believe god used my greed to bring me to my punishment and my calling." Mendez handed Tomás the three pages. "These are translated so far. "When they kill a large animal, usually a deer, they let me cut up whatever skin is left over for pages."

"I see you are dating them," said Tomás. "And judging by those dates, it looks like you are getting about one page done in a week."

"Once I worked out the meanings and assigned Latin characters to the sounds, I was able to work faster. I find several hours each night."

Tomás studied the pages, then pronounced the strange words slowly, using the familiar symbols. He could see that they were Nahuatl, the meanings of which he had begun to learn himself. He read out loud, "'At first God made the sky and the world. The world was formless and void. Darkness covered the deep, and God's Spirit was there, and...'" He looked at Mendez. "One thing I would say: accuracy is extremely important. You left out that God's Spirit 'hovered over the waters.' I am not sure just what that means, but we do not want to change it, do we?"

"Well, 'over the waters' meant it was 'there,' right?"

"Maybe, but if you change it, it is not the Bible, is it? There could be something in it that God meant and that we do not get. But someone else who reads your translation may get it, if you do it right."

"So you are saying, if I do not do it right, God will not heal me?"

Tomás desperately wanted Mendez motivated. But he said, "Ramiro, as I said, you cannot make a deal with God."

"God agreed." Mendez was resolute. "He got me off the fire."

Tomás was amazed that Mendez had already assigned accurate symbols to this strange language, something no one would do without a sincere motive. He said, "God would want you to do it accurately."

"Yes. I feel I can translate this, and do it right. But..." He slumped, staring at the pages. "I fear I cannot live it."

The old Mendez would have claimed high moral intentions. Tomás said, "No one can."

"What? Padre Olmedo does. You do."

"Not him. Not me. No one."

"What have you ever done bad?"

"You mean except for lust, envy, greed, not always standing for the good? How about helping slavers with their legal documents to get around the royal edict? You may have seen where Isaiah wrote that, next to God's ways, our good works are like filthy rags, and the Apostle Paul wrote that 'everybody falls short.' 'Everybody.'"

Mendez seemed puzzled. "I know we are forgiven. Christ died for our sins, my sins. But if that is true, we can sin all we want."

"If your faith is real, you will try not to. And only if your faith is real, will you have this forgiveness. Ramiro, when you were a boy, did you ever choose up sides?"

"I was usually chosen by the side I did not want. But once by the side I did want. I was eleven."

"Were you glad?"

"I was sure we would win."

"How did you play?"

"Not great, but with all my heart."

"That is the way it is." Tomás found the letter to the Hebrews. "Read this. '…let us run with endurance the race set before us, looking to Jesus, the author and perfecter of our faith.' Maybe your 'race' is to translate this Bible."

"I found that passage already. It has been my guide."

Tomás hoped he could deflect the other searchers from Mendez until he finished the translation. But not likely unless the gold was recovered. "Ramiro, how long will this translation take you?"

"I figure seven years."

Tomás said, "If you do this work, and turn the gold over now, I will not tell them where you are for seven years. But in seven years I will come back for you, with soldiers." If Mendez agreed, it would show that he was sincere, and that he would translate sincerely. There was nothing in it for him except seven more years of slavery and his ill-based hope that God would save his life if he finished the translation.

Mendez stared at the pages, then held up the three. "I will have to get these right." He looked at One-Cip', standing nearby. "Only One-Cip' knows where the gold is."

"I will talk to him," said Tomás.

One-Cip agreed to show Tomás the gold.

"You will let a Sant-yago take it?" said Deer of Stone.

"Mendez stole it from them," said One-Cip'. "It is theirs."

"Then let them have it and rust with it," said Deer of Stone.

Tomás said goodbye to Mendez, and he and the other two Sant-yagos followed One-Cip' into the woods.

One-Cip' came back alone.

Chapter 28

Howard woke groggy. He checked on Rachel. The graveyard shift nurse smiled. He studied Rachel's vaguely shaped layers of cloth, thinned and worn by washings, rising and falling slightly and irregularly with each rare, raspy breath. Ehec's Ya-si prayers had changed nothing. He washed her red hot arm with cool water from the bowl.

He knew that to hold her and hug her would not help her. She would not know. But he gently raised her and hugged her. He kept hugging. Rachel, like he, had wanted to know the tribe. She had never even seen the nurses tending her. Finally he let her down.

He found Tee-week and woke him. "Will you guide me?"

Tee-week shook his head.

Fine. Who needed him? Howard would just spot the gap and go. He stopped once more at the hut and shook L.P.

"What?" said L.P.

"I'm going for help."

"What?"

"Antibiotics."

"You're crazy."

"Will you watch Rachel? Don't tell anybody til I'm well gone?"

"If you do this idiot thing, I'll watch her. Probably Blake and Zoe too, and maybe Crauder."

"Good. Don't worry. I'll be careful. I should be back in two days. Maybe three. I gotta go. Bye."

***

He followed the path down to the log bridge, lay on it, hugged it, and slowly crawled across. He followed a trail he knew to be in the direction of the gap.

He walked faster as the light increased, even began to lope. Gusts of wind cleared the fog, and blued the sky. The smooth singing of the wind, rising and falling in the pines, cheered him. As he passed the scattered, swaying trees, the horizontal flashing of the new sun between them switched him on and off like a light, squint-bright, shadow-black.

He marked trees by breaking small limbs or scratching bark with sharp rocks. He quietly entered denser woods, crested the first small mountain, and was relieved to spot the gap across the miles of low, thick forest. Its shape was different in the new angle of view. He ran and walked another two hours downhill as the trail wound and diminished until only soft rotting leaves and limbs covered the ground between scattered rocks and crawling roots in the new, rugged part of the forest he had never seen.

He jumped streams, panting, gasping, searching out each rare new glimpse of the gap through the thick trees in order to know its latest shape and spot it next time, seeing it and its promise less clearly and less often the lower his elevation. That promise alone, of roads and towns and help for Rachel, justified the sneaking off from the team from whom he had pledged never to leave, and drew him as prizes draw lottery players unable to conceive of the odds.

He came to an opening where a tree had fallen. He leaned a shoulder against a huge knotty limb and gulped great quantities of air and tiny insects, hardly able to breathe for coughing and hardly able to cough for breathing. Jagged tree-covered ridges fanned out from him, still downward, divided by small crooked streams. Beyond them gray forests rose again into scattered hanging mists, the whole grand view lush and long and lonely. He searched and spotted the far gap just before it disappeared under the thin edges of a new descending cloud.

He needed a walking stick. He got his knife from his pocket and opened the blade. When he started to cut a straight branch, he saw ahead of him a boy leaning against a tree. Tee-week.

"How did you...?"

Tee-week turned and fell away from the tree into a soundless loping, and vanished in the huge dark woods ahead.

"Wait!" said Howard, and he ran stumbling after him, glimpsing him only now and then, to the left, to the right, sometimes even seeming to double back on himself. Once he was sure he had lost him and wandered in several directions, giving up, then saw him again watching him as if waiting, then quickly darting away. Finally Tee-week stopped where Howard could catch up.

"What are you doing?" said Howard. "You're crazy!" Tee-week laughed and swung limb to limb and reached for Howard's knife. Howard angrily stabbed at Tee-week's hand, not meaning to make contact, but did, and when Tee-week jerked his cut hand back, he missed the next limb and fell, eyes wide. He landed awkwardly, bending his leg under him with a loud snap. He shrieked in pain.

Howard was livid. He shouted, "You're crazy!" then turned and ran away, so not to know if the leg was broken, or how badly, so not to face a decision. It was probably a stick on the ground that snapped. Tee-week didn't deserve help, and besides, he knew the woods much better. So who was Howard to help him?

Howard couldn't outrun the sound of the screaming, but suddenly it stopped, and that disturbed him more. If Rachel who risked her life for him were to live, how would he explain leaving Tee-week? He turned to look back, and realized that nothing was familiar. He had forgotten to mark trees in all that excitement. He ran desperately one way, then another. Nothing was right. He marked trees again, but it made no sense. There was no longer an origin or a destination.

"Scream, Tee-week!" He heard only his echo. "I'll help you!"

Clouds hung lower, darker, and the air began gusting. For a while a vague sense of direction remained, based on the rough memories of the lay of the land, the slopes, the angles, but as he ran one way, then another, those slopes and angles changed, as if the woods and the earth were deliberately deceiving him, and eventually he lost track of all references, and finally knew he was lost.

He needed to hit something. Not the wilderness. It could not think, could not knowingly receive his anger. Tee-week was not there to hit. Maybe Ehec's Ya-si, if he was real, or the god Howard had been told about as a child, if he was real, but those gods were vague and silent and invisible and maddeningly unhittable.

He kicked a painfully rigid old tree, no longer to take out his anger, but to exult in a senseless act, as if doing so would prove the absurdity of everything and thus undermine any reasoning that could be used to assign guilt for abandoning Tee-week. He kicked again, harder, too hard, and the pain shot through his leg. He shrieked. When he did, all insect and bird noises, even the monkey howls, stopped.

He tried to walk in the new quiet, but the pain hit again. He sat down on the kicked tree's huge root-buttresses. Vines thicker than his arm hung and snaked around the trunk.

He rubbed his foot. He and the tree were friends now, like kids who make up after a tiring, undecided fight. He spoke to it. "There was nothing I could do for Rachel. Maybe the far gap is just an excuse to run. My old urge. 'Run for what?' you say? 'Run from what?' you say? I don't know. Something that has hung out of sight since I was a kid. Not run from Ehec and the Greenshirts, not from their Ya-si, not from their songs that almost made me sing. Those frightened me, but didn't frighten me away. If anything, they made me think there's a reason why a man is on the earth. Atlanta and Tech and my old job at Dunhill, my striving for whatever it was I had always felt I was supposed to strive for, those had also made me think there must be a reason, but a reason by contrast, for they had not proven to be it."

Then he said, "Ya-si," just in case, surprising himself. He said it out loud for there was no one around. "Let Rachel live."

The clouds began to thicken. The woods darkened. Stronger, colder wind-gusts came. Yes, the few times he had seen people pray, things got worse. But of course, that's the only time people prayed, when things were getting worse. The gusts invaded suddenly and invisibly, quick rising whispers, cooling his sweaty skin.

Suddenly there came behind him, very close, all at once, a fss-SST with a flash of light so bright, and a great cracking sound so loud, that he clapped his ears and doubled over and hid his face. Then there was a second loud crack, farther away, as if the forest had answered with outrage, then a third, then a fourth, less sharp, tumbling away clumsily through the trees and into the clouds, finally settling into a prolonged woods-wide rumbling. The gusts lashed back. His doubled body tightened like a spring. When he finally eased up it happened again, and the noise reached to his bones, then a third time, even closer than the first. Another flash from behind him lit gray distant trees before him, dimly and instantly, and he could see them frozen in their wild swaying, hanging on as negative after-burns in his eye and in his mind. Then a flash lit the night-mist behind those trees and silhouetted the whipping of their millions of black leaves.

Rain began to spread across the tree tops. Big gritty, familiar drops fell and got into his hair and on his shoulders and soaked coldly into the cotton shirt. Cold blue instant flashes cut the blackness. He began to shake. He saw a strange shape in one flash that was not there in the next, a hundred yards away, black and shiny. El tigre? It could have been upright. It could have been a shadow, except it was shiny. The next flash was blinding and crackling, like phone static. He remembered a phrase from an Aztec poem in his book. "The darkness mocks us..."

The next flash lit the thing again. It was not a shadow. It had moved. It had a long-beaked head, black like the rest of it. The head appeared double, facing to each side at once, making him think of the only ancient statue that had ever given him a sense of terror, Coatlicue, the Earth Mother of the Aztecs, wearing over bared breasts a large necklace of severed human hands, her head replaced by two snakes nose to nose suddenly appearing, if stared at long enough, as the ghastly image of one huge snake's long-toothed, fork-tongued grin straight at him. Rain hissed. Sweat slithered inside his shirt.

The double-beaked head seemed to see or sense him, even to know him. Did it know he had tricked Rachel into el tigre's wood? Refused her hand at that terrible moment? Defied the team? Hated DeSparr? Abandoned helpless Tee-week?

There was another flash, down through the trees, silhouetting the thing this time against the gray dim forest beyond and it looked like a huge, wet, winged Napoleon in broad drooping hat, ten feet from him, staring in its blackness, with its shiny little eyes, directly at him.

And the thunder came again, and again, and it was that moment of greatest activity in the storm, when lightning could not cease before more began, when it seemed he had stumbled into an enormous battle, distant in its causes and sources, moving across the earth and sky.

The thing shrieked, and he could imagine in all the noise that he heard the sound of his name in its shrieking, as if he were being called accountable for something, and he thought that the earth could come horribly alive after all, and could know that it was his time, and could integrate him back into itself, that this was what people and animals who had already died had already seen.

The thing leaped at him, and he kicked at it with his sore foot, and it bent and crouched and shrieked again and he knew it was at least a material thing. But it was not heavy, in the way flying things are not heavy, and that seemed to protect it from the force of his kick.

Again he thought he heard his name and did hear his name, "Howard! Howard!" It was no demon, no angel.

"Miss Margaret!" he shouted.

And in her cheap flying rain cover under the wide black

297

sombrero she had a radio crackling and popping with garbled voices and there were huge flashes and blasts of thunder, and she was shouting at Howard and her words were, "The other way! The other way!"

He was able to struggle and lift her and set her beside him. He had trouble speaking, but finally said, "Where'd you come from?"

"Over there," she said, hitting the radio and motioning distractedly behind her. "I can't tune this piece of junk!"

The next time she hit it, there came, mixed with the static, English words with a Spanish accent. "All the things thirty percent off."

Howard took it. It said, "The sale ends to Wednesday."

There were switches and knobs. The lightning and thunder were moving away now, but the static was still loud. "Hurry and see us."

She lifted her hat and said, "The others? Rachel?"

Howard opened his mouth. Now, when he needed the thunder most, for time to choose the words, there was only the steady rain.

She clasped her hands together in her lap and watched him intently. Finally he began, methodically. He told her of the team and the Jaguar-people and the Greenshirts. When he told her about el tigre and Rachel, her hands suddenly slipped against each other, betraying her tension, and she lowered her head and closed her eyes. Rain washed across their soaked clothes and dripped from the brim of her hat and her elbows and from his nose and chin, and ran through the dark ground cover in glistening streamlets.

"Did you bring any medical stuff?" said Howard, hoping.

She looked up. "We have a nice big kit."

"We?"

"There're three guys trying to catch up with me." She reached for the radio to try another knob or dial to see what it would do. "They know how to use these things."

"Great. Do you have Antibiotics?"

"They do. Lots."

"It's hard to get Rachel to take anything."

"How do we get to her?"

He confessed how he had abandoned Tee-week. "And he's the only one who knows how to get back to the village."

"Can we find him?"

"Maybe in the morning, with daylight. I think he broke a bone. Even if we find him, he may not want to help."

"We have splints and crutches and a stretcher."

Howard was afraid to let it settle into his thinking that help had come. He said, "Do the three guys know the way out?" He found a knob on the radio and turned it from AM to Intercom. Simple.

"We can call helicopters to these signals," she said.

"How'd you know we got lost?"

"Your reports stopped," she said.

"You kept up? Even after you were... dismissed?"

"Sure." The gusts came less often, and less strongly.

"What made you think you could find us?"

"We prayed a lot."

"You and the three guys?"

"My mission board."

"You board is praying?"

"They better be."

The static from the radio was interrupted by a garbled male voice speaking Spanish.

"Hold it higher," she said. "The guys are picking us up."

"It's waterproof?"

"Yep."

He stood and cradled it in the fork of a limb. "How do they know where we are?"

"Don't ask me. They track signals from that thing."

The garbled voice came again in the loud crackling static.

"What'd he say?" said Howard.

"They're getting close."

"How'd you know where we were?"

"Well, I knew the original plans, where you meant to go. There were news reports about floods at the same time you stopped reporting. The papers showed the worst-hit areas. And we did some guessing."

The lightning stopped, but the rain was still heavy and steady.

"Amazing you and I crossed paths," said Howard.

"Just now? I heard screams coming from here."

"Tee-week."

She patted the back of her left shoulder. "Rub there."

"I kicked you. Sorry." He got situated and reached and squeezed her thin shoulders and began pressing a thumb up and down each side of her upper spine. He said, "I guess my next question is, 'Why did you come for us?' You would have had every excuse not to."

"Not and pray right."

Then out of the dark came flashlights. Three men showed, each with a large, stuffed backpack. One of them pulled a small supply cart on a bouncing bicycle wheel with a flat tire. Miss Margaret had introduced them and they looked Howard in the eye and shook his hand as if at a party. Then they got busy and hung a tarp between four trees. Howard, limping, helped them lay out another on the ground below it and they all rolled out five amazingly dry sleeping bags.

Sometime during the night, as they slept, the rain stopped.

***

"Which way to your Tee-week?" said Miss Margaret early, as they ate honey and big two-day-old buttered biscuits warmed on a butane stove. Howard had six.

"He should be that way," said Howard, pointing to his best guess as to the direction, and as he did, Tee-week appeared in the mist beside a tree. He leaned on a bent stick as a cane, favoring a leg. It was badly swollen between the knee and the ankle, but not bleeding.

Miss Margaret and Howard got up and went to him. Tee-week backed up, but she gently offered to help him walk. He let her take an arm and Howard took one and they helped him hop a few times.

"Tee-week," said Howard, "the way back to Tetl and Ehec?"

"You knife?" said Tee-week. He was obviously in pain.

Howard pulled his pocket knife out of its bag. "You want this?"

"For it I show way."

"Deal." But Howard put it back. "When we get there."

"Knife now."

Howard sighed and caved. "Okay."

Tee-week took it and pulled loose and started hobbling away on one leg and his makeshift cane, wincing from the pain.

"Where are you going?" said Howard.

"Hurt, no show."

Howard ran and grabbed his arm and tried to get the knife.

"Tee-week!" said Miss Margaret. "We can fix your leg."

He stopped and looked at her, then at his leg.

"Fix?" he said.

"Make it good."

"Make good now?"

"It will take days. We start today. You show us. We carry you."

300

"Leg and knife," he said.

"The knife when we get there," said Howard.

Tee-week thought, then handed the knife over and offered his arms again and Miss Margaret and Howard each took one and led him hobbling to the tarp.

"That's a pretty bad break," she said.

"Do you really know how to set it?" said Howard.

"I'm no doctor, but I've set more than a dozen in the Amazon." She began working and talking softly to Tee-week. He winced and yelped several times, but otherwise stoically trusted her instinctive mothering. She was able to set it and wrap it in splints.

***

At the Burb, Howard reluctantly gave Tee-week the knife. The first person they saw was L.P.

"Miss Margaret!" he said. "Where'd you come from?"

"The woods, big boy." She pointed at the shabby huts. "What's this mess?"

"Atlanta South." He pointed at the three men. "Guides?"

"They don't know a thing about this place." She winked at one of the men. "But they're volunteers from a mission in Tegucigalpa. And, we've got a magic little radio that'll bring a helicopter in here."

Others gathered. The Crauders hugged Miss Margaret. Dove-Ti, still reeling from Beg's death, made a point of apologizing to her. Blake made a rare smile. Haughton-Alsef stood back.

Zoe said, "Oh, Miss Margaret, I'm just like... too happy!"

Smith spoke sheepishly. "Miss Margaret."

"You big baluba," she said. "Where's Rachel?"

"Is it possible... Can these men help us find our way out?"

"They've got a radio. Don't ask me how the thing works."

Smith looked at Howard and Howard nodded, indicating he had told her about Rachel. Smith showed her the log bridge. He was unusually solicitous. He pointed to four of the young Greenshirts. "These young men can help you across."

She sat on the ground, took off her boots and socks, and stuffed the socks in the boots.

Two of the young Greenshirts approached her, offering to carry her, but she motioned them aside, tucked the tail of her black plastic

301

raincoat into her blue jeans, which made the rest of it puff up like a balloon and made her look, under her wide, ragged sombrero, like a huge walking eggplant. She held her arms straight out with a boot in each hand, curled her bare feet over the tops of the logs, toe-grasping them in the same way the Greenshirts did, and walked all the way across by herself. She scared everybody twice by almost losing her balance.

She glanced back. "Tougher job'n I thought. Who's showing me Rachel?"

Howard shut his open mouth and quickly got himself carried across. L.P. and several others brought the packs of antibiotics.

When she saw the ring of stones, she said, "What do they do here, stone people?"

"How'd you know?" said Howard.

"I was joking. Really?"

"They say it's just symbolic."

"Oh!" Zoe ran to join them. "Miss Margaret! Howard! We've found out more stuff. They don't want to sacrifice Rachel after all."

"What?"

"They just want her to sort of, 'give herself,' actually give the rest of her life, to that Ya-si, you know? If she does, then she knows what 'she's for.' They say Ya-si was the only real sacrifice, did it himself so nobody would have to go through that stoning thing. That's all they mean. They want us all to 'give ourselves.' Not get sacrificed like, to death. And we don't have to. They just want us to."

"But I thought Ya-si was supposed to be still around," said Howard. "Ehec and Tetl talk to him."

"Oh, he got over being dead like... a long time ago." She shrugged. "That's what Ehec told us. It's okay. It's just this like... religion, you know?"

DeSparr seemed oddly embarrassed when Miss Margaret came into the hut.

Chal-chee was there, on her knees beside Rachel.

"This is Chal-chee," said Howard.

"Chal-chee," said Miss Margaret, reaching with two hands and holding both of Chal-chee's hands, staring firmly and affectionately into her eyes. They turned to Rachel. Miss Margaret picked up a damp cloth and rubbed Rachel's hot, red arm. She leaned over her bandage-covered face and listened to her breathing.

DeSparr knelt beside them, crushed one of the new antibiotic tablets, stirred it in water, and slowly and carefully poured the mixture into Rachel's mouth. Gurgling, coughing sounds came, but finally an unconscious swallowing.

Miss Margaret went to Tee-week's mother, who was awake, and felt her pulse and forehead.

DeSparr followed her and gave pills to her. "She'll be okay."

"So will this one," said Miss Margaret, kneeling again beside Rachel. She bowed her head and pressed her arthritic hands together over Rachel. She whispered a prayer from under the sombrero. Chalchee bowed and whispered her own words at the same time.

The rain started up again, loud on the roof.

***

"We needn't delay," said Smith at his called meeting in the Burb. He held a white cloth over his head and shoulders and had to strain to be heard over the noise of the rain and the stream behind him. Miss Margaret stood beside him, about half his height. Her black plastic rain cover glistened and water poured from her wide hat brim. All the team's clothes, still skimpy and ragged and drenched, had been thoroughly cleaned by the villagers.

Some smiled through the rain washing across their faces. Several had apologized for having dismissed Miss Margaret earlier. Her three men sat with the team's guides in one of the huts eating uncooked pork-and-beans out of cans. Now and then DeSparr seemed to study Miss Margaret from under his cloth hood.

Smith said, "Miss Margaret tells me that helicopters can come for us. They can find us using signals from this radio."

"When can they get here?" said Crauder.

"Tomorrow," said Miss Margaret, "if it stops raining. But we need a place a couple of miles away, where they can land and not see the village. If word gets out, there'll be people all over this place."

"There's a flat clearing," said L.P. "We passed it coming here."

They talked and planned for some time. They divided up duties and made a checklist. They vowed not to take souvenirs that would make it easier to slip up and reveal the village's whereabouts to the outside world. They knew it wouldn't be easy.

Haughton-Alsef took a place next to Smith, on the side opposite Miss Margaret. "I think we should all honor our oath of secrecy." His

303

elbow pressed against an odd bulge in his unbuttoned shirt. A large cloth hung over his head. "Don't you agree, Dr. DeSparr?"

DeSparr stepped suddenly toward him, surprising everyone. Haughton-Alsef turned sideways. DeSparr reached quickly under Haughton-Alsef's arm and into his shirt and jerked out several folded papers. "Let's have a look at these!"

Haughton-Alsef groped for the papers but, keeping his elbow pressed against what remained of the bulge, failed. "Those are my private notes," he said, groping again.

DeSparr turned away and flipped through the pages, leaning over them to shield them from the rain. A pencil and a small, triangular object fell from the bundle. All the team watched, dumbfounded.

"This is a violation of privacy," said Haughton-Alsef. "Give those up at once."

Crauder picked up the triangular object. "It's that sorry knife with the face," he said. "The one the Jaguar-guys left when they pushed Tee-week off on us." He handed it to Smith. "That'll fetch a darlin' dollar for Mister Don't-disturb-anything." Smith stared at it unbelieving.

The two hooded silhouettes of DeSparr and Haughton-Alsef moved in the gray rain and fog, bent and dark like conjuring witches.

DeSparr turned away and read, loudly, "'The stream circles the mountain...'" Haughton-Alsef groped again, and DeSparr turned the other way. "'...forming an ideal defensive barrier, illustrating a predictable communal paranoia...'" DeSparr held the papers close to his face in the dimness and had trouble with the handwriting. "'They wear green camouflage and conceal everything when they hear an airplane...'" He glanced at Miss Margaret, then looked up at Haughton-Alsef. "Planning to spread the news?"

"That is my private, scholarly research, not intended for public viewing." Haughton-Alsef held the bulge and the pipe with one arm, and clawed at DeSparr with the other.

"What's this?" said DeSparr, loudly. "'...about ten miles northwest of the river's new waterfall, cut by the flood...'" He shouted, "You might as well draw a map!"

Haughton-Alsef chased him, with his strange, halting dignity.

DeSparr read again. "'...the trail to the village is rough, but not impassible.'"

Haughton-Alsef grabbed again and missed again.

DeSparr read on. "'I was able, with difficulty, to lead the now-distraught team while carrying the comatose woman on my back!'"

"What?" said Crauder.

"These…" said Haughton-Alsef, "These are nothing but ideas jotted down for future reference, a possible… novel, yes, a novel, not intended to be…"

"Ah!" said DeSparr, leafing through the papers again. "'…being a modest man by nature, I had no desire to tell the team how I'd saved the suicidal doctor from drowning!'" He read from another page. "'…saving Pryce from a fall off a cliff, I nearly fell myself. It was worth the risk for my assistant."

"What?" said Pryce. "God! You did nothing! You were right next to me and all I had was a tree limb and it was splitting off! Blake had to climb out on a rock to get me." His voice cracked. "When the limb broke you would have let me fall! Your secrets would be safe!"

"He's got it all wrong," said Haughton-Alsef. "Why would I…?" Suddenly he pointed threateningly at DeSparr with the hand holding the pipe, forgetting the bulge under his shirt. "You…" Pages fell from his shirt, scattering. Not paper this time. Parchment. He dropped the pipe quickly and started to pick them up, but DeSparr was quicker, and grabbed up all the parchments, shielding them from the rain. He handed them to Smith.

Miss Margaret produced a huge plastic bag and handed it to Smith who, bending over to keep the parchments from the rain, slid them and the knife into it.

"Taking back a few souvenirs?" said DeSparr to Haughton-Alsef. "For your 'novel?' Or just a little 'scholarly research?'"

"You question me?" said Haughton-Alsef, picking up his pipe. "You who would have us be cannibals, have us eat Tee-week, or Rachel for Christ's sake?"

DeSparr slumped, obviously stung, then looked up at Haughton-Alsef. "You advocated it yourself, quite seriously."

"You expect us to believe you instead of me. You who…"

"God!" Pryce cried out. "The writings! The parchment! That's what he's been after all along. If you just knew how far all this goes! This 'scholarly research?'" He jabbed the air, pointing at Haughton-Alsef.

"I hardly think," said Haughton-Alsef, an eye still staring out from under the hood at the plastic bag in Smith's hands, "that this is the time or place for…"

"God! What is the time or place?"

305

"Pryce," said Haughton-Alsef, "we have to be discree…"

"Discreet!" said Pryce. "Oh-ho yes. You've been saying that all along! Would you people like to know how Mr. Research came up with this whole expedition idea?"

"It wasn't his idea," said Smith. "Mr. Sands in California…"

"That's the company line, yes," said Pryce. "But …"

"Let's not sidetrack," said Haughton-Alsef, desperately.

"God! This whole 'expedition' has been a sidetrack." Pryce cried loudly as he talked, and his strong, high-pitched bawling drowned out interruptions. Only DeSparr's stage voice could have competed, but the doctor seemed happy to let the accusations fly.

Smith tried to step in. "This may be getting a little out of…"

"No!" cried Pryce. "This must be heard. You probably knew already that Mr. Be-discreet would have let me fall, let me die, when we were hunting for Pedro. He…"

"Now, Pryce…"

"He had good reason! I knew all about his great secret plan. After the cameras washed away, photos for a documentary would be impossible, right? So, who needs me? I might spill the beans. Good riddance! From the beginning it was mainly the parchments, the…"

"Pryce," said Haughton-Alsef. "Let's be honest. This is…"

"Yes! Honest! My god yes! Preach to yourself! A primitive American Indian language in Latin characters! What a find! All indications are that they're five hundred years old. Sands offered eighty-five hundred bucks a page!"

"Now, Pryce…" said Haughton-Alsef.

Crauder blurted, "Eighty-five hundred? What did Sands know about parchments?"

"What do you think this has all been about? After I didn't fall off the cliff, Dr. Scholarly research had to offer me a good portion of the profits to keep my mouth shut, which meant he had to tell me the original plan. Yes, I bargained. Sorry. The cameras and the TV documentary were one thing, but the parchments! If he could get me to help him get his hands on them! Big money!"

"Pryce!" said Haughton-Alsef. "What an absurd imagination! You shouldn't…"

"People knew about the parchments?" said Crauder. "Before we left Atlanta?"

"Of course!" Pryce squinted, still glaring at Haughton-Alsef.

"That little party back in Houston? When was it? Two years ago? Two years you cooked on this little scheme?"

"You're losing it," said Haughton-Alsef. "You're..."

"The cute little nurse from Nicaragua? God! She was so impressed with Dr. TV Documentary. Ask her about her work and she blabs about all the interesting medical records she had seen. At first he was just after her little bod', but when she mentioned the interview, the one from the 80's, the Contra soldier from Nicaragua..."

"What?" said Crauder. "Contra soldier?"

"Yes, yes! This is huge! The soldier is wounded, okay? Separated from his unit. He was interviewed later, in the hospital. He tells how these primitive jungle people, people no one had ever heard of, found him and took him to their village and treated him. While he recovered he saw hundreds of pages of something like parchment with Latin characters, but not in Latin. He happened to see a number, which he assumed to be a date. 1527. After they treated him, they blindfolded him and took him back to a point near his unit and left him. Miss Cute little nurse was impressed with that story."

"I've never heard," said Haughton-Alsef, "such inventive fabrication in my life."

"Well," said Pryce, "when Dr. TV Documentary hears this, he sees green — Sands's green. He flies to Managua. He gets hold of names and records, finds out roughly where the Contra unit had been at the time — happened to be in Honduras, in these woods right here — and talks old friend and ex-hippie-become-multi-millionaire Sands into making an offer. Nothing Sands would like more than adding documents like these to his already huge — and illegal — collection of Maya and Aztec goodies."

"Folks, this is pure fabrication," said Haughton-Alsef.

"How about this?" said Pryce. "You all remember Purple-hair. Ever wonder what was really going on? All a set-up. Tee-week mentioned an exiled man, remember? Mentioned he had a black box? One of my camera cases, right? So after I caved — and I admit I was thinking of the money — I helped Dr. Famous here with his new plan. We planted the boots — the one spare pair the Jaguar-people didn't get — on a log at the edge of their territory. Haughton-Alsef knew the exiled guy, Purple-hair, would be sneaking around for a while before he left all his friends and family for good."

"Pryce, you must stop these imaginings," said Haughton-Alsef.

"Yeah, you figured poor ole Purple-hair would see the boots and be willing to trade the camera for them. Get him to set the camera down, then scare him away with a lot of noise before he picked up the boots, and we'd have the camera and the boots."

"How much time did it take you to come up with this preposterous..."

"But Purple-hair was too quick," said Pryce. "He grabbed the camera back up when he bolted. That only gave Dr. Genius here another idea. Even more lucrative. We could lure him with the boots again, but this time get him inside the forbidden territory. Then hope to grab the camera. But the best part was if his tribe would attack him and better yet kill him, which they did, then we could get the whole bloody mess digitized with the camera. Imagine the money those pics would bring, or the reality in a TV documentary. You'll remember when the guides and I went out without telling anyone? Dr. Famous talked us into it — some of you had to come after us — and all we did was get the poor man killed and me scared out of my wits. No pics. You all thought it was just mix-ups with the guides, didn't you? Oh, he was planning all sorts of ways to make big bucks when we got back to the States."

No one spoke for a minute. The heavy, steady rain and the crashing stream drowned out the sounds of the woods.

"His plan now," said Pryce, "is, before going back to the States to sell the parchments for big bucks, to buy cameras as soon as we're back in Tegucigalpa, hire some people and come back here and take pictures before anyone else can, then tell the world of his 'great discovery.' Why did he always emphasize trust? No disturbing the tribe? It was so he — only he — would have the scoop when we got back."

"I think it imperative that we all see this rationally," said Haughton-Alsef, composing himself. "It's... Can't you see? Pryce is making it up. He's understandably angry over what he thinks is my failure to act when he was in danger, so he's made up this whole thing, a far more complicated plan, I must say..." he made a humble smile. "...than I am capable of."

Smith pointed at Haughton-Alsef's shirt. "You were hiding the parchments."

Haughton-Alsef looked down at his now-lumpless shirt and opened his arms to let it fall open. "There's nothing here... I mean..."

"Milton..."

"I'll split the money with the entire team. Equal shares for each person. As many pages as I think there are, you should each get about eighty thousand dollars to spend as you like. Just one condition: no one repeats Pryce's fabrications."

Again there was silence. Then Smith said, "You're in no position to bargain, Milton. I have to say I am ashamed of myself, falling for this. I thought you were a scholar. You dishonor the meaning of the word. I can't trust you anymore."

"Our great leader," said DeSparr, "whose fear of offending anyone, blinded him to the charlatan."

Smith's embarrassment was obvious, even in the rain.

Haughton-Alsef looked up. "Have you ever had to get an audience for a TV documentary? You have no idea what is required."

"Have you ever stopped to think, Milton," said Smith, "that there are honest people in the news business?"

"But, to get your audience, there has to be a certain amount of… You have to understand. Ours is a free, affluent society. We can't be bound by the arbitrary precepts of a small group of moralists. A vocal minority… Just because I…

"You lied to us, Milton."

"Just a little lie. It would lead to a greater good." The hood turned slowly above the dark bent shape as he looked around for the reactions of the team. A forced, deeply fearful smile showed in the brief flash of his eye. His fingers twisted aimlessly in front of him. "It will be worth millions. Can't you see?" He turned to Smith. "Jerry, old boy. Millions!" Smith turned away. Haughton-Alsef grabbed Dove-Ti by the arms. "Dove-Ti! You can see it! Think what eighty thousand dollars would…" Dove-Ti pulled away, turned her back and began bawling.

DeSparr glanced again at Miss Margaret, as if for approval, then straightened. He threw his head back, and studied the groping Haughton-Alsef with a look of final superiority.

Haughton-Alsef tried awkwardly to appear unawkward, then suddenly grabbed for his notes still in DeSparr's hand, but the doctor stepped away too fast, started to fall toward the stream, and was only able to regain his balance by throwing the water-laden notes out. They dropped and scattered quickly with the rain into the raging water.

Howard left for the log bridge. "I'm going to check on Rachel."

"Me too," said Miss Margaret.

Chapter 29

At the end of the second year of their time in the new village, Atl and Dahlia were married. Dahlia became stronger, and more practical, and more and more Atl saw her as his reason to live. And in the third year, Deer of Stone and Thoughtful Rose were married, and she silenced them all with her poem of joy. Mendez was not healed or even improved that year, and he worried that he was not translating well enough, and he went back over his work, making sure he applied the guidelines Tomás had given him.

All through these years Ocelot taught the men how to fight like the Aztecs, and One-Cip' warned them to fight only in defense of themselves and their village and never for gain from others, which the Aztecs and Sant-yagos had proven would only bring new troubles.

In the third year, the villagers had gained a mastery of their work, and it went well, and they gave Mendez more time which he used for his translating. But their hatred of him had become part of their way of life, and they still beat him. His suffering and his resolve in his promise to God made him stronger, and he endured.

In the fourth year, Dahlia gave birth to a fat little son, and Atl watched his son, and played with him, and began more and more to love peace. Grandfather One-Cip' laughed and danced. Mendez liked to see the little boy wave his hands and laugh and cry.

Then Thoughtful Rose gave birth to a smiling daughter, and said to them all a poem of hope and joy. Deer of Stone was proud and held his daughter up for all to see, whenever Thoughtful Rose would let her go. Grandfathers Two-Rabbit and One-Cip' both laughed and danced.

The new baby girl always smiled at Mendez, from a distance, and he began to care for her happiness, though he was not allowed to go near the children. They were like fresh air. He always returned their smiles. He worried when one of them was hurt or sick. They gave him another reason to work more and more carefully with his translating. It could someday give them peace and hope, and teach them love as he had never known it.

In the fifth year, the daughter of Deer of Stone and Thoughtful Rose became very sick and died, and they buried her. Everyone was sad and silent. Thoughtful Rose's poem was not well said. Aunt Pink, who had loved the baby dearly, cried and cried. Mendez hid his own terrible crying, and hurt more from the loss than from any of the beatings. And for the first time he began to doubt his own healing. But still he worked.

In the sixth year, Thoughtful Rose gave birth to another girl, and spoke a poem better than any before. And again grandfathers Two-Rabbit and One-Cip' danced and laughed. Deer of Stone joined Atl in his desire for peace. Aunt Pink tended the new little girl and gave her much love, but with much firmness, for she did not want her to become spoiled. Mendez again found hope and endurance, watching the new baby smile and laugh.

Later that year Thoughtful Rose said another poem of joy for Dahlia and Atl when their second boy came, and again One-Cip' danced. But this time in his dancing he fainted. He slept for two days, and then he died. All the village was sad and afraid. And so was Mendez, for they looked to Deer of Stone to take his father's place, and Deer of Stone hated Mendez. But Deer of Stone was humbled, and wanted his daughter to see only peace and gentleness, and tried to follow in his father's ways.

In the seventh year Mendez nearly finished the work, but even though he had learned to live with his pain and limitations, his body was no better. He could tell that Shy Petals and Thoughtful Rose and Pink, and even the children as they grew older, saw the ugliness of his burn marks, and heard the disgusting wheezing of his voice. Nothing had changed. His mother and the priests and God had let him hope, but kept sending the punishment.

***

One morning late in the seventh year Tomás and five armed Spanish soldiers walked from the woods into the village. Mendez slumped. The men approached Deer of Stone peacefully.

"We have come for Ramiro Mendez. Is he here?"

311

"What do you want with him?" said Deer of Stone.

"To take him to justice for stealing the king's gold and for murder and desertion."

Yes, his mother had done it again. Again and again and again. But no more. Mendez was tired. He stepped out into view and threw his arms out. "Kill me now!"

All the people looked at him.

Tomás was with the men. In his long robe he came to Mendez. "Ramiro. I have talked to the authorities. They will have leniency because you returned the gold. Padre Olmedo helped me get a ruling. He died a few years later, but the ruling still stands. I withheld your location from them and told them of your captivity, your injuries, your serving in slavery, and your long work translating the Bible."

"They will have leniency? Really?"

"Yes. Really. Have you finished the translation?"

"All but some pages in the Revelation of John," Mendez wheezed. "I was getting confused. Only a month ago, I translated something about this great 'Son of Man,' this 'living one,' who said to a church, 'This I hold against you, that you have forsaken, your first… your first…'"

"First love," said Tomás. "It was a people that had once given themselves, like a living sacrifice, to Jesus. That's his kind of love: sacrifice, small, large. But that church changed, went their own way, like sheep, loose. He holds that against them."

Atl and Deer of Stone listened. Atl wondered how a sacrifice could be a 'living' sacrifice.

"I think I see," said Mendez. "Were they like the church today?"

"Like me at times. Like you at times. And like many Christians past, present and future, from the laity to the authorities. Forgetting our first true, costly love."

"Tomás," wheezed Mendez. "Your dream of the translation gave me my deal with God, my aim, the only aim that was left for me."

"If it pleases God, that is good. But, Ramiro, I have told you: he does not make deals."

"And I am going to prison."

"Yes."

"I was a good slave. They quit beating me years ago."

"Thank God."

Mendez glanced down at his hundreds of pages of translations.

"We could sell these in Europe, you know. This Nahuatl, it is…"

"Forget it, Ramiro."

"Yes, yes. I have worked and suffered for seven years in vain."

"Ramiro, do you remember Rosa?"

"The farm girl near Salamanca," said Mendez. "I do. I have apologized to God."

"In a letter to my sister, I told about Rosa. Last year I got a letter. Rosa is dead."

"You liked her."

"She was always in my mind. I cannot tell you how much I always hoped that God would somehow bring us together."

"And God has denied you," said Mendez.

"Yes."

Mendez was tired, his body battered, his joints aching. He looked at the soldiers and their stern, cold faces. "Who are they?"

"They are new. They mine silver when they can. They have enslaved Indians. They are eager to end their obligation to the army and enjoy their wealth."

"They will be chained to it."

"Yes. As for you, Ramiro, I do not think you will be hanged, but you will surely serve time in prison. I am sorry…"

"No. I am sorry. Sorry for all the pain and death I have caused. I am ready."

"You have changed."

"Tomás, you could explain the pages to these people."

"I have duties with the army. I have committed." Tomás looked at the burned, deformed face of Mendez. "You were not healed."

Mendez sighed again. "I am healed, Tomás."

"Thank God," said Tomás.

Atl and Deer of Stone stood near the Sant-yagos and watched patiently as they talked.

Mendez said to Tomás, "What of your friend… what was his name… Hernando?"

"Fernando," said Tomás. "Fernando was promoted. His unit was the best organized in Cortés' army. He has land now. And landowner friends. Indian servants. Mistresses. I do not see him much."

"He had a limp."

"Still does."

"I think I gave it to him. Do you have other friends?"

"Yes I do. Some very good ones."

"Am I one of them?"

"I cannot save you, Ramiro."

"I just want to know," said Mendez, "that I have a friend."

"It is my hope that we are friends."

Mendez turned to Atl and Deer of Stone and pointed at the translations. "Keep these. Copy them. And if you do not read them I will come back to haunt you."

That frightened Atl, but he had already taken a great interest in the writings and in the talk about a great first sacrifice and even more interest in how sacrifices could be 'living' ones, as the robed Sant-yago claimed.

Atl looked at his sons whom he loved, and he felt even more deeply his heart-pain for having taken such prolonged and angry revenge on Mendez who worked hard and well as a slave. And in looking at his sons he knew that the grudging hatred he and his village had embraced brought only trouble, and he was eager to rise above it, and to read the many pages, which told of such things.

And he was beginning to see that, as more and more of the hate left him, so did more and more of the fear of his unlucky birthday.

Then after a meal served by the families of Dahlia and Thoughtful Rose, all the Sant-yago company thanked them and said their goodbyes. They left with Mendez in chains and Tomás talking to him with his arm around his shoulders.

They never came back.

Chapter 30

Howard woke to Chal-chee's urgent cries, "Come. Come." She stood outside the team hut in the Burb, waiting. Her eyes were red. Smith and Crauder stood behind her. Howard got up and followed them. Young men helped them all across the log bridge.

They walked up into the village, toward the faint glow in the east. Crauder only stared at the ground as they walked, red-faced, uncharacteristically silent.

Smith slowly turned his straw hat in his hands. "I know you had a special relationship with... Rachel."

"Have," said Howard. "Not had."

"Yes, of course. I think there's a certain comfort in knowing that there was really nothing more she could have done to have lived an exemplary life. Caring, thoughtful..."

"She can't be summed up. And she will make it."

"Well, she's... Yes, yes."

Several team members and villagers stood in front of Rachel's hospital hut, staring at the ground, glancing at Howard as he passed.

He heard thumping inside. Chal-chee entered with him. DeSparr was serious, one sweaty hand spread flat on Rachel's green-wrapped chest, the other balled into a fist, pounding. Tears rolled freely down his cheeks and through his black beard.

Miss Margaret was kneeling and praying silently with Ehec.

Rachel was not breathing.

Someone had removed most of the facial bandages and carefully washed the face. Howard was able to make out, in short flashes, partial memories of her face, and each flash, because it was only a memory, was like a painfully bright set of colors or a sudden loud orchestral chord, quickly fading.

She was as still as death. Sight sapped hope. He knelt beside her. There came to him a sense that he, with her, was dying. If there was more to life than physical function, then there was more to death than physical dysfunction. In fact a physical death may not have been so real as the one he would now endure, leaving his mind no more than a brain, his person but a body.

DeSparr seemed to go for her backbone with both hands now. One gurgling gasp came from her mouth, like something from a depressurizing piece of hydraulic machinery. Then he stopped and drew back. He stood. His red eyes looked away, pouring tears, and his shoulders shook. "Three minutes." His voice broke. "No heartbeat."

Finally Howard pressed his ear to her open, distorted mouth, verifying no breath. He held the exposed wrist, angled awkwardly now beside the hip. No pulse. He grasped the limp hand. He would have given all he had ever dreamed of with women for one squeeze, even an unconscious one, from that hand at that moment.

At least now she would not suffer. But he would suffer.

There was one thing he could say, that he, whose old hopes had included little beyond things and ideas, had now known, if only for a moment, oneness of company. Her singular company. It amazed him that so short-lived an experience had twined through his mind and life ever since.

Ironically, the very thing which had finally drawn him to her, her guileless giving, had now deprived him of her. His life was spared for him by the loss of hers which alone would have made his worth living. And the removal of the bandages showed that her healing had been better than expected. Her face, though one side was still scarred and swollen, was recognizable. Oh, sweet face! And ironically, the once-feared People of the First Sacrifice, whom Rachel never even saw or knew existed, had turned out to be peaceful and helpful. And Miss Margaret, whom she had missed so badly, had come.

"Four minutes," said DeSparr. He slammed a hand down on her chest again and hopelessly banged it with the other fist.

Howard stood and walked to the door. The glow to the east was shrouded in mist. Birds sang as if there were no reason for all the world to cry out in agony, or at least respectfully hush for a moment.

Most of the team and quite a few Greenshirts glanced silently and hesitantly up at him. Their faces were soft. L.P. and several others took a step or two toward him, then stopped awkwardly.

Howard smiled and nodded. No one knew what to do or say.

Again DeSparr's pounding stopped. From inside were only the whispered prayers of Ehec and Miss Margaret and now Chal-chee.

Howard turned back and knelt and touched Rachel's hand. To touch and not be touched was a thing as cold and void as he imagined the darkest reaches of the universe to be. Even the intense heat he had learned to expect from her skin since el tigre was now gone.

"They tell me you've grown to love her," said Miss Margaret.

"Oh…" he said, embarrassed to be known to love what was vanishing. "I think from her I may have begun to learn what love is."

She studied his wet eyes with her tough round eyes, then put a hand on his arm and went back to praying. He thought of joining them, awkward as his attempts at prayer would be, but it seemed selfish before a god like Rachel's God. All he wanted was Rachel for himself.

He spread her no-longer-hot fingers and inserted his, squeezing, palm to palm. There was no warm tightening, as there had been on the divide, or through the roof shingles. His chest heaved. Oddly, it was not just his own loss that he felt in that palm, but the world's. Rachel herself had no loss if her heaven was real.

He mumbled out loud, for any witness to hear, "I do not wish her to live just because I want her." Ehec and Miss Margaret glanced up briefly from their praying. Miss Margaret smiled and nodded. He closed his eyes and slowly eased his farewell grip.

And as he did another painful sense of irony came as he felt a slight muscle spasm in the hand, and heard another raspy sound in the chest. And then a halting, gurgling, ugly sound came from the throat and the sound of words may have been in it, which could have been the words, "Who's hand?" and he felt her hand open as if heaven had opened, then squeeze as if heaven had squeezed. "Howard?" came the rasping sound again, more clearly this time, and it was not a sound, but her voice, and she, and he, were not dead.

***

For three hours DeSparr directed Chal-chee, Miss Margaret, and Howard in the work. Rachel's heart stopped and started several times. She said a few more words. She looked at Miss Margaret, and called her name. Howard took the opportunities to describe to her the main parts of what had happened: her coma, the People of the First Sacrifice, the

317

time that had passed. He couldn't tell if she understood. DeSparr said the cooling of her arm that night had actually turned out to be a good sign. The antibiotics would have fought the infection and fever.

L.P. stood in the door. "Did she wake up?"

"Come on in," said Howard. "There's still the question of..."

"Brain damage," said DeSparr, his face as stone-white as ever.

Her head moved a little. "Howard?"

"Rachel?" he said. She couldn't have remembered the attack. People who come out of comas don't remember what caused them.

"Is the thing gone?" She remembered.

"It's gone," he said.

The edges of her mouth made brief frowns. "What will you do?"

DeSparr would hear. That was okay. And Miss Margaret and L.P. And Ehec and Chal-chee. They would all hear and know. Howard answered Rachel. "If you will have me, I will belong to you as long as we live. No matter what."

Miss Margaret studied him. "You're saying quite a lot."

"I mean it."

Everybody waited. Rachel let out a long breath. "I'll have you."

"Yep," said L.P. "She's had brain damage."

Howard leaned close to her ear. "I love-love you."

She said, "I've loved you..." She breathed. "since the ant trick."

DeSparr frowned.

Howard said, "I wasn't in on that"

"I knew you weren't," she said. "But you cared what I thought."

Miss Margaret said, "You'd better treat her right, Buster."

Rachel slept a while, then woke and said, drowsily, "Howard, did we make promises?"

"We sure did," he said. "Were you of sound mind?"

"Yes." She answered quickly, though still drowsy.

"Rachel, I've got to ask you..."

"What?"

"You may think it's a silly question. But..."

"Ask."

"Well... What are you for?"

"For?"

"Your life. What are you for?"

She breathed several times. "Do you mean like... God?"

"If that's your answer."

"It is. Is that a problem?"

"Nope."

***

Howard didn't know how long he had been asleep when he heard the choppers, the whacking and knocking of the engines, miles away. All the team gathered in the Burb, having packed the night before, having carried Rachel, who was better, down and across the stream, with help, on a tribe-made stretcher. The blue-white lights shone through the distant, wildly swaying trees. Above, a bright moon lit lacy clouds. In the dark across the stream, villagers peered toward the distant flashing lights and noise. Chal-chee, having spent the night in her own hut with mid-wives, carried her new, golden-skinned baby boy.

Smith turned to the other team members. "I guess it's time."

Howard shouted to L.P. "I'm going back across!"

L.P. stopped, puzzled.

To Howard's surprise, Dove-Ti followed him across in a loose green shirt and pants, her bag under her arm.

"What are you doing?" he said.

"I'm staying," she said. "I told Smith. I gave him letters for back home. Zoe and DeSparr are watching Rachel. She slept okay. She can take the traveling."

"You're staying?"

"I want to know these people. I'm going to shut up and listen." She spoke with a new resolve. "This will be my seminary."

She hugged him, then disappeared among the villagers.

Ehec looked up at Howard. He had been greatly disappointed when he found out the parchments were stolen. Smith and Zoe had had to do a lot of explaining. It helped the team's credibility that all the pages had been returned and accounted for.

Ehec held his hand out and in it was Crauder's pistol.

Howard took it and dropped it in his cloth pack.

They hugged. Howard was surprised by the old man's strength.

L.P. and Crauder carried Rachel, on her stretcher, to the edge, where all the villagers could see her. She turned her head and opened her mouth. She waved at Tee-week, the only one she had known from before. His leg was in a rough cast. The whole tribe waved back.

Her voice was too soft in the noise, but she said, softly, as if to

319

old friends, "Good-bye."

Howard thought: she hardly knows the people who took her from us and gave her to us.

Ehec said, in English, "Peace and hope, Hyde, to all of you."

"And to you," said Howard.

Ehec said, "Ya-si want you give self."

"Yes. I know. Thank you. I think I gave myself to Rachel."

"Good." He smiled. "Ya-si give you Ra-chul. Still want you."

"Yes, thank you. I… I'll think about that."

The morning light began to spread across the mountain. Howard hugged Ehec once more, and they stared silently at each other.

Chal-chee's baby cooed.

"What's his name?" said Howard.

"Old family name," said Ehec, smiling proudly. "Atl."

Howard tickled Atl's nose and acted silly, making him smile. Then he turned and crossed back over the bridge. He gave Crauder the pistol and looked back at the gathered villagers.

Peets beat his chest. Chal-chee smiled bravely and waved Atl's tiny arm. Tee-week studied the team as if they mattered after all, not because of what he had learned about them, but because of the caring for them he had seen from the People of the First Sacrifice.

***

Smith and Miss Margaret and the Crauders stood at the hospital window, staring at U.S. franchise billboards scattered across the rooftops of Tegucigalpa. Howard and Zoe and DeSparr sat at Rachel's bed. She was asleep in her hospital gown and her tubes. DeSparr had been a rock, tending her, ordering nurses, prescribing medicines, predicting nothing, comforting no one. Zoe helped with warm, persistent affection.

Maria the translator was out showing L.P. the town. Pryce and Haughton-Alsef had parted for good. Each had left the country.

Everyone had shopped when they had a chance, and bought new clothes, except Miss Margaret, who found a flea market and bought used clothes and a plastic raincoat. She gave her sombrero to a woman washing clothes in the Rio Choluteca.

Smith had made two vows. One, to file as many charges against Haughton-Alsef and Sands as the law would allow. Murder. Fraud. His second was to find the funds so the guides would get all their pay plus healthy tips. The team had chipped in and bought bus tickets to their villages. Smith gave their mailing addresses to each team member.

"You know what?" said Smith, unusually open. "I'm going back to being a pastor. Pro-active." He looked at Crauder. "By the way, Jud, whatever happened to that pistol?"

"Chucked it in the Choluteca."

The local doctors had answered questions patiently and professionally, Zoe translating. They predicted a long but full recovery, including the somewhat smooth healing of Rachel's face and neck after some continued special surgery.

Crauder turned and said, "I coulda told ya she'd make it."

"I wish you'd mentioned it earlier," said Mrs. Crauder, smoothing her sweatpants. "We wouldn't have worried so."

"Dang, Pat."

"Less," said Howard to DeSparr, "I want to thank you for…"

"So," said the resonant stage-voice, "The dashing hero of the flood acknowledges the mad doctor's benefit to the patient?"

The others in the room turned to watch.

Howard said, "Well, for your sleepless nights and your…"

"The clever jungle-ant trickster has a polite side."

"I didn't… Just… for your hard work, your skill, your caring …"

"Listen," said DeSparr. "The mad doctor is…" The voice softened. "Well, is mad. Angry mad. At himself. He knows who hatched and did the ant trick. And he knows that in fact it was funny." His mouth turned down, trying not to snicker. "And the mad doctor knows that it was deserved. And that the dashing hero meant to stop it." His voice became low and soft, his mouth alternately frowning and smiling as his eyes reddened and glistened. Finally he turned to Rachel. He blurted, "And he could not go on without knowing that there is living somewhere in this world one like this woman."

Everyone looked down. Howard put his hand on DeSparr's shoulder. DeSparr shrugged it off, then glanced at Howard, and in the red eyes was a faint, desperate need, carefully hidden.

Howard thought: Rachel will keep in touch with him. And I will.

There was a knock on the door, already open. Two men and a woman stood there, Americans. One raised a camera.

"Hi," said the woman, walking in. She named some newspaper. That woke Rachel. Howard stroked her forehead.

The news woman said, "You found the tribe, right? Was it

bodies thrown off a cliff? Drastic things with human hearts?"

Rachel looked at Howard. She said, weakly, "Hearts. Drastic."

Smith smiled at the reporter. "Very sick woman here. I'm sorry. Thank you." He ushered her into the hall.

Howard picked up the rag Zoe had been wiping Rachel with and took it into the bathroom to rinse it. Zoe followed, and said, "Dove-Ti told me something before she, you know, went back to the village."

"Yeah?"

"She said she was glad she wasn't, like… pregnant."

"Oh my gosh."

"She said she always wanted to be a mother. She found it easy to let her guard down a couple of times. From as far back as the like… prep sessions in Atlanta. You know why she's glad?"

Howard made an intuitive guess. "It was Haughton-Alsef?"

"Yep. Blake and I'll see you two back in Atlanta?"

"You bet."

Howard spent the night in a chair next to Rachel.

***

The next morning she was better. When she woke, she said, "Howard. We made promises."

"Yes."

"You know I take care of Daddy. He'll be in a bedroom in the house. He doesn't talk much."

"I'll have plenty of time to get to know him."

Miss Margaret came and helped Rachel with her hair.

L.P. came with Maria the translator. He grinned. "Ready?"

"Ready for what?" said Howard.

L.P. looked at Maria. "We're gonna get hitched!"

"What! Hey, congratulations. Wow!" Howard looked at her glowing face. "My sympathies." She giggled.

Miss Margaret shook L.P.'s hand. "What you're doing is you're promising to treat her right for the rest of your life no matter what. Stick to it." Then she hugged Maria and said, "*Dios te bendiga.*"

Rachel reached for Maria's finger and admired the ring.

Howard almost choked. He hadn't even thought of a ring.

L.P. said, "Did you hear about Blake? He and I each asked our little ladies at the same time, in the same hamburger joint."

"I knew he'd do it," said Howard. "What did Zoe say?"

"She said, 'I'm like, yay.'"

"When are you going to do it?"

"In a couple of weeks," said L.P. "Here, in Tegucigalpa."

"Here? Can we come?"

"You better."

Rachel let go of Maria's ring.

Howard felt his face go red. "Rachel, I…"

"Do you know," she said, "what I will always treasure?"

He remembered her mother's note. He reached for it.

"Three words."

"Three words?"

"When you said, '…no matter what.'"

A nurse came. Time for medicine, time to change the sheets, time to use the potty. She turned off valves and unhooked tubes.

"I'm supposed to get up and walk," said Rachel.

Howard helped her. When she got to her feet, he held her arm and offered her mother's worn note.

Rachel opened it and read and reread silently. She closed both hands over it and held it to her chest. Her eyes were perfect circles and big drops ran in little lines down her cheeks and Howard drew her to him. She seemed weightless in only the gown. He felt the bones of her two hands still holding the note awkwardly between his chest and hers and they stood like that for a long time.

∗∗∗

Next day he found a ring that he, and to his great relief, she, liked. Next week she got around pretty well. The week after that they and Miss Margaret witnessed L.P. and Maria's promises. As the newlyweds left, Rachel said to Miss Margaret, "Do you have to go now?"

"No prolonged goodbyes. I'll see you guys in Atlanta."

"North Carolina. Black Mountain. That's where we'll do it."

"I'll be there on sabbatical in July."

"Maybe we'll schedule it when you're not on sabbatical, to get an extra visit."

"A lot of work has piled up in my little jungle town."

"July, then."

Miss Margaret turned to Howard and hugged him, then hugged Rachel for a long time.

After she left, Rachel said, "How long 'til our flight?"

"DeSparr says he needs three more weeks with you."

***

Three weeks later, in the early morning, their plane climbed northward over the vast crumpled mountains. Their seats were on the right, forward of the wing. She had the window.

He looked past the fine, zigzag edge of her profile, which caught the brightness of the new day like lightning. Far below them was the soft gray-green of a million trees. Scattered white wisps hung above a twisting, glimmering river.

He leaned closer to the window, closer to her. Her eyes, kept round with effort, were direct to him. He let his own eyes follow the faint mottled softness of her pale cheek leading back from her lightning-profile, down to her mouth, which made again the funny crinkled smile, the smile still scarred, softly now, by the remains of el tigre's work. And he smiled, and it felt to him as if his smile had the same shape, the crinkle and the scar, and they turned easily, both of them, to the window.

His ear touched, pressed, her healing ear and she returned the pressure, lightly, and he could feel and hear the rushing of their bloods, and he knew she felt and heard it too.

And they looked down and saw that the river tumbled through the thick woods on the long northern slopes and broadened and reached the low, flat, leafy land where it spread out among tiny islands, too slow to beat out the thickening impurities and too wide to be shielded by trees from the glare of the day. And it seemed hardly to move, but to merge with the waters of the Caribbean, its tiny, changing droplets drawn upward like long mist-fingers into the vast, gleaming spread of new sky.

Acknowledgements:

Thanks go to Wycliffe Bible Translators, who are the real deal, for consultation about translating in remote regions, to Jenny Humphries, author of *Where the Buffaloes Roam* for invaluable literary advice, and to more friends and family than I know how to list, but who know who they are, for proofing, suggestions, and encouragement.

Special thanks for days of hard work proofing and/or suggesting to my brother Doug, my son Jim, my daughter Fran, and my wife Betty.

About the author: Doc grew up in Georgia, where he and his wife Betty and their two married children and five grandchildren live. He

graduated from Georgia Military Academy (Now Woodward Academy). He led a rock band, delivered coffee, and worked in construction while finishing his studies at Georgia Tech. He has a BArch, MBA, and MDiv. He practices architecture and taught design, drawing, and history at Southern Poly. He served as president of American University of Biblical Studies for five years and is now a director. He has been fascinated with pre-Columbian culture and architecture since college, and how the events of history interact with matters of the heart. He has done short term mission work in Mexico and Honduras. He likes to spend time with his kids' families, read, write, hike, draw, paint, work with wood and metal, build bridges in the woods, shop at thrift stores, and sing when no one can hear.

www.ingramcontent.com/pod-product-compliance
Lightning Source LLC
Chambersburg PA
CBHW051938220626
47052CB00004B/697